# The Cowboys

A Smitten Historical Romance Collection

*Healing Hearts* by Cindy Ervin Huff
*Becoming Brave* by Jennifer Uhlarik
*Trail's End* by Sandra Merville Hart
*Loving a Harvey Girl* by Linda W. Yezak

SMITTEN
HISTORICAL ROMANCE
LIGHTHOUSE PUBLISHING OF THE CAROLINAS

Other Smitten Historical Romance Titles by *The Cowboys* Authors

*Secrets & Charades* – Cindy Ervin Huff
*Sand Creek Serenade* – Jennifer Uhlarik
*A Stranger on My Land* – Sandra Merville Hart
*A Rebel in My House* – Sandra Merville Hart
*A Musket in My Hands* – Sandra Merville Hart

Other Lighthouse Publishing of the Carolina Titles by
*The Cowboys* Authors
*A Southern Season* – Linda W. Yezak
*Writing in Obedience* – Linda W. Yezak

THE COWBOYS BY JENNIFER UHLARIK, LINDA W. YEZAK, SANDRA MERVILLE HART, CINDY ERVIN HUFF
Published by Smitten Historical Romance
an imprint of Lighthouse Publishing of the Carolinas
2333 Barton Oaks Dr., Raleigh, NC 27614

ISBN: 978-1-946016-90-4
Copyright © 2019 by Jennifer Uhlarik, Linda W. Yezak, Sandra Merville Hart, Cindy Ervin Huff
Cover design by Elaina Lee
Interior design by Karthick Srinivasan

Available in print from your local bookstore, online, or from the publisher at: ShopLPC.com

For more information on this book and the authors visit: https://jenniferuhlarik. wordpress.com/, https://lindayezak.com/, https://sandramervillehart.wordpress.com/, https://jubileewriter.wordpress.com/

Brought to you by the creative team at Lighthouse Publishing of the Carolinas (LPCBooks.com): Eddie Jones, Pegg Thomas, Shonda Savage, Stephen Mathisen, Christy Callahan, Jennifer Leo

Library of Congress Cataloging-in-Publication Data
Uhlarik, Jennifer; Yezak, Linda W.; Hart, Sandra Merville; Huff, Cindy Ervin
The Cowboys / Jennifer Uhlarik, Linda W. Yezak, Sandra Merville Hart, Cindy Ervin Huff 1st ed.

Printed in the United States of America

# Praise for *The Cowboys*

I recommend these four novellas, each with different style and mood. Good old cowboy conflicts and fighting for justice struggles ... from gritty, tense classic western stories to sweet cowboy romances. Romance wins out every time over dealing with murderous ambush, racial prejudice, secret pasts, gambling addictions, strict rules of Harvey House girls training, a disapproving preacher, and a conniving rival. Loved the life-changing poker game twist. If you're looking for humor and pathos, inspirational and heart-tugging, along with tests of courage and healing of wounded hearts, try this collection of down home on a western trail tales.

~**Janet Chester Bly**
Author of *The Trails of Reba Cahill Series*

Get ready for a handsome cowboy to lasso your heart! *The Cowboys* is a wonderful collection of heartfelt romances you'll fall in love with before you finish the first pages. Each story is lively, enchanting, and rich with historical detail. I was especially spellbound by Sandra Merville Hart's *Trail's End*. A seasoned writer, Hart spins a romantic yarn that is tender, uplifting, believable, and peppered with plot twists! Only, her heroine's cooking left me drooling for homemade pies and biscuits! Hurry and round up all these clean, wholesome romances today. Though, you might want to eat first.

~**Heather Blanton**
Author of *A Lady in Defiance*

Swoon-worthy cowboy heroes. Heroines full of spunk and grit. Each story a Wild West adventure. What's not to enjoy?

~ **Lisa Carter**
Award-winning author of *The Stronghold* and *Under a Turquoise Sky*

If you're looking for clean, exciting Western romances, this collection will delight you. I thoroughly enjoyed these four novellas that carried me off to the Wild West and plopped me in the middle of danger and drama, from outlaws and crooked gamblers to ranches and saloons. I especially enjoyed the excellent writing style of each author whose story grabbed my attention from the beginning and kept me reading to the exciting end while entertaining me with realistic cowboy lingo and attitudes. I highly recommend you step out West and get to know these cowboys!

~**Marilyn Turk**
Award-winning author of *Shadowed by a Spy*

What a great read. *The Cowboys* features four inspirational stories of four strong women doing their part to settle the American West. While the collection shows us some of the challenges these women faced, it reminds of the ever-present soft side of women and the presence of godly cowboys who will appreciate them.

~**Rebecca Waters**
Author of *Libby's Cuppa Joe*

# Healing Hearts

By

Cindy Ervin Huff

# Dedication

*Linda Ervin*
*My Sister with a Cowgirl Heart*

# Chapter 1

*Kansas, 1866*

*IF I ONLY DO one good thing in my life, I'm getting my brother home.*
The bitter temperature and steady snowfall slowed the Holt brothers'
progress. Lonnie nudged his brother's shoulder to wake him.

"Hey." He dusted snowflakes off Jed.

Jed's chin drooped deeper on his chest.

*Don't you dare fall asleep in this cold.*

"Jedidiah Ezekiel Holt, wake on up." Lonnie imitated their mother's
gentle tone.

"Ma, I'm up." Jed rubbed his eyes then glared at his twin. "Ain't
funny. A grown man resortin' to such a childish prank."

Jed's chuckle relieved some of Lonnie's anxiety.

"Figured it'd be better than slappin' you headlong into the snow." He
held the reins one-handed and adjusted the lap robe securely around
his brother. Jed pushed his hand away.

"You're freezin' too." Jed spread it across their laps and shoved his
gloved hands into his pockets.

"I'm fine," Lonnie growled and then whistled to encourage the
plodding horses to pick up their pace. He switched hands on the reins
and shoved the other between his legs to warm it.

"You still need to gain a mite more weight. Since you got back from
the war, you ain't et enough to keep a squirrel alive," Lonnie said. Jed's
appearance had startled him when he'd met his train in Omaha. *Father,*

*forgive me for listening to Jed's insistence. We shoulda waited until spring to come. In a few more months he'd be stronger.* That Confederate prison camp had nearly taken his last brother from him.

Jed flipped his collar up. "Last week you said I et like a sparrow, so I must be improvin'." He ducked his head lower in the too-large coat.

The bracing wind twisted the whiteness in circles before them. The horses trudged on as the snow deepened. Lonnie sure hoped they were still on the road. He looked back to see how his saddle horse, Drake, was fairing tied to the back of the wagon.

Jed fell silent again. He better keep talking, keep him awake. "You'll always be the better-lookin' one even if you're skinny as a garter snake."

Jed shook his head. "We're both good-lookin'. Your scar makes you more distinguished. The ladies will swoon."

Lonnie cringed. Jed's reference to the C branded on his face for refusing to take up arms caused his jaw to tighten. He brushed his gloved hand over the scraggly part of his beard that barely covered the brand, then glanced at Jed's hollow cheeks—a gift from prison camp. Though twenty-five, someone could mistake them for much older men.

"I miss Ma." Jed sighed and pulled the lap robe closer.

"And Willy and Leroy too." Guilt and grief encircled Lonnie like the snow. He hadn't been able to stop his younger brothers from enlisting in the Confederate army any more than he could have saved Ma from the fire.

"The boys woulda loved workin' Uncle Clyde's ranch." Jed smiled.

Lonnie words grated past his tightened throat. "I shoulda tried harder to stop 'em."

Jed nudged him. "Shouldas are past, and the ranch is our future. Keep your mind on that, brother."

Jed made it sound so easy …

"Lookin' forward to a fresh start." Jed's dark-ringed eyes danced with excitement. "Back east they're clamorin' for beef."

Lonnie gripped the reins harder. "I reckon."

"You spent too much time as a hermit." Jed put his gloved hands into his armpits. "Time to come back to the world."

Three years in a mountain cabin in Colorado hadn't lessened Lonnie's pain. *I failed the family. I shoulda stayed insteada runnin'. Pacifist turned coward. God forgive me.*

The prospect of rebuilding the ranch they'd inherited from Uncle Clyde seemed to revive Jed. That was the only reason Lonnie had agreed to accept the inheritance and join his brother on this venture in Kansas.

The long days on the trail from the train station in Omaha, Nebraska, had been uneventful until the snow. Now he regretted not purchasing a covered wagon. Jed could be nestled between the supplies, protected from the elements. *I gotta get him home safe.*

Lonnie glimpsed a cross atop the barn in the distance. Uncle Clyde's familiar declaration of faith. He sighed.

"The ranch be just around the bend." Lonnie whistled to the horses to pick up their pace and nudged his brother, who'd slumped forward again.

"Hey, lookee there." Jed pointed at the ranch house as they drew near. Smoke billowed out the chimney.

"What in the Sam ..." Lonnie slowed the horses and pulled the wagon behind the barn. "You stay here."

"I ain't sittin' and waitin'." Jed grabbed his rifle. "I can handle myself, and you ain't goin' alone."

No sense arguing. The snow silenced their footsteps.

Jed peeked in the window. "Someone's tendin' the stove wearin' Uncle Clyde's coat."

Fire burned in Lonnie's belly as he stared in the window. *Not again.* He reached the front porch before Jed. His fury in check, he eased opened the door.

A shotgun greeted his chest. "I know how to use it." The tiny female held the gun awkwardly, her hands shaking.

Lonnie almost laughed. "I doubt it."

"You doubt I'll shoot you?" She repositioned her feet and aimed higher toward his head.

Jed joined Lonnie in the open doorway. Her eyes widened, but she didn't move. "Get out. Both of you."

Lonnie handed his rifle to Jed, stepped forward, and yanked the shotgun from her hands. "Hard to shoot with the hammer not cocked."

The woman ran toward the window. Lonnie caught her by the waist in a few steps. She squirmed away and fell to her knees, his uncle's coat almost swallowing her tiny frame, her arms protecting her face. "Don't hurt me."

He stared at the glistening brown eyes of the frightened creature, his tongue lifeless.

Jed came into the house and shut the door behind him. "We ain't plannin' on hurtin' you." He helped her to a kitchen chair while Lonnie stared. His brother, ever the gallant one. "Who are you and why are you in our house?"

"Your house? Liar." The woman spat the words out. Fire in her cinnamon-colored eyes. "This is Clyde Holt's ranch."

"Was." Lonnie found his voice. "He died, and now it's ours."

She gasped. "Did you kill him?"

"Well, no." The false accusation stung like so many from his past.

The innocent face bore no malice, though fear trembled in her voice. No doubt due to his scars. Pain rested in his chest.

Jed shook his head and smiled at the quivering woman. "We inherited it. Clyde was our uncle. We can show you the legal paper." Jed always explained things better.

Tears glistened in her eyes. She sniffled, then straightened her back and stared at Jed.

"I'm so sorry. Months ago, he hired me by correspondence. He wrote he might not be home when I arrived. He told me to wait for him."

"How long you been waitin'?" Lonnie asked.

"Two months."

"Two months? Land sakes, woman, after a few days a sane person woulda gone on their way." She cringed, and Lonnie wished he'd said that a whole lot nicer.

"Don't mind my brother, he speaks without thinkin'." Jed winked at him while rubbing his hands before the fire. Lonnie joined him, positioning himself so his scarred side was hidden from her.

He let the fire's heat chase the chill from his body while his mind fought to find some manners. A glance out the window at the thickening snowfall told him the scared filly would not be leaving anytime soon … which both irritated and intrigued him.

# Chapter 2

"I've no place to go." Genevieve Collins stared at the pair of blond-haired and bearded men. The thin one's hollowed cheeks and haunted eyes contrasted the other's scowl, the scars on his face giving him an angry air. Another red scar slashed across his hand.

"What do you mean you got no place to go?" The cranky one didn't look at her as he grabbed the poker and jabbed at the logs in the fireplace, increasing the flames. "What's a little gal like you doin' out here alone?"

Genny caught the concern underneath the gruffness. She resisted the urge to tell them everything. "I can take care of myself." Crossing her arms, she glared at his back. "My business is none of yours." *They may be acquainted with Malachi Morgan and his ilk.*

"I understand." The thin one held out his hand. "Then let's make introductions. I'm Jedediah Holt and that's my twin brother, Zebulon."

"Twins? I mean, I see you're brothers, but …" Her face pinked as she extended her hand. "I'm Miss Genevieve Collins."

"You can call me Jed and that's Lonnie. Calling us both Mr. Holt would be confusin'." Jed shook her hand. Lonnie kept his hands in his pockets.

"As soon as the storm lets up, one of you can take me into town, and I'll find a new position." Her chin rose as fear shivered through her. *Towns are where he'd search for her.*

*"If you ever leave without my permission, I'll hunt you down and show no mercy."* Malachi Morgan's final instructions conjured the old dread she'd laid to rest since coming to the ranch.

"We won't be headin' to town for a while." Lonnie stared out the window. "No tellin' how long this blizzard's fixin' to stay." Lonnie turned sapphire eyes her way while sadness cloaked his shoulders. "We got provisions in the wagon." He put on his gloves and frowned. "I gotta tend the horses. In all the commotion I left 'em out in the cold."

He shot out the door.

Jed stood. "Miss Collins, I'll go help my brother. If'n anythin' happens to his matched pair of blacks and his favorite stallion, he'll never forgive himself. If we hadn't seen the smoke from the chimney, he'd have taken care of Drake, Sally, and Prissy first."

Genny recognized the reference to the smoke as a polite reminder of her invasion. Jed wrapped his red scarf around his neck, making his pallor even grayer. He seemed nice enough, considering she was an interloper. Lonnie was … best not to judge him just yet. She'd trusted the wrong people based on first impressions.

Jed pulled on his gloves and reached for the doorknob. "Miss, some hot coffee would be nice after tendin' the horses, if it's not a bother."

After two months alone, the few minutes of conversation had been like nectar to a lost bee. She hurried to grind the beans and reheat the vegetable soup.

"What are we goin' to do with a woman?" Lonnie brushed Drake while Jed tended Sally.

"You could marry her," Jed teased as he finished currying his horse.

"That's the stupidest thing—"

"Life in that mountain cabin musta got mighty lonely. If you were willin' to pull up stakes and come here, a wife's the next step."

Lonnie scowled. Quiet filled the barn as the men worked until Jed found a new subject. "Are you gonna tell me why you needed to sell our family home?"

Chest hurting at the prospect of explaining, Lonnie put Drake in the stall and began working on Prissy.

"I know what really happened." Jed filled the feed bins from the sacks they'd hauled in from the wagon. "Your letter left a few details out."

Lonnie stopped brushing the black horse and stared at his brother.

"Our old neighbor, Silas Morgan, worked as a guard at the prison camp where I spent the last two years of the war."

That name sent a chill down Lonnie's spine. "I can't prove Silas and Malachi was behind all the coward-hazin'. But their voices under those hoods the night the house burnt down …"

"They're troublemakers for sure."

Lonnie gave Prissy a firm pat. "He and his brother lit out of town after the fire."

"Silas elected hisself my personal tormenter. He took great pleasure in tellin' me how Ma died. When he mocked your cryin', I smashed his ugly face and got tied to a fence post in the rain overnight." Jed stroked the mare's muzzle.

Lonnie's heart clenched. He touched his branded cheek. *Maybe I am a coward.* "Back in Texas, I lost my trust in people. Lookin' at 'em, wonderin' if they help set the fire. Did they know who poisoned the livestock? After Ma's funeral, I couldn't stay."

"But why'd you sell the ranch for so little? It was worth more than the six hundred in gold you got from Cousin Randall." Jed shook his head. A frown formed for a moment.

"That's all the gold he had. I didn't want his Confederate paper." Lonnie sighed and gave the horse a few more brushes. "Sellin' it to Randall kept it in the family in case … some day—I'm sorry I didn't do better by you."

"Better?" Jed stared across the mare's back at his brother. "You survived so I'd have family to come home to. You're my twin. Without you, I'm half a man."

The familiar declaration sent a tremor though him. "I shoulda stayed and fought for what was ours."

"No." Jed's voice stern, his eyes glistening, he took a few breaths and whispered. "After what I went through, I never want to see Texas again." Jed wiped his face with his sleeve. "I'm thankful God made a way."

Lonnie shook his head. "By lettin' the kindest man we ever knew die?"

"Well, Uncle Clyde was eighty-three."

"You got a point."

"Yep, and his mind was muddled. He'd gone back to Texas to see Pa."

Lonnie laid his curry brush aside. "Pa's been dead nigh on twelve years."

"But ain't it better Uncle Clyde died at the family ranch in Texas than alone in his cabin here in Kansas?" Jed tugged his gloves back on. "Cousin Randall wrote he buried him next to our folks. It was providential he carried his Last Will and Testament in his jacket pocket."

"Good thing he weren't robbed like when he carried the gold mine deed in his saddlebag."

Jed shook his head. "He didn't trust banks. Wonder if he buried any money around here."

*Is that why the gal is here?* Lonnie stroked Prissy's ear, and the horse nuzzled close.

"And with his mind gone, he coulda told a stranger." Jed patted Sally's back then threw hay in the manger.

Lonnie moved the last of the feed from the wagon to a corner of the barn, while Jed rested.

"Makes me wonder if'n that gal is being truthful." Lonnie shoveled moldy straw from a stall. His life had become one big pile of the stuff. A female only added to the stench. Especially if she was squatting on Holt land with a motive to take what was theirs.

"We got plentya time to sort it out durin' the storm." Jed readjusted his hat. "Scripture says to worry about nothin' and pray about everythin'."

*As if God was gonna hear a coward's prayer.*

Lonnie rewrapped his scarf. "We best get these two crates in before it gets so bad we can't see nothin' but white."

"I tied a rope to the hook by the barn door. Figure Uncle Clyde has a hook near the back door of the house. Don't want to get lost twixt the two."

"I'll take this crate to the house then fetch the other." Lonnie grabbed the heavier one full of dry goods and mason jars of canned vegetables.

"No need." Jed stepped toward the boxes. "I'll grab the other and let the rope unroll from my hand as we walk."

"I'll get 'em." Lonnie stepped between his brother and the supplies. The men glared a standoff.

"No, I'll carry it." Jed hefted the lighter crate and adjusted the load in his hands.

Lonnie followed behind at the turtle pace his brother set. The icy wind wrapped around his fingers. He shouldn't have left his gloves in his pocket. At the door, he stepped inside and placed the crate on the table, then grabbed more firewood from the pile near the fireplace and stoked up the flames. Once he was satisfied with the fire, he took a seat at the table.

Miss Collins extended a cup of coffee to him. "I've been very frugal with the wood. I never learned how to chop firewood. My father felt it was unladylike."

Their fingers touched, and heat spread through his body. Startled, he gulped the coffee. He set the cup down and gripped the edge of the table as the hot liquid travel down his throat. Schooling his face, he waited for the pain to ease. "I'll check behind the bunkhouse. Uncle Clyde's ranch hands cooked their own food, so there may be firewood there."

"Don't go in there." Miss Collins paled.

He paused and glowered at her. "Why not?"

"There's a family of skunks living in there."

So much for the idea of sleeping there. He nodded, grabbed his hat off the hook, and went to find more rope in the barn to guide him through the snow to the bunkhouse.

"Wait. I'll go with you." The tiny thing had his uncle's coat on in a flash. "I may not know how to cut wood, but I can certainly help carry."

"No need. I can handle it."

"Please let me help. I feel like the little girl who intruded on the three bears. Well, two bears."

*Maybe if I growl, she'll stay put.*

She followed in his tracks. There was a fair supply of firewood behind the bunkhouse.

He knocked the snow off the pile. "How come ya never found this durin' your two months of free lodgin'?" The icy wind kicked up in his face. He pulled the scarf over his mouth.

She lowered her scarf to speak. "I'm frightened of skunks. The first week here the family marched to the soddie. I steered clear of it."

"They're hibernatin' now." Lonnie found the hook on the bunkhouse frame.

"Good to know." Miss Collins hooked her elbow around the line and held out her arms for firewood. The snow clung to her hair and eyelashes like a snow fairy from one of Grandmother Strauss' stories. She looked every bit as beautiful as he'd imagined the childish imps.

*Them fairies caused all matter of mischief.*

The wind whipped around them as they struggled to carry wood and hang on to the rope. The cold reached through Lonnie's long johns their third trip. They stomped the snow off their shoes as they stacked the last of the wood near the back door. The aroma of soup made his stomach growl.

"*Brr*, I wish I had shoes as warm as this coat. I can't feel my feet." Miss Collins hung up her coat.

"Sit near the fire." Jed moved the rocker closer.

She sat and removed her shoes.

"Let me see your feet." Lonnie squatted before her and reached for her left foot. She jerked it away. "How dare you be so forward."

He jumped up and straightened. Heat ran up his neck. "Just checkin' for frostbite."

She tucked her feet underneath her dress hem. "I assure you, my toes are not frostbitten." Her face flamed as she fanned her hand before him. "You're blocking the heat from the fireplace."

Lonnie shrugged and took three deliberate steps to his left. "Suit yourself."

"Look away, both of you. It's not proper for you to see my bare feet. I'll need to remove my stockings and let them dry. I have no others."

"Yes, miss." Lonnie's answer stumbled over the top of his brother's.

"The soup should be hot by now, and there is bread on the counter and peach pie." Miss Collins pointed toward the stove, reminding him their last meal of dry jerky had long faded. "Go ahead and help yourself. I'll eat later. It will be a bit before my stockings dry."

While Jed grabbed the bread and pie from the counter, Lonnie filled two bowls with soup. The scent of vegetables tickled his nose while he waited for his brother to bless the food. Lonnie scooped the soup into his mouth. The flavor almost made him groan. He'd been eating his own tasteless cooking for three years. "Eat up, brother, this oughta put meat on your bones."

Jed shoveled it in and had seconds. More meals like this should put him to right.

Between them, they finished the pie. Jed grabbed the coffeepot and refilled their cups. "Mighty fine meal, Miss Collins. You always cook like you're expectin' company?" Jed looked around the room. "Where did you get the provisions?"

With his peripheral vision, Lonnie watched her check her stockings.

"Your uncle has a well-stocked larder in the cellar out back. I bring enough in for a few days at a time, mostly canned vegetables and peaches." Miss Collins slipped on her stockings, and Lonnie focused on his coffee cup. "And yes, I cook expecting Mr. Holt any day. He'd hired me as his housekeeper. I've spent my days cleaning this place from top to bottom, except the locked room over there." She pointed to the door near the back entrance. "Bachelors don't keep house very well."

"Housekeeper?" The idea of his persnickety uncle hiring help, a female at that, was laughable.

"Are you accusing me of lying?" Her voice shook. "I can show you the letter." She grabbed a cup off the sideboard and poured herself coffee. "I also have a letter of recommendation from Mrs. Sparks."

"No worries, little lady." Jed got up and held her chair. "It's your turn to eat."

Lonnie grabbed a bowl and filled it with soup. No way was his brother showing him up regarding manners.

"Thank you, gentlemen." She put her napkin in her lap.

Jed smiled at her. "Uncle Clyde wrote me he was considerin' gettin' help."

When Jed grinned that way, it generally meant he was up to something. His brother held up the empty pan. "Sorry, there's no more pie."

Miss Collins returned his smile. "I don't mind. As I said, there are lots of canned peaches in the cellar. I can make more."

She turned Lonnie's way. Her smile ignited heat around his collar. What was she up to? He crossed his arms. She wasn't looking at him for a possible husband. No woman would. *Thank you, brother, for planting the thought of marriage in my head.* Back home, Ida Hargrave had admired his pacifist stand, and they'd come to an understanding. However, after the fire, she'd taken one look at his scarred face and left to visit her sister in Canada. She'd never returned. Yep, his appearance chased women clean out of the country. He placed his hand on his chest, his heart pounding against his scarred fingers.

# Chapter 3

LONNIE BANKED THE FIRE as darkness cloaked the cabin. A lone lamp glowed from the tabletop. Fierce winds searched for entrance, but the house was solid. "Which room is yours, Miss Collins? We'll bunk in the other."

"Neither, I've slept on the floor in front of the fireplace."

"That's rid—why?" Lonnie gazed at the flames for a few moments to settle his thoughts. Now a different kind of flame sparked in his heart. He rose and glanced at her. "No need to sleep on the floor if there are two bedrooms."

She pushed an errant tendril of hair from her forehead. "I thought with limited firewood it made sense to only heat one room."

Jed rose from his chair. "How'd you get here on your own?"

She wrapped her arms around her like a fortress. "I walked."

Lonnie raised his eyebrow. *She ain't making this easy.* "From where?"

"Carter Town, south of here." She stepped to the dry sink, her back to him.

"In them flimsy shoes?"

His brother once gazed at a lady snake charmer from the circus in the same way he was eyeing Miss Collins. Was she planning on picking his pocket too?

"Why'd you stay?" Lonnie asked.

Miss Collins grabbed the kettle from the stove and poured hot water into a tin wash pan. She added a dipper of cool water and a few flakes of soap from a jar.

Lonnie brought the dirty dishes to her.

She took her time washing the first bowl.

"I fell on hard times a while back. A kindly church woman, Gladys Sparks, took pity on me and let me stay at her homestead. Mr. Sparks sent a letter to your uncle. They used to be neighbors, and the last letter they received from Mr. Holt said he was considering a housekeeper."

Lonnie's jaw hurt from holding his tongue. She was a might skittish when they'd first come. Now, her eyes shuttered afore she answered. *Maybe she was usin' womanly wiles to keep us from discoverin' the truth. Not sure what womanly wiles look like but she's … somethin' ain't right with her story.*

Jed picked up a towel and dried the bowl. "I visited Uncle Clyde before I enlisted." Jed's hand swept the room, "This place was a maid's nightmare. We joked about it."

"I'm surprised he was willin' to hire someone." Lonnie squinted her way. Her face crimson, she turned attention toward the dishpan. He grabbed a towel and stepped to her right, so she'd not be distracted by his scars and he could observe her responses. "The man was set in his ways even when we was kids, and he didn't take to strangers in his house."

Jed gave him his you'd-better-shut-your-mouth look. "I recall Jethro Sparks. He and Uncle Clyde were good friends before they moved to Nebraska." He addressed Miss Collins as he dried the ladle. "How'd you get from Sparks' place to here?"

"Mr. Sparks had some neighbors with a son in Abilene, and since they planned to visit him in the fall, I hitched a ride with them. They dropped me off near the mercantile in Carter Town."

"Abilene." Jed rubbed his chin. "The name is from Luke 3:1. King Herod gave that province to his son to rule during the time of Christ. Wonder why they changed the name from Mud Creek to Abilene?"

Jed knew his Bible, even the little details. The Union army had been lucky to get him as a chaplain.

"When I arrived in Carter Town, your uncle wasn't there to meet me. At the mercantile, I purchased a few essentials and asked for directions. They said I'd see the cross on the barn from the road." She glanced Lonnie's way, sadness in her eyes. "They never mentioned he died."

"They didn't know." He resisted the urge to pat her shoulder in comfort. Instead he took extra care drying the spoons. "Uncle Clyde died in Texas."

"Sounds like he might have left right after he sent that letter," Jed said. "It was months ago. He was gettin' forgetful."

"That makes no sense." Lonnie couldn't imagine the smart man becoming so feeble-minded. But then again, he'd not made the effort to visit in recent years. Another failure on his part.

"Before I joined up, Ma encouraged me to seek Uncle Clyde's

counsel. Even then he was a little confused. Add four years, and it's no wonder he went away without a thought of Miss Collins coming."

*Kinda makes sense. But I ain't sure about nothin' right now.*

The metal spoon scraped against the soup pot bottom as Miss Collins scrubbed it. "You both must think me foolish for not seeking help or employment in town. I never made your uncle's acquaintance, yet I waited like he asked in his letter." She studied the dry sink. "I guess after all the cleaning was finished … well … it started feeling like home."

Lonnie didn't doubt she had no place to go. But why would a citified woman want to stay here? If she was afraid of skunks, what would she have done if a cougar or a wolf came calling? Made no sense. The sooner she was gone the better.

"Our home is yours until you find a job and new accommodations," Jed said.

Miss Collins perched near the fireplace. "I can't take your charity, and it's not proper for me to be unchaperoned here with two men."

"Well, we ain't leavin'." Lonnie stood taller and glowered at her.

"Seein' as the blizzard has us trapped in here, you'll take our uncle's room. I've set the fire in the bedroom fireplace. It'll keep the chill off." Jed swung his arm toward the bedroom.

"No, you two take the larger room. It's your home."

"Jed and I slept in the other room afore." Lonnie didn't relish the prospect of a bunk bed.

"But there's no fireplace. It's not right. I'll take the colder room." She started in that direction.

Lonnie barred her way. "Gentlemen don't allow ladies to be uncomfortable." He made sure his scarred side was away from her when he spoke. "Go on now. Take a kitchen chair to bar the door."

She paused at the door, her cheek moist. "Your kindness is too much. Thank you." She wiped her face with her hand. "I'll not be a burden. I'll keep house for you and your brother until the storm is over and the roads are clear. Then I'll go to Carter Town and find work." She grabbed the chair and closed the door, leaving the brothers staring at the wood grain in silence.

Lonnie stomped into their bedroom. "She's gonna be trouble."

Sweat beaded on Jed's brow, and fatigue rested in his eyes. "Stop fussin'."

"How you feelin'?" Lonnie stood ready to catch his brother if he got weak-kneed.

"Tired and cold." Jed shook as he pulled on his nightshirt. Lonnie averted his eyes from his brother's emaciated frame. He pulled the blanket off his bunk and laid it over Jed's blanket, then searched for more.

He shouldn't have insisted that Miss Collins take the bedroom with the fireplace. "I'll get the extra blankets, and you'll be right as rain by mornin'." He opened the empty wardrobe. "Where would Uncle Clyde keep blankets?"

"In the trunk at the end of his bed." Jed's teeth chattered, and his shivering pushed away any debate about knocking on the woman's door.

"Yes?" Miss Collin's voice quavered.

"I'm sorry to disturb you, miss. There's extra beddin' in the trunk, and Jed's a mite chilled."

She appeared in the door in Uncle Clyde's too-large nightshirt, a shawl around her shoulders. "Take whatever you need." Genny moved aside for him to enter. "Is he sick?"

He gathered two quilts and another blanket while averting his eyes at her presence in bedclothes. "He's tuckered out and cold from the ride."

"Perhaps you should have delayed your trip until spring." Her tone soft. "Less chance of snowstorms."

*And there was the slap.*

Anger mixed with guilt brought a snarl to his words. "I didn't take him out in a storm. The storm took us by surprise." His voice rose, and he gripped the blankets like a drowning man his rescuer. "Who are you to tell me what I shoulda done? You know nothin' about our situation." He stepped back. "You took over our home without our permission. Be grateful we didn't kick ya out in the storm."

He stomped to the door.

Before he could slam it good and hard, she called, "Wait."

He turned, and lavender scent surrounded him as she drew near.

"Forgive me. I spoke out of turn." Another blush came to her face. She drew the shawl tighter. "If Jed needs any doctoring, I've learned a few things."

Lonnie nodded and closed the door between them, the sound of the chair secured the knob.

The mention of his lack of thought mimicked the taunts from his neighbors when he refused to take up arms. The truth of her words hurt to the core. He'd failed his family again.

He returned to their room and placed another blanket and a quilt on Jed. "How's that?"

"Better."

"Holler if you need anythin'." Lonnie changed into his nightshirt and hauled his tall frame onto the top bunk. He curled up to keep his feet from dangling off the end, pulling the remaining quilt tight around his neck, grateful for his red flannels and wool socks. *Father, help my brother get strong again.* Once the quilt's warmth enveloped him, his mind vacillating between a curly-haired beauty and worry over his twin, he drifted into a fitful sleep.

"Ahh."

The bunk bed creaked.

Lonnie's foggy mind came alert.

Another moan.

"I'm comin', Jed." A chill of fear matched the shiver of cold from the icy floor as he knelt near his brother.

"Jed, y'all right?"

"Water." Jed tossed about fighting his covers. Lonnie straightened the blankets to free him from his imagined bonds, then touched his warm, sweaty brow.

Lonnie lit the lamp on the wall hook in the predawn shadows. The pitcher on the dresser was empty. He sprinted to the kitchen, his hands shaking as he lit another lamp. He clasped his hands together to still them. Then took a cleansing breath before he dipped a cup in the bucket of water on the counter. Beside the bed, he lifted Jed's head. His brother drank it all in gulps. Rattling breaths followed by a deep cough shook Jed. Lonnie threw on his clothes and stepped to Miss Collins' door.

She opened with his first knock, fully dressed. "I heard someone cough." Concern filled her eyes.

"Come." Fear muted his words. His brother had nearly succumbed to pneumonia at the army hospital after his release from the prison camp. *Please, Lord. He's all I got.*

After placing her hand on Jed's forehead, Miss Collins pulled down the quilt and placed her ear on his chest. Then she rose and secured the quilt under his chin. "We're going to make you well."

Jed nodded and fought another cough.

She turned to Lonnie. "Stay here while I gather what I need."

"Thank you." His brother's present condition was proof her earlier scolding was deserved. *Why hadn't he insisted they wait until spring?* Because Jed had argued the open road would do him good. Why had he listened?

He followed her to the door and kept his voice low. "Forgive me, miss, for bein' ornery and sharp with you earlier."

"Home is where you hoped your brother would heal." Her brown eyes lingered until he felt uncomfortable. "I forgive you." She left the room, taking with her his momentary peace.

# Chapter 4

GENNY SEARCHED THROUGH HER carpetbag for the few medical supplies she'd purchased. Pneumonia had taken her mother when Genny was ten. Papa's smile hollow, he'd patted her face. "I promise, little princess, I shall return with the doctor as soon as the Faro table yields to me." *Why hadn't Papa sold his pocket watch to pay the doctor?*

His watch fob was empty when he'd returned three days later, having traded his timepiece for another chance to win. He'd returned to a dead wife and grieving daughter. *I'll not witness another die.*

She pulled out her volume of *Home Remedies for the Homemaker* and searched the pages for lung ailments. It was limited in its recommendations. What had the doctor done for her mother? Bled her.

At fifteen, Genny had persuaded her father to allow her to take a nursing apprenticeship. Her mentor, Dr. Carver, frowned on bleeding and purging as barbaric and ineffective. *Lord, what do I do?*

A conversation with a schoolmate from years past came to mind. Her classmate had been so excited when her little brother had recovered from pneumonia. She repeated the treatment to anyone who would listen. *Thank you, Lord, that I listened.*

In the kitchen, she pulled out a large pan and poured the remaining water from the bucket in it. The pan was only half full.

"Lonnie."

He appeared beside her. "I need more water. We're going to steam his lungs."

"I'll haul in some snow."

"Perfect."

Lonnie opened the front door. The entire doorway was blocked by whiteness.

Trapped. She trembled like she was ten again, and her heart raced as the key turned in the tiny, dark closet's lock. The wretched woman's voice echoed across the years. *Your ol' man don't pay me enough to take a brat like you out in public.* She ran her fingers through her hair as she pushed those three weeks after her mother's death from her mind.

Lonnie filled the bucket with snow and dumped it in the pan. Then he grabbed another large pan. "I'll fill a few more pans, then try diggin' out later."

"How will you tend your horses?"

Lonnie opened the back door. "This one's passable. The snow drifted on the front of the house. I'll dig a path to the barn." Cold seeped into the room.

He closed the door, and Genny moved closer to the stove. She pulled the willow bark from her bag and two tin cups from the cupboard. Searching for something to add to the water, she spied some dried leaves. Mint. That would do. Water bubbling in the pan caught her attention. "The water's hot." She grabbed the handle of the heavy pot. Lonnie did too.

"Where do ya want this?" Her hands dropped from the handle at his husky voice.

"On the table." She mixed mint into the water. "Bring Jed."

Voices rose from the bedroom. "Put me down."

Lonnie entered with an aggravated brother in his arms.

"Let a fella walk."

He squirmed out of Lonnie's grasp and scowled as he sat at the table. Lonnie straightened the quilt around his shoulders.

"Stop. I may be sick, but I'm not ..." A deep cough choked Jed's words.

She unfolded a blanket. "I want you to lean over this pot and breathe deeply. I'm going to cover your head so none of the steam escapes."

Jed nodded.

Lonnie stood like a sentry over his brother. Envy squeezed her heart. *If only I'd had a brother or sister.* Her childhood had consisted of doll friends.

Genny glanced around the room. "There is no clock to time it."

Lonnie produced a pocket watch. "How long?"

"Twenty minutes."

Lonnie fixed his eyes on the timepiece, looking up only to check his brother. Jed's muffled coughs brought a worried scowl to his face.

She busied herself preparing willow bark tea for his fever. The poultices she'd hope to apply lacked some essential ingredients. *What else can I do, Lord?*

*Incline.* During her training, the doctor had placed pillows behind a lung patient, so her breathing was easier.

"Time's up."

Genny jumped and clasped her hand to her chest. "Good." She lifted the blanket. Jed's hair was plastered to his head, his beard held water droplets, but his face appeared more relaxed.

"How are you feelin'?" Lonnie sat in the chair beside him.

Jed turned to her. "My chest don't feel so tight. I'm breathin' some better."

Genny smiled at his declaration. "We'll have to do this every few hours until your lungs are clear."

She placed the cup of willow bark tea in front of him. "It tastes terrible, but you've got to drink it all to bring down your fever."

Jed took a sip, shuddered then gulped it down. Genny's lips puckered with him. "Here." She placed chamomile tea before him. "There's honey on the second shelf of the cupboard."

Lonnie retrieved it.

"This tea should help you sleep." Her confident voice disguised her fears. "I'm sorry I don't have any laudanum."

"Laudanum gives me nightmares. As a child, I woke up screamin' spiders was crawlin' all over me." Jed shuddered as he stirred honey into his tea.

She patted his hand. "I'll do my best with what we have."

"Miss Collins." Lonnie spoke her name in reverence, and he nodded toward Jed. "We trust you."

Would either of them trust her if they knew the whole truth behind her misfortune? She glanced at Lonnie, whose face had relaxed into a rather handsome peace. Maybe she could heal his brother. She'd used her knowledge to help a few ladies who worked in the tent saloon, even delivering Lucy's baby. If only Papa had let her continue her apprenticeship with Doc instead of selling her off like a prize cow.

# Chapter 5

LONNIE MOVED THE COOLING pot back to the stove as Miss Collins refolded the blanket, placing it across a chair. Doubts about her story still nettled him. But the panic of losing his brother was lessened with her to nurse him. He'd never seen anyone steamed before, but his brother's breathing eased. He trusted her nursing skills, even if her past was in question.

"Jed, you'll need to sleep in the larger bedroom." Miss Collins touched his brother's forehead with the back of her hand.

"No, miss, the bunk's fine." Jed readjusted the quilt over his shoulders and stifled a sudden cough.

"It wouldn't be proper," Lonnie added his protest. There was no way he'd share a room with a woman not his wife.

She crossed her arms, eyes full of determination. "Don't be ridiculous."

Jed caught his eye, and both spoke at once. "It ain't proper."

She dipped a spoon in the honey pot. "Jed, take this. It will help soothe your cough."

Then she turned to Lonnie.

Her serious expression darkened her brown eyes. His heart took off at a gallop. He placed his hand on his chest, trying to still it. *Hope what Jed's got ain't catchin'.*

"I need to prop your brother up with pillows, so he's at an incline." With her hands, she demonstrated the position. "He'll breathe more comfortably, and it will help keep his lungs clear. It is easier to manage when the bed is free on both sides. That room has a fireplace so he can stay warm." She sat in the chair across from Jed. "We'll be steaming him throughout the night and catching sleep in shifts."

"That sounds reasonable. Still ..."

"Zebulon Holt, we are far from the watchful eyes of those who would judge our actions as improper."

The use of his formal name, even if it was in a scolding tone, pleased him. Mentally, he shook himself. He had no right. She was sent from God to help his brother. That was the whole of it.

"Good."

"Hey, I'm right here." Jed rose from his seat, and Lonnie stepped to his side. "I'm sick but not nearin' the pearly gates. I can make my own decisions."

"Sure thing, little brother."

Jed laughed at his reference to the five-minute difference in their age. The laughter brought on a fit of coughing. Lonnie scooped him up and deposited him on the bed.

"Stop haulin' me around like a crippled calf."

Lonnie ignored his brother's scowl. "When you get strong enough to stop me, then I will."

"If you want to be so all-fired helpful, grab the chamber pot from under the bed."

Miss Collins blushed as she gave the pillow a fluff. "I'll leave you to help your brother."

The deed done, Lonnie placed the pot near the back door.

Miss Collins turned from the window where the snow continued to fall. "I imagine you'll need to dig a path to the necessary right away unless there is another chamber pot."

"True." Lonnie peeked in on his brother, who was sleeping soundly, then he glanced around the cabin before retrieving his coat. "Ain't no shovel handy. Can't imagine Uncle Clyde not havin' one."

Lonnie shoved his hands in his pockets while nervousness overcame his tongue. Fidgeting with the contents, he pulled out a key. "Lawyer found this key with my uncle's things. I got a front door key, so let's see if this one's for the storeroom. Might be a shovel in there."

The key squeaked, and the door opened to a little light flickering through the snow-covered window. A variety of smells and a hail of dust filled his nose. He coughed as he stumbled through the maze of miscellaneous things on the floor.

"Where's that gull durn …" He struggled to extract a shovel from a pile of tools, stumbling over several of them, then stepped out of the room. "Seems he put anythin' he wanted handy in there. He was quite a trader. Preferred it to cash. Ain't no tellin' what we'll find." Lonnie shook his head. "Near broke my neck findin' this shovel."

He wrapped his scarf over his hat and around his neck before heading out the back door.

Freezing wind and bits of snow gained entrance to the cabin, blocking the door open as Lonnie shoveled the knee-high drift from in front of the door. Genny pulled on old Mr. Holt's coat and scurried to stoke the fire. She'd sorted the items from the crates the brothers had brought with them. Among her finds was a glass jar of chicken and a bag of flour. "How clever to can meat. Chicken and dumplings would be nice for dinner."

"You need somethin'?" Lonnie popped his head through the open door.

"I was just saying that chicken and dumplings would be nice for dinner."

"Haven't had them since before my ma ... in a long while." He moved back to his work, then hollered into the house. "Coffee would be nice when I'm done."

She put the coffee on, then pulled the frying pan toward the front of the stove when her stomach reminded her they hadn't had breakfast. Just as she found the slab of salted bacon in the crate, the door slammed, and her quivering hands dropped the bacon on the table. She sucked in a breath. Lonnie had removed enough snow from the entrance to close the door. There was no intruder. Her former boss hadn't tracked her here. Her racing heart slowed.

She removed the coat and grabbed her apron. From the jar on the shelf near the stove, she scooped out some sourdough starter. In a few hours, she'd have bread ready to go in the oven.

Mrs. Sparks had shown her how to prepare it. The time she'd spent with the kind woman had been her training ground. She wanted to impress the Holt brothers with her skills. Until Papa had gambled away her mother's wealth, they'd had servants to do the cooking. Eventually, she and Papa'd eaten at soup kitchens. Cooking gave her a sense of independence.

"Thank you, Lord, for Your provision." She'd used the last of the flour yesterday. Mrs. Sparks had said God would provide exactly what she needed, and the brothers had brought flour and much more.

Yesterday, loneliness and abandonment had overwhelmed her. She'd cried the morning away. Then a peace had come over her a few hours before the Holt brothers showed up. The days she'd spent here alone had given her time to read through old Mr. Holt's Bible. A book she'd never read for herself. Even after reading it, she'd told a half-truth to the Holts.

No, she'd lied.

She set the bacon in a frying pan. "I wonder if there's something more interesting for breakfast in the storage room." She pushed the pan away from the flames. Careful not to trip over the clutter, she made her way to the closest shelf. Light shone through the open door. Crockery lined the shelf filled with an assortment of pickles, molasses, and maple syrup. Removing the largest jar's lid, she found her prize, preserved eggs. Replacing the lid, she struggled with removing the heavy crockery from the shelf.

"Coffee smells good." Lonnie filled the doorway of the storage room, blocking most of the light.

"Ahh." Her grip loosened as she jerked in surprise. Lonnie placed his hands over hers to steady the jar. "Can you not sneak up on me?" His large hands covered her small ones, and his closeness made her voice husky.

He took the jar from her and placed it on the table.

"Sorry, didn't mean to scare ya. Wasn't my intention."

"I didn't hear you come in. My mind was woolgathering."

"Woolgathering?" He smiled. "My ma used to say that."

"She was a daydreamer too?"

"Guess so. You daydream a lot?"

"More so since I've been here alone."

Lonnie opened the lid. "Are these pickled eggs?"

"No, preserved eggs. Our cook, Miranda, used to preserve eggs in slaked lye water."

"So, we're havin' some eggs with that bacon?"

"I hope so. If the eggs were preserved correctly, we'll have some all winter." She meant to say *you'll*, but correcting her word would only draw attention to her fumble.

"I'll see about gettin' chickens in the spring when I buy livestock. Uncle Clyde hadn't kept any critters for several years, him gettin' up in age and all." Lonnie sat at the table, and she brought him a cup of coffee. "Thank you, miss."

Genny nodded as she mixed her sourdough bread dough. "I'll make biscuits for breakfast, and the bread should be ready for our midday meal."

"All your good cookin' oughta help Jed get his strength back." Lonnie sipped his brew. "You know Jed's a preacher. At least, he used to be. Enlisted as a Union chaplain."

"Now he's a rancher?" Genny shaped the dough into biscuits.

"He's the one wantin' my help to make this a workin' ranch again, somethin' Pa and Uncle Clyde would be proud of."

"Sounds like a good plan." She wiped her floured hands on her apron and placed the biscuits in a cast iron skillet and then in the oven. *What a blessing to have a home and a plan for the future.*

Coughing from the bedroom sent them both to Jed's side. Lonnie helped him sit upright, and Genny gave him another spoonful of honey. Jed barely finished when Lonnie shoved a glass of water in his face. "Land a Goshen, give me a minute to swallow." Jed pulled himself more upright, then took the glass, downing the contents. "Satisfied?"

Lonnie took the empty glass.

Genny checked for fever again. Lonnie tucked the quilt around his neck.

"Thunderation. The two of you are gonna smother me." Jed batted his brother's hand away. "I smell somethin' burnin'."

"Oh no." Genny ran to the kitchen. Smoke oozed around the burner plates. She opened the oven door with her apron-covered hand. The biscuits were fine. She moved the pan of bacon to the side.

"You forgot to adjust the damper." Lonnie turned the handle on the stovepipe and then opened the back door. In minutes, the frigid breeze had lifted the smoke from the room. Genny closed the door while Lonnie stoked the fireplace in the bedroom.

"Jed, you cold?" Lonnie's anxious voice carried to the kitchen.

"I'm fine. That bit of cool air was refreshin'. When we gonna eat?"

Genny grabbed the plates and utensils and set them on the table. "I'll have the eggs ready in a few minutes. Better start on the biscuits while they're still hot."

Lonnie carried the protesting Jed to the table. "The next time you grab me up against my will I'm gonna ..." Jed straightened his rumpled nightshirt. "I'm gonna smack that smirk right off your face."

"All right, little brother." Lonnie ducked a playful swing from Jed. "I'll let you walk."

Genny set a crock of butter she'd found in the crate on the table and went back to the stove to finish cooking the scrambled eggs. The Holts ate heartily. Her heart fluttered with pleasure knowing her meals were appreciated. "More coffee, boys?"

"Yes, miss." They said in unison.

"I never had any brothers or sisters, and you two fussing at each other makes me envious."

"It's a high compliment, you considering me your brother." Jed smiled and gave a slight nod. "We never had a sister, only brothers."

Lonnie pushed away from the table. "Now that I dug a path to the barn, I'll give the horses some extra hay and check their water." He donned his winter gear and headed out the door.

Jed left his chair. "I'll take myself back to bed."

Genny took a few paces toward the door to be sure he got in bed without help.

Jed's hacking cough filled the room. He pulled the quilt over himself. That cough worried her. Once the roads were passable, Lonnie should go for a doctor. What if there wasn't one? Her hand went to her throat. *Please, Lord.*

# Chapter 6

DEEP HACKING COUGHS WOKE Lonnie. *Lord, help.* He rose from the chair beside his brother. The smell of onions told him Miss Collins was already up.

Jed's red face from coughing had returned to a sickly pallor. "Stop lookin' at me like I'm dyin'. Miss Collins'll make me better. The Lord sent her to us."

Lonnie nodded, knowing if he spoke, his fears would tumble out rather than encouragement. He headed toward the kitchen.

Miss Collins stirred the onions. A piece of cheesecloth lay on the table. She smiled at him from the stove. "My maid put an onion poultice on her husband every time he got a cold."

"Do you think that'll help?"

"She swore by it. He was prone to lung ailments because of his bout of ague as a youth. This should work well. Let's steam Jed, then I'll add this poultice to his chest. I'm hoping he'll breathe easier."

"Hopin'?" Lonnie caught the growl before it tainted his words.

"Yes, my medical knowledge is limited. I'm praying for wisdom."

"Thank you." He turned his scar away from her. "I'll fetch Jed."

After the steaming, he assisted his exhausted brother to bed, and Miss Collins applied the poultice to his chest.

"Feels good." Jed closed his eyes and sleep overtook him.

"I'll keep watch."

She nodded and left the room, closing the door softly behind her. Jed's chest moved with an occasional twitch as a cough slipped through the calm. The steaming, honey, and the poultice seemed to be working. Wind rattled the windows, sending a shiver of foreboding through Lonnie. *Lord, don't let this brother die.* Guilt lay heavy as the faces of his younger brothers, Willy and Leroy, filled his mind. His mother had begged them not to join the Confederate cause. Leroy's words slashed out from the past. *We ain't cowards like Lonnie.* They echoed in his mind when sleep left him. Even in the peaceful mountains of Colorado, he couldn't escape them. If Jed had stayed a little longer, he might have persuaded them to at least wait until they were eighteen. The war ended before then. He unclenched his aching hands one finger at a time.

Jed's coughing fit brought Lonnie's full focus on his living brother. *Please, don't let him die and leave me all alone.*

"Miss Collins." Lonnie squatted beside the lower bunk. A mumble escaped her lips as she swatted his hand and pulled the blanket over her head. She'd been working with him nonstop for days. Jed's fever had broken in the night, and Lonnie had persuaded her to take the bunk. Her sweet face framed in curls drew him. Before the desire to run his fingers through the strands overcame him, he shoved his hands in his armpits.

"Genevieve Collins, get out of bed right now," Lonnie barked.

She sat up with a start, nearly bonking her head on the top bunk. "You are so mean."

He chuckled as he rose from his squatting position near the bed.

An embarrassed grin formed on her sleepy face. "When my mother wanted my attention, she added my middle name."

"Tell me, Genevieve Collins, what's your middle name?"

She threw back the covers and ran her hands down the wrinkles in her dress. "I need to change into a clean frock and comb this unruly hair."

"You look right pretty to me." Lonnie winked, enjoying his attempt at flirting. He stepped back a few paces. "Is your middle name that awful?"

She grabbed her shoes. "Skedaddle." She pushed him toward the door.

He planted his feet. "It must be something downright embarrassin'." He chuckled as she shooed him out of the room, closing the door behind him.

"Well, you two are gettin' along right fine." Jed's chuckle stopped his.

"How-w-w lo-ong you been there?" He hadn't stuttered since he was a child. "What are you doin' out of bed?" He scowled at his brother to cover his embarrassment. Then busying himself, he added a few pieces of kindling to the stove and lit it. Hair prickled on his neck. "Stop starin' at me."

Jed laughed, stepped closer, and whispered. "She'd make you a fine wife."

Lonnie growled, "You don't know nothin'."

"You just keep tellin' yourself that." Jed's smirk needed smacking. But Lonnie didn't want to explain to Genny why they were brawling. Genny. When had he stopped thinking of her as Miss Collins? What had he been thinking about? Oh yes, smacking Jed, but his brother was still on the mend. Once he got well, then … A shiver passed through him. What if he never did? What if he stayed skinny and weak? Great-Uncle Luther had fought in the Revolution and spent time on a prison boat. He'd survived but never gained back his youthful vigor.

An ache formed in Lonnie's chest as he watched Jed take his seat at the table. His shirt and trousers hung from his bony frame. The cough had lessened over the last week. Maybe Genny's cooking would restore him. If she married Jed, he'd have her delicious meals every day. Lonnie scowled again.

Jed's shoulder punch interrupted his thoughts. "Now what you mad about?"

The center of his thoughts entered the room. She wore a deep-blue dress that brought a sparkle to her eyes. Her hair was neatly pinned in place. He missed the messy locks that cascaded down her back.

"Well, did I interrupt something?"

Lonnie squirmed in his chair and shot his brother a warning look.

Jed winked at Lonnie before turning to her. "Can I have coffee before the remedy?"

"I'll start the coffee, and by the time your therapy is done, it will be ready." Genny held up the empty water pail.

"I'll fill it." Snow no longer blocked the entrance when Lonnie opened the door. "It's melted considerable, then froze. Lots of hardpacked snow." He took his knife from its sheath on his belt and chopped a few large chunks into the pail. "I best clear this afore it melts into the house."

After the treatment, Genny knelt close to Jed and placed her ear on his chest then his back. Lonnie's fists clenched and unclenched. *What's a matter with me? She's doctorin' him.*

She rose. "I don't hear any rattling, so we can stop the steaming."

Jed took Genny's hand in his. "I thank the Good Lord, for providin' you for my care before I'd be needin' it." He raised his hands in praise.

"It was certainly the Lord every step of the way." She patted Jed's shoulder. Lonnie fought a frown. He was grateful for God's provision for his brother's sake.

"I'm mighty hungry." Jed poured himself coffee.

"Good to hear." Lonnie held out his cup, and Jed filled it.

"There's no more bread, so I'll make biscuits and gravy." Genny put on her apron.

"Well ain't that somthin'?" Jed declared as he returned to his chair. He lifted an eyebrow at his brother. "That's Lonnie's favorite breakfast."

"It's yours too." Lonnie punched his shoulder gently and shook his head. "I'll go tend the horses."

The sooner he got away from Genny and his brother's foolish matchmaking, the sooner he'd get his mind onto rebuilding the ranch for Jed. Never again would he fail his family or God. He may be a coward, but his brother deserved better. And better he would get.

Genny placed the biscuits in the oven while Jed read near the window. Thoughts of Lonnie's flirting and playful looks took her woolgathering to a sweet place. Working together to save his twin had shown her a softer side of the grumpy man. She stole glances when he wasn't aware. He was quite handsome despite the brand on his face. She mixed the gravy and wrestled with her foolish thoughts, knowing a fine man like Zebulon Holt deserved someone much better than a saloon girl. A tear trickled down her face.

"What's wrong?" Jed stood near, concern in his eyes.

Now she'd done it. She'd promised herself no more lies. But how could she confess her feelings to his brother?

"You're wore out." Jed handed her a hanky.

She wiped her eyes. "I am. Now that the crisis has passed, I'm exhausted." That was the truth. She offered a half smile. "After breakfast, I'm taking a long nap."

"You should." He headed to his chair. "Me, I'll stay up a while. I've been stuck in Uncle Clyde's bed too long. I'll go back to the bunk tonight."

Genny pulled the biscuits from the oven and placed them on the stovetop.

"Are you sure you'll be comfortable in that small bed?"

"You were."

"I'm tiny compared to either of you."

Jed's chuckle grew to a belly laugh so full it took Genny along. She was catching her breath when a cold breeze swept into the room.

Lonnie came in with an armful of firewood. "What's so funny?" His scowl had returned. She wished the man would confide in her. Talking often helped. What a hypocrite—she hadn't told either of them what was troubling her.

Once they sat down for breakfast, Lonnie's good-natured disposition returned as he watched his brother eat almost as much as he did. Here was a man who cared deeply. That caring had scarred him on the inside too. *Father, bring him a wife worthy of his big heart.*

# Chapter 7

LONNIE SPENT THE DAY clearing snow. He'd hacked out the ice near the front entrance and then kept shoveling. Once that chore was done, he'd have no excuse for keeping his distance. The more time Jed had with her, the better chance she'd fancy him. Then they'd marry, and he would hightail it to his cabin in Colorado. *Wait. I promised to help Jed with the ranch. Why'd she have to come and make things so complicated?*

"Lonnie, you gonna play in the snow all day?" Jed called from the back door. "Why'd you shovel a path from the front door to the barn?" He shook his head.

"Miss Collins made a peach cobbler, and she cooked that ham we brung. Come in before you get sick, and I have to carry you to the table." Jed's chuckle disappeared behind the closed door.

Lonnie slogged to the house. The promising aroma of another wonderful meal mellowed him. "Smells mighty good, miss."

"Hurry before it gets cold." Genny's sweet voice warmed his heart faster than the fireplace warmed his hands.

His pulse raced, but he fixed a scowl on his face and sat at the table. Jed said grace and they dug in. Jed ate slower than usual, no more shoveling in the food. He'd placed his napkin in his lap and chattered between bites. Lonnie hardly heard a word while watching the way she tucked a loose strand of hair behind her ear. How daintily she ate, dabbing her mouth with her napkin every few bites. Gold flecks formed in her brown eyes when she laughed. A deep sigh escaped his lips, and he forced his eyes on his plate.

"Are you coming down with something?" Genny placed the back of her hand on his forehead.

A tingle slid to his toes. He jerked his head away. "What's wrong with you, woman? Stop lookin' for a new patient. I'm fine."

She crossed her arms. "You've hardly touched your food, and you were out in the cold all day."

"Can't a man keep to his own thoughts without you lookin' for a fever?"

"What's trapped your tail to make you so snippy?" Jed asked.

Lonnie scrambled for something to distract his wayward thoughts. "I was wonderin' how the roads are." He paused. "If they're clear enough, I can escort Miss Collins to town. Now that you're well, she needs to find a job."

The shocked expression on Genny's face glowed, then faded in an instant. She took another bite of ham and began to cough. Lonnie leapt up and pounded on her back. She motioned for him to stop and took the glass of water Jed offered.

"You all right?" Lonnie's hand lingered on her back.

Genny gasped as she sipped. She signaled for them to sit and finished her water. "That's better. My goodness, you two, I wasn't choking that bad."

She schooled her face, then picked up her knife and fork, slicing her ham into tiny pieces. "When were you planning on checking the road?"

"Tomorrow." Lonnie forced himself to leave not a crumb of the now-flavorless meal. He'd said she needed to go. Pride kept him from taking it back. It was probably for the best. When the spring thaw came, Jed could court her proper-like, and he could … Genny's sweet voice interrupted his misery.

"There's a few chores I want to finish before I leave. And I'll make several loaves of bread." She took her untouched food to the stove. Jed shook his head.

Lonnie jumped to his feet. "Gotta check on the horses and bring in more firewood."

"I'll help." Jed followed him and grabbed his coat. "I need some fresh air and exercise."

*Can't a man be left alone to think? If only Jed'd stay quiet.* Lonnie lit into his task like a racehorse straining for the finish line. Maybe Jed would tire right quick and leave him to finish in peace. The steamy stench of fresh manure as they placed the dirty straw in the wheelbarrow fit his mood. His heart as gloomy as the dark corners of the stalls untouched by the lantern's light. A draft of frigid air crossed his neck, sending a shiver through him. Once the wheelbarrow was full of dirty straw, Jed spoke.

"You're like this icy snowstorm."

"What?" Lonnie rolled his eyes, sure as shooting a sermon was coming his way. "Don't start."

"Your heart—" Jed wiped sweat from his brow and laid the pitchfork aside. "You was like that blocked doorway after the storm the whole trip here."

"Hey, I looked after you, didn't I?"

He grabbed his pitchfork as Jed picked up his sermon. "The whole trip you blocked out others. You growled at everyone, even refused to tip your hat. The old lady at the tradin' post where we bought supplies was shakin' in her shoes. While you cared for me, you stared daggers at the world."

Lonnie groaned as he stepped in manure trying to distance himself from his brother's tongue lashing. Scraping his boot with some fresh straw added frustration to insult. Being a monster had cost him more than standing up for his convictions.

Jed laid his pitchfork aside. "Comin' here, the icy part—the meanness—started meltin'. Miss Collins is touchin' the deep places. Shoot—you're too stubborn to admit it. Shovel away that ice blockin' your life. Forgive yourself for your imagined failures."

"No one stared at you like they did me."

"Lonnie, you saw what you wanted to see."

"Shut your mouth." His growl startled the horses, their whinnies and snorts an amen to his brother's words.

"Open your heart." Jed's words were quiet, his eyes pleading.

Conviction surrounded Lonnie. Why'd his brother have to take up the call to preach? He grabbed Drake's lead rope and took him into the clean stall. He patted Sally's muzzle, drawing comfort from the mare. Horses he could trust.

"These two will produce fine colts. A great start for horse-breedin'." Lonnie's change of conversation lightened the heaviness between them.

"You're the breeder."

"You'll learn." Lonnie placed his hand in his brother's shoulder as they headed out the door.

"What is your vision for the ranch?" Jed matched his long stride.

Lonnie stopped and stared at his brother. "Once you're strong again and this ranch is up and runnin', I'm goin' back to Colorado."

"That's just mule dumb stubborn." Jed crossed his arms and planted his feet. "Ranchin' is in your blood. No one's a better horse breeder'n you."

"I lost the will after they burned me out and Ma died." A knot formed in his throat. A chilly wind scooted across his neck. He raised his collar and shoved his hands in his pockets. "It's too hard." Lonnie headed into the house, knowing Jed would say no more in front of Genny.

# Chapter 8

"BE CAREFUL." GENNY PULLED her shawl close. Chilly winds stung her cheeks as she stood near the corral hating the memories this moment would bring.

Lonnie mounted his horse and tipped his hat toward her. "Be back by noon. If the roads are bad, I'll turn back sooner."

Jed glared at his twin and shook his head. He took her elbow and escorted her into the house.

Eyes still sore from a night of tears, she regretted being drawn to Lonnie while they'd tended Jed. Not seeing him every day, even when he scowled and fussed. *What is wrong with me? I don't need a man … especially not a grumpy one.*

She lifted her head high. It was for the best. Hanging her shawl on the peg, she grabbed the broom. Once he knew the *whole* truth, he'd be glad he sent her packing. Tonight, she'd tell them. Jed wouldn't be so friendly after that, him being a pastor, but she'd promised the Lord no more lies. The feeling of family would fade with the truth, and loneliness would become her companion again. Living in town would be easier, as long as Malachi Morgan never showed up. A shiver rippled her spine. Her former boss always tracked down those who escaped his grasp— just like the slaves he'd owned before the war.

"I'm gonna lie down for a spell." Jed headed to his room muttering, "Stupid fool."

*Was he calling her a fool?* Her sweeping intensified to chase away the shame.

She finished setting the kitchen in order, then started on the storage room. While her hands stayed busy, her mind searched for a solution. When she'd walked to the cabin from town, her mind had contrived this crazy idea, to hide from her past and the man looking for her. What would she do now? She wiped perspiration from her brow with her sleeve as she cleaned and sorted. Flour dust billowed as she tidied a pile of empty sacks. She coughed.

"More canned vegetables and peaches." She moved to the rows of neatly built shelves and wiped them before placing on the canned goods. The room held piles of things that needed sorting through. "Old Mr. Holt saved everything."

Genny found places for a variety of odds and ends. Her nose twitched as she arranged three blocks of chaw.

"Hmm, an army stretcher. How odd." She placed it under the bottom shelf.

"Quite an undertakin'," Jed said as he stepped inside.

She blushed at being caught talking to herself.

"Was your uncle a trapper?"

"No." Jed reached for a pile of pelts. "Land sakes, these furs will bring a nice price. I reckon he did some tradin'." Jed tied them with string and hung them from a hook overhead. "Let me help."

"Can you move that saddle over there?"

Jed lifted it and placed it where she'd indicated. "These things goin' to the barn?"

She nodded and pushed a stray hair out of her eyes. "There are wagon traces over there." He shifted the mass of leather, examining it in the light from the door. Something glinted from the three jars that had been buried in the jumble. Genny's breath caught. "Jed." She handed the jar to him.

"What in the name of heaven?" Jed grabbed the jars.

They headed to the kitchen table. He opened the first jar and poured gold coins onto the table. The second jar held paper money and the third gold dust. Jed smiled and shook his head. "Lonnie needs to see this." He glanced out the window. "Speakin' of my half-wit brother, he oughta be home by now. There's a new storm brewin'."

Genny turned back to her work when hoof beats echoed outside. She went to the window. "It's Drake—and he's riderless."

Jed grabbed his winter things from their pegs on the wall.

"I'm going too." She shrugged into old Mr. Holt's coat.

"I'll saddle Sally. Grab what we might need."

Her breath coming in shallow pants, she stuffed her rucksack and flung it over her shoulder. *God, keep him safe.*

"Lonnie trained Drake to stay put and not bolt," Jed explained. "No tellin' when he fell off the horse."

She patted the stallion and whispered in his ear, "Please show us where Lonnie is." Her oversize coat got in her way as she struggled to mount the mare. Jed pushed her into the saddle, then mounted Drake. She trailed Jed as he followed Drake's tracks. It wasn't twenty minutes before they reached a patch of icy road. Drake balked and bucked. Jed calmed the horse, then urged him forward. The horse twitched his ears and whinnied, Genny scanned the area.

Jed pointed ahead. "Ain't that Lonnie's hat?"

Genny leapt from her mount, struggling for footing on the slick surface.

The Stetson lay in the middle of the icy road. Some of the ice was cracked and hoof prints cluttered the area. They tied the horses to a tree, then Jed grabbed the rope from his saddle and led the way to an outcropping over a copse of trees in a ravine.

"Help." Lonnie's voice filled her with joy and dread. She spied his coat sleeve several feet below under an evergreen with broken branches.

"Stay here." Jed headed toward Lonnie after tying a rope to a sturdy tree.

"No, I'm coming with you." Panic forced Genny forward. She followed the path made by Jed's boots in the crusty snow and clung to the rope for balance as they descended over the outcropping and down the hillside. For the first time in her life, she wished she were wearing trousers as snow clung to her dress.

Heart pounding, she made her way with the rucksack. Lonnie's pale face wrenched her heart. "Where do you hurt?"

"Everywhere. Ice patch. Horse threw me." His words came in broken bits. The evergreens lay thick around them. He flexed his left leg and fell back. "Ribs hurt … head spinnin'."

Jed squatted beside him. "You're freezin'." He rubbed Lonnie's hands.

Genny covered him with a blanket. She supported his head and offered him water from the canteen. He took a few sips, then closed his eyes. "Lonnie."

She tapped his cheek. "Stay awake. Take another sip." After a few more swallows, she replaced the cork in the canteen.

Jed ran his hands over his brother. Lonnie moaned. "Genny, look at his leg."

Her light touch brought a tight-lipped groan. "It's broken. We need to be careful moving him."

"I'll make a travois to haul him home."

"There's an army stretcher under the shelves in the storage room, would that work?"

Jed stood and scanned the path they'd come down. "I'll fetch it. We can use it to haul him up the hill. He's too heavy, and the hill's too steep for me to tote him over my shoulder. We'll rope him to the stretcher and use the tree up yonder for leverage."

He glanced at her. "I'm taking both horses home and bringing Prissy and Sally back with the wagon."

After cutting dead branches and clearing a place in the snow, Jed took his flint and tinderbox from his pocket to start a fire. Crouching near her, he whispered, "Keep him warm while I'm gone. He's been out here too long." Jed left as Genny secured the blanket around Lonnie's shivering form.

"I need to make a splint." Genny searched through her rucksack for bandages.

Lonnie pointed to the knife in his boot. Then his eyes flickered shut.

Genny tapped his cheek several times.

His eyes jerked open. "What ..."

"Don't you dare fall asleep. You could have a concussion." Fear clutched her heart and pounded through her body. She fashioned a splint with two branches and bandages.

Lonnie continued to shiver, his skin ice-cold. There was only one way she knew to bring up his body temperature. *Father, my motives are pure. Help me be brave.*

"I need you to sit up." Genny tugged, and he moved forward with a moan. She sat behind him and opened her coat, stretching it around them both, molding her body around him.

"No ... ain't proper." Lonnie's teeth chattered. He tried to pull away, but she held fast. Too weak, he sagged against her, pushing her back toward a tree trunk giving her the support she needed to hold him up.

"Medical science has proven close bodily contact is the fastest way to warm someone."

Lonnie's shivers lessened as the fire and Genny's closeness thawed him. She wrapped a scarf around his snow-dampened head. "Sorry ... to inconven—"

"Inconvenience me?" Genny's breath warmed his neck. "You scared us half to death when you didn't come home. Your horse brought us to you."

"He waited. I whistled ... Jed."

"I had no idea you could train a horse to do that."

Genny's arms sent a tingle through him. If not for the cold, he'd keep his distance.

"Drake's smart." Lonnie forced himself to talk through the pain raking his body from the fall.

Genny pulled the blankets closer, pressing against him. Fear had gripped him after he'd regained consciousness. Her presence gave him hope.

"Somewhere I heard that ranchers don't name their horses."

"Raise 'em to sell. Train 'em to get a nice price."

"If you name them, do you keep them?"

"Sally, Prissy, and Drake are great breedin' stock. Won't be sellin' 'em." He leaned back against her, struggling to keep his eyes open.

"Sounds like you love ranching."

"Not no more," he whispered.

"Lonnie Holt, I never took you for a liar." She gave his shoulder a gentle nudge. Her sigh tickled his ear producing an oddly warm shiver that spread to his toes. He'd stay like this forever if it weren't so cold and painful. Genny's presence made the horror of losing his family and the loneliness of the past few years fade into a distant memory.

"You're a good woman, Genevieve Collins." His eyelids drooped.

She sniffled against his shoulder. "No, I'm not." He was fully awake now.

"Genny?"

"I'm a big old liar." Her body quivered against him as she expelled a breath. "Please don't tell Jed." Before he could respond, she moved her head off his shoulder and readjusted the blanket. "I didn't tell you the whole truth about where I came from."

He'd been right, but now it didn't matter. "No need."

"Yes, I must." She tensed. Cold air sent a path down his back. Genny shuddered and closed the gap between them. Lonnie pulled the blankets toward his neck. Her head rested on his shoulder once again. The hole in his heart seemed to seal shut.

"Papa loved to gamble more than he loved his family. Mama's wealth kept us well enough until he gambled away every last cent. We ended up living in a hovel because my grandfather would only take us in if she left him. Instead, Mama honored her wedding vows. She took in sewing clothes for the women she once had to tea. When I was ten, she contracted pneumonia. Papa tried to win enough to pay the doctor and left me alone to watch her die. After that, he promised me he'd quit and got a job in a factory. We had no friends from our old life, and the new neighbors judged us as 'uppity' because we were once wealthy."

Lonnie placed his gloved hand over hers under the blanket and squeezed. He'd gone to the mountains of Colorado to avoid people. His loneliness was a choice. Hers had been thrust upon her.

"When I was fifteen, I found an apprenticeship with a doctor. My life had purpose for the first time. Then a few years ago, Papa confessed he owed a huge sum of money to a gambler. He said he'd arranged for me to work off his debt." Bitterness covered her words. "Being an obedient daughter, I agreed. I thought I'd be cleaning the man's home."

Genny fell silent and moved her head to his other shoulder, her anguish a palpable thing.

"You don't need to say more."

Genny sniffled then snuggled closer and tugged the blankets tighter.

"I gave up my apprenticeship and dealt cards in a tent saloon that followed the railroad across the country." Her voice quavered. "Papa had taught me how to count cards. I'm ashamed to admit it, but I manipulated them, so the house won. My worthless father taught me that one lesson ... and it saved my virtue. Last year, I completed the contract. I'd received a telegram a few weeks prior from Papa's friend telling me he'd died. Mr. Morgan was unaware and claimed Papa owed him more money."

Alarms went off in Lonnie's head. *Surely, it wasn't Silas. Was it his brother Malachi? Could Malachi be trackin' her? Please, Lord, keep her safe.*

"Six hundred dollars might as well have been six million." She nestled closer.

Lonnie's fists tightened.

"Mr. Morgan suggested a way I could pay it off in full." The wind picked up and flakes of snow landed on the blanket. "For the first time since I'd come to that horrible place, I prayed for deliverance."

"How'd you get away?"

"Gladys Sparks, the woman I told you about, grabbed my arm when I left the gambling tent and told me God had said to rescue the next woman who walked out of that den of iniquity. She and her husband smuggled me to their farm. Mr. Sparks wrote your uncle. His pastor had told him he'd better get rid of me quick before I contaminated their children."

"That ain't right." No wonder she didn't want him to tell Jed.

"If your uncle hadn't said to come, I don't know what I'd have done."

A rustling interrupted her story. Jed descended the hill.

"You two all right?" Sweat glistening on his face, Jed dragged the stretcher behind him. He stopped and panted.

Genny moved from behind Lonnie then secured the blankets around him. "Jed, rest a spell." She led him to a fallen log. "You don't want to overexert yourself." Genny shared the canteen with him. "Better?"

Her bright smile set off a string of jealous thoughts. She'd cuddled close only to keep him from freezing. While he was her patient, Jed got her smiles. After a few minutes, Genny helped Jed execute his rescue plan.

Lonnie gritted his teeth to smother a scream as the two struggled to move him to the stretcher.

"Sorry to cause you additional pain." Genny stroked his cheek, then adjusted the blanket around him.

Lonnie woke in twilight, his body stiff and achy. Memories of lying in the snow, Genny's closeness, the pain of rescue. He lay on a mattress from the bunkbed in front of a roaring fire. No wonder his bones had finally stopped shaking. The new splint from wood planking ran from his groin to his ankle. Bandages wrapped his torso and head. He turned his head and groaned.

"Miss Collins, bring him that laudanum." Jed appeared in his line of vision.

"Where'd you get some?" Lonnie squeezed his eyes shut to stop the walls from tilting.

"Uncle Clyde had medical stuff in a crate in the storage room."

Genny put her arm under his head to assist him with the medicine. "Drink it down. I've cut it with water to help with the pain but not overpower your senses."

After swallowing, Lonnie lay down with a sigh. "How long have I been sleepin'?"

"Several days." Jed leaned close. "How you feelin'?"

"Like I been in a cattle stampede." He tried to sit up, and a smooth-faced Jed shoved a pillow behind his back. "You shaved?"

"After I shaved your face so Miss Collins could be sure there weren't any hidden wounds under that scraggly beard." Lonnie's fingers flew to his face. Shame overwhelmed him, bringing a growl of protest. "You shoulda asked."

"It's retribution for carryin' me around like a rag doll when I was sick."

Lonnie scowled while Jed laughed.

"You two are a pair." Genny straightened Lonnie's blanket. Her touch brought unchecked yearning.

"A matched set." Jed leaned his face next to Lonnie.

She put her hand to her chin and her eyes sparkled. It took Lonnie's breath away.

"I think Lonnie is the better looking."

*Don't torment me, woman.*

Jed sat up and placed his hand on his heart. "You wound me, madam."

Their laughter sent jealous tendrils tangling through his heart.

"Lookee here, brother." Jed grabbed the three jars from the table. "We got no money worries for sure."

Lonnie examined each one. Uncle Clyde had truly provided. "Ain't that somethin'?"

Jed grinned like a possum. "Well Doggie, no need for credit, and we can get one of them special bulls you mentioned."

"We got enough land for more cattle. Now we can afford 'em." Lonnie let the idea of growing the Single Cross Ranch circle in his mind. "We can double the horses we was planning to buy."

"Maybe you could build a church in town." Miss Collins smiled at Jed.

"Sure thing." Lonnie's enthusiasm waned as his brother nodded and shared a knowing look with Miss Collins. Or was it a loving look? Did she want to be a pastor's wife?

Lonnie allowed the medicine to push him back to blissful unconsciousness lest his jealousy cause him to say something he'd regret.

Genny moved the chair closer to Lonnie's sick bed. *Thank you, Lord, for no infection so far. It's been three days of storms. Please, he needs a doctor.*

She placed the bowl of warm water on the chair and sat on the floor near his mattress to bathe his face. His eyes moved underneath his lids. She'd memorized every line of the C branded on his cheek. Without thinking, she reached out and lightly traced it with her fingertips.

Lonnie's eyes sprang open and his hand captured hers. "It stands for coward."

Genny kept her gaze locked on Lonnie. "I see courage."

He shoved her hand away, anger flaring in his eyes.

Genny cupped his chin and turned him to her. "I see a man of conviction, one not afraid to stand up for his principles." She once again ran her fingers over the C.

"If there were more men in this country with your convictions, maybe there'd have been no war." She pushed a wayward strand of hair off his forehead. The feel of his face invited further exploration. Her fingers avoided his lips as they ran down to his neck. She pulled away before she acted on her impulse and embarrassed them both by kissing him. Once well, he'd insist she leave. Yet, his eyes shined at her touch, allowing hope to blossom in her heart. Then a scowl stamped out the shine.

"You're a fool to think I'm courageous." Lonnie struggled to turn onto his side.

Genny adjusted the pillows so he was facing the fireplace, glad he couldn't see the tears on her cheeks. "You sleep now."

She rose and wiped her face before Jed returned from chores. *Why am I crying? Men are untrustworthy, selfish brutes.* But her heart rebelled. *Why must I love the one who won't love me in return?*

Lonnie feigned sleep while his mind replayed her pleasing voice and gentle touch on the mark that defined him. Could he view his scar as courageous? His neighbors had branded him with their opinion. Could he stand tall in this hateful world knowing he'd done the right thing? Only an angel would view that C as brave. Genny didn't deserve the scorn she'd endure if he asked her to be his wife.

A cold breeze wafted over him. Lonnie kept his eyes closed so Jed wouldn't talk to him. His twin dropped the firewood nearby and then pulled Lonnie's blanket over his shoulder. As soon as his leg healed, he would return to Colorado. *If I leave, that'll get the notion outta both our heads about me marryin' Genny. Jed needs the kinda care she gives him. She'd make a right fine rancher's wife.*

The idea brought him no joy. Joy was something he'd have to learn to live without. *Then there's my promise.* His brain hurt from trying to sort it all out, almost as much as his leg.

# Chapter 9

LONNIE STARED OUT THE window from his new bed near the fireplace, made from planking Jed found in the rafters of the storage room. The thwack of Jed's ax gnawed at him. "I should be out there, and he should be restin' inside." Uncle Clyde's calendar mocked him. Six borin', lay-about weeks.

Genny pulled dry shirts from the clothesline strung across the room. "He isn't sick anymore. Exercise is good for him." Her calm demeanor irritated. "You're the one who needs rest."

He ran his fingers through his hair and huffed. "It's too cold. He's too puny. What if he hurts hisself?" He shot her a furious glower.

Genny shook her head and folded a shirt. "I imagine he has been cutting wood since a lad. He's wise enough to pace himself."

Fighting the stirring in his heart toward this woman was maddening. Jed had praised God for bringing her. They worked around the house like an ol' married couple. If he hadn't been a fool and broke his leg … He glanced at the floor. Once his cheeks cooled, he turned toward the window again. "Where'd he go?"

The ax lay on the ground, but there was no sign of his twin. "I gotta check on Jed." Lonnie grabbed the crutches Jed had fashioned and struggled toward the door. Walking was a challenge even with the new shorter splint.

Genny held up her hand. "Stay right here." She blocked his path and with a furious look of her own added, "You need to go rest that leg."

"Get out of my way, woman." His roar brought a visible shiver to the tiny thing in his way, but she refused to move. He stood his ground letting shame at his nasty behavior take second place to his concern for Jed.

"He isn't lying out on the ground. Jed is well enough to handle things. If you're not careful, you'll rebreak that leg."

The crack of ax against wood filled the silent space between their determined stares.

She pointed to the window. Jed, now coatless, set another log on end for splitting.

"He'll catch his death, and you'll be to blame." He hobbled to a chair and propped his splinted leg on another chair while rearranging his nightshirt to cover himself.

"Well, mother hen, I will go check on him." Her smirk annoyed him.

"Laugh all you want, but Jed needs his rest."

Genny pulled on her coat and stepped outside, closing the door behind her. In a few minutes, they entered with their arms full of wood.

"I heard you yellin' from the outhouse." Jed laughed as he piled his load near the fireplace. "Since when did you become my mother? I'm fine. The weather's not bitter today. I'm pacin' myself. I told Miss Collins to come get me in half an hour if I wasn't in." Jed grabbed his watch from the table.

Lonnie looked between the two and slapped the table. "Been nice if'n you'd told me."

Jed winked at his brother. "It was kinda funny seein' your worried face through the window."

"If you weren't so puny, I'd smack that smile off your face." Lonnie swallowed the knot in his throat. "There's always risk of another bout of pneumonia."

Jed squeezed his brother's shoulder as he walked to the stove and poured a cup of coffee. "I appreciate your concern. Choppin' wood is good exercise. And accordin' to Miss Collins' medical book, exercise is the best thing for me."

He frowned. "When I'm better, I'll teach Miss Collins how to chop wood, so she don't have to bother you."

"A lady don't need to when gentlemen are present." Jed glared as he replaced the pot on the stove. "I can do it."

"I'm no lady, and it's a very practical idea." Genny reached for another shirt to fold.

The angry expression Jed shot his way was well-deserved. He hadn't meant to imply … Why'd he say it? What was wrong with him? The last few days Genny and his brother had laughed together as they worked side by side. Little jokes betwixt them that he couldn't hear. It got under his skin and sent the sting of envy through him. *Lord, forgive me.*

Lonnie hobbled into Dr. Murdoch's office with assistance from Jed and

Genny. After the long wagon ride, his leg screamed at him, but he kept his expression blank as the doctor unwrapped the splint and examined it.

"It's healed well." Dr. Murdock set the splint aside. "You won't need a splint anymore, but it's going to be very painful to walk on. Give it some time. Your wife did a fine job of setting your leg."

Before Lonnie could correct him, Jed spoke up. "Yes siree, she once worked for a doctor."

Lonnie struggled to find the right way to correct the doctor's misconception. But everything sounded wrong when he formed the words in his head. Admitting she shared a house with two bachelors not her kin was … fuel for gossip. If Genny found a room in town … and if Doc mentioned her being his wife to someone. That'd just complicate things. His lower teeth raked across his new mustache as he tried to catch Jed's eye.

Dr. Murdoch turned to Jed next. "I'd say you've recovered nicely." The doctor glanced at Genny. "Could I call on you to assist me with a patient from time to time? I have yet to hire a suitable nurse." His eyes lingered on her.

Oh, how Lonnie wanted to punch the man.

"Thank you for thinking I would be suitable." She crossed her arms and stared at the floor a moment before answering. "I'm afraid I'll be too busy."

She headed out the door ahead of the men. Jed helped Lonnie onto the wagon next to Genny, then climbed aboard.

Without waiting until the wagon moved, Genny leaned toward Jed. "What were you thinking to imply Lonnie and I are married?" she spoke through gritted teeth.

"To protect your reputation." Jed released the brake and headed the horses out of town.

"But Lonnie hates me." Her words barely audible.

"Ain't so." Jed nodded at Lonnie. "Tell her."

Here was his chance. He looked into her eyes and froze. No. He couldn't chain her to his past. He faced forward as they rolled out of town.

The wagon ride home was silent.

# Chapter 10

ONCE THE WAGON STOPPED, Genny fled into the house. Jed shook his head. "Well, brother, there was the perfect opportunity to speak your mind."

Lonnie's chest tightened as he entered the house, sobs coming from the bedroom. He knocked on the door. A loud thud answered him.

"Don't blame her for throwin' things." Jed glowered at his brother then grabbed his Bible. "I'm headed to the barn. Fix this."

Misery rooted him to the spot. Glancing at the firewood, he imagined building a raging bonfire and throwing himself on it. *Father, I deserve her wrath. But how do I fix this? If I admit my feelin's ... She said she preferred Jed. Or did she? God give me words.*

"Genny."

Silence answered him.

"We gotta talk. Please."

When the door opened, his heart palpitated with both hope and fear.

Genny's puffy eyes chastened him. He spoke around the lump in his throat. "I ... come to the table, please ... I need to sit."

She followed him and once seated, she spoke first. "I'm sorry my presence pains you so."

"I never said that," he whispered.

"You implied it with every growly, grumpy remark."

A stubborn glint rested in her cinnamon eyes. Shame filled him.

"I like you bein' here ... you're a godsend ... Jed mighta died." His words came out low and husky. "He's scolded me about my surliness. More'n once." He cleared his throat. "I apologize for my behavior. Please, forgive me."

He waited, staring at her every beautiful feature.

Without replying, Genny rose to make coffee.

Maybe if he resurrected the old Lonnie, things would be easier. The one who'd went into hiding when living got difficult. "What can I do to gain your forgiveness?"

"You don't need to gain it. I give it freely." Genny offered a brief smile. "Your brother means the world to you. I'm a bit jealous. I have no family now."

He reached for her hand then drew back. "I appreciate your understandin'. I—" The door slammed against the wind that blew Jed inside.

"*Brr*, the barn is a perfect place for prayer except for the cold." Jed looked between the two. "I see you are sortin' things out." He took off his coat. "Time with the Good Book always settles my heart. I hope this oaf apologized proper-like." Jed laid his Bible on the table, then huddled at the fireplace.

Genny nodded his way. "Yes. I need to start supper." She reached for a basket she kept near the back door. "A cobbler might be nice tonight. I'll get some canned peaches from the cellar." She shrugged into her coat and slung the basket over her arm. Neither man mentioned there were still jars of peaches in the storeroom. Once she was gone, Jed leaned toward him.

"Did you ask her to marry ya?"

"When you gonna stop kicking that dead horse? She favors you."

He stared at Lonnie, then cleared his throat. "Don't know where you got that fool notion. 'Sides, we'd have to go to the preacher in town to get hitched. How'd that look?"

Lonnie held his head in his hands, elbows on the table. "I can't. I'd be a saddlin' her with a monster and a coward." *Did he just admit he cared?*

The door creaked. Genny entered, cheeks flushed from the cold. Lonnie took in the vision. She put her basket of canned peaches on the table. "You boys all right?" Genny placed the back of her hand on his head. "Are you feeling poorly?"

He gently removed her hand. "No, miss."

Jed opened his Bible, and Lonnie rose. "Doc was right about the pain in my leg. Jed, I think I'll lay on your bed." The farther away from Genny the better.

# Chapter 11

GENNY STOOD IN THE now neatly organized storeroom. Its fresh appearance reminded her of Lonnie's new attitude. He smiled more, spoke kindly, and shaved daily. Her neck flushed as the focus of her thoughts appeared in the doorway.

With a pleased expression, he scanned the room. "Thank you for organizin' in here. Everythin' you lay your hand to is always better for it."

*Be still, my heart.* She cleared her throat. "I found paper and pencils." His gaze unnerved her. "It's a good thing too. I need to make a list of supplies."

"Jed and me'll have the barn set to rights by lunch. We'll go after."

She nodded as another bright smile beamed her way. She appreciated the new Lonnie. Maybe God was using her to heal both brothers. Doing something good after years of relieving men of their hard-earned wages brought healing to her own heart as well. *Thank you, Lord.*

"You sure you don't want to come to town?" Lonnie mounted the wagon.

"After Dr. Murdoch's misunderstanding, I think not." She wrapped a scarf around Jed's neck. "Don't need to catch your death, brother."

"Sure don't, sister." Jed tipped his hat and joined Lonnie.

The men rode in silence. Jed glanced his way. "Don't go back to that dark place you camped in for years."

Lonnie ran his hand over his face. "What if she leaves in the spring?"

"You can't let her go. You'll regret it all your life."

"I ... But ..."

"But nothing. Don't prove that brand."

"What's that supposed to mean?"

"You're the bravest man I know. I've said it, we both heard Miss Genny say it. But you keep tryin' to prove you're a coward. Especially regardin' that little gal."

"She don't want me." Lonnie pressed his hands to his forehead, attempting to erase her lovely face from his mind.

"I ain't marryin' her. She claims me as her brother. However, I ain't heard her refer to you that away."

"I'm the monster who growls."

"You've done a good job of slayin' that dragon."

They pulled up in front of the mercantile, leaving the knight analogy to ruminate in his head.

The dragon sparked to life in the mercantile when he spied his old enemies. The thin, wiry frame of Silas Morgan with his bulky brother Malachi stood like a bad dream before them, chatting with the storekeeper. Lonnie replayed the branding and the fire. Long before rumors of war, he'd promised Pa he'd not take up arms to end a man's life. Here stood the men who tested his conviction.

Malachi hovered over the proprietor. "We're openin' an establishment that will offer fine spirits. Can you order what we want?"

"'Fraid not. This here's a dry county."

"Surely, you could make an exception?" Malachi stroked his long mustache.

The shopkeeper leaned forward on his counter. "Me and the missus are God-fearing temperance supporters, and we won't live where liquor flows free."

Silas' whiny nasal voice resonated through the shop. "I told you Kansas was strong on temperance."

Malachi took his brother's arm and turned him away from the storekeeper. "And I told you I'd handle it."

Silas paled as his eyes met Lonnie's. He nudged his brother and pushed a sneer on his lips. "I wondered at the stench driftin' this way."

Lonnie's nails bit into his palms.

Malachi smirked. "This where you decided to run to?"

Lonnie walked toward the men.

Jed stepped closer to his side, his voice low, "War's over."

"And you was rottin' in a prison camp most of it." Silas lifted his chin. He eyed Lonnie. "I imagine there's enough southern sympathizers in this town who'd like to mete out some justice to a coward ... and a Yankee."

The storekeeper pulled a rifle from behind the counter. "Well, as for me, I fought proudly for the North alongside several in this town." He aimed the rifle at Silas. "If I was you, I'd not go boasting about the

Confederacy around here." The man's eyes flashed. "We all just want to get on with our lives."

Malachi tipped his hat to the storekeeper. "As do we."

Lonnie tamped down his anger as the two left the store.

Jed stepped up to the counter. "We got a list."

"Sure thing."

"I'm Jed Holt. This is my brother Lonnie."

"I'm Martin Clemens." They shook hands. "Happy to make your acquaintance. I'll get this list filled right away. I got new stock in yesterday, and my wife's a seamstress. You'll find her ready-mades over in that corner. Some homesteaders ain't handy with the needle, like my Polly."

Lonnie spied a dress on display. Was Malachi the man Genny ran from? Did he track her here? Lonnie stroked the dress sleeve. *I'll protect you, whatever it takes.*

"That'd look right nice on her." Jed's voice made him jump.

He dropped the sleeve and blushed. "I suppose."

"Buy it for her." Jed nudged his shoulder. "It might let her know how you feel without …"

"Sayin' it." Lonnie stared at the blue creation, imagining her umber eyes sparkling with delight. He had nothing better to spend his share of Uncle Clyde's money on. His only excuse not to buy it would be fear.

As Mr. Clemens tallied their purchases, Lonnie noticed a flyer on the counter. A five-hundred-dollar reward attached to a passable likeness of Genny. He snatched it off the counter and crumpled it before shoving it in his pocket.

Once in the wagon, he handed the crumpled paper to his brother before he took the reins.

Jed stared at it. "I don't believe a word of it."

Lonnie whistled to the horses and they headed out. "Me neither."

Anger soured his stomach. No way were those men taking the woman who made him feel whole again.

"Among their many talents, the Morgans are liars and cheats," Jed said.

"And murderers." Lonnie ground his teeth. "We need to get the truth from Genny—Miss Collins—before they go spreadin' rumors and stirrin' up trouble."

"How'd those scalawags track her here?" Jed's face mirrored Lonnie's feelings of foreboding.

"I reckon it's time I told you all I know." Lonnie filled Jed in on the tale Genny had told him in the snow. "No tellin' what Malachi told people."

Passing an empty storefront, Jed moaned. Lonnie turned to see a giant staring at them from the sidewalk. Silas Morgan emerged from a nearby storefront and hailed the man. "Gunt, we need you."

Jed's face blanched.

"You know him?"

"Gunt was Silas' lackey at the camp. He beat a couple men near to death. Everyone feared him."

"Did he hurt you?'

"Beatin' a chaplain would have ended both Silas and Gunt's careers as prison guards. They mighta had to be real soldiers." Jed shook his head and sighed. "What we gonna do?"

"We got to keep her safe, even if she won't marry me."

"She will."

"Then I best get back and propose."

The poster exaggerated the amount of money Genny'd claimed she'd owed—that her father'd owed. Just like Malachi to post a huge reward he'd probably never pay. Lonnie'd find a way to make things right. No way were the Morgans taking someone else from him.

# Chapter 12

GENNY HURRIED TO HOLD open the door. "You made good time."

The men carried in the first load. Lonnie hefted a sack to the storeroom. "The roads are clearin."

She caught herself staring. The fifty-pound bag of flour appeared featherlight on his shoulder.

"You look nice." Lonnie's eyes lingered.

She'd pulled her hair back with combs. His compliment brought out a schoolgirl blush. Her eyes followed him out the door.

He bore the mark of his convictions. Jed had told her Lonnie'd risked his life attempting to save their mother. Now he'd fought for Jed's health. A longing for that kind of care overwhelmed her.

Jed placed the last parcel on the table. "The new storekeeper has an icehouse. He stores meat there. Winter weather kept these steaks cold the whole ride home."

"Wonderful." She put the skillet on the stove. "We'll have a feast."

"Hey, she baked a cake." Jed hollered as he took off his coat.

Lonnie came toward the table and swiped a taste of frosting with his finger.

Genny gave him a gentle swat. "Stop touching it with your dirty fingers."

His heart fluttered with her playful pat. "It was only one finger."

The teasing was rewarded with a smile. A nervous thrill swept through him as he thought of her gift still resting underneath the wagon seat. "I hope by the time I unhitch the horses and tend to 'em, supper will be ready."

"Absolutely."

"I promise to wash all my fingers before I sample that frosting again." He hurried through the chores. The flyer crinkled in his pocket as he hid her gift in his room. *I ain't ruinin' the surprise … not right away.*

He cleaned his plate of the delicious steak and wolfed down his piece of cake—which was larger than Jed's.

When she went to the stove for the coffee pot, he retrieved the gift. "We thought you'd like it."

Her eyes sparkled as her hands stroked the dress, then joy dissolved into sadness. "I can't accept this." Genny pushed it toward him.

"Sure you can." Lonnie froze as a tear rested on her face.

Jed mouthed, *Go to her.*

Lonnie wrapped his arms around her. "What's wrong, Genny?"

"This is too much. I don't deserve it." She leaned into his shoulder.

Lonnie savored the closeness, not knowing what to say as his shirt absorbed her tears.

Red-faced, Genny jerked away. "That was inappropriate."

"I kinda liked it." The schoolboy words resting in his head tumbled out his mustached lips.

Lonnie took her hand, stroking it with his thumb. "You deserve so much more." He nodded toward the parcel. "Try it on."

She squeezed Lonnie's hand, scooped up the brown paper wrapped dress. "Why not?" She ran to her room, a skip in her step.

When she emerged, his breath caught. Every fold and ruffle of the blue dress caressed her figure, stirring a longing to run his fingers through the curls that fell to her waist.

Lonnie found his tongue. "Beautiful."

Jed nodded approval. "Lonnie sure has good taste."

"Thank you both." She gave Jed a hug. Jealousy raised its ugly head only to be vanquished by a delightful kiss on his cheek. A wisp of promise, like the fairy princess in Grandma Strauss' tale when the hero rescued her from the evil troll. All his senses embraced the sweetness of her kiss. If his brother wasn't watching with that silly grin on his face, he'd kiss her smack on her lovely lips.

"You're welcome." The only words he could manage.

"I'll put this away. It's too special to wear every day."

She spun around and swished the skirt before she closed the bedroom door behind her.

"Appears she got the message." Jed grinned at his brother.

Lonnie traced the brand on his face. *Can I be courageous for her?* Recalling the joy on her face, he decided no more backing down from his feelings.

When she reentered, the boys had set the kitchen in order. Genny's hair, still flowing to her waist, distracted his thoughts from the poster. Rather than reaching for her hair, he pointed to a chair. Then he pulled the wrinkled paper from his pocket. Smoothing it out, he passed it to her. "We ran into the Morgans in town."

# Chapter 13

GENNY STARED AT THE drawing, images of perpetual servitude danced through her mind. "What did they say?"

Jed cleared his throat. "Lonnie told me everythin' on the way home." He nodded to Lonnie. "They said you stole two thousand dollars."

"I didn't." She searched Lonnie's face. "I would never steal."

He stood and pulled her to him, the blue in his eyes darkened as he gazed upon her. "I know." His voice soft. "But what haven't you told us?"

She drew in a cleansing breath, stepped away from the safety of his arms, and stared out the window, gathering her thoughts. "Everything I told you about Papa owing Malachi Morgan and my dealing cards in his tent saloon is true."

Humiliation softened her speech. "The winners tipped well, I kept a part of it back. We were required to give all our tips to Mr. Morgan. So, I suppose I did steal. I used most of it to help Lucy, one of the soiled doves who found herself with child. After I delivered her baby, I paid someone to smuggle them away. Then God sent Mrs. Sparks to rescue me."

"Does Malachi always track down runaways?" Jed's question held no judgment.

"Always." Genny's face paled. "And a dealer who wins for the house is …"

"A pot of gold." Jed finished her sentence.

"I was so grateful for the housekeeping job." Her hand went to her throat. "My worst fear has come to pass."

Lonnie took her hand. "I'll take care of you." Those comforting words were full of passion. He squeezed her hand and peace flowed through her. Lonnie wrapped her in a delicious hug full of hope and promise. "Will you marry me, so I can keep you safe?"

*Lonnie is willing to marry me to save my reputation. But does he love me?*

She pulled away and ran to her room, leaning against the closed door, her mind racing. Should she marry Lonnie? *God, give me a sign. What's your will? I lived with a father who loved me but didn't care for me. Can I live with a caring man who doesn't love me?*

A loud pounding echoed in the room. "Genevieve Collins, you come out right now. We're goin' discuss this like men. I mean adults."

Genny's heart leapt at his determination. Unlike Papa, Lonnie would always care for her. She opened the door.

"I'm sorry for yellin'." Lonnie's repentant expression touched her heart.

"I'm sorry I ran. I needed a moment to sort things out. Malachi will demand his money. I can't ask you to pay my debt, especially a mostly false one."

"We have issues with 'em too." Lonnie took her hand. "They set fire to our home back in Texas, killing our ma."

"I can't let anythin' happen to you." His hand stroked her face, then he released her. "Marry me and your reputation is one less thing they can bring into question. We won't let him hurt you."

She never imagined a marriage proposal so logical, yet so right. A burden lifted from her shoulders. Genny rested her head on his chest. His heart beat a wild rhythm. "Yes." *Because I love you.*

"Then let's get to it." Jed retrieved a black book from his room. Genny had forgotten he could perform weddings.

She held her hands up. "Wait."

Bewilderment overwhelmed Lonnie when Genny headed to her room again.

Jed chuckled. "She'll be back."

Lonnie was about to barge in and fetch her when Genny reappeared in her new frock. She'd dressed for him. He trailed a soft curl through his fingers. It'd been worth the wait.

"I reckon you'll have to tell me your middle name now." Lonnie flashed a mischievous grin.

"It's Brunhilda, after my father's maternal grandmother." Genny ducked her head then peeked up at her groom.

"Why, that's right ..."

Genny pressed her finger to his lips. "Zebulon, don't say it's beautiful."

Laughter stole the tension from the air. Jed opened his book to the wedding service, and the two repeated their solemn vows.

Once said, Lonnie drew Genny to him and kissed her gently, then with more intensity, letting her know the feelings he couldn't put into words. She matched his ardor and pulled back first.

Jed slapped his brother on the back. "That was my first weddin'. How'd I do?"

"You done good, brother." Lonnie squeezed his new wife closer.

Genny's blush took a long time fading. She placed her hand on her heated cheeks and smiled.

Jed headed toward the door. "I'll sleep in the barn tonight."

"You will not." His words tangled right over the top of hers, saying the same thing, and it felt … right.

"You'll catch your death out there," Genny said as Lonnie hugged her from behind and nodded agreement.

Pounding on the front door caused Jed to step back.

"Holts, you in there?"

Genny paled. Lonnie signaled her to go into the bedroom. Jed grabbed the rifles. Lonnie's moist palms gripped the stock when his brother handed one over. A chair scraped as she secured her door before they opened the other.

They glared at the Morgans and kept their guns pointed at the two. Malachi and Silas filled the door as if to block their escape.

"Don't want any murderers in our house." Lonnie's anger simmered below the surface. His sweaty hands held his rifle steady.

"We'll be turnin' you boys over to the authorities for murdering our mother," Jed growled.

"You can't prove nothin'." Malachi lit a cigar with a steady hand.

"Silas told me as much while he was my prison guard." Jed pointed his Winchester in the man's direction.

"It's your word against Silas'." Malachi smirked. "My, my, you boys with guns. Lonnie, you claimed to be a pacifist before the war. We know the truth. You're too yellow to haul back on that trigger."

Lonnie cocked the rifle. "Ain't no way on God's green earth we're lettin' you inside." A knot formed in his throat.

Jed did the same. "You two belong behind bars."

"Genny owes me money, and I intend to collect." Malachi stood his ground. "The little vixen was my best dealer. Accordin' to town gossip, she's married to one of you." Malachi tugged his jacket smooth as he added. "No one steals from me and gets away with it."

Silas smirked and adjusted his hat to a slight angle before adding.

"That five-hundred-dollar reward would do a lot for this shabby place."
He glanced behind him, then nodded to his brother.

Malachi took a long draw on his cigar and blew smoke rings. "As I
said, I always get what I want." Both men stepped away from the front
door with their faces toward the Holts.

Genny kept her ear to the door. Familiar voices rose beyond the wooden
barrier. Prayer for her new husband and brother-in-law rose from her
heart right before a rough hand shoved a cloth across her face. Her jaw
trapped in the paw-like grip, fear overtook her as chloroform filled her
lungs.

# Chapter 14

JED STEPPED TO THE window, his rifle at the ready. After several minutes he relaxed his grip.

"They gone?" Lonnie glanced over his brother's shoulder.

"Appears so."

Lonnie released the hammer and some of his anger with it, then set his rifle back near the door. Jed propped his Winchester beside it.

"You forgot to release the hammer," Lonnie said as he retrieved it and inspected the gun. "It ain't even loaded."

Jed let out a big sigh. "I'm a man of God dealin' with hateful thoughts. A loaded weapon is too temptin'."

"You're braver than me. At least a loaded rifle gave me a bit more confidence. Facin' down them two snakes." *This ain't a foolish war—it's my family.* Lonnie stared out the window. "What we gonna do?" His fingers itched to choke the life out of the Morgans. A vision of Malachi's smirk turning to gasping horror … He shook his head to mentally toss the idea away.

"We go to the sheriff tomorrow and sort it out," Jed said.

"That'd get Genny arrested." Lonnie glared at Jed, stepped away, and ran his fingers through his hair. "I promised to keep her safe."

"We will." Jed put a calming hand on Lonnie's shoulder.

"The gold dust is probably worth more than her debt. We give it to Malachi, and then we ask the sheriff to arrest them for the murder."

"All that gold dust and no way to spend it in prison." He relaxed. "I like it."

He knocked on the bedroom door. "Genny, it's safe to come out."

Silence.

"We got a plan. Everything's gonna be fine."

Silence.

Jed put his ear to the door. "I don't think she's in there." He tried to open the door, but the chair behind it held.

*I always get what I want.* Malachi's words haunted him. "Where is she?"

They ran out the back door. Large footprints to and from the bedroom window said it all. Jed climbed in the open window, and Lonnie hurried back inside to meet his brother at the bedroom door. Jed opened it, a cloth in his hand.

"Take a whiff."

A vile odor hit him. "What is it?"

"Chloroform. Doctors use it to put patients to sleep before surgery. The army hospital reeked of it."

"Gunt?" Lonnie slammed his hand on the door frame.

Jed threw the cloth on the floor. "Those two kept us occupied while Gunt stole her."

"Malachi's a rabid dog when he wants somethin'."

Jed looked heavenward. "Lord, give us wisdom." He continued in fervent prayer while Lonnie's chest hurt, and his stomach knotted. Once his brother's prayer ended, he sprang into action. "I'm goin' after them."

"We need the sheriff and a posse." Jed grabbed his hat from the peg.

"You fetch 'em, and I'll leave a trail." Lonnie gathered a few supplies and his gun, then pulled on his coat. The rifle felt heavy with the prospect of breaking his vow. But for Genny ...

They raced to the barn. Lonnie's fingers fumbled as he saddled Drake and pushed his rifle into its scabbard. Pain shot down his leg.

"You plan on using that gun?" Jed asked.

Lonnie clenched his jaw and rubbed the painful ache in his chest. "I ain't never raised a gun with the intention of harmin' any man. Pray my convictions don't conflict with savin' Genny."

"Wait." Jed dashed to the house and returned with the jar of gold dust. "Take it."

Jed mounted Sally and galloped toward town.

Lonnie walked Drake following the tracks until the footprints turned to hoof prints. He mounted. The tracks were too deep to be a man riding alone.

Gunt hadn't bothered to cover his tracks. Lonnie kept his eyes on the snow as Drake moved forward to the top of a hill. The light was fading, and he dismounted to check the ground and the direction of the hoofprints. His breath fogged as he exhaled dread. His leg screamed for rest, but he ignored it.

The tracks stopped at a shallow creek bed. The search for tracks on the other shore frustrated Lonnie. *God, please. You blessed me with*

*Genny. I can't lose her. I give up doin' things on my own. My courage comes from you, Lord. I trust you to protect my family.* As "Amen" passed through his lips, he found the trail again. Dry grass peeked through the melting snow, and the tracks descended toward a soddie covered by a snowdrift. The trail disappeared inside.

It was a barn. Lonnie eased open the door. Three horses were tied inside. His breath caught as he spied a piece of blue fabric. A roar rose in his throat. He forced it down. The blue fabric smelled of lavender. *Lord, please.* He stuffed the cloth in his pocket. Lonnie led Drake to a space beside the barn in the dark shadows. He grabbed his rifle from its scabbard. "Easy, boy. Keep an eye out."

He crept from the shadows. Two dugouts stood a few feet from one another. A light shone from a window. Lonnie moved toward it, struggling to keep his balance on the icy surface.

He peered in and spied crates marked *Irish Whiskey* and *Boston's Finest Spirits*. Gunt stood beside Silas whose voice carried through the loosely framed window. "Malachi is a fool. He should cut his losses. I'd tie that harlot to a tree and let the wolves get her." He pointed for Gunt to pick up a crate. "But no, he has to prove to himself he's still somebody by openin' a fancy, high-class saloon."

Gunt held the crate, waiting for instructions.

"You and I." Silas pointed at the giant. "We ain't that far from Indian Territory. They trade furs for firewater, and we'll sell them back east for a tidy sum."

Gunt nodded. "Good plan."

Silas opened the door, and Gunt passed through.

Lonnie ducked to the side of the building and flattened himself against the snow. The men headed past the dugouts and into the woods. Lonnie rose to a crouch and moved toward the other dugout's window. Genny lay still on the bed, her dress soiled and torn. The chloroform must not have worn off.

Where was Malachi? Lonnie slid on the slick first step landing in front of the door with a thud. His backside protested its connection with the ground as pain shot through his leg. No sounds of rushing footsteps headed his way. He opened the door and hurried to Genny's side. Every button was in place and, other than a tear on her skirt, she appeared unmolested. He snatched a blanket and wrapped her in it. His rifle across his back, he scooped her up and sprinted toward the darkened barn and Drake. Halfway there, he stopped to get a better grip on Genny.

Cold steel rested on his neck. "You're the one who left the barn door open." Malachi chuckled.

His heart pounded in his ears. *Lord, give me wisdom.*

Genny groaned in his arms. Her eyes opened and she screamed, her heart racing against his chest, matching his own. Malachi pointed toward the door of the dugout. Lonnie set Genny on her feet and supported her until she could walk on her own.

"Drop the rifle."

He glared at Malachi and dropped it as he gave a high-pitched whistle. Drake plowed into Malachi knocking him to the ground. Lonnie grabbed the reins and leapt into the saddle. He caught Genny up and pulled her in front of him. She shrieked as Malachi rose from the ground. Lonnie held her close while Drake took off like Pegasus.

After putting some distance between them and the homestead, he slowed their pace. Genny pulled his hand to her lips and kissed it. "You're my hero."

He kissed her hair and squeezed her tight. "Anytime, my lady." He glanced behind them and then guided Drake through a slick patch.

Genny wrapped the blanket around her shoulders and relaxed against him. They picked their way down the hill guided by the full moon and a bright sprinkling of stars.

"When I saw Mr. Morgan ... I ... You came for me." She pressed against his chest.

He wrapped his arms around her. "You're my wife."

He turned her chin up to steal a kiss when a bullet slammed into a tree nearby.

Genny screamed. Hoofbeats pounded behind them. Lonnie gave Drake his head. Lantern light flickered from across the creek. More bullets sprayed the air around them. They splashed their way to the opposite shore where Jed, the sheriff, and six other men sat on their mounts.

"You found her." Relief colored Jed's voice.

Lonnie maneuvered his mount behind the posse, giving Drake an *attaboy* pat, and they dismounted. He held Genny in his arms again. She leaned into him, quivering.

Malachi, Silas, and Gunt crashed across the creek. Out in front, Malachi raised his hands. Silas and Gunt wheeled their mounts and fled. The sheriff nodded to the posse. Three men dashed after them.

Gunfire and shouts echoed on the other side of the creek.

Malachi, trapped in the circle of men, kept his hands up. "There's been a terrible misunderstandin'."

"Really?" The sheriff signaled for one of the posse members to take Malachi's gun.

"Yes, this woman stole a great deal of money from me." He pointed at Genny, his eyes full of fire. Lonnie glared back, wrapping a protective arm around his wife.

"I was merely collectin' a debt."

Dr. Murdoch put his horse between Malachi and Lonnie. "If you'd spoken to her husband, you might have worked something out."

The sheriff tied Malachi's hands to his saddle horn. "But being as you kidnapped this woman from her own home, I'm arresting you."

"I didn't kidnap her. Helmet Gunderson did."

"We'll sort this out at the jail."

Protesting voices accompanied the splashing of horses crossing the creek.

The three deputized men returned with Silas and Gunt tied to their horses.

"I'm bleedin'," Silas whined. Malachi scowled at his brother but said nothing.

The taller of the three deputies smiled. "I'm freezing from crossing the creek too many times, but it was worth it. Tell 'em, Matt."

A short man in a bowler hat nodded. "That big fella got so scared when we shot the other fella, he jabbered like a parrot. Sheriff, they got a stash of liquor at the ol' Judson homestead."

The taller spoke again. "You can add selling liquor in a dry county to the charges."

"Can you get them for planning to sell liquor to the Indians?" Matt pushed his rifle into Gunt's face. The bully responded with a whimper. "Yeah, this big fella told us all about it."

The sheriff and his men corralled the kidnappers between them.

Jed dismounted and hugged Genny. "Sis, you all right?"

She nodded.

Lonnie pulled off his coat and wrapped it around her. It hung past her hands and reminded him of the first time he'd seen her. "Warmer now?"

"Yes, but now you're cold." She peeked up at him. "We could share your coat and the blanket."

Jed chuckled and mounted his horse.

Lonnie took his coat back and helped her onto Drake. She wrapped the blanket over her, and he wrapped his arms around her with his coat open. "Seems I remember you teachin' me this trick."

She snuggled into his chest, then straightened. "What's in your pocket?"

Lonnie pulled out the jar. "Here, sheriff. There's more than enough to pay whatever *Mister Morgan* claims she stole."

"See, you could have avoided all this by coming to the law." The sheriff adjusted his hat. "I'll be unraveling the particulars tomorrow at the jail. I got me a lot of questions, but it's late and cold, and I want to get home to the missus." He tipped his hat toward Genny. "Mrs. Holt, your charges will probably be dropped." The sheriff then turned to Malachi. "But yours are starting to pile up."

The deputies gathered the reins of the criminals' horses. The sheriff tipped his hat to Genny, then added, "All you Holts show up at my office at ten tomorrow, and my brother, the judge, will have court. I'll lock the gold dust in my safe for now." The sheriff signaled for his men to head out.

Jed turned his horse toward home.

Genny touched her husband's brand. "You needn't give up your dreams for me."

He brushed her forehead with a kiss. "You're worth every speck of gold dust and more." His hand held her cheek close to his chest. Wetness fell across his knuckles. "I say somethin' wrong?"

"No, you said everything right." She snuggled close again. "I am in love with a very courageous man."

"I'm in love with the smartest, bravest, and most patient woman in the world." He whistled to Drake to pick up the pace as the cross on the barn came into view. They trotted into the yard. This time with a different intent toward the woman who'd invaded his home and now his heart.

Jed waited for them by the barn. He grabbed Drake's reins. "I'll get Drake settled, then I'll head to the hotel in town."

"Appreciate it." Lonnie grinned, heart overflowing with gratitude for a brother who knew what he needed before he knew himself.

Lonnie carried his bride into their home. Setting her down, he stared into her love-filled eyes. He ran his fingers over every feature of her face. She smiled and stroked his brand. "I knew you'd save me ..."

and without harming anyone."

He pulled her close, their bodies molded together. Their lips touched, and the lingering kiss removed any doubts about his worthiness to be loved. Their ardor increased as he explored her neck with his lips. He pulled away and lifted her into his arms "Shall we commence with the honeymoon?"

A blush covering her face, she leaned up and kissed his scarred cheek.

"Unlike Jed, I like being carried in your arms."

Lonnie took her into the bedroom and pressed the door closed with his boot.

# Acknowledgments

I WANT TO THANK my awesome editor Pegg Thomas for asking me to be a part of this collection. I'm grateful to my fellow authors in the collection, Sandra Melville Hart, Jennifer Hough Ulrich, and Linda Yezak for all their words of encouragement. I'm honored to be counted among your number. And special praise to my Lord Jesus for the gifts of words.

Extra hugs and kisses for my husband, Charles, who kept the rest of life in order while I finished this.

Cindy Ervin Huff is a multi-published writer. She has been featured
in numerous periodicals over the last thirty years. Her historical
romance *Secrets & Charades* won the Editor's Choice, Maxwell Award,
and Serious Writer Medal. Cindy is a member of ACFW, Mentor for
Word Weavers, founding member of the Aurora, Illinois, chapter
of Word Weavers, and Christian Writer's Guild alumni. She loves
to encourage new writers on their journey. Cindy and her husband
make their home in Aurora, Illinois. They have five children and eight
grandchildren. Follow her on social media.

Facebook: www.facebook.com/cindyehuff
Twitter: @CindyErvinHuff
Instagram: @CindyErvinHuff
Website: www.jubileewriter.wordpress.com
Secrets & Charades: https://www.amazon.com/dp/1946016144/

# Becoming Brave

By

Jennifer Uhlarik

# Chapter 1

*Indian Territory, 1870*

Five. Five bodies.

Sweat snaked between Coy Whittaker's shoulders as he stared over the crest of the hill at the ghastly scene below.

"Lord have mercy!" Mitch Tanner whispered, inches from Coy's right shoulder. "No wonder there's so many vultures circling." He shook his head. "Those bodies probably ain't even cold yet."

Three men lay sprawled in different places around the half-acre meadow, arrows protruding from their chests or backs. A fourth man, scalp missing, had died sitting up, slumped against the jagged end of a fallen log near the edge of the meadow. Coy suppressed a shiver as his attention slid to the last body. An Indian, from what tribe he couldn't tell, lay on his back near the fourth gent, his buckskin shirt stained with fresh blood, and strands of his long hair splayed across the ground.

"We need to get out of here." He shot a glance at Mitch.

His friend's blue eyes were full of compassion. "Why don't you ride back and tell my pa." He shifted his attention back to the scene as a vulture landed near one of the bodies. "I'll stay, get these men ready to bury before we lose the light."

Coy's chest tightened. "Something caused that brave's people to abandon him." The fact that a lone Indian lay just feet from where several white fellas had died set his teeth on edge. "Just a matter of time till they return." He, for one, didn't want to be here when they did. "It's not safe for either of us to stay."

Mitch shook his head. "We're not leaving these men for buzzard bait. I'll choose a spot for burying whilst you ride back with the news."

His friend was right, of course, and even if Coy could talk him into leaving, the moment Mitch's pa had the Bar CT's herd settled, he'd be along to investigate the scene himself. The boss'd make sure they buried these men proper.

Heart pounding, he shot a sidelong glance at Mitch. They *really* needed to leave here, before … "Fine, but you ain't staying here alone." Coy gripped his Colt Navy pistol a little tighter, scanned the area one last time, and, mustering his courage, pushed off the ground. "Let's go."

"Coy."

He ignored Mitch and kept moving.

*God?* A shiver snaked through him as the Almighty's name passed through his thoughts for the first time in many months. *If You're up there and You're listening, I'll keep this short. Would You mind making sure we're not about to get bushwhacked?* He didn't want no truck with anyone, least of all Indians.

As they strode down the sparsely treed hill toward their horses, Mitch latched onto his shoulder and tried to spin him around. "Would you stop?"

He shrugged free of his friend's grasp and, mounting his big black gelding, pinned the other man with a hard glare. "You ain't gonna get ambushed alone."

"No one's getting ambushed!"

Urging Rogue up over the hill, he searched for a likely burial place. Two of the men lay off to the right, paces from each other. A third, almost directly ahead, died near the base of a small rise. And the fella leaning against the tree was to the left. He and Mitch halted at the center of the clearing, and Coy turned his horse in a slow circle.

"What about there?" Coy indicated the rise ahead, tucked in the long shadow of a huge old tree lining the clearing. Not waiting for an answer, he dismounted and, turning toward the fella reclined against the tree, shoved past Mitch's horse.

From behind him, saddle leather creaked. "It's a durn good thing I consider you my brother. You're about the most bullheaded, ornery cuss I know. Sometimes you're a little hard to abide, that way."

"Yeah?" He slowed as he passed the Indian, an eerie pull drawing his steps off their intended track. Was it morbid curiosity that drew him toward the Indian? Coy hesitated, trying to force himself back to his original purpose, though his focus stayed trained on the Indian. Unable to resist it, he walked the final few paces and, throat knotting painfully, squatted next to the pungent body.

The Indian's unwashed form stank of blood and death. Coy mopped his face in disgust, and his muscles coiled with the nearness. "Mitch, did you ever stop to think it's because I consider you my kin that I'm being such a bullheaded, ornery cuss?" He lowered his voice. "His kind's already stolen too much from my family."

"His ki—" Shock and sadness laced Mitch's tone.

Coy cursed himself. Such talk wasn't permitted by Bar CT ranch hands. In the eight years he'd lived and worked at the ranch, he'd learned that lesson well. But despite the lessons ... despite Chet Tanner's careful tutelage, it was impossible to forget the hatred his ma spewed for all Indians.

Pushing past his repulsion, Coy twisted the Indian's face his way, noting the warmth still lingering in his cheek. Perhaps the sweltering summer heat wasn't allowing the body to cool. The Indian's head lolled, a few long strands of black hair webbing across his face. The brave's eyes were half open, mouth slightly agape.

"He ain't wearing any war paint." Hopefully that was a good sign.

Looking to the Indian's torso, he caught the slightest hint of movement—a tiny rise and fall of his bloodied midsection. He darted a glance again to the brave's face. Just as a faint flicker of life sparked in the dark eyes, something tugged at his hip.

Grabbing for the butt of his Colt, Coy lunged up. Something pulled hard at his trouser pocket, then popped loose with a clatter. He backed up a step and leveled the gun at the brave's face.

"Don't shoot him!" Mitch's footsteps pounded as he ran toward them.

Nerves pulsing, Coy slapped the torn pocket at his hip.

Empty.

The blasted Indian clutched the strand of earth-toned beads, bone, and grizzly claws that Coy had dug from his saddlebags and stashed in his trouser pocket as they'd neared Indian Territory. Stupid thing must have worked its way loose. The Indian's eyes widened for the briefest instant, then sought Coy's face.

"Give me that." He settled his boot across the brave's wrist and snatched the trinket from his limp fingers, the gun never wavering.

The Indian squinted at him, and a soft phrase Coy didn't understand trickled from his lips.

"Shut up." Shaking, Coy cocked the pistol and trained the barrel between the Indian's eyes.

"Coy, don't!" At his side, Mitch redirected the pistol's barrel and pushed him away from the dying man. "Shooting him won't solve anything."

When the brave's eyes slid closed, Coy looked away with a stuttering breath. Mitch gently wrested the pistol from his fingers, uncocked it, and slid it back into the holster tied to Coy's leg.

For a moment, he gulped air and tried to calm the fear surging through his veins.

"You all right?" Concern dripped from Mitch's voice.

"I'm fine." The words were thick and unsteady.

Mitch gave him a shove toward his horse. "Go get yourself some water. Take a minute, all right?"

Coy did as he was told. At Rogue's side, he wiped the bloody fingerprints from the necklace and, wrapping it in his handkerchief, crammed it deep into his torn pocket. He took a long swig from his canteen and, with his nerves thrumming, leaned his forearms on his saddle.

The scene played over and over in his mind. From the unnerving draw he felt to walk to the Indian's side to the way the brave almost seemed to come back from the dead. And the blasted idiot pulling the necklace from his pocket. The unintelligible words he'd mumbled. The images haunted every corner of his mind.

Mitch knelt at the brave's side, so Coy drew the necklace from his pocket. Despite holding the abhorrent thing, his pulse returned to normal as he studied its grizzly claws. His mind drifted to the story Mr. Tanner told him about the string of beads. Coy shook his head. Hang it all. The boss never should've given him the trinket in the first place.

Movement drew his attention from the necklace. Vultures landed near two of the bodies. Durn things. They'd not get these men if he had anything to say about it. Coy wadded the necklace back into his handkerchief and shoved both into his pocket. He donned his slicker to avoid bloodying his clothes, then strode toward the fella still leaned against the tree.

"The vultures are ready to feast," he called as he passed Mitch, eyes focused on the white man this time.

"Be there when I can. Our friend here's gutshot, and I think the bullet severed his spine. He ain't long for this world, but I don't figure he ought to die alone."

"No friend of mine …" He breathed the words, recalling what his ma always said. Indians were nothing more than filthy heathens. *Every. Last. One.*

Yet even as he thought it, something gripped his chest, and he looked again at the brave, an uneasy feeling roiling in his gut.

Coy shoved the sensation aside and focused on the white man. With a single arrow buried deep near the center of his chest, there was no chance this fella was still alive. The arrow alone would've killed him. But the man's face and clothes were painted red with blood after the Indian had scalped him. Just like his ma's first husband, the man whose last name Coy wore. A man he'd never met, but who his ma had always elevated to the status of saint for the way he fought to protect her from the Cheyenne as they swooped down on their wagon train some twentyish years ago.

The gent's holster sat empty, but no pistol lay in his lap or anywhere nearby. No rifle or shotgun either. Had the brave taken it?

"You see a pistol laying anywhere around that Indian?"

"No." Mitch paused. "Why?"

"This fella's wearing a holster with no gun." He stood and scanned the area but found only grass and blood. No weapons.

A curiosity, to be sure.

Steeling himself, Coy broke the arrow shaft near the deceased man's chest then, drawing a deep breath, grabbed the fella's arms. The limp frame slumped against him, and, stomach rebelling, Coy hoisted the body up and dragged it a step or two.

A strange whimper sounded from the direction of the log, and with it, a scuffing sound. Warning bells clanged in Coy's mind. He dumped the dead man and pawed for his revolver. Pistol drawn, he leveled it at the log, only to find … *a woman.* Filthy. Blood-soaked. Crawling from a hidey-hole in the hollow trunk.

She stood, her brown eyes panning the scene in a blink. Two-fisted, she hoisted a revolver far too big for her hands, training it on his chest.

Heart hammering, he lifted his hands, letting his own shooter dangle from his index finger. "I don't mean you no harm, ma'am."

She wore the look of someone half crazed. Her jaw cracked open a bit, and for a second, Coy thought she might speak or scream. Instead, the little gal took a shaky half step toward him before her knees buckled and she pitched into his arms.

"Ma'am. Can you hear me?"

The unfamiliar male voice roused Aimee Kaplan from her stupor, though the enveloping blackness pulled at her. Everything grew still again.

"Ma'am?"

At the repeated word, she stirred and drew a deep breath. The strong scent of dirt filled her nostrils.

"Ma'am."

It was a pleasant enough voice. Deep and rich, though colored with a tinge of concern.

When something wet swiped across her forehead, one eyelid, and to her cheek, the murkiness fled. Her eyes flew open to two shadowy faces staring back at her. Aimee bolted up and turned on them. Her petticoats tangling about her ankles, she tottered on unsteady legs.

"Whoa, now." A dark-haired, dark-eyed young man also stood and caught her elbow. "We're trying to help you."

"H-h-help me?" Why?

The other man, this one with lighter brown hair and blue eyes, bobbed a single nod. "You remember hiding in a hollow tree trunk?"

Hiding. In a …

*Oh.*

With a horrified grunt, Aimee jerked free of the first man's grasp. Her knees went soft, and she sank into the ground, dress billowing around her. She cradled her head in her hands, but something stuck to her hair. She pulled back and looked at her palms.

Blood. *Edouard's blood.*

A sob boiled out of her as she stared at her hands.

The man with the dark eyes squatted next to her, canteen and handkerchief in his grip. "Let me help." He sloshed water over the cloth, then looked her way with an expression that begged permission. At her shaky nod, he wiped the dripping cloth across her palms, and when he was done, she snatched it and scrubbed her face.

"Coy," the second man spoke. "The others are coming."

*Others?* She blinked water from her eyes and peered past them. Several riders and a wagon approached. Her chest seized. Was the man Louis spoke of among them?

"I'll let Pa know what we found." The blue-eyed man ambled toward two horses and mounted the buckskin. With a cluck of his tongue, he cantered in the direction of the approaching riders.

She took a long, dazed look at the sparse trees that filled the land, even far into the distance, then finally turned to the man. "Who are you?"

"Name's Coy Gentry Whittaker, ma'am. And you are …"

She flicked a look at the holster tied to his thigh. "Where is my gun?" Edouard's gun—that she'd used to shoot the Indian.

"It's nearby. You won't need it. You're safe now."

Her skin prickled as the unknown riders drew nearer, one breaking from the pack to meet the blue-eyed man. "I'll thank you to return it to me." She needed that gun. These men didn't know who was after her.

Mister Whittaker shoved his hat back on his head, his expression tinged with worry. "I assure you, you'll be safe with me, ma'am." His brows arched.

Aimee cast a glance around, searching for the easiest path away from here. But where would she go? And how would she protect herself without that gun?

A choking cry escaped as a fresh wave of memories of all she'd seen in the meadow bombarded her. *Oh Lord Jesus, help me. They're dead. Edouard and Louis and Paul and Marc—all dead.*

"Ma'am, I'll ask again. What's your name?"

She sucked a huge breath and flicked another anxious glance toward the approaching riders. "Miss Aimee Le Chapela—" Horrified, she shook her head. "Aimee Kaplan."

His brows rose slightly. "Miss … Le Cha—"

"Kaplan."

"My mistake, Miss Kaplan." Mr. Whittaker's dark gaze turned somber. "The men in the meadow. Was one of 'em your husband?"

After a moment, she shook her head, and her limbs trembled. "My brothers."

His jaw hung open a little. "All four of 'em?"

Aimee nodded feebly, but when the lone rider turned their way, she drew a sharp breath and again tottered onto unsteady feet. Mr. Whittaker matched her actions.

Was this rider the man she'd heard her brothers discussing in hushed tones? They'd spoken of a young man. Tall, lean, wearing a gun slung low on his hip. For that matter, was it Mr. Whittaker—or his blue-eyed friend?

"Where'd you come from, ma'am?"

"Arkansas."

"And why're you and your brothers in Indian Territory?" He ducked his head, trying to catch her eye.

Her mind spinning, Aimee stared at the ground.

"Miss Kaplan, are you in some kind of trouble? Other than what happened in the meadow, I mean."

Yes. Yes, she was in trouble. Her brothers were dead, their horses—with all their supplies—had run off during the attack, and she couldn't begin to guess which man was pursuing them. Mr. Whittaker fit the description her brothers gave except—she pinned her focus on Coy Whittaker's almost-black eyes—except his were *not* the cold eyes of a killer. There was a warmth and concern there that drew her in.

Dare she trust him? The odd stirring in her chest said she could—him and no one else.

The lone rider arrived ahead of the approaching group and dismounted near the black horse. As he strode closer, Aimee darted behind Mr. Whittaker's back, one hand settling gently on his back as she stood on tiptoes to peer over his shoulder.

"Coy? Everything all right?" The voice belonged to an older man, probably *not* the one her brothers had spoken of. Despite that, her pulse quickened.

"Reckon it hasn't been one of my better days, sir." He attempted to draw her forward into the other man's view, but she shifted, keeping him between her and the newcomer. After a confused instant, Mr. Whittaker gave up and faced the man. "Chet Tanner, this gal here is Miss Aimee Kaplan. Miss Kaplan, meet part owner of the Bar CT Ranch outta Texas." He paused. "Sir, Miss Kaplan's brothers are needing some *final* attention just over that rise."

Mr. Tanner touched his hat brim. "Miss. I'm sorry about your brothers. We'll see they're attended to. In the meantime, you're welcome in the Bar CT camp for as long as you need. Just as soon as our cook gets the chuckwagon settled, we'll rustle up some clothes, and you can freshen up and change in there."

Aimee glanced at the once-sunny yellow calico of her dress, now stained from neckline to hem with black, brown, and red. What had he said to her after promising to attend to her brothers?

"Miss, would you mind if I had a private word with Coy for just a moment?" Mr. Tanner continued, "I'll return him to you directly."

Brushing at the stains, she nodded absently. Mr. Whittaker and Mr. Tanner moved off a good ten paces to stand by the horses.

What now?

She would need to find her horse—all their horses. Gather whatever belongings they'd brought. Had her brothers thought to pack her a clean dress? They'd left in such a hurry.

"Gather my things," she whispered, blinking at the rise separating her from where she'd last seen their horses.

A chill swept the length of her. *Her coat.* She'd hid it in the tree. Edouard was always admonishing her. Lower lids stinging, she recalled the urgency of his last words. *Aimee, don't forget your coat.* And yet, she'd exited the tree and left it. Panting for breath, she marched up and over the rise. She must get it back.

For Edouard.

# Chapter 2

LOOKING INTO CHET TANNER'S grizzled face, Coy was once again the twelve-year-old boy who'd come to the Bar CT eight years ago. Especially with his guts still quivering over the actions of an almost-dead Indian and a frightened young woman.

"Son." The older man pushed his hat back. "You all right?"

Coy forced a nod. "I'm fine."

"Fine?" The elder man gave a sardonic huff. "You got the bejeebers scared out of you—twice—and you were about a hair's breadth from shooting an Indian. But you're fine."

Coy squirmed under the scrutiny.

"I know you as well as I know my own son. You wanna answer that question again, and give me the truth this time?"

He swallowed. "A little rattled." A *lot* rattled. Bordering on downright quaking-in-his-boots flustered. But he couldn't admit that just yet.

If only he were that twelve-year-old boy again, back when Mr. Tanner knew just what questions or statements to make to force the walls around Coy's heart to bust. It had been uncomfortable, all that confounded prying Mr. Tanner did back then. And Coy had *hated* him for it. But once those walls weakened and he began to spew the hurt and anger from his mother's neglect and her husband's abuses, Chet Tanner only held him as he'd screamed and cried, held him so tight Coy thought he might suffocate—until all the anger and tears were spent, and the fight was gone. And not once had Mr. Tanner ever judged him less of a man.

So why, after all these years, was it suddenly so hard to tell this man—the only man who'd ever shown him a father's love—his true feelings?

Maybe because something new was stirring in his chest, and he couldn't make sense of it. And admitting it aloud was too foreign.

"I *am* rattled, sir, but I'll be fine. You say the word, and I'll be ready to help bury those gents."

Mr. Tanner clamped a firm hand on his shoulder. "Figured you'd say that. But I got a more important job for you."

He perked a little. "Oh?"

"Need you to stay with Miss Kaplan, keep her compa—"

"Boss, no." He shook his head vehemently. "You know I'm not the righ—"

Chet Tanner held up a hand, stopping him short. "Did you notice the way she hid behind you, son?"

How could he not? Coy straightened his spine, still feeling the heady little tingle of her touch. That odd sensation was all part of his frustration.

"With what she's been through, it's understandable she's afraid. But you're the one who found her. She might trust you, leastways more than she does the rest of us. Like it or not, you're elected."

"Yes, Boss." He mumbled the words, heart pounding at the idea of watching over Miss Kaplan. So much for wading through the agitated feelings.

As he turned to face Miss Kaplan again, an unbidden oath slipped from between his lips.

She was gone.

Coy ducked around the boss's sorrel and swung onto Rogue's back. Urging the black up the rise, he peered into the unholy scene again to find his new charge standing over her brother—the one nearest the hollow log. Her slim shoulders quaked.

Something welled inside Coy, and despite the hellish images around him, he clucked his tongue to move Rogue into a lope. The big horse covered the distance in easy strides. As he neared, Miss Kaplan turned distraught eyes on the Indian and, almost as if she didn't see Coy at all, stumbled toward the buckskin-clad form, clutching something—a blanket? No, a coat, it appeared—to her chest.

"Miss? Come with me. I'll see to it you get a chance to freshen up some."

She ignored him, wholly focused on the brave.

"Miss Kaplan?" He dismounted and strode after her. "Please. This ain't a fitting place for a woman."

The petite gal hesitated at the Indian's side. Just before Coy reached her, she dropped the coat, and sunlight glinted on metal. His muscles coiled as she leveled a pistol at the brave's head.

"No!" Coy darted to her side and, just in time, knocked her

hand away.

A gunshot roared, and dirt exploded near the Indian's skull. Without thinking, Coy wrestled the heavy gun from her fingers, even as a primal cry tore from her throat. They grappled for a moment before he twisted the weapon from her grip, and once more, her knees went soft. This time, before she could collapse, he pulled her to him.

The little woman grabbed fistfuls of his shirt, a keening wail rising as she clung to him.

"He killed my brothers!"

The gut-wrenching screams launched his thoughts backward eight years, and, his own limbs trembling afresh, Coy scooped up Miss Kaplan and turned toward Rogue.

Mr. Tanner drew his horse up next to Rogue. Coy extended the pistol, butt first, to his boss. "This'll be safer with you for now, sir."

An approving look on his weathered features, he took the gun as Coy walked past, cradling the sobbing Miss Kaplan.

Aimee clutched her soiled coat and stared into the campfire's flames. She was an orphan. An adult, but an orphan nonetheless. First Papa during the war, then Mama of a broken heart, and now her brothers.

*Lord, what do I do now?*

She'd prayed those words incessantly as strangers buried her brothers, throughout that evening, and now as the dozen Bar CT hands bedded down for the night.

She was the last of the Le Chapelains. No. The Kaplans—she must remember to use the *other* name. It was still new, strange to her tongue, a change that Edouard and Louis mandated to avoid the unknown outlaw who'd chased her brothers into Indian Territory. But she had no idea who the outlaw was and only a vague understanding of why her brothers felt they must run. Something about an altercation between Louis and the unknown man in town. A gambling debt, maybe. She wasn't sure of that, nor of the man, so how could she protect herself?

At the edge of the camp sat the older man—Mr. Tanner, was it?— beside the Indian who'd killed her family. Earlier, he'd insisted they move the dying brave to their camp, and now, he continued to sit next to the vile being. Why? And why had Mr. Whittaker stopped her from shooting him earlier? Hadn't she seen him turn a gun on the same Indian while she hid in the log? Surely he should understand.

Footsteps rustled in the grass, and the approaching shadow cleared his throat.

"Miss Kaplan," Mr. Whittaker said. "It's late. I've laid out a bedroll for you. You should try to sleep." He squatted beside her. "I reckon you'll feel better if you do."

She stared again at the fire. As empty and numb as she felt, it was a mystery whether she'd ever feel anything again—least of all *better*.

"Please. You hafta take care of yourself."

"Why?" Her voice cracked with the question. "I've no one to live for. Nowhere to go." She looked toward Mr. Tanner and the Indian. "That wicked heathen stole all that was good in my life."

His Adam's apple bobbed, and he nodded. "I understand."

"Why is Mr. Tanner sitting with the enemy?"

A momentary silence hung between them. "Reckon it's his way. It don't matter to him if a person's white, black, Chinese, Irish. Or Indian. He extends respect and decency until a person's actions say something else is called for."

A derisive laugh gushed from her. Hadn't this godless animal's actions warranted harsher treatment than to sit with him while he died? "Do *you* think this Indian deserves such respect?"

"I …" He heaved a breath and sat. "I struggle some."

"You hate them too."

"I don't rightly know how to feel. My ma was captured by the Cheyenne whilst traveling the Oregon Trail."

Aimee clutched the coat even tighter.

"Her experiences with them turned her into a bitter woman. She hated everyone, including me."

The raw emptiness that was her heart broke a little more. "I'm so sorry."

"I grew up hating everything Cheyenne. But when I was twelve, Mr. Tanner took me in. He's been trying to reshape my thinking ever since."

Her chest aching, she pondered Mr. Whittaker's words. "Is it working?"

He shrugged. "Depends on the moment." He rose and extended his hand to her. "I'll show you to your bedroll. Things'll look better in the daylight."

How?

She loosened her death grip on her coat enough to slip her fingers into his calloused palm. As she stood, the clothing he'd given her to change into—a pair of men's trousers and a shirt—chafed in awkward places. Oh, she'd balked at being seen in such unseemly attire until Mr. Whittaker offered her his duster to further cover herself. Her cheeks burned afresh. Judging by how many of the men had stared throughout the day, she must look unladylike to these rough strangers. They'd *said* they would wash her dress and return it, but she'd later seen the paunch-bellied cook talking to Mr. Tanner, her dress and petticoats rolled up under his arm. She hadn't seen anyone wash it, and she guessed it wouldn't be returned. She was stuck wearing men's clothes, and until she found a ribbon to tie back her hair, it would remain unpinned and dangling down her back. At least someone had thought to bring her one of her brothers' hats to wear. She kept it pulled low over her eyes. It was good for hiding under, though Paul's scent clung so strongly, the ache of missing her brothers grew almost suffocating.

Her escort tucked her hand into the crook of his elbow just as if she were a woman in high society.

"This way, miss."

A sea of bedrolls lay before her, and she stopped. "You don't intend for me to sleep in the midst of all these men, do you, Mr. Whittaker?"

Despite the dim firelight, his stubbled cheeks reddened. "Well now, I figured you'd be uncomfortable amongst all these fellas, so I settled your bedroll underneath the chuckwagon. It ain't much, but it'll afford *a little* privacy. That all right?"

A stack of blankets waited beneath the wagon, and relief washed through her. "That'll do nicely."

Arm in arm, he led her to the wagon. Beside the hulking structure, he took off his hat and an awkward smile crossed his lips. "Miss, we don't hardly know each other, and I didn't want to presume by putting my bedroll too close. If you need anything, I'll be sleeping just a few paces away." He motioned to an empty bedroll near the men.

Nodding, she slipped between the layers of blankets and laid her head on her coat. He took his place on the bedroll he'd indicated.

Her cheeks burned at Mr. Whittaker's kind attentions. With four overprotective brothers, she'd never had much opportunity to speak to young men outside of pleasantries at church or in town. No one had dared call on her, surely because Edourard and Louis, perhaps even Paul, shot any interested suitors such withering glares, they walked the other way.

Her chest constricted. Never again would they frighten away

gentlemen callers. Ever. Nor would they protect her from dangers. Or reminisce about Papa and Mama—or anything else.

A sob tore from her chest, and she rolled onto her stomach, burying her face in her coat to stifle her cries. Minutes ticked by, her body quaking. She was utterly alone.

As she attempted to stifle the waves of hiccupping sobs, the chuckwagon creaked.

"Miss Kaplan?" Mr. Whittaker squatted beside her, one hand braced against the wagon's side, the other extended toward her, something resting in his palm. "Take my handkerchief, if you need."

She reached toward him, but rather than plucking the cloth from his palm, she clamped tightly to his hand and cried all the harder. After a couple seconds, he curled his fingers around hers and eased to the ground.

Sometime later, when her anguish had dulled again, she released her grip and took the offered handkerchief. "Thank you." Aimee dabbed away the wetness on her cheeks. "For staying with me."

He flexed his fingers several times in the flickering firelight. "Don't reckon I had much of a choice, now did I?"

A tiny chuckle bubbled through her, though she stifled it just as quickly. "I'm sorry."

"That wasn't a complaint." After the briefest hesitation, he nodded. "Now I figure it's well past time we both tried to sleep. Have a good night, Miss Kaplan."

He stood, but before he got more than three steps, she rose onto her elbow. "Wait. Mr. Whittaker?"

His shadowy form paced back and squatted beside her again. "Yes?"

*Lord God, forgive me.* "Please. Would you move your bed closer? I don't want to be alone."

# Chapter 3

Heat crept up Coy's neck as yet another Bar CT hand shot him a discreet, if teasing, grin. Thankfully, no one had said anything to upset or embarrass Miss Kaplan about how close they'd slept. A mere two feet apart, her underneath the wagon, and him just outside the wagon wheels. None of 'em would dare besmirch her character. In fact, some had offered their condolences, friendship, or help. But the moment they turned, they grinned his way, as if promising to rib him just as soon as she wasn't within earshot.

Aimee sat in silence, her filthy jacket wadded in her lap as she hunched forward, breakfast plate balanced on her knees. He'd heaped it full of biscuits, sowbelly, and flapjacks, but she'd barely nibbled at it.

"Miss, if you want, I'll roll that jacket in your bedroll, and we'll stash it all in—"

"No." She hunched even more, pinning the coat between her belly and legs. "I'll keep it with me, thank you."

It was far too warm for such a garment. "Maybe tonight, we can work on washing it for you."

She set the plate aside. "Like you all did with my dress?"

Coy hung his head. "About that." He smiled apologetically. "I'll see we get you something more appropriate just as soon as I can, but your dress was so soiled. It couldn't be salvaged."

The poor gal still hadn't come fully back to her right mind. Perhaps once they pushed on, moved past her brothers' graves, she'd think more clear-headed.

"Miss Kaplan, can you tell me what you and your kin were doing out here in the middle of Indian Territory?"

A haunted look crossed her features.

"Were you heading someplace specific? Or passing through, maybe?" He hated to pry, but—

"Whitt." Baz Freeth approached. "Boss wants to talk to you and Mitch."

"Be there directly." Coy nodded, then turned back to seek the woman's attention. "Miss?"

She scanned the nearby men, eyes distant.

"Miss Kaplan." He spoke a bit more firmly. "I need to talk to Mr. Tanner. Reckon it's best if you stay here. Try to eat, please."

She nodded, though she didn't pick up the breakfast plate again.

Coy rose and stalked toward the far side of camp. Mitch approached, leading both Mr. Tanner's best horse and a spare. They arrived at the same time, and Coy slowed. The blanket had been pulled over the Indian's face.

An odd feeling twisted through him—a strange mix of relief and regret.

"Morning," Chet Tanner spoke, rousing Coy from his thoughts.

"Morning," Mitch called.

"Sir." Coy nodded in greeting.

"Didn't figure he'd last as long as he did. He passed a couple hours ago."

Mitch cleared his throat. "You want I should send someone to the meadow to dig another grave?"

Mr. Tanner shook his head, then turned to Coy. "How's Miss Kaplan?"

He slid nearer, stationing himself so the horses stood between them and the camp. "Still pretty shook up, sir. She hasn't come back to her senses fully, but she's better."

"She causing you any difficulty?"

"No, sir." Not if he discounted the awkward discussion the previous night about his opinion of the brave. "Nothing I can't handle."

"Good. Has she told you where she was headed?"

"She said she's from Arkansas, but I haven't gotten her to say why she's in Indian Territory or where she's headed."

After a pause, Mr. Tanner turned to his son. "Mitch, I'm putting you in charge while I'm gone. And Coy," the boss shifted in his direction, "you're Segundo."

*Him*—second-in-command? "You're joshing." The startled statement burst forth unchecked. The position of Segundo was typically the cook's place, and Dixon Ramshaw was a good second-in—

Wait. What had he just said? *While he was gone...*

"What d'ya mean *gone*, Pa?" Mitch sounded as stunned as Coy.

"I'll be gone a few days, and I'm leaving you two in charge. Now you rely on Dix as much as you need. He's a good man."

"Where are you going?" Mitch asked.

"I spent the last few hours praying about what to do with our friend's remains. I believe the right thing is to take him to his people, allow them to bury him according to their customs."

A horrified gasp drew their attention. Coy's belly dropped when Miss Kaplan turned a betrayed expression on them.

"Miss, is everything all right?" Coy stepped toward her. "Did you need som—"

"How dare you! Have you forgotten? He killed my brothers!"

Mr. Tanner stepped forward. "I haven't forgotten, Miss Kaplan. But—"

"He doesn't deserve such accommodations. Let him rot. Let the wild beasts tear him limb from limb."

She spun and raced away, headed toward her brothers' gravesites.

Aimee ran for all she was worth, leaving the Bar CT's camp behind. Good riddance. If they thought an Indian—the very murderer who'd killed her family—deserved a proper burial, she wanted no part of them. But …

*Lord, help. Please.* She had no horse, no money, not even a proper set of clothes. Just her filthy coat, which she wouldn't leave again. Aimee held it all the tighter, as if someone might wrestle it from her grasp.

No one had returned Edouard's pistol to her. Indian Territory was a dangerous place, and she was unprotected. Icy fingers gripped her heart, but Aimee shook away the sudden fear. It didn't matter how dangerous. She must escape the men who'd taken her in. They didn't understand— *or didn't care*—what their reckless actions meant to her.

Which way should she go to leave Indian Territory—and once she'd departed, where on earth would she go? *Father, I need guidance.*

Lungs burning, she surged up the rise leading to the meadow. She crested the hill, and momentum carried her down the other side. But at the sight of five men standing between her and her brothers' graves, backs to her, Aimee skidded to a halt. Fear rooted her to the spot, and she dropped into a squat, working to regulate her breathing.

On the far side of the meadow, several horses stood cropping grass. Among them, Paul's mount and—she squinted—perhaps Marc's. Their horses had run off during the Indian's attack. It was a comfort to see *anything* familiar.

"You figure it's them?" A man's voice cut the silence.

"Are you stupid? Of course, it's them." A second man, tall and thin, turned slightly to look at the others. "Those are some of their horses, ain't they?" He flung a hand at the animals. "We tracked 'em here, didn't we?"

"Sure, but how do we know it's them buried here? Maybe they dug some holes, turned their horses loose, and set off on foot. Anything to get us off their trail."

*Oh no. These* were the men.

"You're overthinkin' it, Gray," a third man spoke.

"No. He's right." A different man's voice this time.

Aimee froze. The voice was unmistakable. *That* was the one whose thinly-veiled threat caused her brothers to run.

"One way to tell. Start digging."

*Oh Lord, no.* Aimee struggled to unroot her feet as the men moved off to follow the order. She managed to take a backward step, then another, but her heel caught, and she tumbled onto her backside with a grunt.

All five men turned in her direction.

# Chapter 4

"PAL!" COY RACED TO the remuda, bellowing for the wrangler. "I need Rogue."

At fourteen, Pal Hinkle was already a solid hand. The rail-thin kid stepped out from the horse herd leading Coy's saddled mount. "Saw that gal marchin' across camp and figured things mightn't go too good, so I saddled him for you."

Coy breathed easier. "Thanks." He checked the cinch, then swung into the saddle.

"Whitt?" Pal called.

"Hmm?" He stood in his stirrups, eying the distance in an attempt to keep Miss Kaplan in sight.

"You figure Miss Kaplan'd be interested in a younger fella—a fella like me? She's right pretty."

Coy glared at the red-faced kid. "Reckon I don't know, but it's hardly the time to be wondering such things, now is it?" Not with his charge racing from the camp into Indian Territory. Unguarded. Before Pal could respond, he spurred Rogue and set off after her. Blast it all. He couldn't blame her for running. If he'd just lost all his kin like she had, he might run too.

Who was he kidding? He was ready to argue with Mr. Tanner about his plan to take the Indian back, and he'd not lost anyone. The whole idea unsettled him.

Coy shook away the thoughts and focused on following Miss Kaplan. As expected, she headed to the meadow, probably to seek solace near her brothers' graves. But what if she wasn't? What if she ran on past the graves and got herself lost? A sudden surge of fear pulsed through his veins, and he turned a reluctant glance heavenward.

"God, Mr. Tanner says to pray when we're worried. To ask You for our needs." He willed himself to overcome his hesitance. "I ain't asking for me, but for Miss Kaplan. Please keep her safe."

*You figure Miss Kaplan'd be interested in a younger fella?*

Confound it. Coy gritted his teeth at the idea of Pal Hinkle fawning after their charge. The question rankled. Despite his youth, Pal should know better than to ask.

Coy neared the meadow, his belly knotting with recollections of the horrors he'd seen there. As a tendril of dread wound through him, he slowed Rogue and blew out a breath. He wouldn't find corpses there today. He'd find graves, and hopefully, Miss Kaplan would be near them.

He touched his spurs to the horse's side. Rogue scrambled up the small rise, and as Coy caught a first glimpse of the meadow over the hill, her head and shoulders bobbed into view. Beyond her, several men approached.

His nerves crackled with danger. That many rough-looking men in Indian Territory meant trouble. Probably outlaws. He removed the leather thong from the hammer of his Colt Navy before he crested the hill. Then, as if surprised by coming up on her, he rode past and swung his horse sideways, maneuvering Rogue between her and the men.

"There you are." Coy smiled, hoping to put her at ease, even as his mind scrambled for a quick and easy exit. "We found the horse. He's safe back at camp."

She trembled. Despite wearing her brother's hat pulled low to shade her face, she was pale as death. That set his teeth on edge. Had they hurt her? Doubtful. She hadn't been gone long enough. And, thank heavens, her present attire mostly hid her feminine form. She'd braided her dark curls and dropped the braid under his duster, further masking her identity. She could pass for a boy Pal's age, perhaps younger.

Someone cleared a throat. "Morning."

Coy turned Rogue slightly, keeping the big horse between them and his charge.

"Oh." He acted as if it was the first he'd noticed of them. "Howdy, gents." Coy dismounted. Before he stepped out from behind the horse, he looked at her. "Get in the saddle and wait for me."

"Didn't mean to come busting in on you like that." He stepped into their view. "We had a horse wander off in the night, so ol' Joe was looking for him."

"Happens sometimes," the man in the middle of the pack said. A young fella wearing, of all things, a battered top hat.

"Reckon it does at that." Coy forced a good-natured laugh. "Pardon the intrusion." He refocused on Miss Kaplan. Thank God she'd hoisted herself onto Rogue's back. "Let's get after it, Joe. We're burning daylight."

He mounted up behind her, and as he shifted positions, he dipped his mouth closer to her ear. "Take the reins but hold steady." Despite her trembling, she passed him her coat, then did just as he asked.

Coy looked back with a wave. "Again, didn't mean to intrude."

"No harm done," the top-hatted fella said.

He faced front, shoving her coat between them. His instinct said to wrap his arms around her, spur Rogue, and ride for the Bar CT's camp. Instead, he placed his left hand loosely at her waist, and settling his right on his thigh near his gun, he clucked his tongue.

"Keep Rogue to a canter," he urged under his breath. The big black carried them up over the rise and down the other side. "Good. Keep steady a little longer."

He resisted glancing back. Were they leveling their guns at his spine? Images of the Indian, gutshot and unable to move his lower extremities, flooded his mind. A head-to-toe shiver swept him at the thought of a bullet leaving him wounded and forcing Miss Kaplan to fend for herself. A fine lady like her shouldn't have to defend herself. It was a man's place. And blast it all if there wasn't some thrill in being the one doing the protecting.

*All right, God. Maybe I am asking for both of us. Keep us safe.* Please.

Aimee's tongue bonded to the roof of her mouth, and she quaked with the knowledge that those men had chased her brothers to their deaths. Yes, they'd died at the hands of a savage Indian, but those men, particularly the top-hat-wearing outlaw, were ultimately responsible. She and her brothers would never have been in Indian Territory if they hadn't threatened them. And except for Edouard's quick thinking to hide her in the log, she'd have died too.

Coy released his grip on her waist and just as quickly handed over her coat. She received it without a sound. Then, his arm circled her frame and pulled her a little nearer. Her breath caught as he hunched forward and, hand wrapping over hers, took the reins. Rather than spurring the horse into a run as she expected, he settled his mouth near her ear.

"You did real good, miss."

At his gentle words, a shudder ran through her.

"Do you know those gents?"

*Oh, Lord.* She gulped. Would Coy leave her if she told him … told him … told him what? She didn't even know what trouble her brothers had been in. "I don't *know* them."

He hesitated. "There's something you ain't saying." Another pause. "Am I right?"

She gave a feeble nod but couldn't bring herself to speak.

"I can't help you unless I know what we're facing. What kind of trouble are you in?"

*Lord, please. I know I just ran from this man, but …* Somehow, that didn't seem so important. *Please don't let him leave me once I tell him what I know.*

They neared the Bar CT's camp before she pulled herself together enough to answer. He maneuvered his mount toward the chuckwagon, stopping when it stood between them and the camp. There, he dismounted and plucked her out of the saddle.

Taking her by the shoulders, Coy bent in an attempt to see under her hat brim. "Who are those men?"

Her coat trailing on the ground, Aimee leaned her forehead against his shoulder. Before she knew it, she'd slipped her arms around him. "Thank you for coming after me. I didn't mean to cause trouble."

He straightened, body going rigid for a second before he relaxed and, awkwardly at first, circled her frame with his arms. Her ear so near his chest, it wasn't hard to hear the beating of his heart. A smile tugged at her lips. It was *pounding*.

"I told you. You're safe with me." He pushed her back a half step. "Didn't I?"

Once again, she wadded the coat into her arms and nodded.

"Please trust me." He cleared his throat roughly. "Now who are those men?"

"I don't know." Her voice squeaked. "About a month ago, Louis and Paul went into town, and when they returned late that night, my brothers talked. They thought I was asleep, but I wasn't. I overheard something about some trouble. And a game of poker." She shrugged. "There was a heated discussion about leaving, moving further west, but come morning, it was as if the discussion never happened. Then"—she hung her head—"a week later, someone pounded on our door in the middle of the night. He woke the whole house. I didn't see who it was, but I heard the voice. It was the man in the top hat."

"You're certain?"

"I couldn't forget it."

"Why? What'd he say?"

Her cheeks burned. "He said to return what was his, or ... he'd take me instead."

# Chapter 5

COY BALLED HIS HANDS into fists. "That ain't gonna happen." He mounted, then helped her up behind him. Once settled, he turned toward the camp. The Bar CT riders might rib him for moving his bed beside Miss Kaplan's or for being so gentle with her in her time of need, but not a one would let the likes of that silk-hat-wearing hooligan lay a hand on her.

He turned Rogue toward Chet Tanner, who knelt to roll his bedding. The Indian's body had been wrapped in a blanket and tied over the spare horse.

"Boss." Coy helped her down, then dismounted and stepped away from Rogue, motioning for her to stay. "We got an issue."

"What's that?"

"Miss Kaplan ran to the meadow and came across a group of five men. Outlaws, I reckon. She says one of 'em is the cause of her and her brothers hiding out in Indian Territory. A young cuss, by the looks of him. A couple or three years younger than me, fairly short with curly hair. And he wears a top hat." He met Mr. Tanner's concerned gaze again. "She said that fella threatened 'em. Said to return what was his, or he'd take her instead."

Mr. Tanner's jaw popped. "What is it they were supposed to return?"

"I dunno. Sounds like her brothers were keeping a lot of information from her, but she thinks it might've been relating to a card game."

"Did the men recognize her?"

He shrugged. "I ain't rightly sure. I did my best to spirit her outta there before they got too close."

Coy could all but see the thoughts churning in his boss's head.

"Have her ride with Dix in the chuckwagon. And when you and Mitch take the herd out of here, skirt wide of that meadow. Cut those gents a hefty berth. But keep an eye on your back trail, make sure they ain't following."

His heart stalled. "You ain't coming, sir?"

"I told you where I'm going."

"Yeah, but I said we might have trouble with outlaws."

"Son, you know me. I wouldn't be leaving if this wasn't important."

He had to be joshing. "Respectfully, sir, what's more important than getting the herd to Kansas?"

"Nothing. That's why you, Mitch, and Dix will see to that while I carry out this goodwill mission."

"A goodwill mission. *To the Indians.*" Had his boss lost his mind?

"Yes. We're in *their* territory. It'll go a long way toward keeping us on their good side."

Coy's muscles knotted. "Or they'll kill you for riding into their camp with one of theirs tied over a saddle."

"That's a risk I'll take, but in my dealings with the Sioux and Cheyenne, I've found they value bravery. They won't likely kill me before they discover why I rode to their camp. It'll give me opportunity to explain about their warrior's death."

The explanation didn't ease his concern but arguing would prove futile. "Yes, sir." He extended a hand to shake.

Mr. Tanner pulled him into a hug. "I'll find you all in a few days." He released Coy and grinned. "In the meantime, look after my herd—and that little gal."

"Yes sir, I will."

Chet Tanner walked to his horse, tied his bedroll behind the saddle, and mounted up. With a tip of his hat, he bid farewell and, leading the spare horse, set off.

The slump of Mr. Whittaker's shoulders as he approached tugged at Aimee's heart. It also sent fear winding through her. Obviously, his conversation hadn't gone well.

"Is everything all right?" The timid question tumbled out as he mounted. *Lord, please don't let Mr. Tanner have said to leave me behind.*

Hypocrite. Had she not just wished these men a good riddance because Chet Tanner said he'd return the Indian's body to his people? And now she was begging God to let her remain with them. Her cheeks burned.

Mr. Whittaker settled into the saddle and helped her up behind him. "He's making a mistake." His words dripped bitterness. "Now's *not* the time to ride away for a visit with the Indians."

Coat between them, Aimee wrapped her arms about his waist. "I was afraid perhaps he told you to leave me behind. For the trouble I've caused."

Stiffening, Mr. Whittaker looked over his shoulder at her. "Of course not! This ain't no place to leave a lady. In fact, he told me to take good care of you."

A bashful grin curved her lips.

"And you haven't caused us trouble."

She doubted that, though his sweet words caused warmth to rush through her. Aimee held him a little tighter. His presence was a comfort she needed right now. Similar to the safety she'd felt with her brothers, but different too.

Returning to the chuckwagon, he helped her down, then dismounted. "When we move out, you'll be riding with our cook."

Her breath leaked from her lungs. "Where are we going?"

There was a gentleness in his nearly black-eyed gaze. "For now, to Ellsworth, Kansas. Once we get the herd sold, I reckon we'll take you wherever you want."

Aimee swallowed hard, then nodded.

"As I was saying, you'll ride with Dixon Ramshaw."

She looked at the curmudgeonly, bespectacled man with the hefty paunch as he readied the wagon. Heart beating a little faster, she looked back at Mr. Whittaker. "Can't I ride with you?"

He shook his head. "That wouldn't be wise, miss. I'll be busy with the cattle. That's some hot, dusty, and dangerous work. You'll be far safer with Dix, even if he does open his mouth and show what a sharp-tongued devil he is."

"I wouldn't hafta be so sharp-tongued if you knot-heads possessed even half the wisdom God gave a toad. Someone's gotta keep you in line." He shot a pointed glare Mr. Whittaker's way, then turned a much gentler smile on her. "But I don't figure I'll need to speak so harsh to you, young lady. Will I?"

Her heart stuttered. *Lord, I'd rather stay with Coy ... Mr. Whittaker. I need him.*

"Why don't you settle yourself on the bench there, missy. Your chariot awaits." Mr. Ramshaw grinned, and Mr. Whittaker helped her climb to the wagon seat.

"You're sure I can't stay with you?" she whispered as soon as she'd settled herself.

"Yes, miss. But you'll see me plenty. I'll be checking in throughout the day."

Her stomach knotted. She'd come to rely on him more than she realized. Coat in her lap, she faced front.

*Father, take care of me … and Coy.* Her cheeks flamed. *I mean, Mr. Whittaker.*

The two men stepped away a few feet, and though she didn't look their way, their hushed words reached her.

"Please, Dix. Treat her good. Like you would—"

"Son, please." The cook snorted. "I was married longer than you been alive. I know how to treat a lady. She'll be safe."

"Yes, sir. Thank you."

"Now, can we git?" Mr. Ramshaw's tone turned snappish. "Reckon we're all restless to get moving."

Mr. Whittaker remounted and maneuvered his horse so she could see him. He gave a broad smile and touched his hat brim. "Miss Kaplan. I'll check on you soon."

Aimee fought the urge to scramble down and take her former place behind him.

Within minutes, Mr. Ramshaw sat beside her. "Iffen you want, miss, you kin stash your coat in the back. You don't gotta hold it the whole way to Kansas."

It *was* hot, clutching the heavy garment at all times. As she loosened her grip just a little, the cook reached for it.

"No. I can't forget it."

His features lit with surprise, but he smiled. "No, miss. That wouldn't be good. How's about under the seat where you kin keep an eye on it, get to it whenever you need."

She finally nodded, and he tucked the garment under the bench.

"There, now." He started the wagon rolling northward.

With her arms empty, she untucked her long braid from inside Coy's duster and fidgeted with the softly curling end. To her right, the huge herd moved out like a sea of cowhide and horns flooding across the landscape. One man rode at the front, the tip of the flood's wave. As the sea spread out, more Bar CT riders positioned themselves around. Aimee searched for Coy and his big black horse. Once she found him about a third of the way back in the herd, she took off her hat and leaned forward, as if for a better view.

"You ever seen a cattle drive before, Miss Kaplan?"

"No." Her gaze never left Coy's lean frame.

"That's Mitch Tanner up front. He's what you'd call the point rider. He scouts the way and leads the herd. Then, there's Whitt, and on the other side of the herd about even with him, Baz Freeth. Them two are swing riders. You look further back, and you'll see the next pair—Jeff Lange and Alex Jansik. They're the flank riders. Them four keep the herd bunched and look out for any cows making a break for freedom. And at the back, Gus Mabry and Sam Ulster are riding drag, pushing the stragglers to keep up. And Pal's the wrangler. He keeps the remuda, saddles the mounts, doctors the horses."

As he explained, one huge animal turned from the rest, wide curving horns bobbing as he ran for some trees in the distance. Coy wheeled his horse and circled wide around the large animal. In a quick charge, he got beside the steer, stopped it, and with a wave of his hat, got it moving back toward the herd.

Aimee turned to Mr. Ramshaw. "Is he good at his job?" To her, he seemed born to the saddle, more comfortable atop a horse than on his own legs.

"Who? Whitt?" He huffed softly. "Shucks, he's about the best we got." Admiration tinged his words, though he cleared his throat roughly. "But don't tell him I said so. I got a reputation as a grump to keep intact."

A timorous chuckle sputtered out as she swept her gaze back toward the herd. However, on the crest of the hill to Mr. Ramshaw's left, she glimpsed a figure some twenty yards away, near where her brothers were buried.

Aimee tugged her hat on and discreetly pushed her braid over her shoulder. Too late. The figure, a top-hat-wearing man, stared directly at the wagon—*at her*—as they passed.

# Chapter 6

HANDS FOLDED UNDER HIS head, Coy lay in his bedroll just outside the chuckwagon's wheels. Inches from his left shoulder, Miss Kaplan lay inside the perceived protection of those wheels. Her breathing was even. For once, she slept, seemingly not plagued by nightmares of her brothers' deaths.

He listened to the singing of those on night duty with the herd. Despite the music that calmed the cattle, his thoughts churned. It had been almost a week since Miss Kaplan had tearfully reported the outlaw watching their passage. She'd feared the man might've seen her braid, seen her without her hat, and pieced together her identity. Coy had circulated word amongst the men to be on guard, to watch for anything suspicious. Everyone had been vigilant, and it appeared they'd passed the outlaws without any trouble.

*Thank You for that much, God.*

The grudging prayer flooded his mind, and he shoved it away. Yes, God had kept the outlaws from stirring trouble, but He hadn't made Chet Tanner return—and Coy was concerned.

*What about that part, God? Did You let the Indians kill my friend?*

Each day Mr. Tanner didn't return, Coy's fear grew. Was he lying injured—or worse—at the hands of those to whom he'd meant to show kindness? Coy blew out a frustrated breath.

*God, if You're as good as Mr. Tanner says, then prove it. Bring him back, unharmed—*

Miss Kaplan burrowed deeper into her bedroll, blankets tucked under her chin, and a contented moan escaped her lips. Intrigued, Coy also rolled onto his side, though sharp pain jabbed his hip. He rolled back, retrieved the necklace from his pocket, then curled onto his side again.

She slept soundly, at peace in the flickering firelight. In the six days since he'd found her, he'd come to care for her—fiercely. It pained him to leave her with Dix each day whilst he worked. But herding cattle was no place for a lady, and the more he saw of Aimee—Miss Kaplan—the more he was convinced she was a true lady. Kind, gentle, proper. In spite of her great losses in that meadow, she'd kept a sweetness about her. A tender side. Very seldom did it falter. Only the once, when Mr. Tanner said he'd take the Indian to his people.

He stared at her delicate features—the curve of her cheek, the long lashes resting against her smooth skin, her perfect mouth. His heart beat a little faster. Hers was a face he could enjoy studying. Particularly her soft, shapely lips.

*Idiot.*

With a frustrated sigh, he flopped onto his back, the necklace heavy in his fist. Aimee Kaplan might be beautiful and sweet and perfect in nearly every way, but nothing could ever work between them. He was a fool for dreaming. Thoughts churning, he held the wad of beads, bone, and grizzly claws up to see in the firelight.

*If You're so good, God, bring Mr. Tanner back safe.* His attention strayed again to Aimee's perfect face, though he snapped his eyes shut before he could start memorizing every detail. *And make this whole blasted drive more bearable.*

With a huff, Coy sat and shook out his boots to dislodge any unwanted critters. Certain any spiders were gone, he pulled the boots on, stood, and shoved the necklace back in his pocket. Snatching up his gun belt, he stalked toward the campfire, where the customary pot of coffee sat warming over the fire. Before he sat, he fastened the belt around his waist.

"You all right?" Dix's voice cut the stillness as he stepped from the shadows and handed Coy an empty tin mug.

Taking it, Coy poured himself some of the strong brew. "Can't sleep."

"What's occupying your thoughts?"

Not ready to admit it was as much Aimee Kaplan as anything else, he hoisted the pot and raised an eyebrow at Dix, who thrust his own mug forward. "Don't like how long Mr. Tanner's been gone," Coy spoke as he poured.

The cook grunted, then sipped from the mug in silence. After a moment, someone else emerged from the dark camp.

Mitch blinked at both men, eyes still full of sleep. "Anything wrong?"

Coy took a sip of the coffee. "Your pa's been gone an awful long time."

"Five days." Mitch crossed his arms.

He stared at each man in turn. "Am I the only one concerned about that fact?"

"You ain't," Dix answered.

Mitch gave a resigned shake of his head. "I'm feeling it too, but what do you suggest we do? Pa said to keep moving north, and he'd find us."

Coy swirled the coffee. "I think it's time we rest the herd for two or three days."

"I can see resting a day, but two or three?" Mitch's brow furrowed. "That's a lot, Coy."

It was, but …

"The longer we delay, the shorter we'll run on supplies," Dix reminded.

"There's plenty of space here, good grazing and water. Won't hurt to fatten the herd a little before we push on. Besides, the next leg will include another river crossing. Waiting a few days'll give your pa some time to catch up if he needs." By waiting, they could scout for sign of Mr. Tanner, which would put his mind at ease. "And whilst we're stopped, we can rustle up some prairie hens or something to add to our stores."

Mitch and Dix exchanged thoughtful glances before the cook spoke. "Reckon I could make a case for two."

A grim smile tugged at one corner of Mitch's mouth. "Two da—"

"Coy!"

At Aimee's high-pitched shriek, Coy drew his gun and ran for the wagon, Mitch and Dix keeping pace.

Aimee cowered next to the wagon wheel, one arm looped through the spokes, when Coy and his friends raced up. In a flash, he was at her side.

"What happened? Are you hurt?" Worry creased his handsome features.

Her breath came in tiny gasps.

"Miss Kaplan?" His concerned gaze pierced to her soul.

She slid free of the spokes and all but launched herself into his arms. He caught her, pulled her close, and cradled the back of her head in his hand.

"Were you dreaming again? Nightmares?"

If only. "*He* was here." Cheek pressed against his shoulder, Aimee stared at the growing crowd of men as they stumbled from their bedrolls to see about the commotion.

Coy's hand slid to her shoulder, and he pushed her back to arm's length. "He who?"

Panic shrouded her heart. Was he among the shadowy faces surrounding her, standing in their midst?

"Who? Talk to me."

She gulped. "Kid Heller."

"Who?"

"The outlaw," she all but screeched. "He was right there." She jabbed a finger toward the spot where he'd knelt at her left side.

Mitch urged one of the men to light a lantern, and he scrambled away to do his bidding.

"He was *here?*" Coy whispered.

She nodded, eyes brimming with tears. "He clamped his hand over my mouth." She could still feel his grimy palm pressed to her face. With a hiccupping breath, she pressed on. "He said Louis stole from him. Cheated, then ran off with his winnings. He said I have until tomorrow night to give them back or …"

The man returned with the lantern, and he and Mitch circled the wagon to view the ground.

At that sight of matted grass beside her bed, a murmur rippled through the group. Coy's features turned stony.

"Or *what?*" he prompted.

Aimee swallowed hard, her throat knotting painfully. "He'd take me, and I'd *eventually* end up dead like my brothers."

# Chapter 7

EXHAUSTION PULLED AT COY'S muscles and his mind. After Miss Kaplan's frantic middle-of-the-night announcement, not a single Bar CT man had slept. Several wanted to charge out in search of the outlaw and his friends, but Mitch elicited promises that they'd wait until morning. Level heads had prevailed, though it was a long, sleepless night for all.

"When're we leaving?" Jeff Lange asked from across the fire.

"The sooner the better, if I have my druthers," Gus Mabry answered.

Coy eyed Aimee—Miss Kaplan—pushing her scant breakfast around her plate.

Sam Ulster cleared his throat. "We'll defend your honor, miss."

"Ya'll, hush." Mitch ground out the words. "Leave Miss Kaplan in peace."

Once they fell silent, she leaned close to him.

"Will we all go?" Her voice barely reached a whisper.

Coy shook his head. "No." He matched her tone. "You'll stay with Dix, Pal, and a couple others."

"With you?"

The question stopped him. "Uh, no. I'll be going. We need to make a strong show, change these fellas' minds about harassing you."

She looked up, her face inches from his. "Please don't go."

His head spun with her nearness.

"Why? Dix and the others'll watch over you."

Confound it, she was so close. If he leaned in just a little, he could kiss her. How easy it would be. *Just lean in, steal a kiss.* He ached to.

"I know they will, but I *trust* you."

The words stopped him cold. Pulling away, he wiped the back of his fist across his mouth. The last thing she needed was to trust *him*. She didn't even know him.

And by no means should he kiss her.

After an instant, she turned away. "I've lost so much already. I don't want to lose you too."

He hauled in a huge breath, hoping it would calm him.

"Please? I feel safe with you."

As if on cue, Mitch stepped up, a knowing smile curving his lips. If Coy didn't know better, Mitch had been watching their whole interchange.

"Everything all right?" he asked.

"Fine." Coy reached for his coffee mug to avoid Miss Kaplan's pleading glance.

She rose. "Does Mr. Whittaker have to go this morning? I'd feel much safer if he stayed with me."

The tepid coffee hit Coy's throat wrong, and he coughed. When Mitch looked his way, Coy gave a discreet shake of his head.

Mischief in his smile, Mitch turned back to Miss Kaplan. "No. In fact, I think it's a real fine idea, him staying to look after things in camp and provide you the security you need."

Her smile blossomed. "Thank you. I'd feel ever so much better."

Again, Coy shook his head to dissuade Mitch. Didn't he see? She was growing too fond of him, and he of her. That spelled disaster for both.

"Then that's what you'll have, Miss Kaplan. Right, Coy?"

Both she and Mitch turned his way.

It took an instant to find his tongue. "Reckon I'm staying."

Just after breakfast, the Bar CT crew had ridden off to confront Kid Heller and his gang, leaving only Coy, Dix, Paladin Hinkle, and Alex Jansik in camp. Coy and Alex had promptly headed toward the waiting herd and Pal to tend the remuda, much to Aimee's dismay. Since they weren't moving the cattle, she'd hoped they'd be left to graze, and she could wait with Coy.

But something had happened as they finished breakfast. Coy, normally attentive and caring, had pulled away. Perhaps because she'd forced him to stay in camp rather than going to confront the outlaws. Maybe he thought she was mollycoddling him. She wasn't. She'd been honest, saying she didn't want to lose him like she had her family. He'd become her anchor, the one person she felt some little sense of peace with. As kind as the other men were, Coy was … Coy. Sweet, kind, attentive, accommodating. And handsome. His was an exotic look, with those almost-black eyes and dark hair that shone in the sun anytime he took his hat off. She often tried to study his features without staring.

"Those boys better return soon, or they'll miss supper," Mr. Ramshaw grumbled as he checked on the meal he was cooking.

Tension gripped her muscles at the out-of-the-blue comment. As the day had dragged on, worry had crept into her thoughts. Were they safe? Had they dealt with Kid Heller's gang? It was kind of them to fight for her, but now, hours later, she would be happy they'd returned. "How long do these matters usually take?"

The cook mumbled something unintelligible.

"Pardon?"

Mr. Ramshaw rolled his eyes. "Nothing. Weren't fit for delicate ears." He lifted a pot lid, checked the contents, then lowered it again. "Reckon they shoulda been back a while ago."

"You're concerned too, then." Dear God, she wasn't the only one.

He heaved a breath and scrubbed the back of his head. "Tried to tell Mitch it wasn't smart, sending the bulk of our crew out to deliver a warning."

An ache formed between her temples. "What happens if they don't return?"

"Hoping we ain't gonna find out."

From the direction of the remuda, Pal approached. "Something sure smells good, Dix." The boy stopped at the fire and, grabbing a rag, lifted the lid to a pot. "Food about ready?"

Mr. Ramshaw swatted him with his hat, and Pal dropped the lid with a clatter. "Git your grimy hands outta my cooking. You wash those filthy mitts before you touch anything."

Pal slinked away, grinning as the cook continued to grumble. A chuckle on her lips, Aimee looked toward the cattle to keep the cook from seeing her laughter.

She sought a glimpse of Coy in the distance like she'd done throughout the day. This time, several familiar riders skirted the herd, trickling in across a fair distance.

"Mr. Ramshaw?" Aimee stood, shading her eyes against the setting sun. Was that them? Hard to tell, the way several of them slumped in their saddles.

Both the wrangler and cook stared toward the herd, then Mr. Ramshaw burst into motion.

"Pal, get a horse saddled and get out there. We got wounded," the cook barked. "Miss Kaplan, dump the coffee pot and fill it with water whilst I get the medical supplies."

Heart pounding, Aimee jumped to action.

# Chapter 8

COY'S HEART RATCHETED INTO his throat at the sight of the Bar CT riders. Mitch's face was pale, his shirt bloody at the shoulder. Gus and Baz shared a horse, Gus nearly lying across the sorrel's neck as Baz kept him in the saddle. Jeff Lange's blond hair was matted with blood above his left ear, and the other men rode with the look of exhaustion.

"By all that's holy. What happened?" Coy skidded his horse to a stop near the first men.

"They were expecting us," Baz answered, wrestling Gus' hunched form into a better position.

Coy edged nearer. Sunlight glistened on a wet patch darkening Gus' shirt, and the man's breath rasped. Not good.

"Go. Get him to Dix. Now." He scanned the other men and urged them toward camp with a sharp nod. "All of you."

Baz spurred the sorrel and headed into camp, the others following. Pal Hinkle arrived, stopping to stare at passing men.

Mitch met Coy's gaze for a second before he looked away.

"You all right?" Coy urged the sturdy paint horse he was riding toward his friend.

"You said there were five of 'em?" Mitch's words slurred with pain.

"That's what I saw in the meadow."

Mitch shook his head. "Heller had to have eight, maybe ten guys, but half of 'em were hidden." He gulped a breath, wincing as he did. "They had us dead to rights, Coy. Only reason any of us are alive is because they weren't ready to kill us. *Yet*."

Kill them. Why? Who in blue blazes was Kid Heller, and what did he think Aimee Kaplan had that was important enough to kill for?

A groan from Mitch's direction drew him from his questioning.

"Let's go. That wound needs attention." He slapped Mitch's horse on the rump with his hat, sending the horse toward Dix, then turned to the wrangler. "Pal."

The young man looked Coy's way.

"Take my place out here and keep a close watch. Expect trouble." He scanned the perimeter of the herd and found Alex Jansik on the far side. "Make sure Jansik knows to be on his guard. Understand?"

"Yes, sir." Pal took up his new job without hesitation.

Eyes on Mitch's slump-shouldered form, Coy's chest tightened at the sight of a second bloodstain down the back of his friend's shirt.

As Coy caught up, Mitch struggled to form words. "I think some of the hidden shooters might've been—"

"Quit jawing. Save your strength."

Reaching the chuckwagon, Coy slid from his saddle and scrambled to Mitch's side, all but pulling him from his mount. He guided him toward the other wounded.

Dix and Baz worked on a gaping hole slightly off-center in Gus' back. Aimee stood nearby, the same lost appearance she'd displayed after he'd found her in the meadow had returned. He looked at the three men awaiting attention.

"How bad's your head?" He twisted Jeff Lange's noggin so he could see the wound.

"Got me a thumper of a headache, but I was lucky, I'd say. It's a crease, nothing more."

Coy grinned. "Reckon you can function?"

The man straightened a little. "Yeah."

Coy turned to Sam Ulster. "Where are you hurt?"

He nodded to his bloody pant leg. "Just a flesh wound. Ain't nothing serious."

"Good. Help each other if you need, and I'll see to Mitch."

As Lange rose to collect supplies from Dix's medical kit, Sam cleared his throat. "I recognized that Heller fella and a couple in that bunch with him today."

"Yeah, from where?" If he had time, he'd give Sam his full attention, but Mitch's wound needed tending.

"They're from my neck of the woods. Arkansas."

That tracked with Aimee's story.

"You know 'em?" He helped Mitch out of his shirt, straining for Sam's answer.

The bullet had struck the meaty part of his shoulder, wound still oozing blood. "Went all the way through?"

At Mitch's nod, Coy fished the handkerchief from his pocket, dislodging the necklace in the process.

"Ain't had dealings with 'em myself," Sam said. "But they got quite a reputation."

Coy shifted for a better look at the exit wound, a nasty-looking hole. A tendril of fear wound through him.

"They been stirring trouble since before the war ended. Ain't let go of the South's loss, and they're doing all they can to keep fighting. If memory serves, they're suspected of attempted murder of a couple delegates from the state's constitutional convention about three years back, and more recently, they were involved in robbing a railroad. All sorts of things."

He pinned Sam with a firm look. "I want to hear more once we got all this under control."

"You got it."

Coy tucked the handkerchief against the entry wound. "You hold that there and sit still. I'll be back."

He wiped his bloody fingers in the grass. "Baz, you hurt?" he called.

He shook his head. "Only one who ain't."

Thank heavens. A bit of good news. Coy grabbed the necklace and hurried toward Aimee.

"Hey," he called as he drew near. "You all right?"

Her breath came in ragged gasps, but she met his eyes and nodded feebly.

He reached toward her cheek, realizing too late that he still clutched the necklace. She drew back, brow furrowing, and stared at the strange sight.

"What is that?"

He cursed himself and shoved it in his pocket. "Nothing important."

Questions filled her hazel eyes.

"Are you all right?"

After an instant, her eyes strayed to the men. "Are they?"

"They will be." He forced more confidence into his voice than he felt. "But I need you to do something for me."

Trepidation flashed across her features. "What?"

"Search in the chuckwagon and find something we can use for more bandages. We're gonna need 'em."

She pulled her eyes from the wounded men, nodded at him, then scurried toward the wagon. Coy returned to Mitch's side to study the wounds.

Mitch grinned. "You and her have really taken to each other."

Coy ignored the comment, dabbing blood away for a better view. "You're good together."

He liked her plenty, but … "I ain't no good for her, and you know it."

"I don't know nothing of the kind."

For the briefest second, his mind wandered through what life with Aimee might look like, but quick as the woolgathering started, he slammed that mental door. "She don't want a man like me, so hush."

"Why?" Mitch's tone was challenging. "Because you're half—"

"Yeah," he growled, snatching rags from the stack Lange had brought over. Balling a rag against each wound, Coy applied pressure to the injuries to staunch the bleeding. Mitch sagged in pain. "Because of that."

Aimee scrambled onto the wagon and clambered into the back. The scent of warm canvas permeated the air in the chuckwagon.

Something for bandages. She cast a frantic glance around the wagon box. The bedrolls. She could tear blankets and sheets into strips, but that would leave someone without bedding.

Only if she had to.

Bags of flour, oats, sugar—the staples they needed—were stacked against the sides. Rifling through those bags, she found one at the bottom of the stack unlike the others. Not heavy and dense like the bags of food, but soft. Flimsy, not firm. She jerked it free and peeked in.

Her dress and petticoats. Of course. They would make for excellent bandages.

She pulled the rolled clothing from the sack, the sight bringing both a strange comfort at their familiarity and a revulsion to the stains. Pushing the latter aside, she grabbed the edge of the clothes and shook them, the fabric unfurling. As it did, something heavy clattered against the wagon bed and skittered across the planks. She pulled the garments aside.

*Edouard's gun.*

Aimee scooped it up and checked to see it was loaded, just as her brothers had taught. It was. Relief flooded through her.

*Thank You, Lord.* She hadn't seen it since Coy had handed it off to Mr. Tanner. She wouldn't give it up again.

"Aimee?" Coy called from outside the wagon. "How you coming on those bandages?"

"I have something. I'll be out in a minute."

"Hurry."

At his urging, she grabbed the least stained petticoat and tore it. Once she had a few strips, she looped one around the butt of the pistol and knotted it, making sure to keep it free of the trigger and hammer. She unbuttoned Coy's duster, looped the long strip around her neck and tied it off, then tucked the gun barrel into her borrowed belt. Refastening the duster, she prayed the oversized garment would hide it.

She returned to tearing the petticoat into lengths for bandages, but as she neared the center, an odd thickness of material gave her pause. A second layer of fabric. How had it gotten there—and why? She'd hand-stitched the garment herself several years ago, and she'd not sewn such a patch in this awkward position. Fingers straying over the clumsily-stitched flap, she felt an odd thickness of—what?—inside.

It took her only a moment to find an extra-wide space between stitches and work her finger between the layers. Loosening the patch, she found a long strip of paper—a much larger sheet folded until it was a one-inch-tall strip. She started to unfold it.

"Miss Kaplan." Mr. Ramshaw barked. "Hurry, girl!"

Of course. The men. They were of utmost importance. She refolded the paper and dropped it in the only safe place she had—inside her borrowed shirt. With the strips of material she'd already torn, she climbed over the wagon bench into the fresh air and approaching dusk.

A distant gunshot rang out. Aimee stalled, clinging to the wagon's wheel. Another shot. Followed by a cacophonous volley. She jumped free of the wagon and stared in the direction of the sounds—*the direction of the herd*.

"Stampede!"

*Oh Lord, no.* Her scream died in her throat.

# Chapter 9

AT THE FIRST SHOT, Coy jerked to face the herd. To his horror, the noisy barrage sent the longhorns into motion. Straight toward them.

*Oh, God. Keep everyone safe.*

The Bar CT hands launched into action around him.

"Go." Coy grabbed Mitch's good arm and hauled him to his feet. "Get to the wagon."

"I can ride."

"Not in a stampede, you can't. Now go." He gave the man a rough shove.

The other men scattered as Baz and Dix wrestled Gus' limp frame toward the wagon.

Ground rumbling with the approaching herd, Coy ran for his paint pony. Halfway there, he spotted Aimee. Eyes huge, she stared at the approaching stampede.

"Aimee!" Coy launched himself into the saddle and turned toward her. "Get in the wagon!" He fanned the air as if that might force her to move.

She remained stock-still, her face a mask of terror.

Dix and Baz huddled under the wagon with Gus' unconscious form, screaming for Aimee's attention. Mitch was on the wagon seat already, also calling for her. Mounted, Lange and Sam charged out ahead of the herd, surely in hopes they might be able to turn the cattle and eventually stop them. Yet Aimee still stood frozen.

He charged nearer and skidded his horse to a stop. "Get in the wa—"

The first cattle raced past, just feet from them, one plowing through Dix's cookfire. Aimee screamed.

Too late.

Coy slid behind the saddle and, leaning down, caught her about the midsection. Before he could straighten, the herd was on them, and his horse bolted. With all the strength he could muster, he hauled her into the saddle, both legs dangling down the right side of the horse's body.

He clamped his arms firm about her.

Cattle surged around them, bumping and jostling, his paint horse carried along in the flood. Thick dust billowed, coating his tongue. He had to get to the outside, or when his mount's strength waned, they could be trampled. But he wouldn't attempt anything until Aimee was secure in the saddle.

"Throw your leg over his neck," he shouted above the thunderous noise.

She only trembled in his arms.

"Do it," he growled.

*God, please. Make her cooperate.*

As if something snapped, she moved. Her hand braced against his thigh, she raised her leg. When one of the cows slammed into them, she screamed. His horse stumbled but recovered.

Coy held her even tighter. "You won't fall. Do it now!"

Aimee worked her leg over the paint's neck and twisted frontward. And with that, Coy leaned in, his body curling around hers.

*God, get us out of here.*

Coy searched for any opening in the crush of bodies to their left. When the cattle separated a little, he jerked the paint's reins hard, and he ducked into the space. Distance disappeared under them. Minutes later, another space opened, and Coy deftly shifted his horse into it.

The herd surged hard to the right, and hope sprouted. If Lange and Sam had gotten positioned, maybe they were driving the herd, working to bunch the cattle and drive them into a tighter and tighter circle. As they turned, Coy jostled positions again. Over and over, he kept moving left until finally, the edge of the herd was in sight. Only a few longhorns between them and freedom. None too soon. His horse was tiring fast.

The cattle once more banked right and, seeing his break, Coy charged the paint out of the sea of horns and hooves. As they turned, he kept the horse on a straight path. Only when he was sure they were free of the threat did he draw to a halt. The horse's sides heaved.

Coy slid from the horse's back and, muscles quivering, pulled Aimee down. Her feet barely touched the grass before her knees gave way. Grasping the saddle horn, he caught her, pulled her to him.

Durn, but she felt good.

"You're not hurt, are you?"

After an instant, she shook her head against his chest. "I don't think so."

He blew out a breath and lifted his eyes toward the ever-darkening heavens. "Thank you, Lord."

Shifting his attention to her, he rocked back a step. "You scared me to death. You've got to listen to me. When I say get in the wagon, *get in the wagon.*"

"I'm sorry." A tremor ran through her, and she latched onto his shirt. "I couldn't move."

Coy pulled her nearer, drawing on her inner strength for his own quaking muscles. He rested his cheek against her temple. "It's all right. You're safe."

*Thank You, Lord, for bringing us through that.*

He brushed a gentle kiss across her cheek and lingered there, savoring the feel of her. With a tiny sigh, Aimee twisted ever so slightly, her mouth hovering near his, breath stirring against his skin. He pulled back and found a timid question in her fine dust-covered features. An invitation. Heart pounding, he arched a brow at the unspoken request with a question of his own. She dipped her chin slightly, a shy, rosy-cheeked smile creeping across her lips.

It was all the answer he needed. Coy kissed her again, this time full on the mouth.

Aimee melted against him with a soft moan, and every fiber in him ignited. His hand strayed to her hair, his fingers twining into her once-neat braid as he deepened the kiss. Muscles still shaking after the stampede—or were they shaking anew with Aimee's nearness?—he dragged her closer still and hoisted her off the ground. His senses spun nearly out of control.

From behind them, someone cleared his throat roughly. Startled, Coy broke the kiss and spun to face the sound, hand hovering near the pistol on his hip. Aimee's featherlight touch came to rest between his shoulder blades, and he sensed rather than saw her stand on her tiptoes to peek over his shoulder.

"You done?" Still mounted, Chet Tanner leaned on his saddle horn in the looming dark, the last shreds of daylight illuminating a look of— what? Annoyance? Perhaps amusement.

Feeling like that blasted twelve-year-old kid he'd been the day Tanner caught him trying to swipe his billfold, Coy nodded. "Yes, sir."

"Good. We got a herd to catc—"

"Coy." Aimee's fingers twisted into his shirt. He sidestepped while she stared at a shadowy movement in the distance.

A man rode toward them on an unfamiliar bay horse, bare-chested, dark hair trailing down his back, with a bow slung across his body. Coy's heart, only now slowing after the breakneck rush of the stampede—and their unexpected kiss—again leapt into a gallop.

Beside him, Aimee fumbled with the duster's buttons, then hefted a gun with both hands.

"No," both Coy and Mr. Tanner shouted as she steadied the pistol.

Aimee darted a glance between Coy and the approaching rider, her body once more spasming with fear.

Coy wrapped a hand around the gun's barrel and forced the muzzle toward the ground. "You could spook the herd again."

"Black Moon is here by my invitation, Miss Kaplan," Mr. Tanner spoke, nudging his horse between her and the Indian.

"By your invita—" She gaped as he dismounted. Why on earth would he ask an Indian into their camp? He *had* to remember that the brave he took back to them had killed her family. She was the one who'd shot him. *Oh, Lord.* Had he come for revenge?

"Give me the gun." Coy's expression held a firm pleading.

He wrapped gentle fingers around her left wrist and pried it away from the pistol, though when he attempted to twist the gun free, she clung to it.

"Please don't take it."

Chet Tanner approached. "You can't shoot him, Miss Kaplan. He's a friend." The elder man eyed Coy. "The son of Ten Bears."

Coy's grip on her wrist faltered. His face paled, and a haunted look flashed on his handsome features.

"Not now." Coy gave a tiny shake of his head.

Aimee's stomach knotted. "Who is Ten Bears?"

"Not now, meaning you don't want to talk about it? Or not now, you won't meet him?" Mr. Tanner skewered Coy with a glare.

He clenched his jaw. "I mean, not *here.*"

Tucking the pistol back in her belt, she buttoned Coy's duster. Why *not* here? They were alone, but for a couple of horses. And her. Aimee's breath hitched. Coy didn't want to discuss whatever this was in front of *her*.

"Who is Ten Bears?" She ground the question out between clenched teeth.

"You need to face this, son." Mr. Tanner spoke as if she weren't even there. "Put those beads around your neck and wear 'em, proudly."

Beads? After the injured men rode into camp, Coy had held some beads when he approached her. When she'd asked about them, he'd dismissed the question. Aimee twisted to look at his hip. Even in the growing darkness, she found a few inches of earth-colored beads trailing from his pocket. Without hesitation, she grabbed them and pulled.

Coy's jaw went slack as they tumbled free. He latched onto her wrist roughly, his almost-black eyes flashing with—was it anger? No, *horror*.

She stared at him for a breath, then looked at the strange beads, interspersed with some kind of claws, which dangled from her fingers. Just past Mr. Tanner, the Indian appeared near enough she could make out his features in the deep dusk. Dark hair. Almost-black eyes.

Realization struck. Twisting free of Coy's grasp, she dropped the beads.

"You're one of *them*."

# Chapter 10

THE REVULSION IN AIMEE'S tone struck Coy like a mule kick. Shame cascaded through him, like when his mother spewed her whiskey-induced rants about the Cheyenne.

*Only good Cheyenne's a dead one.*

*Indians are filthy heathens. Including you, you little brat.*

*You're so much like your father. Vile. Loathsome. I hated him. You ain't any better.*

Unable to meet Aimee's gaze, he stared at the ground. "Reckon I am," he growled. "Leastways, I been told the Cheyenne brave, Ten Bears, was my father."

Throat knotting until he could barely breathe, he led his tuckered paint pony away.

"Coy," Chet Tanner called.

He shook his head as he retreated. "Leave me be."

This was Mr. Tanner's fault. Coy had developed thick calluses on his heart due to the constant barrage of hate his mother spewed. He'd come to expect her vile words. Oh, they'd hurt, but he'd learned to harden himself. Then Mr. Tanner plucked him out of that life, taught him what it was to be loved and accepted. How to accept himself. For a few short years, he'd lived in a world where he thought his heritage wouldn't matter.

Then Miss Kaplan came along. Oh, he knew. He knew from the minute Mr. Tanner said to look after her that she was gonna be trouble. He shoulda just said no then and taken whatever consequences the boss wanted to levy against him. But had he done that? No. Because he'd grown soft.

Every time she turned those big eyes on him or called out in that quavering, fearful little voice, he'd come running. Like a blasted fool. Lying next to her every night, she'd awakened something in him. Desire. An itch for more than sleeping every night of his life in a bunkhouse full of sweaty, stinkin' men. He'd allowed himself to dream that he could love and be loved by a pretty woman. But he was Indian. Vile, filthy, loathsome Indian. And she hated his kind.

The rustle of footsteps in the grass alerted Coy to Mr. Tanner's approach before the elder man touched his shoulder.

"We've got a lot of work ahea—"

Coy spun to face him, one open palm smacking Mr. Tanner's chest. "I told you I wasn't ready to talk." He darted a tiny glance in Aimee's direction, thankful the darkness had obscured her from view. "Not in front of her. But all these years, you've picked at every sore spot in me until it bleeds."

"That's God's way, son. He leads you back to those sources of hurt long enough to clean out the rotten parts an—"

Coy's right fist landed square on Mr. Tanner's nose. The Bar CT owner tumbled backward into the grass, blood sprouting from his face.

"You ain't God! You ain't my pa! And as of now, you ain't my boss! I quit."

"Coy."

"I'm done." Grabbing the paint's reins, Coy swung onto the horse and spurred him into a gallop.

*Oh, Father. Help.* What is happening here?

Coy—an Indian. Even as he charged off, the drum of hoofbeats fading in the darkness, Aimee gulped for air. Her thoughts flew too fast to grab hold of, the swirl leaving her nearly light-headed. He'd left, and she remained—with Mr. Tanner and an unknown Indian brave.

The Indian approached her, and his piercing eyes met hers. Aimee's heart launched into an erratic beat. But he only scooped the strand of beads from the grass, then walked to Mr. Tanner's side and helped him up.

"I will go after him."

Aimee gasped. The Indian's words, spoken in English, were clear as a mountain stream.

"No. As dark as it is, we're not going to find him tonight." Mr. Tanner gripped the brave's arms as he got his feet under him again. "Maybe he'll grow some sense and return to camp on his own. We'll head that way, and if he's not returned by dawn, Mitch and I'll look for him."

At the mention of Mitch, Aimee toddled forward. "He's hurt."

"Who? Mitch?"

"Mitch, Gus, Lange, and Sam. All shot." When had she started thinking about them this way? By their first names … like family?

"Lord God above." Mr. Tanner approached, settled his hand at the small of her back, and with a gentle pressure, hurried her toward his mount. "Let's go."

Before she could blink he had her on his horse, riding behind him. The English-speaking Indian kept pace to their right. Somewhere ahead, they'd find the Bar CT men, hopefully alive. Galloping across the distance behind them, Coy.

In the midst of it all, Aimee was even more lost than the day her brothers died.

# Chapter 11

IN SPITE OF THE paint's fatigue, Coy charged the horse into the darkness. He'd go only until Chet Tanner wouldn't be likely to follow. Then he'd dismount and allow the horse a well-deserved rest.

His mind flashed to camp. He'd left Rogue behind. And his bedroll. He had his pistol and rifle, a half-full canteen, but nothing else. Fear clawed at his insides but quickly died. What did any of it matter? Aimee knew the truth, and she'd turned on him.

*You're one of* them.

He was. Half Cheyenne and half white. Mr. Tanner had spent the last eight years filling his head with the lies that if he lived an honorable life, worked hard, loved God and his family, that his heritage wouldn't matter.

It did.

Aimee's horrified reaction was all the proof he needed. He was everything his mother had told him.

*Why, God? Why would You create me if I'm all the things Ma said I was? You coulda saved—*

The paint's gait faltered, and a terrifying scream rent the air. Coy pitched forward over the horse's neck, his body tumbling through the air. And then the ground grabbed him, driving the air from his lungs, shards of pain slicing through his head, shoulders, and torso.

*Oh God, help.*

Aimee stared, breathless. A small fire burned at what had been the Bar CT camp just an hour before. Now, it was in total ruin. The ground was churned from the stampede. Cattle gone. The chuckwagon was tipped on its side, wheels spinning in the wind. The few horses that were left watched them from the far side of the wagon.

Icy dread enveloped her.

"Helloooo?" Mr. Tanner's voice rang over the cicadas' song. "Hello, the camp."

"Pa?" Mitch's weak voice perked from the other side of the wagon.

Pal Hinkle stood, craning his neck, also from the other side of the wagon. A relieved smile flashed across the young man's haggard features.

Aimee's heart brightened, at least until Pal looked toward their unexpected companion.

"Uh, Boss?" The young man stiffened, his hand inching toward his pistol.

"Keep that gun holstered, Pal. Black Moon's a friend." Mr. Tanner urged his horse around the wagon. There, Mitch leaned against the seat, legs outstretched. His shoulder was freshly bandaged, arm in a makeshift sling. Nearby, Baz, Sam, and Dix waited with him. They seemed none the worse for wear, except Sam, sporting a bandage around the gunshot wound he'd received earlier.

Just outside the circle, two forms lay draped in blankets, head to toe.

The dread returned, this time knotting her throat. Which men were they—Gus, Lange, or Jansik? All had cared for her when she had no one. An all-too-familiar ache lodged in her chest.

"Get down, now." Mr. Tanner offered his elbow, and she latched onto it and slid from the saddle.

"What happened?" he asked, voice full of disbelief.

Baz looked apologetic. "There was a stampede, Boss—"

"I can see *that*," he grumbled.

"That outlaw bunch has caused us trouble, Pa." While Mitch detailed Kid Heller's midnight visit to harass her and their ensuing confrontations, Aimee wandered toward the two dead men.

*Father, why do the people I love, even those I like, keep dying?*

She bent beside the nearest body and reached for the blanket. Before she could lift it, a large boot settled across the corner. Startled, Aimee twisted to face the owner.

Dix squatted, his eyes full of grief. "You *really* don't want to take a peek. What you'd find would haunt you forever."

Her chin quivered as she released the blanket. "Who's under there?"

"Alex Jansik and Gus Mabry."

She looked at the other men, all watching her. "What about Jeff Lange?"

Sam shrugged. "Lost track of him in the stampede. Once dark fell, I didn't know whether to keep searching or come back here, so I made a choice." He shifted toward Mr. Tanner. "Hope I did right, Boss."

The elder man shook his head. "We all did what we thought best tonight."

A momentary pause hung between them.

"Where's Coy?" Mitch struggled to stand, but Baz restrained him with a firm hand.

"Stay down, durn it," he hissed. "You're weak as a newborn calf."

Mitch settled back, though he pinned his father, then her with a hard glance. "Tell me. Where's Coy?"

Her heart stuttered. Chet Tanner's expression, shadowed by his hat brim and further obscured by the play of dancing firelight, was nearly unreadable. She held her breath. Surely his answer would pin the blame for Coy's disappearance on her—squarely where it belonged. But when he spoke, his voice was filled with regret.

"Coy and I had words. He ran off, but I'm hoping he'll come to his senses and return." He shook his head. "Let's get this wagon upright and see if we can't get some rest. We got a lot of work ahead tomorrow, and not near enough men to do it."

In a matter of minutes, the Bar CT men cleared a space, got Mitch and her a safe distance out of the way and, with Black Moon's help, lifted the wagon onto its wheels. Dix fetched the bedrolls from inside, and each man rolled out his bedding near the fire.

"Miss Kaplan," Mr. Tanner said, "I think it's best if you sleep in the midst of the rest of us tonight."

Aimee's throat clogged, both with the embarrassing closeness of her companions and the realization that Coy wouldn't be by her side tonight. *She* was the reason he'd left. *Her* startled outburst. Not anything Mr. Tanner had said.

Why had she spoken so? It had been a shock to realize Coy Gentry Whittaker was part Cheyenne, but that didn't matter to these men. They respected him for his character—not his parentage. Hadn't he treated her with kindness, dignity, and tenderness, in spite of their rough surroundings? He was no savage like the Indian who'd killed her brothers.

He was Coy, the gentle soul who'd made her love him, and come morning, she'd do everything within her power to find him and tell him exactly that.

# Chapter 12

SOMETHING STABBED AIMEE BETWEEN her shoulder blades. For a terrified instant, her mind raced with thoughts of Kid Heller. But when she squinted at her surroundings, all was calm. The sun had yet to crest the horizon. Only Mr. Tanner and Dix Ramshaw, both seated near the campfire, stirred. Their conversation, hushed though it was, carried on the still air.

"Dix, we're in a mess. We gotta round up cattle, horses, and get those men buried."

The cook hung his head. "I know, Boss. And for my part in this, I'm sorry. I shoulda kept these young bucks under better control."

"I'm not laying blame. I'm asking for ideas. Mitch is weak. Sam's not a whole lot better. That leaves four of us to do the work of ten—and really, we need *more*."

Mr. Tanner kept speaking, though his words muffled as he scrubbed his face.

"Saw him slip away not long after we bedded down," Dix answered.

Her ears perked. Who had slipped away—Heller? Her skin prickled. Hopefully not. Or perhaps they meant Coy. She strained to hear more, but they quieted until she couldn't catch their words. If Coy, it wasn't a good sign that he'd been in camp and left.

She shifted, and the same odd poking sensation jabbed her. Reaching to scratch the spot, her fingers brushed something. Ever so slowly, she rose up on an elbow, and it shifted inside her shirt. *Oh, Lord ... a snake.* At that, she bolted up in her bed and untucked the garment. The thing slipped out and fell to the dark blanket.

The long, narrow paper she'd found before the stampede stared up at her, and Aimee clasped a hand over her mouth to stifle her laughter. Nothing quite so heart-stopping as a snake, thank goodness.

"Miss Kaplan?" Mr. Tanner stood. "Anything wrong?"

"No, sir."

He seated himself to continue his hushed conversation with

Mr. Ramshaw. Aimee rubbed her eyes and unfolded an official-looking paper. Without enough daylight to read, she stopped, pulled on her boots, and looped the strap she'd rigged for her pistol around her neck. Gun tucked into her waistband, she walked to the far side of the campfire, affording herself some privacy. There, she smoothed the document, and a second sheet of paper fluttered loose, this one with Edouard's neat script. The sight of it sent a wave of grief crashing over her, and she struggled to breathe.

*Lord, I miss my brothers. And Coy. And Gus and Alex and Lange. Please, can this end? I don't want to lose anyone else.*

Aimee took a moment to pull herself together and turned again to the papers—starting with Edouard's note.

My dearest sister,

Forgive me. I tried to hide this in a place you wouldn't notice immediately. I'd intended to remove it once our dangers were past. If you've found it, I suspect something has happened to us.

Aimee paused, cheeks flaming. Edouard had sewn something into her underclothes? Were he here, she'd reprimand him for taking such intimate liberties. But he wasn't. She gulped down a sob.

*Oh Lord, help me get through this.*

After several moments, she calmed and read on.

First, know that Louis, Marc, Paul, and I love you very much.

Second, this certificate is a bearer bond. You'll find nine more just like it hidden between the layers of your coat.

Louis won them in a game of poker from an outlaw named Jimmy "the Kid" Heller, and he wants them back. But as the name, bearer bond, indicates, these belong to whomever possesses them. They are yours now and will provide you a good start.

<u>Do not</u> tell anyone you have them unless you are <u>absolutely</u> certain you can trust them. Please, Aimee. It could be a matter of life and death.

Love,
Edouard

Again, she smoothed the other paper, then angled it toward the firelight. Across the top of the certificate was MEMPHIS AND LITTLE ROCK RAILROAD, and in each corner, the amount of—

Her jaw fell open. Squinting, she skimmed Edouard's note for the information she sought.

You'll find nine more just like it…

She tilted the certificate's corner toward the firelight. One thousand. *One thousand dollars.* And there were nine more exactly like it in her coat. That was … *ten thousand dollars'* worth of bond certificates. Belonging to *her.*

No wonder Edouard had been so adamant she not forget—

*Her coat.*

Aimee's thoughts ground to a halt. It had been stashed either under the wagon bench or in the wagon bed when the stampede started. She'd not seen it since. Fumbling, Aimee refolded the papers and tucked them out of sight, then ambled toward the wagon, far calmer than she felt.

"Stay close, Miss Kaplan. Hear?" Dix called after her.

She nodded, unable to trust her voice as she searched the seat, then slipped into the dark interior, which was a mess after the stampede. She struggled to sort what was what. But after several moments of rifling, her fingers latched onto the thick coat, and she pulled it to her chest.

As she did, the whinny of a horse split the air.

Coy? She peeked through a hole in the chuckwagon's tattered canvas cover. A shadowy line of Cheyenne raised the hair on the back of her neck. She reached for the butt of Edouard's pistol.

From her hidden vantage point, she watched as one brave nudged his horse out from the group. "Tanner."

The loud call sent fear rippling across her scalp.

*Father, no. Please don't let anyone else die.*

Aimee fumbled—and failed—in cocking the hammer. She tried again, though the shaking of her fingers hindered her progress.

"Black Moon?" Mr. Tanner's voice sounded close.

Peeking once more, the one who'd ridden from the group dismounted, and Mr. Tanner stepped up to meet him.

"We weren't sure what happened to you. Dix said he saw you ride off in the night."

Black Moon nodded. "You need more men. My people wish to help."

Aimee blinked. *Help?*

Lingering silence. Then Mr. Tanner laughed. "Well then, welcome. We can use all the help we can get."

Aimee rode beside Mr. Tanner on one of the few horses remaining from the remuda. The more seasoned Bar CT riders rode Indian ponies borrowed from the Cheyenne. They moved along the stampede path gathering cattle, though certainly she, with her inexperience, and Mitch and Sam with their respective wounds, were slowing the progress. Mr. Tanner hadn't wanted to further scatter his men, so they all rode together, the two wounded under strict orders to take it easy.

As they combed the miles of country, gathering strays, she kept watching for any sign of Coy or his paint pony.

*Lord, I said the wrong thing last night. I wounded him. I was startled. Scared at first. But I'm not now. Not of Coy. Please help me fix my mistake.*

To their right, a Cheyenne brave drove seven head of cattle into the small herd they'd gathered. He then directed his horse straight toward Black Moon. The two conferred before Black Moon turned his bay in their direction.

"Tanner," Black Moon called. "Come."

Without hesitation, Mr. Tanner followed, and Aimee with him. As they reached Black Moon, he turned his horse in the direction his friend had come.

"Yellow Bird says a man hides in the rocks." Black Moon jutted his chin at an outcropping of boulders in the distance.

Chet Tanner dismounted, dug through his saddlebags, and produced a small telescope. Extending it, he raised it to his eye. Aimee also dismounted and led her horse off a few feet, scanning the area.

*Lord, please help me find Coy.*

With her focus on the distance, a flutter of motion to her left drew her attention, and Black Moon appeared at her side. Aimee sucked in a startled breath and rocked back a step, every muscle locked tight. Her chest constricted as he stared at her.

"I am sorry," he finally whispered.

Her jaw loosened. "Sorry?"

"Tanner says your brothers are dead."

"Yes." Her throat knotted with grief.

"By the hand of a Tsitsistas brave."

"A Tsitsi ..." Aimee's tongue knotted around the foreign sounds.

"Tsitsistas. You call us Shy-Ann."

As understanding came, anger and fear shrouded her heart. "Why would one of your people murder my brothers?" she demanded. "We were going to make camp in that meadow. We weren't hurting anyone. He attacked us. From hiding."

Black Moon's eyes clouded. "That one ... was evil. He turned from the Tsitsistas people and our customs many summers ago. He went his own way. Abandoned our people. Found new friends. White men who steal and kill for pleasure."

Aimee's thoughts churned. "Outlaws?"

He nodded. "Outlaws."

Her heart pounded. Had the brave that killed her brothers been one of Kid Heller's band—after the bearer bonds she hadn't known she'd been carrying? Aimee darted a glance to her horse to be sure the coat was still tied behind her saddle.

Black Moon continued, "He has led others to this bad path, turned them from our ways. Three other young braves." His jaw clenched. "My people do not grieve for him. It is good he is dead."

Good heavens. What sort of reception did Mr. Tanner receive when he rode into their camp with this Cheyenne—Tsitsistas—outlaw's body? Had he been celebrated a hero for returning this villain dead? Or was he reviled for bringing the body of one so hated back to their camp? He'd risked much, going there with that corpse.

"That's Lange." Mr. Tanner stashed the telescope in his saddlebags. Facing the herd, he scanned the area, then whistled sharply. "Dix. Get over here. We might need your doctoring skills."

As Dix approached, they all hurried toward the stone outcropping. Nearing the spot, Mr. Tanner pulled ahead of the others.

"Lange? You up there?"

"Boss?" Relief dripped from Lange's pain-tinged voice. "Real glad you found me."

"Wasn't giving up till I did." Mr. Tanner slid from his saddle.

Beside him, Dix dismounted, then snatched a canteen and his medical kit. "I take it you're hurt?"

"Busted my leg, and my dang horse ran off. Couldn't get back to camp."

As both men started into the rocks, Mr. Tanner looked back. "Miss

Kaplan, stay with Black Moon. Don't need anyone else twisting an ankle or something. You two use my telescope and keep watch. Understand?"

"Yes, sir."

Beside her, Black Moon nodded.

The men disappeared into the outcropping, and she slid from her saddle. Silence hung between her and Black Moon. He remained on horseback, tall and proud and watchful, though every now and then she caught him flicking a quick glance her way.

*Lord, he tried to explain about the Indian who killed my brothers.* And the explanation did help—at least a little. Though it went only so far to ease the tension in her muscles as she looked at the strange man wearing only a breechcloth, leggings, and moccasins with his bow and quiver slung across his bare torso. *I don't want to be rude, Lord. What would You have me say to him?*

She wobbled a smile at him, though as she did, Mr. Tanner's voice rang from the rocks above.

"Black Moon, we could use a hand."

Black Moon looked at her, then slipped his bow from around his lean body and disappeared on the trail into the rocky hills.

An odd sensation—a heaviness, perhaps?—settled across her shoulders as she kept watch. Had she grown that used to being with the Bar CT hands? She stood alone for the first time in days, and it left her almost ready to crawl out of her skin.

She was being silly. Aimee retrieved the telescope from Mr. Tanner's saddlebags and, extending the glass, peered into the distance. She'd allow herself to linger over every shadow, tree, and rock in hopes she'd find some sign of Coy. Maybe that would help her shake the awkward feeling.

Minutes ticked by in silence. Then a muffled scream split the air. Aimee spun to face the sound, chills snaking down her spine. Behind her, the horses pranced uneasily. Telescope still in hand, she dashed a few paces into the narrow passage into the rocks, though she stopped when Mr. Tanner's warning to stay echoed in her thoughts. "Is everything all right?"

When no answer came, Aimee unbuttoned Coy's duster to draw the pistol from her belt.

"Lange might disagree," Dix hollered, "but everything's fine. Just setting his leg before we move him."

Relief swept over her, even as she cringed at the thought. "Do you need any more help?"

"Nah. Three growed men can wrestle these bones back in place." Dix chuckled, though the sound was more subdued than usual. "We'll be down in a few minutes."

Aimee rolled her neck to release the tension between her shoulder blades, then eased down the narrow path.

As she stepped out from between the walls, someone grabbed her from behind, an arm around her torso and a hand over her mouth. Her scream muffled behind it. A second man bobbed into view, and she dropped the telescope.

Hands trembling, Aimee managed to cock the Colt and pull the trigger. As the gun roared, the second man—one from the meadow—stumbled sideways, his eyes going wide just before he fell.

A vile curse lodged in her ear, and her captor dragged her to the nearest horse. "Mount up." He released her with a shove.

Aimee's feet tangled in the long coat, and she tripped, sprawling face-first into the grass. Pain rattled her teeth, but she reached again to cock the Colt's hammer. Tasting blood, she rolled over and hefted the gun at him.

As she squeezed the trigger, Kid Heller kicked her hands aside. The gun bucked, though the bullet flew wild. He dropped to a knee over her, his own gun in one hand, even as he pinned hers to the ground with the other.

"That's enough." Wresting her weapon from her grasp, he leveled his Colt at her forehead. "Now get up and get on that horse." He jerked the makeshift strap from around her neck and tossed the gun aside.

*Lord, help.*

He hauled her up with him as he stood.

"Heller," Dix shouted from the direction of the pathway. "Let her go."

The outlaw dragged her close, pistol to her temple. "Not until I have what's mine."

From her vantage point, she could see both Dix and Mr. Tanner hiding near the edge of the pathway.

"What're you after?" Mr. Tanner called. "Maybe we can work out a deal."

"No deals. She gives up what her kin stole, and I'll leave y'all be. I'll even return your cattle."

A tiny pause lingered. "What'd they steal?"

"This pretty little thing knows." He twisted her to face him, the gun's barrel lodging under her chin. "Don'tcha, darlin'?"

She gulped, something like lightning crackling through her. "They didn't tell me anything. Please. Let me go."

Aimee eased back a half step, her feet tangling again in the unbuttoned duster. Kid Heller grabbed for her arm to steady her, but she dropped onto her back.

As Heller leveled his gun at her, a fearsome scream from the top of the rocks raked across Aimee's senses, and at the same moment, an arrow sailed at Heller from above. It struck him near the crook of the neck with a sickening *thwack* and sunk deep. The arrowhead protruded through his belly, and blood sprouted across his shirt. The outlaw went to his knees, eyes huge and mouth agape as he gasped for breath.

Aimee clamped a hand over her mouth to stifle a scream. From the top of the rocky outcropping, Black Moon loosed another primal cry and, bow in hand, leapt down the jutting rocks like a mountain goat.

Mr. Tanner and Dix rushed to her side, guns drawn, and one of them pulled her a safe distance away from the carnage. At nearly the same time, Black Moon reached Kid Heller, then dragged the outlaw around the rocks by his hair.

"Are you hurt?" Dix looked her up and down.

Aimee's whole body trembled, and her thoughts spun. At first, she couldn't pry her hand loose from her mouth, her cheeks puffing out as she gulped air. But as her nerves settled, her breathing slowed, and she sank to the ground.

Black Moon had *protected* her.

"Aimee." Dix's voice pitched sharply. "Look here, darlin'. Are you hurt?"

She finally lowered her trembling hand from her mouth. "No."

All thanks to an Indian. She was shaken, but unscathed. Though a powerful urge lodged in her chest for one of Coy's tender hugs.

"Mr. Tanner, we need to find Coy. Please. I'm worried about him."

"I'm worried too, but we're so pulled in different directions now. I don't know how I can spare anyone to look."

"Tanner." Black Moon reappeared, carrying Kid Heller's top hat and— Her stomach knotted at the bloody scalp in his other hand. The man jutted his chin in the direction of a dense line of trees in the distance. "The outlaw says your cows are that way. My people will help you gather them, fight for them if they must."

"Thank you."

"I go to find my brother." He turned to Aimee. "Come if you wish."

Stunned, Aimee glanced to the scalp, then back to Black Moon's face. She rose, legs shaking, and retrieved her discarded pistol. *Lord, protect me.* "I'll go with you."

# Chapter 13

Soft, golden laughter roused Coy from darkness. Inhaling, he fought to open leaden eyelids to see who produced the musical sounds, only they wouldn't comply.

The scent of woodsmoke wafted toward him, and a fire warmed his right side. Somehow he knew that daylight had come, but the bright sun didn't reach him directly. Wherever he was, this place was shady and peaceful. Comforting.

Whispers from two female voices caught his ear, and his attention perked. He attempted to call out, but his tongue was so dry it stuck to the roof of his mouth.

"Coy?"

A soft rustle sounded, then split and moved around him on either side. He turned toward his left.

He managed to loosen his tongue, though his words were thick. "Who's there?"

A gentle touch tipped his face back toward the firelight. "It's Aimee."

*Aimee?*

When a bright light flashed nearby, he jerked toward it, and pain sliced through him at the sudden movement.

"Hold still."

She wiped something cool and damp across his forehead, then over his eyelids. Despite her tender touch, pain lanced his right cheek, but her ministrations allowed him to blink his left eye open.

Aimee lifted his head and tipped something to his lips. Cool water splashed across his tongue, and he drank greedily until she lowered his head.

He stared until her pretty features came into some sort of focus.

Her eyes brimmed. "You've had me worried."

The sight sank talons through his chest. "Why?"

"You've been unconscious for three days." She paused. "Coy, I'm so sorry for what I said to you."

"What'd you say?"

"After the stampede. Don't you remember? You kissed me, and then Mr. Tanner was there …"

Hazy recollections formed, but before he could latch onto them, daylight brightened the dusky space. Startled, he turned, sending pain crackling from around his right eye into his shoulder and chest. He fell back, stifling a groan.

"Coy?" Mr. Tanner dropped to a knee beside him, relief brightening his face. "I was praying you'd wake up today."

A second figure—Mitch—filed in, arm in a sling, and stood a pace behind his father, grinning. More shadows entered, making the light flicker.

Coy glanced around at the sloping sides of his surroundings and the tall poles that jutted up toward a small patch of blue sky above. An Indian lodge.

"You brought me to the Cheyenne?" He lolled his head toward Mr. Tanner.

"*He* didn't. Your brother and I did."

At Aimee's soft words, the fogginess in his head evaporated. Why would she bring him here? She hated the Indians. She hated *him*. "I don't understand."

"No, son, you don't." Mr. Tanner's expression was grim. "You've missed a bunch in the last few days." He nodded toward the entrance where the brave he'd seen with Mr. Tanner stood. Beside him, a lithe young Cheyenne woman watched. A wife, maybe? Or a sister? "You and Miss Kaplan are staying here a while with Black Moon."

He turned again to look at Aimee as she offered a tiny smile and a nod. "But I gotta help with the herd. We gotta keep pushin—"

"You're bruised from head to hip." Mr. Tanner laid a gentle hand on his shoulder. "You ain't helping with anything for at least a few weeks—more likely a month or two."

That would explain the pain. "What happened?"

"You remember riding off into the night?"

He tried to grasp the elusive recollections.

"When Miss Kaplan and Black Moon tracked you down the next day, they found your paint pony with its leg stuck in a deep hole. Snapped clean."

Coy cringed at the thought of the horse's suffering.

"You were thrown clear. Musta landed face-first and skidded a ways, given all these scrapes and bruises."

Aimee tipped his face toward her again. "The Cheyenne will help Mr. Tanner get the herd to the railroad, and Black Moon and Gray Willow Woman have invited us to stay with them as long as we need."

"You're willing to stay here—with me?"

She sat a little straighter. "Very."

What in the world had happened? Fatigue crept through him, stealing any fight he might have put up. "Black Moon?"

The brave squatted next to them.

"You said this—that we can stay?"

The brave smiled. "We feel honor that you would stay in our lodge, my brother. While you are here, I will teach you anything you wish to know about the Tsitsistas people."

How many times had he pondered his other half, the one he'd been led to believe was something loathsome and vile? How many nights had he wished to ask his mother questions about the man who'd sired him? He'd never had the freedom, but he did now. "Will you tell me of our father?"

The brave called something in his native tongue to Gray Willow Woman, and she quickly retrieved an object from a pouch near the edge of the lodge, then handed it to her husband.

"The necklace you carry. Our father gave it to your mother the day the soldiers took her away from our camp. He made her promise to tell you of him."

"She never did." Coy didn't have the strength to tell Black Moon of her hateful comments about Ten Bears.

His brother's eyes clouded, but as he moved to Aimee's other side, a grim smile spread on Black Moon's face. "He was a great warrior." Gently, he settled the necklace around Coy's neck. "And you were much loved, Brave Eagle."

"Brave Eagle?"

Black Moon's brow furrowed, and he eyed Mr. Tanner. "Does he not know his own name?"

"I told you. His mother was a bitter woman."

For a long moment, Black Moon remained silent, visibly bothered by the news. Finally, he laid a hand on Coy's uninjured shoulder and nodded. "You are Brave Eagle, son of the Cheyenne, and once you grow stronger, I will teach you our ways."

Emotion choked Aimee, particularly when she saw the way Black Moon's pronouncement seemed to steal Coy's breath. As much as he needed this moment, this acceptance, worry nibbled at her. "Thank you, Black Moon." She glanced at the others in turn. "Thanks to all of you. But I think Coy should rest now."

The voices silenced. Black Moon, Mr. Tanner, and Mitch each filed out. Gray Willow Woman walked to Aimee's side.

"You need anything, Ai-mee?"

She shook her head. "No, thank you."

Gray Willow Woman nodded, then slipped from the tent.

Aimee dragged several heavy buffalo robes over and made a pallet for herself next to Coy's.

"Aimee?"

"Yes?"

"You sure you want to stay here with me? Mr. Tanner would take you with him."

She stretched out on her pallet and curled her fingers around his. "I don't want to be with Mr. Tanner."

"But … you hate the Indians." He swallowed hard. "And *I* am Indian."

Her throat knotted. "Like Mr. Tanner told you, there's been a lot that's happened since you rode off. The Cheyenne came to help gather the herd. While we were doing that, Black Moon explained about the Indian that killed my brothers."

"Explained what?"

"He was a Cheyenne, but he'd left the tribe. I think he might have been one of Heller's outlaws, Coy."

He turned a questioning glance on her, and she nodded.

"Then, when Kid Heller and his friends tried to grab me, Black Moon was there."

"What'd Heller do?"

Aimee squeezed her eyes shut. Hopefully, after one more retelling, she could forget about these men. "We were gathering the herd, and Heller and one of his men found me alone while the Bar CT men were occupied elsewhere." She drew a shaky breath. "I shot the one, but Heller grabbed me and wrestled my gun away. Mr. Tanner and Dix tried to get to me, but it was your brother who came to my rescue." Her stomach knotted at the recollection of Kid Heller's scalp in the Cheyenne's hand. "All I could think of then was how sorry I felt for what I'd said to you. I had to find you, to explain. It was Black Moon who took me." She squeezed his fingers. "I am so sorry. The moment I realized you were part Indian, I ..."

"You're surrounded by 'em here."

She paused, features creasing just a little. "Yes, and I'd be lying if I said I wasn't uncomfortable. But these are *your* people, and they've been very kind to us so far. You deserve a chance to know them." Her eyes brimmed. "I *love* you, and it's not right of me to stand in your way."

He cracked a glance at her. "And you're *sure* there's nowhere else you'd rather be?"

"Coy Gentry Whittaker, what will it take to convince you? I want to be where you are, even if that means being *here*."

A faint smile pulled at his lips. "All right, Miss Kaplan."

Kaplan. Now that Kid Heller's gang was out of the way ... "Coy?"

"Hmmm?"

"I should tell you. My name's not Kaplan. It's Le Chapelain."

Would he think her dishonest for changing it?

"Le Chape—" He pulled his hand back, and his brow furrowed.

"My brother, Edouard, thought we'd be less conspicuous if we changed it."

He hesitated only an instant before he laced his fingers in hers. "Doesn't matter. One day soon, I'll make you Aimee Whittaker."

Her shy grin grew. Aimee Whittakar. Coy's *wife*. "So you'll want to live among the whites?"

"I dunno. Why?"

"If we lived among the Cheyenne, then wouldn't I be Mrs. Brave Eagle?"

Coy chuckled, but the sound quickly dissolved into a groan. "Don't make me laugh."

Aimee cringed. "I'm sorry."

She rested her forehead against his left temple.

"Where would you want to live?" he whispered.

She drew back, studying the way his dark hair fell across his forehead in a sweet, boyish way. Aimee leaned in and brushed her lips gently against his.

"Wherever you are, Coy Brave Eagle."

"Do that again."

"What?"

"Kiss me."

Her face flamed, but she complied, brushing her lips against his.

This time, she lingered, and her heart leapt. Heat rushed through her, and she longed to kiss him more soundly, though she dared not—not now. Oh Lord, how she loved this man—and yet there was still so much to get to know about him. So much he didn't know about himself. Coy lifted his head from his pallet but immediately sagged back, breaking the kiss with a groan.

"Are you all right?"

His mouth twisted into a slow, lopsided grin. "Once I'm better, I'll expect more of those."

Aimee bit her lip and wiggled back to her own pallet. If they were to share many more such kisses, she'd have to press for a quick marriage.

Minutes ticked by in silence before he roused a little. "Where *would* you want to live? Arkansas?"

"No. There's nothing for me in Arkansas. Well, maybe one bit of business."

"Business?"

"Yes, I need to speak to someone at the Memphis and Little Rock Railroad headquarters."

"Why?"

The stern warning in Edouard's note came to mind. Be careful who she told.

But this was Coy, the man who'd claimed her heart.

She smiled. "Oh, just a little matter of about ten thousand dollars' worth of bearer bonds I need to cash in."

# Acknowledgments

THANK YOU TO MY wonderful critique partners who helped me so much with getting this story down. Sarah, Ruth, Michele, Cindy—you all are invaluable. Shannon, thanks for all the late-night reads and the never-ending encouragements that, "No, this does NOT totally suck!" Susie, thank you for praying me through this one from afar—your sweet emails and quiet support were so valuable through this process. To my husband and son, thank you both for putting up with my deadline craziness. You both are amazing, and I am blessed to have you. And to Pegg, thank you for inviting me into this project and for the bang-up job with edits. You make me a better writer!

Jennifer Uhlarik discovered the western genre as a pre-teen when she swiped the only "horse" book she found on her older brother's bookshelf. A new love was born. Across the next ten years, she devoured Louis L'Amour westerns and fell in love with the genre. In college at the University of Tampa, she began penning her own story of the Old West. Armed with a B.A. in writing, she has been a finalist in, and won, numerous writing competitions, and been on the ECPA Bestseller lists numerous times. In addition to writing, she has held jobs as a private business owner, a schoolteacher, a marketing director, and her favorite—a full-time homemaker. Jennifer is active in American Christian Fiction Writers and lifetime member of the Florida Writers Association. She lives near Tampa, Florida, with her husband, college-aged son, and four fur children.

Website: www.jenniferuhlarik.com
Facebook: https://www.facebook.com/JenniferUhlarikAuthor/
Twitter: https://twitter.com/JenniferUhlarik
Pinterest: https://www.pinterest.com/jenuhlarik/
Instagram: https://www.instagram.com/jenniferuhlarik/

# Trail's End

By

Sandra Merville Hart

# Dedication

*To my niece, Stephanie, who inspires me*
*with her sweet spirit*
*and steadfast heart.*

*This story is set in Abilene, Kansas,*
*partly as a tribute to her ancestor*
*who lived there.*

# Chapter 1

*Abilene, Kansas, May 1870*

A GUSTY BREEZE SHIFTED Wade Chadwick's wide-brimmed slouch hat sideways. He shoved it down on his ears, blocking the midday sun. The smell of fresh pine lumber testified to the recent formation of unpainted town buildings. He sniffed again. Baked ham? His stomach flopped in anticipation.

Dirt swirled around him as he crossed Texas Street toward a frame building nestled like an oasis between a saloon and a hotel. The sign in the window whetted his appetite, *Abby's Home Cooking*. After two months of trailing longhorns from Texas to Abilene, a home-cooked meal appealed more than anything else in this Cowtown.

Unnatural silence greeted him as he stepped over the open threshold. Five tables of diners stared at something in the back of the room. Wade's lip curled as he followed their gaze.

A dust-covered cowboy swayed drunkenly as he lunged for a beautiful young woman. "Aw, com'on, Miss Abby. Give me a little kiss." He grabbed her arm.

"Let go of me!" Cascades of honey-colored curls, swept back with combs, shook as her head jerked with a pointed stare at the cowboy's hand on her arm.

"I ain't had such good cooking since my ma died." He leaned close to her face. "You was meant for me. Just a little kiss."

Wood scraped against wood as three men pushed back their chairs, but Wade got there first.

"Only gentlemen are allowed in my establishment." Miss Abby shoved a loaded plate into her captor's chest. The plate crashed into the floor with a slab of ham. Mashed potatoes smeared his red wool shirt.

He let out a yell that could have curled Wade's hair, had it not been cut by the town's barber an hour ago. "Why you—" The cowboy raised his hand, falling against an empty spindle-back chair.

Wade grabbed the irate man by the knotted bandana around his neck. "Lose your manners, cowboy? Been so long since you've seen a lady that you don't recognize one?"

The belligerence left his eyes as he looked up at Wade. "Reckon I didn't 'spect to find a lady on Texas Street in Abilene."

"Pay attention next time." Wade loosened his hold. "You owe her an apology."

Scarlet tinged his face, giving the culprit a boyish look. The kid was younger than he'd thought. Maybe a score of years.

"Meant … no harmmm." His gaze dropped.

Quirking an eyebrow, Wade met the bright green gaze of Miss Abby. A ruffled white bib apron hid part of her pink gingham dress.

"You're welcome to return to this establishment"—she folded her arms across her chest—"when you find your manners."

"Yes'm." The cowboy reached for a hat on a table and missed. He tried again, nearly overturning a full cup of coffee next to a pink rose-patterned plate scraped clean. He shoved it onto his head as he reached the open doorway. Weaving, he grabbed the door jamb before stumbling into the dusty street.

Wade released his breath. For a minute he thought he'd have to toss the drunken cowboy out onto the boardwalk.

The men who'd stood in Miss Abby's defense sat. Conversation resumed among the dozen or so diners. Knives scraped across the plates. The corners of Wade's mouth lifted. Most of the cowboys ignored the forks beside their plates and ate with their pocketknives. He looked up to meet the snapping green gaze of the proprietor.

The drunken cowboy stumbled, spurs jangling against the boardwalk, as he left Abby Cox's diner. If only she'd had her wooden spoon handy to whack the fool across the face. He deserved a slap for his boldness. Though most visitors to Abilene treated her with respect, this was the second time a man had grabbed her since the Texans had arrived. After driving cattle up the Chisholm Trail, they needed haircuts and new clothing. That fool boy had spent his money on that Stetson hat and fancy boots instead. Then, like so many trail-weary cowboys, he'd found the saloon. At least he wasn't whooping and hollering and shooting his gun into the air. Too much of that went on.

Pa would never stand for a drunken fool treating her that way. It had been difficult to persuade him to concentrate on building their new ranch and allowing her to run a restaurant in Abilene for cowboys starved for home cooking, but she had managed. She must think of her own future. Cooking for a hungry crowd usually suited her ... until one of them tried to take liberties.

"I'm grateful for your assistance." She eyed her rescuer. Clean shaven. Close-cropped blond hair, so he'd already visited the barber. New red wool shirt and corduroy trousers. Plain, long-legged boots—he hadn't yet been to Thomas McInerney's Boot Factory to buy a pair of high-heeled, red-topped boots with a Lone Star design. New to town. Once he visited one of the many saloons, he'd probably shoot his revolver in the air and act foolishly too.

He tipped his hat and removed it. "My pleasure. Name's Wade Chadwick."

"Miss Abigail Cox." She nodded, liking his deep voice. "Customers have been calling me Miss Abby since my family opened this eatery."

"Miss Abby." He inclined his head.

"You probably saw what I'm serving for lunch." She picked up broken shards of the plate the drunken cowboy had cost her. If he'd drunk his coffee, he might have sobered enough to avoid all this. "Baked ham, mashed potatoes, biscuits, and coffee. Fifty cents. Hungry?"

"Starved." Grinning, he stooped and picked up a broken shard. "Been living off corn bread and sowbelly for two months—and grateful to get it too."

His brown eyes lit up in anticipation of the meal. She almost smiled back when gunshots rang out. Everyone stiffened. Abby peered over Mr. Chadwick's shoulder through the window. So far, the eatery's windows had escaped flying bullets, thank the Lord. Just last week, men had broken into the jail and freed a prisoner. No marshal the town hired stayed long ... some hired at breakfast left by suppertime.

She sighed. The town had at least five months before the cattle drives stopped for the year. No matter. Her family had lived through worse than this before the war ended. "Take a seat. I'll bring your lunch."

"That was my lunch you dropped, Miss Abby." A cowboy dining alone spoke up.

"Yes." Abby stood, hands full of one of her mother's precious plates, broken. If business remained this good, she hoped to have money to buy new plates and store her mother's set away. Gordon took all their surplus cash to Pa every Sunday to purchase supplies for the property. Every cent went into fence posts until he completed the fencing. "I'll bring your lunch first."

Pushing open the kitchen door, she hurried inside. "Gordon, we lost another plate. I need two orders." She set the shards and dirty food on a side table and then surveyed the messy room. A black pot of potatoes, ready to serve, covered nearly two burners on the large stove. The aroma of baking biscuits wafted in the air, reminding her that her last meal had been before sunup. She sighed. Her meal must wait until the customers left.

Hands in a soapy pan of dishes and brown hair falling across his forehead, her brother turned to her. "What happened out there?"

"Just another drunk cowboy." She pressed her lips together. Before the dark moods had overtaken Gordon, he'd have rushed to her defense. She lifted her chin. No matter. He was a mere boy. She'd convinced Pa she could care for her brother else he would never have left them. Their new ranch was close—a quarter hour's walk, fast paced—so it was no problem.

At least it hadn't been. She'd handled everything so far.

But she never expected her brother's sullen mood.

Gordon flicked a glance at her. "There's a stack of clean dishes on the table. And you'd best get the biscuits out of the oven before slicing the ham."

Pursing her lips, she picked up a towel and retrieved golden-brown biscuits from the oven. Gordon could have done this. Then she stifled her frustration. The fourteen-year-old already resented quitting school to help her. She cooked and served—he washed dishes and helped clean after customers left. Best not ask for more. "Thanks, Gordon. I don't know what I'd do without you."

"I don't either."

She lifted her eyebrows. What was eating him?

He grunted. "Thought Pa was going to help us with this place. But no, he's too busy."

"I convinced him we'd be fine here." The restaurant had been her idea. Pa, who loved her cooking, supported her plan. "He's working hard too."

"Ain't even no house there yet."

"Fences first. To keep out the longhorns." She stifled a sigh. Gordon knew all this. She and Pa had explained everything.

His frown deepened. "Maybe I'd rather work with him than wash dishes all day. Or enjoy the sights of Abilene. Everyone else is."

Slicing a generous portion off a slab of ham, Abby bit her lip to hold back a reprimand. It wasn't the first time he'd voiced that desire. Boys little older than Gordon—five years her junior—often drove cattle up the Chisholm Trail and then drank and gambled in the several saloons on Texas Street. She didn't want him in the saloons where women wearing low-cut, fancy dresses coaxed men to buy them drinks. But with Pa rarely in town—how was Abby to keep her brother from *enjoying the sights*? "Well, I appreciate all you do. Sorry that you had to quit school early to work in our restaurant. I couldn't do half what I do without you."

More gunshots. Abby peeked out the open back door for the culprits. Of the Texans roaming around, no one in sight held a smoking gun. She tugged at her apron. Memories earlier that month of cowboys tearing down the jail to release a buddy were too fresh. Then the fellows made matters worse by shooting windows of many businesses. Thankfully, those troublemakers seemed to be gone for good.

"I know." His half smile barely warmed his brown eyes. "And I'd worry about you sleeping alone here at night if I joined Pa."

The second floor housed three bedrooms and one storage room. Sleeping wasn't easy with yelling and laughter going until late into the night. "Thanks, brother. Having you in the next room makes me feel safer."

Then she stole a glance at Gordon's rigid back. He hadn't promised not to seek adventures. Mama would turn over in her Missouri grave if her son took up drinking and gambling.

Abby'd have to keep an eye on him. With a swift glance at Mama's old mantel clock decorated with gold cherubs on a kitchen shelf, she poured coffee into a cup and grabbed a filled plate before pushing the dining room door open with her shoulder. Another hour to go before they closed for the afternoon. Then she'd cook and clean to ready the dining room for the supper crowd.

# Chapter 2

WADE PUSHED BACK HIS empty plate. First satisfying meal in months—made by a pretty cook to boot. He took a long swallow of his third cup of Miss Abby's coffee. He looked over his shoulder at the closed door leading to savory smells from the kitchen, hoping she'd offer to freshen his cup.

Idly running his finger around the rim, he glanced around the vacant room large enough to hold six square tables with four chairs each. The scent of pine lingered on the new-looking floorboards. One large window next to the front door had the name of the establishment painted in red letters. Not even faded yet.

Change jingled in his pocket as he shifted in the wooden chair. The number of coins had dwindled this morning. A wall sampler embroidered with the alphabet and numbers at the top caught his attention. Roses bordered a stitched verse, *Be not wise in thine own eyes: fear the LORD and depart from evil.* Abigail Cox had stitched her name in 1860 with her age—nine years.

His ma had nailed a similar embroidered sampler on the wall when he was a boy. Those were his happiest years—before she died, the Yankees killed his pa, and his Uncle Buck gambled the family's small ranch away before teaching his gambling ways to Beau, Wade's younger brother. He clenched his fist. If he never saw his uncle again, it would be a mercy.

Wade's face tightened. His brother had learned his uncle's lessons well.

His chair scraped against the pine boards as he pushed himself from the table. Time to get busy. His trail boss wouldn't need him until their herd was on the Union Pacific's eastbound train—when he'd draw his wages. After paying for a bath, new clothes, and a visit to the barber, he needed to earn money.

Not just for daily expenses. No, he aimed to own his own ranch someday. With Beau as part owner? He shook his head. Not as matters stood. But if it saved his brother from his destructive path …

Clanging mingled with snatches of conversation behind the door. Miss Abby must be washing dishes. Would she hire him? The day stretched endlessly until evening when he'd bed down near the herd better than a mile away. With so many drovers already here, they might have to wait weeks for their herd to load onto the train cars.

And he sure didn't mean to while his hours away at the saloons' gambling tables.

The door between the kitchen and dining room swung open, and Abby jumped. Mr. Chadwick, the man who had come to her rescue, stood there. "No one but family is allowed back here." She glanced at the open outside door and sucked in her breath. Gordon was fetching water. She took a step backward. "We're closed until supper. I forgot to take your payment. Just leave it on the table beside your plate."

"I did," his gaze swept the messy kitchen, "but I could use a job. Maybe washing dishes."

No one—including her brother—had ever offered to help her clean after a meal. Gordon did it because he was her brother. Searching Mr. Chadwick's sheepish expression, she inclined her head. Cowboys weren't to be trusted, as last week's jailbreak had taught her. "Why?"

"Won't get paid for a month or better. Came north without much money in my pockets." His face flushed dull red. "Fellows I rode the trail with went to the saloons as soon as we got the herd settled. Ain't seen hide nor hair of them since." He twisted the hat in his hands. "If you need help …"

He had come to her aid when that obnoxious cowboy tried to kiss her. Abby bit her lip. She was *always* behind—and those apple pies for supper wouldn't bake themselves. "Free meals plus fifty cents a day. We're closed Sundays."

"Sounds fair."

His slow smile warmed his brown eyes. Her heart skipped a beat. Mr. Chadwick was more handsome than she'd first thought. Best keep her guard up, or her loneliness might prompt her to take more notice of the tall man with kind eyes than she ought. "My brother took two buckets to the well. You can start by fetching more water. The well is behind Hixson's Groceries."

"Much obliged." He rested his hat on a wall hook and rolled up his sleeves.

"Since today's half over, I'll pay you beginning tomorrow. Your lunch and supper will be free today. Does that suit you, Mr. Chadwick?"

He nodded. "If you call me Wade."

Though he'd saved her from a humiliating situation, she wasn't certain she trusted him. Still, a growing number of customers meant more cooking. Best start on those pies. She measured flour into a large bowl. "You may call me Miss Abby, Mr. Chadwick." Most of the customers did anyway, with or without permission.

"Yes, Miss Abby." He picked up two empty buckets. "Be right back."

Wade washed dishes while Gordon dried and stacked them on one of the numerous shelves lining most of the available wall space. Wade glanced at the beautiful Miss Abby. That woman sure was distracting as she rolled out pie dough. Wondering whether the boy always talked this much or if he was just happy to find a man who'd listen, Wade turned his attention back to her brother's explanation on how they'd come to live in Abilene.

The family had seen their share of hard times, starting with the War Between the States.

"We moved to St. Louis from Tennessee after the Confederacy surrendered." Gordon stacked plates on a shelf. "Things looked up when Pa got a job with the railroad. Then Ma died." His gaze shifted to something outside the window. "Pa changed."

"That happened with my pa too," Wade said quietly. Memories flooded back. He'd been ten and Beau barely seven when their ma died of pneumonia. Tough times.

"We heard about the cattle drives and the money to be made in Abilene. Cheap land too." Plates scraped together. "We moved to Abilene in January. Pa helped Abby open the restaurant and then bought a quarter section of land. He planned to get his share of the Texans' business to build the ranch." His jaw hardened.

"You're doing that." Wade dipped a plate into rinse water.

"*We* are. Abby and me." He tapped his chest. "Pa's fence'd get built quicker with me helping. I'd rather build houses and fences than wash dishes any day, but did anyone ask me?"

Wade gave him a sidelong glance. Gordon's resentment was too similar to Beau's when he'd gotten them jobs on a Texas ranch.

"It's temporary, Gordon." Miss Abby rubbed flour on a rolling pin. "I need your help until everyone goes back down the Chisholm Trail. That should be by October. You'll return to school then."

"That's months away." He tossed a damp towel onto a table. "I'm done." Grabbing a Stetson from a wall hook, he stalked out the open back door into the sunshine.

"Gordon?" Miss Abby ran to the door. "Where are you going?"

"For a walk."

"Best let him go." Wade joined her at the door. "Let him cool down."

"It's hotter out there than it is in here."

"I meant his temper." He met her troubled gaze. Truthfully, he shared her worry. If he could have seen the signs earlier with Beau, maybe he'd have handled things differently, listened more carefully. "How old is he?"

"Fourteen." Her shoulders drooped. "Maybe he's going to our land. To talk to Pa."

"Maybe." Telling his side of the story had only seemed to frustrate Gordon. He hadn't seemed to be in a talking mood by the time he left, to Wade's way of thinking.

"I'll go after him." She reached to untie her apron.

He frowned.

"What?" She paused.

"You heard him. *Miss Abby's Home Cooking* isn't his future." He returned to the pan of dirty dishes and scrubbed on a plate. "Your pa's ranch might be—I don't know. Looks like you need my help now."

She leaned her forehead against the doorjamb.

Her pinched face tugged at his heart. "I'll be here at least a month. Maybe two. Do you have a friend who needs a job after that?"

"I don't know." Eyes closed, she shook her head. "I don't have many friends in town. The ones I know from church don't walk on Texas Street any more than necessary while the cowboys are in town."

Shots rang out from the west. Wade gazed out the window, bowing his head briefly in thanks that the boy'd headed east. What a town. He'd never seen the likes of it.

Miss Abby ducked her head outside. She was back inside in a moment. "Gordon headed toward our ranch—away from those shots." Her body sagged against the wall. "Those cowboys get wild with their six-shooters sometimes. I feel safe in here unless someone rides by shooting into windows and doors."

A chill shot up his back. Things were worse than he'd been told. "I'll work here as long as I'm in Abilene. I'll bed down near the herd and return every day."

"What should I do?" She covered her face with her hands.

"Finish your pies. Prepare supper."

She shook her head. "I meant about Gordon."

"Pray for him. Tell him you'll hire a woman to help in the kitchen. That may ease him some." He hoped so. "After that, send him to your pa. He wants to work on the land."

"I'll think on it. I promised Pa I could handle everything. Gordon takes every penny we can spare to Pa on Sundays." Her chin lifted. "You're hired, Mr. Chadwick. Temporary-like."

He smiled. "Reckon I'd best get these dishes clean then."

# Chapter 3

MORE EXPENSES. WHAT HAD she gotten herself into? Yet business was growing.

Abby shot Mr. Chadwick furtive glances while slicing bread for ham sandwiches. He worked quietly, only talking when seeking direction for the next task she assigned. Pretty handy around the kitchen—must have fended for himself a while. He'd even washed the red-and-white checked napkins from breakfast and dinner. These hung on the line Pa had strung behind their building. The cloth napkins ought to dry in an hour in the heat. Then she'd shake them free of dust from the constant wind.

The aroma from baked apple pies that cooled on the windowsill and on the worktable set her stomach to growling. She'd forgotten to eat in her worry over Gordon. She peered out the back door for his familiar lanky stride. Nowhere in sight.

Dinner was her big meal—sandwiches, pie, and coffee were enough for supper. She made coffee, the routine steps requiring almost no thought. Had Gordon gone to see Pa?

She glanced at Mr. Chadwick. Was he always this quiet? He seemed content—not grumbling as Gordon always did.

Five o'clock—time to open the front door again. She'd prefer to leave it open all day for the cross breeze, but cowboys entered at all hours when the door was open.

Five men sat on the boardwalk. She greeted them cordially, having learned the hard way that some misinterpreted a friendly smile for flirting. Until customers realized she wasn't like the women who drank whiskey with them in the saloons, she'd keep her guard up.

A strong whiff of liquor lingered after the men crossed the threshold. She'd serve coffee right away and hope that sobered them. Somehow, Mr. Chadwick's presence in the kitchen comforted her.

Wade, preoccupied with concern for his brother *and* Miss Abby's brother, kept an eye out the back window for Gordon. The restaurant had closed at seven. Twilight … and still no sign of the boy.

Miss Abby cleaned in the front room. There'd been little time for conversation once diners arrived for supper. Just as well. Her tense face showed more than words that Gordon's actions weren't normal.

He might be with his pa … or he might be drinking at one of the several saloons around town. Or gambling.

Wade's jaw tightened. He'd learned from Beau that many of the games were rigged in the saloon owner's favor, though players who kept their wits about them had a fair chance of winning at faro. Poker could be another story. Dealers often cheated by manipulating the cards and bottom dealing—dealing from below the deck. If Gordon brought money to gambling tables, he'd likely leave with empty pockets.

Occasional gunshots reminded Wade of other dangers on Abilene's streets. Miss Abby was beautiful enough to turn any man's head, his included. Yet it was her compassion for her brother that had really snagged his interest. He'd rather search for her brother than risk her searching for him and being accosted on the streets at night. Her actions with that rude cowboy had proven her courage. She'd look for Gordon if Wade didn't.

The door between the kitchen and dining room swung open. Miss Abby balanced a wet towel and three cups in her hands. "This is the last of it. Front door's locked."

"Good. Everything else is done." Wade dried his hands on a towel. "Think I'll mosey around town a bit before heading back to the herd. I'll send Gordon home … if I find him."

Her green eyes widened. "That would be a kindness." Her gaze flew to the ceiling.

"You live upstairs."

She gave a wary nod.

He hated to learn they lived in the midst of so much danger and temptation for a boy still wet behind the ears. He rubbed his forehead. With saloons all around—one next door—and a house of ill repute behind another saloon down the street, this area wasn't as safe as he'd like. "Stay here and lock your door."

"I will." She glanced at a pile of soiled napkins. "There are things to finish up first."

Something about this short, feisty woman appealed to his protective instincts. He considered staying until she finished. A gunshot nearby decided him. Gordon might be in trouble. "See you at breakfast."

"Thank you."

He plopped his floppy hat on and left before her forlorn look changed his mind.

It took a half hour's search through boisterous streets to find Gordon inside a noisy saloon. Men stood at a long mahogany bar, glasses of watered-down green whiskey and beer on the gleaming wood in front of them. Wade spotted Gordon lounging against one of the gambling tables. Green cloth with painted images of thirteen playing cards covered the table.

Faro.

Wade steeled himself. Visions of his brother's last visit before Wade left Texas rose unbidden. Beau had needed twenty-five dollars to settle a gambling debt. Wade had lectured him and then pleaded for him to ask for a job on the cattle drive set to depart the next morning. It was useless—Beau wanted no part of a cowboy's work. In the end, Wade gave him ten dollars—almost everything he owned. Beau's promise to repay was meaningless.

Wade hadn't been able to save his brother—yet—but Gordon was still young.

"Evenin', Gordon." Wade raised his voice to be heard over the din in the room behind him.

The boy's head jerked toward him. "Wade. Didn't expect to see you here." Alcohol fumes rolled out with his words.

Miss Abby wasn't going to be happy.

"I could say the same." He folded his arms.

"Abby sent you, didn't she?" He thrust his chest out. "Well, I ain't ready to leave. Not when I'm winning."

Then he'd probably be ready to leave soon. Most bets went in the house's favor.

The table's lookout gave Gordon a five-dollar chip.

Grinning, he placed a chip on the painted eight card. Three other fellows placed a chip on a five, a seven, and a four card.

Wade was happy to see a casekeeper move a disk on an abacus. Smart players watched this tool that tracked the cards already played.

His brown eyes feverish, Gordon didn't even glance at the casekeeper.

Should Wade explain this feature of the game? No. Best for his young friend to lose money. Losing wasn't fun. If Gordon lost, maybe he wouldn't return.

The dealer turned up his first card—the loser. Seven. A cowboy's chip was removed as the house won. The next card was an eight.

Gordon grinned and placed his winning chip on the eight again.

Wade rubbed his jaw. The abacus showed that three eights had been played. Only one left.

The game continued for the next half hour. Gordon won once again and then steadily lost the rest of his chips. He turned his pockets inside out. Empty.

Wade placed a hand on his shoulder. "Let's go outside. I need some fresh air." Cigar smoke hung like a rank fog, warring with liquor smells as they strode past the bar.

They stepped out into the twilight. The day's heat had turned mild. "Pleasant evening."

"What's good about it?" Gordon's shoulders slumped. His gaze strayed to the dusty street. A rider on a mustang kicked up dust clouds as he passed them, making Gordon sneeze. Wade steered him from a woman wearing a red silk dress cut indecently low, who giggled as she clutched the arm of a cowboy too bashful to meet her gaze. Wade and Gordon weaved past groups of men standing outside saloons and leaning against hitching posts. Unaccustomed to crowds, Wade focused on the fourteen-year-old at his side.

Gunshots.

Wade halted and looked behind him. Whoopin' and hollerin', two cowboys sat on their mustangs in the middle of Texas Street, smoking six-shooters aimed at the moon.

He rolled his eyes. The town needed a marshal, all right.

Wade's spurs jangled as they traipsed the boardwalk toward the restaurant. "You ain't the first to lose all your money at faro." His thoughts flew to his younger brother. "And you won't be the last."

"I reckon."

The boy's steps were steady enough. Good. He must not have drunk much before gambling. Or his drink was watered down. They stopped outside the dark restaurant. "Looks like your sister locked up for the night."

Gordon glanced up. "That's strange. Abby didn't light a lantern yet."

Wade's heart skipped a beat as he followed Gordon to the side of the building.

"Hope she's not looking for me." He climbed the outside stairs leading to the second floor.

Wade's shoulders tensed. She'd promised.

Gordon unlocked the door and ran inside. He was back within seconds. "She's not here."

Outwardly calm, Wade's blood turned to ice.

"She's too smart to be out on the streets after dark." Gordon half ran, half stumbled down the stairs. "Where is she?"

Fearing the gutsy woman might march into a saloon looking for her brother, Wade straightened his shoulders. "We'll find her."

# Chapter 4

Abby encountered another bold stare and lowered her gaze. Texas Street didn't feel all that friendly during the daylight hours since the jailbreak—it was far worse as darkness fell.

She'd paced the narrow twenty-foot hallway of their upstairs living quarters for thirty minutes before deciding to search for her brother. She'd promised to watch over him. Relying on a man she'd known only a day had been foolhardy. Mr. Chadwick was probably back with his herd.

Good riddance too. She'd seen the wild side of these men. Forget the compassion in his eyes, the strength of his muscular arms. She'd best remember that he was one of them.

A horse tied to a hitching post whinnied. A lone rider on a sorrel horse watched her. She averted her eyes.

Gunshots drew her startled attention. Two riders at the end of the street had their guns pointed at the sky. An exuberance of high spirits? Looking for trouble?

Once past the man with the brazen stare, her eyes skimmed the crowded street. Searching for Gordon's blue shirt and brown trousers secured in place by suspenders, she avoided looking directly at men's faces. Recalling her promise to Pa, she followed every turn of the street in the gathering darkness. Where was her brother?

Another saloon loomed on the right, its false front making the building appear taller. It drew her eyes in spite of her anxiety over the way men emerged—staggering from too much drink or dejected from losing at gaming tables.

A group of cowboys watched her from outside the saloon's open door. Two held half-empty whiskey bottles. Gordon's blue shirt? Not there. Legs wobbling, she stepped off the boardwalk. She hesitated. What if Gordon was inside? Someone had to fetch him before he lost all his earnings.

Two gunshots halted nearby conversations. She shuddered—worse things could happen to her little brother than losing his money.

"Hello, darlin.'"

A smiling cowboy with a slow drawl stepped beside her.

He tipped his Stetson. "Lookin' for someone to buy you a drink?"

Chills ran up her back. With trembling hands she lifted her skirt off the dust. Raising her chin, she stepped forward.

He blocked her path.

Wade lengthened his stride to keep up with Gordon's frantic pace. Twilight had given way to darkness on a street crowded with horses, riders, loungers, and pedestrians. Odors of unwashed bodies mingled with the familiar stable smell.

Except for raucous laughter and a few feminine giggles, he could almost believe that he still rode the Chisholm Trail and this was all a bad dream.

Only Abilene was nothing like his imaginings.

Stores were dark. Saloons and other businesses that catered to men were lit like beacons.

"You don't think she's inside a saloon, do you?" Gordon's rapid glance bounced from left to right.

He frowned. He sure hoped not … yet the dark street also held danger for a woman alone. "Doubt it. Let's walk to the end before we worry about searching saloons."

Accustomed to darkness, his attention flew to a commotion ahead.

"Kindly step aside." Miss Abby, her stance rigid, faced a muscular cowboy a half foot taller than her.

Wade sucked in his breath. Clem Harley had ridden for the same trail boss as him—and all the fellows gave him a wide berth when he drank.

"Well, now, that ain't friendly." Clem grasped her upper arm. "I'm buying you a drink."

"Get your hands off my sister!" Gordon rushed toward the man ten years his senior—in years and strength.

One swipe of the back of Clem's hand sent Gordon sprawling, his face in the dirt.

Wade's pulse escalated as Gordon pushed himself to his knees. Men standing near Clem went silent. Still. Yet they didn't protest their buddy's behavior against the siblings. His frown deepened.

Miss Abby gasped. "Why, you—"

"Let her go, Clem." Wade wedged himself beside her. "She's a lady."

Clem spat without releasing his hold on her arm. "Then why's she alone on Texas Street after dark?" He slammed her against his body. "Find your own woman, Wade."

She pushed against his chest. "Release me!"

Body tensing, Wade touched the gun in his holster. "I'd listen to her if I were you."

"You saying you'd draw on me?" His jaw slackened. "I never figured you for a fool."

"And I never figured you for a man who'd accost a lady ... no matter what time of day." His fingers rested on his revolver, poised to draw if necessary. He was likely on his own dealing with Clem. Wade looked past him to the silent men—some he'd ridden with. This could get really ugly if he didn't maintain control. He refocused on Clem, hoping the man wasn't drunk. The smell of cheap whiskey in the air could be coming from any of them.

Abby struck Clem's chest with her fist. "Let go of me!"

Gordon pushed himself to his feet.

Wade couldn't risk Gordon launching himself at Clem again. His revolver was in his hand faster than thought. "Release the lady."

"Plenty more where she came from." Clem pushed her at Wade.

He caught her. Steadied her with one arm while his gun never wavered. "She's a lady, Clem. Her dress is modest. Any of them women in the saloon dress this way?"

"If I see her out alone after dark ..." His menacing glare dropped to Miss Abby.

She shivered.

The back of Wade's neck heated up. "You'll tip your hat like a gentleman and allow her to pass."

His gaze fastened on the six-shooter in Wade's hand. "Sure thing. Didn't know you had claim to her."

She stepped away. His arm fell to his side.

Clem adjusted his shirt. "Com'on, fellas. Let's see what's happening at the Alamo."

Wade eyed the half-dozen men who followed Clem to a saloon. None had intervened. Because he had the situation in hand? Or were they afraid of their leader?

The evening suddenly felt hotter than Fourth of July sunshine.

Clem wouldn't take kindly to another confrontation. Wade didn't have money for hotels or boarding houses. He didn't know if Clem stayed in town or not. Until he figured out whether the man held a grudge, he'd sleep with one eye open.

Best worry about that later. He holstered his gun. "Let's get you home."

# Chapter 5

PRIOR CLAIM INDEED. ABBY huffed as she matched her brother's wobbly stride. The nerve of that man to accost her, hit her brother, and then hold her against his sweaty wool shirt. The odor of sour whiskey breath lingered even after he shoved her at Mr. Chadwick.

She stopped when they'd put a building between them and the saloon. "Thank you, Mr. Chadwick, for standing up for me." She'd been proud of the way he'd confronted the bully.

"Any gentleman would have done likewise." He tipped his hat. "Hate there was need for it."

Her fault. Resuming their walk, she shivered uncontrollably.

His spurs jangled as he followed them, booted steps clopping against the boardwalk.

Her breath came in shuddering gasps. Wade had saved her. The cowboy that grabbed her, though not drunk, had been drinking. She believed the cowboy's threat—he intended to force his attentions on her if she ventured out alone after dark again.

"You all right, Abby?" Gordon studied her in the glow of a lantern hanging on a building they passed.

"Just fine." What would have happened tonight if Gordon tried to rescue her alone? A chill spread across her back. A far worse beating at the very least. Respect for Mr. Chadwick escalated. "I'm tough."

"It's the truth."

"How brave you were." She forced her trembling lips upward. "Did he hurt you?"

"Nah." His chest puffed out. "Been hurt worse playing baseball back home."

She laughed, pleased that he acted more like his old self. The wobbliness had worked out of his step. Outside her restaurant, she turned to Mr. Chadwick. "Thanks again. The situation with that cowboy would have gone far worse without your intervention."

No fooling. Miss Abby's brother would have required a doctor's attention if not for Wade. Not to mention what Clem had in mind for her. So why did he sense uneasiness toward him? Did she imagine all cowboys were like Clem?

"My pleasure, Miss Abby." He tipped his hat. "Lock your door."

"That man aimed harm to my sister. I couldn't stop him." Gordon's shoulders slumped.

"That was the whiskey talking. A gentleman would have listened." Wade thumped the boy's shoulder awkwardly. "You got no call to feel shame."

"That's right." Miss Abby took Gordon's arm. "You acted courageously." Her smile included Wade. "Can I expect you tomorrow?"

He nodded. "What time?"

"Breakfast is served from six to eight. Six o'clock?"

After tonight's confrontation, wages weren't the only reason to work for her. She needed protection. "See you then." He widened his stance. "I'll wait till you're inside."

Face stiffening, she looked up and down the street. "I'm obliged to you. See you in the morning."

Gordon's boots struck the top landing. Miss Abby's skirt brushed against the pinewood steps. She gave a little nod before disappearing inside. She sure was pretty—no wonder she'd caught Clem's eye.

Lantern light brightened the curtained windows. He relaxed. She was safe.

He turned to traipse the now less-populated road toward camp in the moonlight.

Yes, Abby—Miss Abby—was a beautiful, spirited woman. She deserved better than a cowboy who had failed his own brother.

Sporadic shooting overnight wasn't the only thing that disturbed Abby's sleep. Worry for her brother finally drove her, bleary-eyed, from her bed before the rooster crowed. He wanted to build the ranch with their pa. She'd send him there today with their surplus cash. Pa needed money for supplies anyway.

Mr. Chadwick would fill Gordon's place at work. She'd just have to trust him. The man had earned her respect last night for bolstering her brother's confidence.

Gordon hadn't explained where he'd been yesterday—another reason to send him to Pa.

Biscuits were already rolled out when someone tapped on the door. Abby glanced at Ma's shelf clock. Five-thirty. Gordon hadn't come down, and he never knocked anyway. That fellow, Clem, didn't know where she lived. Did he? No. More likely, a hungry customer arriving early for breakfast. "Who is it?"

"Brian Hixson delivering your groceries."

Abby drew a shaky breath at the familiar voice. She unlocked the door with a smile. "You're early."

"Didn't mean to frighten you." The father of seven set a large crate on the counter. "My wife noticed your lantern was lit over an hour ago. We got today's order together early. Been awful busy since the cowboys arrived. We've got to get an early start these days, or we fall behind quick."

"It's fried chicken for dinner today. Ugh." She pulled a face. "Word travels fast. Tuesday dinners are one of my busiest meals. I understand wanting to get an early start on the day."

Booted footsteps with jangling spurs approached. Mr. Chadwick stopped in the open doorway.

"Miss Abby opens at six." Mr. Hixson stepped between him and Abby. "Come back then. And use the restaurant's entrance around front."

Warmth filled Abby's heart at Mr. Hixson's fatherly protection. He and his wife, Katherine, had been helpful in many ways since she opened her restaurant. It had been Katherine's suggestion to serve the same meal to all customers. The advice had saved her sanity. She did have friends in this town.

A few.

"It's all right, Mr. Hixson. Wade Chadwick is working here the next few weeks." Abby introduced the grocer to Mr. Chadwick, who extended a strong hand to Mr. Hixson's hearty handshake.

"Call me Brian." His open face invited friendship. "I expect we'll see one another daily."

Abby glanced at the clock. Twenty-five minutes until the restaurant opened. She shoved a pan of biscuits into the oven. Time to fry a skillet of bacon. "Unpack the box for me, will you, Mr. Chadwick? And take the chickens to the cellar. I'll cut them up after breakfast."

"I can cut up the chickens for you." He took a slab of bacon from the box. "You have a cellar?"

"Not many people in town have one like we do." Brian helped stack the chickens, beefsteaks, eggs, milk, jars, and cans on a side table. "Yes, her pa dug a deep cellar, five foot wide and the length of this room. Too much trouble to traipse to a springhouse on the muddy Smoky Hill River when you've got a restaurant to run."

Abby listened to their conversation with half an ear. Gordon always came down before the first customers arrived. When there was a lull in the service, she'd give him the good news about sending him to join Pa.

Wade wiped his brow with his sleeve. It had to be ten degrees hotter in this kitchen than outside … and the sun was hot today. Digging a small pit near the back door for Miss Abby would give her more space for cooking—and remove some heat from the building. He'd dig one his first opportunity.

He'd washed more dishes this week than in the past four years. A cook made breakfast and supper for them at the ranch, and a chuckwagon cook took care of meals they ate on cattle drives.

The good definitely outweighed the bad at this job. He'd eaten delicious, free meals for a week and earned fifty cents a day. Besides dishes, he fried the breakfast meats, ran errands, and made multiple trips to the well. Miss Abby promised to pay him every Saturday. Tonight, he'd receive his first wages since leaving the ranch. His tendency to save had hounded him since the first time Beau borrowed money to pay a gambling debt. That reluctance to spend was difficult to overcome, but wasn't everything he earned here a bonus? He planned to buy another set of clothes and a Stetson. Maybe.

The snap of bullwhips took him back to the recent cattle drive. Cowboys shouted and cursed at longhorns to prod them onto train cars. The tracks were a hundred yards away yet the voices were loud enough to distinguish some of the words.

From his position at the back window, the familiar sounds bombarded him all day. The ruckus went on well into the night. His herd still waited their turn. It might be weeks before those cattle were sold and headed east.

Ears attentive to any sign of trouble from the dining room, he looked out the back window as he washed another stack of plates. Just the hum of normal conversation.

He dumped the dishwater outside the back door. Must be lots of folks on the street because plenty roamed behind the buildings. Sighing, he emptied a bucket of fresh water into his dishpan. The restaurant's popularity guaranteed he had to wash every dish three times per meal to have enough for service.

Miss Abby must be pleased with the business.

She bustled in with plates wiped clean of crumbs and bowls empty of gumbo soup. "We close in a quarter hour, and customers are still coming." She stacked plates on the counter beside him.

"Your good cooking brought 'em."

Her cheeks flushed a pretty shade of pink. "Three cowboys are ready for plum cobbler. I've been thinking. We might need one more worker. There's been twice as many customers the past two days as we've had all week. Too bad Gordon …" Lips pursed, she dipped a generous portion of cobbler.

"Probably for the best." Gordon had packed a bag on Tuesday morning and left for their pa's ranch. "Lots of temptation for a boy his age in Abilene."

She slanted her green eyes in a side glance at him. "When you put it that way, he's better off with Pa."

"Reckon so." Wade hoped that losing all his money had cured Gordon of wanting to gamble—for Gordon's sake and his sister's.

But he wasn't certain that trouble was over.

Abby—Miss Abby—left with the cobbler and returned with more dishes and cups. Her eyes were huge.

"What is it?"

"That cowboy just walked into the dining room."

# Chapter 6

CLEM. THE CUP IN Wade's hand splashed into the dishwater. "Did he see you?"

"No," she whispered. "I hurried back here. What should I do?"

"Stay put." He patted the side of his thigh for his gun. Right. His gun belt hung on a wall hook.

"It was dark that night." She crept closer. "Do you think he'll recognize me?"

"We're not taking the chance." When sober, Clem wouldn't do anything to her. What were the chances that he was sober now? Better he not see her at all. "I'll serve the rest of the supper shift."

"Agreed." Despite the heat, she shivered. "A table of four is ready for cobbler." She prepared the desserts. "He walked in with two others. Serve them coffee right away."

He arranged the small plates between his fingers and pushed open the door. Every table was occupied by three or four men. Only one had empty plates pushed aside. Clem and two strangers sat at a table by the window, staring out at the street bustling with wagons, riders, and pedestrians. Conversations and laughter lent comradery to the dining room's atmosphere that with any luck would last.

He dropped off the cobbler and then strode over to Clem's table. "Howdy, folks. Clem." He forced his arms to relax at his sides. "We're serving roasted beef sandwiches, gumbo soup, plum cobbler, and coffee. Sixty cents." Miss Abby charged an additional dime for an extra dish on Fridays and Saturdays.

"You got a job in a restaurant?" Clem guffawed. "Don't tell me you cook."

"Not hardly." He grinned as if he didn't mind the jabs. "Mostly cleaning and running errands."

"What about the herd?" Clem's eyes narrowed.

"Not much to do until the sale is negotiated." The extra hands hired for the cattle drive were mostly idle in Abilene. "I'll get your coffee and then bring the rest."

Abby had the coffee poured. "Did he give you a hard time?"

"Nope."

"Anyone else need anything? More coffee?"

He shrugged. "Didn't ask."

"Then ask." She sliced bread for sandwiches. "Two tables should be ready to pay. Sixty cents per meal today."

"I know." Extra dishes to wash too. "I'll take their coffee out and check with the others."

"Thank you."

Abby was glad that cowboy and his friends got lukewarm coffee. It seemed little enough reward for his rough treatment of her.

Too little. Her body broke into a cold sweat. She gripped the table. Her legs weakened at memories of his callused hands jerking her against his hard chest.

Hmm. A bowl of salt. Impulsively, she rubbed a pinch of salt on his roasted beef. Then another pinch. Not knowing which sandwich he'd get, she made all three sandwiches alike. After all, the pair with him might have stood silently outside the saloon and allowed him to mistreat her.

This was too much fun. What could she do to the gumbo soup? Extra pepper? No, he might like extra seasonings like pepper or dried parsley that were already in the soup. She had ground cinnamon left from yesterday's apple pie. Just the thing.

Mr. Chadwick came in with dirty dishes and money. "Two tables are empty. I'll close the door in five minutes."

"Take these to that cowboy's table." She turned away to hide her glee. Revenge tasted sweet. That was it—sugar. She sprinkled sugar over an already sweet plum pudding. He shouldn't enjoy any part of his meal. Best not give him any reason to return.

Mr. Chadwick pushed open the door, a stack of plates balanced on his arms. "Seven people are ready for dessert." He glanced at the side table. "I'll need four more."

Abby rushed over. "Take those to that cowboy's table. I'll have the rest prepared by the time you return."

His brow creased. "They're still eating."

"That's fine." Abby avoided his eyes. She prepared another serving.

"It's almost seven. That will stir them along."

He was back with three full bowls of soup. "They said to bring these back. Don't want more coffee. They're slow about eating their sandwiches too."

"Soup have an odd flavor?" She giggled.

His eyebrow quirked. "What did you do?"

"Cinnamon."

He chuckled. "And cold coffee." He grinned. "That'll get him. All of us ex-soldiers cherish our coffee."

Abby giggled. "There might be too much salt on that cowboy's roasted beef sandwich."

His smile lit up his face. "Can't say I blame you. He'll probably hightail it out of here before long. No need for my six-shooter tonight."

Miss Abby's lips tightened. Wade fumbled with the plated desserts. They'd just laughed, sharing a joke on Clem. What had happened to chase the joy from her face? Bad memories from Clem accosting her earlier? "You all right?"

She picked up a cloth and a dirty bowl. "You'd best get those cobblers to my guests and start collecting money."

Shaking his head, he delivered the desserts. Clem and his buddies had left money on their table, dessert plates scraped clean. Good. This saved him from hearing another dig about "dishboy."

Wade hoped that Miss Abby's wreckage of their meal kept them away. He grinned as he cleared the last table. Abby was a feisty one all right. Life with her would never be dull.

Shots nearby—did they never stop?

His smile died as he locked the front door against whoops and hollers in the street from cowboys. Men just like him.

Miss Abby was meant for a better man than him, that much was certain.

Abby had eaten lunch with the Hixsons after church and now the rest of the day was hers—the only day she didn't cook for others. Or herself. Leftover cobbler sounded like a mighty fine supper.

Exhaustion claimed her most evenings, so Sunday was the day she counted the money left after expenses. She descended the few stairs leading to the cellar, candleholder in hand. Ah. That cool air revived her from the day's heat. And to think, summer hadn't even arrived yet.

The candle's glow cast dim shadows on two floor-to-ceiling shelves and one cupboard. A quart-sized mason jar nestled in the back of a bottom shelf. She grunted as she lifted it.

Counting the money away from the kitchen's heat appealed to her as much as a tumbler full of cold water just drawn from the well. Standing in the cramped space, she poured the coins and bills onto an empty shelf. Mr. Hixson had a hefty order to bring tomorrow, including a set of inexpensive dishes he'd ordered for her from St. Louis. She laid aside money for all supplies then counted the rest.

Surely she miscalculated. There should be more than four dollars left over, even after paying Mr. Chadwick. She recounted. Still only four dollars.

That number made no sense. Usual weekly earnings were between twelve and fifteen dollars after expenses. Gordon had taken two days of profits to Pa on Tuesday. With the number of customers the past two days she'd expected over twenty dollars ... maybe twenty-five. Food costs had certainly increased. Was that the difference? What had changed between last week and this?

Her heart skipped a beat.

Wade—Mr. Chadwick.

Though she handled all the money, he fetched supplies from the cellar daily. The money jar wasn't hard to find.

She squeezed the folds of her pink cotton dress. He seemed honest. Trustworthy.

Though other cowboys continued to shoot off guns and rule the town, Abby had grown to like the broad-shouldered man who'd come to her rescue more than once. Maybe more than like him. He treated her with respect. Kindness. Like she was special. He even dug a pit out back for cooking, something she'd not considered. It helped with breakfast and cooking vegetables and soup.

And he'd treated Gordon compassionately—even after rescuing him from his poor decisions.

Mr. Chadwick's actions, his words, had proven him to be a good man. A man to be trusted.

She must have miscalculated the food cost. Arithmetic had never been her best subject in school. Yes, that must be the reason.

It had been too busy to worry with updating her ledgers. She'd have to do a better job with calculations—and maybe keep an eye on her new employee.

# Chapter 7

THREE DAYS LATER, WADE asked Brian Hixson where he could buy a new coat. He hadn't been to church since late February, a week before the cattle drive started. His coat and vest were in the bunkhouse back at the ranch—the only possessions he hadn't brought with him.

"I hated missing church last Sunday." Wade unpacked Brian's latest delivery. "Didn't know how the good folks of Abilene feel about cowboys showing up in wool shirts and bandanas."

"I reckon it's like anything else." Brian lifted a basket of eggs onto the table as Miss Abby waited on customers in the dining room. "There's always someone who doesn't like something. Personally, I'd be happy to see you in church dressed as you are. But if you'd like to purchase a coat—"

Miss Abby pushed open the connecting kitchen door. "Oh, Mr. Hixson. Not too hot for you, I hope." She lined three plates on the table and tossed two biscuits on each.

He chuckled. "Not this early in the day. With your orders growing bigger every day there's no need to ask if business is booming."

She sighed. "Too big. I need another woman to help cook and serve my customers."

"I might be able to help you with that." Brian placed a bag of flour on the table. "I'll talk to Kathleen about our oldest daughter."

"Christina." Abby nodded.

"Yes. She may be able to work a few hours a day. Say five hours daily? Would that help?"

"Is she a good baker?" Abby ladled a generous portion of gravy over two biscuits. "Bread for sandwiches? Pies? Cobblers?"

"I'll say." He patted his stomach with a grin. "She can even do part of the baking from our home. Free up your oven."

"Then how about noon to five o'clock, six days a week." Abby arranged three pieces of bacon on a plate. "The pay is fifty cents a day plus her meals."

Wade shifted. That was his pay—for over double the hours. Then again, the money wasn't the main reason he stayed here ... her protection was.

"Think about it." Balancing three plates, Miss Abby disappeared into the next room.

"She comes in like a whirlwind, doesn't she?" Brian chuckled.

Wade laughed. "Reckon so. About the tailor ..."

"I'd better explain how to get there before she comes back." He laughed again.

Wade grinned and listened to the simple directions, itching to sit with Abby in church on Sunday. The long ride he'd taken on Dusty, his mustang, had done them both good last Sunday. Truth was, he missed church. His ma had taken her boys to church every Sunday. Read to them from the Good Book on Saturday evenings.

Some habits were too good to break.

A noise jolted Abby from a deep sleep. Booted steps. Spurs that jangled. Was someone outside the restaurant or next door at the saloon?

There was no chance that she'd investigate the cause armed with only the wooden spoon she kept stashed in her apron pocket.

Her thoughts swirled. A drunken cowboy? A fellow sleeping on the boardwalk near her window? That had happened before the jail was dismantled by disgruntled Texans rescuing an incarcerated buddy. There were a lot more strangers in town every day.

That cowboy? The one who'd grabbed her?

All alone. She shuddered. Gordon didn't sleep across the hall any longer. Wade had left hours ago.

Cowboys shouted at longhorns at the railroad tracks but other street noises had died down.

A door creaked.

Downstairs? Next door?

She put a fist against her mouth to keep from crying out. *God, please save me.*

All went quiet.

She laid back against her pillow, the sheet knotted in her cold hands. When the sounds weren't repeated, she gradually relaxed.

A train chugged to a stop beside the station. Shouts and curses accompanied longhorn steers to the train.

Abby flopped to her side. Why didn't those cowboys have more consideration than to load their cattle in the middle of the night when hardworking folks tried to sleep?

A bullwhip cracked. Then another. More shouts easily reached her through her window, open to coax a cool breeze inside.

Abby groaned. That ruckus made the earlier creaking door sound peaceful. Someone must have been passing by.

Morning came too soon not to snatch all the sleep she could get.

The hair on the back of Wade's neck stood up when Abby mentioned on Friday morning that she'd heard footsteps outside her home, and then a door opened.

In the warm light of day, her features relaxed as she casually described how jangling spurs awoke her.

Breakfast was over. Three pans of chicken baked in the oven with three ready to go in as soon as those were done. He was caught up on the dishes. Four buckets of fresh water waited by the back door. Food supplies were put away.

"I'll wipe the tables."

She waved him on.

Best investigate while Abby concentrated on meal preparations. He took a wet cloth into the dining room, locked until eleven o'clock.

He unlocked the door and walked around the building, searching for boot prints in the dirt. Nothing. Shutters open on the windows. Normal.

Mindful of Abby's presence in the kitchen, he studied the back door from a distance. Nothing broken. No splintered wood.

The front door showed no signs that someone forced their way in.

Had the noises come from next door? A vivid dream?

Back inside, he scanned the dining room. Six tables and twenty-four chairs pretty much filled the room. Nothing new.

Wade tapped his finger against his mouth.

A possibility occurred to him that made his stomach churn.

When the restaurant closed this evening, he wouldn't be heading back to the herd.

# Chapter 8

WADE AMBLED ALONG THE crowded boardwalk, finally choosing to walk in the streets around the horses tied to hitching posts. He avoided men riding past in an exuberance of high spirits. Instead of the crowds decreasing with every trainload of longhorns that left, the population grew.

In one sense he couldn't blame his fellow Texans for staying in Abilene. Danger filled the lonely Chisholm Trail. Hunger when a fellow couldn't find a jackrabbit to shoot for supper. Many made their own way back to ranches if the cattle drive north hadn't cured them of a desire to make a living as a cowboy.

Rough life. After being around Abby the past two weeks, Wade wasn't certain a cowboy's life was going to be his. Abilene might be a fine place to buy his ranch.

After all, Abby lived here.

A gunshot riveted him back to the War of Northern Aggression. Fingers resting on his six-shooter, he searched for the source. A boy barely old enough to shave whooped and hollered outside a stable, gun smoking in his hand.

Relaxing, Wade shook his head. Men used to sitting in the saddle purt near from dawn to dusk suddenly had days on end of idleness. Caused no end of trouble. Just yesterday a man had been accused of cheating at cards. His accuser drew a gun across the table and killed him. Not the first time that had happened since Wade came to town, either.

Another saloon. Having already searched two saloons, he crossed the street toward the building. He had to admit the false front gave the establishment an air that invited folks inside.

Like his brother, Beau.

But tonight he searched for a different brother.

The smoky aroma of cigars almost strangled him as he stepped through a double-glass door. Polished mahogany bar. He raised his eyebrows. A brass rail. Fancy.

He averted his eyes from the painting of a woman to four bartenders drawing beer or pouring whiskey.

None of the customers standing in front of the long bar looked familiar. Good.

He made his way around smoking cowboys toward gaming tables covered with green cloth. A boy stood in front of the faro table, a frenzied look in his eyes. The boy should still be in school but in reality was the same age Wade had been when he mustered into the Confederate army.

Gordon.

Not living with his pa ... at least not the whole time. He'd either been lying to his pa or his sister. Probably both.

Wade stifled a groan. Flashbacks from Beau's refusal to work on a ranch, his insistence on living a life of leisure rose up to haunt him like a life-sized ghost. Wade's dream had been saving to buy a ranch for him and his brother—two of them sharing the load as their father had done. All for naught. Beau's dream had been a life of gambling. His greatest fear was that Beau ended up on the wrong end of a gun at a poker game.

He had been unable to save his own brother. How could he hope to save Abby's?

The sun rested on the western horizon when a key turned in the kitchen door. Abby dropped a tablecloth back into her washtub. Only Pa and Gordon had a key, besides her. "Pa? Is that you?"

Gordon pushed open the door. "Just me. Still working on a Saturday night? Glad that's behind me."

"It's good to see you." Chilled by his condescending tone, Abby gave him a brief hug. "It's nice to have company tonight. Wa—Mr. Chadwick left an hour ago. You can go to church with us tomorrow."

His lip curled. "Can't do that. Me and Pa have been working hard on the new fence. With longhorn herds spread out for better than five miles, it's the only way to keep them off our land. He sent me to get the money from you tonight and get back to the ranch. A hundred sixty acres requires a lot of fencing. Need to order more wood for posts."

The loneliness that struck her when Wade—when had she started to think of him by his first name?—left that evening attacked her again. Was her company not worth her men's time? Was the only reason for her existence to run the eatery and give Pa every spare cent? No, she'd asked Pa for the chance to earn her own way. She could do it. "I haven't counted it yet."

Gordon raised the cellar door. "I'll do it. You keep working on the laundry."

Abby surveyed the heap of red-and-white checkered tablecloths on the floor. Three more to go. "All right. Hold out twenty dollars for food purchases."

"Twenty dollars?" Frowning, he lit a candle. "Seems like a lot."

He'd never questioned her before. "We have more customers since you left. I had to hire Christina Hixson to help cook in the afternoons. How much does Pa need?"

"Every dollar helps." The candle's glow illuminated the dark cellar as he descended.

Change clinked against glass underneath her feet. Abby rubbed at a coffee stain on the cotton tablecloth in the washtub. Pa should be pleased with the amount for almost two weeks. Hard work kept him from town, but she missed him. She sighed. No doubt the labor rubbed the worst of the grief from his heart. They all grieved for Ma, but Pa had taken her death the hardest. If building a new ranch was what he most needed, she was all for it. Even if it did leave her lonely at night.

Her thoughts wandered through familiar ruts back to Wade—Mr. Chadwick. He'd been quieter than normal today and had left as soon as she'd paid his weekly salary. He'd hinted at worries that troubled him. Maybe he was ready to talk about them. She'd ask him tomorrow after church.

He'd offered to walk her to services. A smile touched her lips. Her ma would be pleased she found a churchgoing man.

Booted steps climbing the cellar stairs brought Abby back to reality. "Well? How much was it?"

He frowned. "I reckon Pa will be happy with twelve dollars."

"Twelve dollars?" After the record number of customers this week? She'd expected three times that amount—maybe more. Abby's heart shriveled. Wade must be helping himself to the spoils. He'd mentioned buying a new coat and vest.

"That's all he'll get." Gordon sighed. "Pa wished for more. Hate to rush off, but I want to get back to the ranch before nightfall."

She understood his rush. It got awful dark away from town. "Take a candle."

Removing the candle from its holder, he snuffed out the flame with his thumb and forefinger. "I'll take this one. Thanks, Abby. I'll be back next week for more."

She relocked the door against the boisterous street sounds. Lonelier than ever, she wrung water from the last tablecloth with more force than necessary.

No. It couldn't be Wade. Arriving early, his tasks now included frying meat for breakfast, peeling and cutting vegetables, running errands, and keeping a watchful eye on foods cooked outside. He voluntarily took on these extra jobs. She'd even toyed with raising his wages.

And he always treated her with respect. Proved himself to be an honorable man.

Yet no one else made multiple daily trips to the cellar. Alone.

But it couldn't be him.

She rubbed her aching temples. Had she been wrong to trust a cowboy?

# Chapter 9

ABBY SAT NEXT TO Wade at the church service, though she heard very little of the sermon that droned on and on. Normally content to listen to the pastor, worry for the lost money whirled about in her head. Money was placed in the jar several times a day. She was now certain her restaurant had been robbed.

But was it Wade?

He sat silently at her side, hand tapping against his leg as if he couldn't concentrate either.

Conscience bothering him?

If guilty, he deserved to be fired. Yet, she needed him and Christina sharing the load.

Hmm. Christina preferred to bake at home yet was still at the restaurant a while each day. Sometimes alone. In fairness to Wade, she had to consider Christina as the possible culprit.

Hiding the money and then counting it every night, no matter how her tired body protested, was the only way to know exactly what she made.

But where was the best hiding place? Not the cellar. Coins were too heavy to tote in her apron pocket. Where else?

Crossing her arms, she stole a look at Wade. She had enough to worry about without this added burden.

Yet his head bowed in prayer. He'd treated her with unfailing courtesy.

More courtesy than she was giving the pastor. She bowed her head for the final prayer, listening impatiently for the *amen*.

She stood when Wade did, moved by the conviction in his deep bass voice as he sang "Amazing Grace" to end the service. Was she doing him a disservice in suspecting him?

Mrs. Hilby craned her neck to look at Wade during the last stanza. Eyebrows raised, she stared at Abby.

Wonderful. The biggest gossip in town wanted more fuel for the latest fire. Abby glanced up at Wade and melted under the warmth of his smile. More than one female head had turned when she walked in beside the tall Texan, handsome in a dark blue coat, red vest, and string tie.

He couldn't smile at her like that and then rob her the next minute, could he?

Wade tried to shake off his failure with Gordon as the last notes of the hymn died away. Abby surely wouldn't smile at him as warmly if she knew that her brother gambled in nearby saloons—and no longer heeded Wade's advice not to throw away his money.

A thin woman with inquisitive eyes appeared at his side as soon as the minister released the congregation. "Why, Abby, I saw you two exchanging glances during services and thought I'd better meet your beau."

"I believe you're mistaken, Mrs. Hilby." Abby's smile wavered. "Mr. Wade Chadwick is in my employ." She gave a brief introduction that did nothing to alleviate the curiosity in the woman's eyes.

Wade gave a polite nod. A chill shot through him that Abby only thought of him as an employee. He wasn't good enough to court her, yet he'd considered her a friend. He'd lingered after the day's work was finished several times. Though reserved with him the past week, she'd seemed to enjoy his company.

"For the short time he's in Abilene."

Neither woman gave him time to respond. Wade ran a finger between his collar and his neck. Must have tied his new string tie too tightly. Abby sure did look pretty in the blue dress with little red flowers on it that matched the silk roses on her hat.

He appreciated Abby's reminder that working for her was temporary. Even if he stayed in Abilene, he didn't fancy himself washing dishes, frying bacon, and running errands the rest of his life. His dream of owning a ranch, raising a family with a woman like Abby, seemed more out of reach than ever.

Her honey-colored hair, gathered back in combs, fairly bounced as she nodded to Mrs. Hilby.

What would it be like to watch Abby walk down this aisle to him in her prettiest dress? Raise a family with her? He shook his head. Best not let those dreams take root.

Abby tilted her head. "You disagree, Mr. Chadwick?"

"I ..." He hated to confess he hadn't heard a word of their conversation.

"No matter." Abby inclined her head at Mrs. Hilby. "Good day." She tugged on Wade's arm.

"A pleasure making your acquaintance, ma'am." He reached to tip his hat and realized he held it in his hand since they were still inside the church. He shook the pastor's hand at the door, smothering a sigh at not meeting the congregation's men.

Kicking up a dust cloud, Abby headed toward her home "It would have been more polite to simply agree Pastor Langford preached a fine sermon. You weren't raised in a barn."

Ouch. He ate her dust until she stepped onto the boardwalk. "No, Miss Abby." His words were clipped. "I didn't hear the comment. My attention had wandered."

Bright green eyes flashed up at him. "Then don't shake your head for no reason. That woman's the biggest gossip I know. Mrs. Langford will hear of it before she steps outside church. What were you thinking?"

Best not tell her. "Sorry." Her reaction seemed a bit too strong. "Something else eating you?"

Her lips clamped shut, heels clanking against the boardwalk.

He followed her. "Did I leave something unfinished last evening?" He'd searched for Gordon—without success—the better part of an hour before heading back to the herd.

One hand on the bannister outside her home, Abby wheeled around to face him. "Gordon came last evening. Shame you missed him."

Best place for him. Wade folded his arms. "How is he? And your pa?"

"Working hard putting up a fence strong enough to keep longhorn herds off the property."

Why was she angry about that? "Thousands of them outside Abilene."

"Exactly." One small fist rested on her hip. "It takes time to build a fence around one hundred sixty acres."

Wade whistled. "Nice size for a small ranch."

"Quarter sections were more affordable for us. We spent all our money buying that property and this building." One hand tapped on the bannister. "The restaurant's customers pay for the fence ... and someday the house."

A sense of foreboding swept over him. "Does your pa collect the profits from you?"

"Too busy." She shook her head. "Gordon used to take it to him every Saturday night and return on Monday morning. Last night was the first time he's collected the money since moving to the ranch."

Wade's mouth went dry. "Must have been a pretty penny with all the business we've had."

Her eyes narrowed. "Not as much as you might think. Twelve dollars."

He shoved his Stetson over his eyes. "That's what you counted?"

"Gordon counted it. He said Pa'd have to make do. They both hoped for more."

Something was wrong here. He washed the dishes—there had to be fifty dollars in the money jar hidden in the cellar. Maybe more.

Only one explanation. Gordon stole the money from his pa and sister and then gambled it away.

She'd be crushed. Too soon to voice his suspicions without proof. Maybe he could take her mind off her worries. "W-will you be my guest today at the Drover's Cottage? You shouldn't have to cook on Sundays."

The hand on her hip went to her throat as her eyes widened. Then she looked away. "No, thank you. I appreciate your escort to church." She turned with a flounce of her blue dress.

"My pleasure." Wade's chest constricted as she climbed the stairs to her living quarters. There went his plans for spending the day together. "See you tomorrow morning."

She turned to him from the landing. "I expect so. Good day." After inserting a key into the lock, she stepped inside and closed the door without another word.

Why was she angry?

Maybe she did suspect her brother of thievery.

Or maybe she objected to a cowboy buying her lunch.

Either way, he'd double his efforts to track down Gordon. If Wade was a betting man, he'd wager the boy wasn't on his pa's ranch past sundown.

Sun scorching the back of his neck that his bandana usually hid, he strode past the crowded Drover's Cottage on his way back to the herd. His appetite for the expensive meal had dissipated with Abby's rejection.

He'd swap this hot coat and vest for an old shirt and bandana. A long ride on Dusty might clear the cobwebs from his thoughts.

# Chapter 10

ABBY KEPT HER GUARD up against Mr. Chadwick the next few days as a hot May drifted into a hotter June. He cooperated by leaving as soon as the kitchen was cleaned. Whether she was sorry to see him go was a mystery to her.

Late Thursday afternoon, Christina baked peach pies in her mother's kitchen to allow room for two large skillets of pork and beans in Abby's oven while she fried potatoes on the stove top.

Wade—Mr. Chadwick—entered the kitchen from the dining room and sniffed. "Something burning?"

"Oh, no." Abby threw open the oven door. Steam escaped as she removed a heavy skillet. Her heart sank. The beans were darker than usual. Setting the pan on the wood table, she stirred gently. "Pork seems fine, even with me slicing the meat smaller to go further."

"Customers won't complain. They love this meal." Wade extracted a second skillet and set it next to the other. "This one doesn't smell burnt."

"That one hasn't cooked as long. It can go back in until half past five." He put it back without a word of censure for her mistake. Gordon had always been a little critical—probably because he'd been unhappy here. At least her brother was happier with Pa. "This will have to do." She marveled at Wade's sympathetic expression. "My saving grace is that this meal stretches pretty far."

Wade brushed a loose tendril from her temple. "The customers love your cooking."

Her heart raced at his gentle touch. "Thank you. I hope so."

"Abby?" His brown eyes searched hers before dropping to her mouth.

Face uplifted, she leaned closer, his breath on her lips.

A fist pounded on the front door. "You open?"

Even though no one could see them in the kitchen, Abby sprang back, her face flushed that she'd invited his kiss. "C-coming!"

"My apologies. I forgot myself." Wade's arms fell to his side.

Abby took a gasping breath, realizing just how much she had wanted him to kiss her.

Another loud knock. "Miss Abby? Supper ready yet? I'm like to starve."

"I'll unlock the door." Without glancing her way, Wade left the room.

Abby closed her eyes. His lips had been mere inches away. A cup clanged against its saucer as she reached for it. Probably wouldn't get another opportunity for a kiss from him. The heat in her cheeks had nothing to do with steam from the hot coffee she poured.

The connecting door swung open. "Three tables of customers already. Want me to take them coffee?"

Nodding, she kept her back to him. "Don't know what's keeping Christina." The clock showed five o'clock. She often worked at her family's kitchen because it had more room, but she'd never been late. "Will you fetch the pies from her?"

"Right after I serve the coffee."

Abby's sigh came from deep within her heart as he walked out the back door. All week she'd toted the money to her bedroom after every meal ended. The money jar was now stashed beneath a loose floorboard under her bed. She counted it each night after her employees left, for Christina had almost as many opportunities to steal the excess cash as Wade.

Suspecting Mr. Hixson's daughter of robbery went against her nature though fairness to Wade demanded it. Christina worked from noon until five every afternoon, finishing out the lunch service and beginning preparations for supper. Abby didn't believe, deep in her heart, that the fifteen-year-old stole from her.

And her heart whispered for her to trust Wade.

Even after paying for supplies, she averaged about twenty dollars profit daily. The amount staggered her. Profits hadn't been that high when it was just her and Gordon.

Pa'd be happy with more money. So would Gordon. Wade got paid a daily wage. So did Christina.

Abby got more hard work.

And a growing love for a man who might be betraying her trust.

Wade left work on Friday night a week later and stopped to talk with his trail boss, Lance Nye.

"Any closer to selling our herd?" Wade leaned against a hitching post outside Abby's restaurant.

"Nah. Too many ahead of us." Lance chewed on the end of a cigar.

"Another three, four weeks?"

"Mebbe more. Ain't much to do with our herd until then that a few cowpokes can't handle. Work here?"

"Yep." Frilly white curtains hid the tables from view. Not as hard on a man as cowpoking.

A man stumbled out of the saloon next door and flipped over the hitching post. Laughter erupted around them.

"Clem drew his pay today so's he could go back to Texas. Got into some trouble in Abilene." Lance, gazing at the drunken man sprawled on the ground, blew a ring of cigar smoke. "Seemed best. Let another rancher worry about that foul drunken temper of his."

Wade grunted. It would have been nice to have gotten his pay early too, but at least Abby was safer now.

"Don't need every man at the ranch anyway." A laughing cowboy lifted the man to his feet. "Make your own decision about coming back to Texas."

Plain speaking. "I'll think on it." He'd considered staying in Abilene anyway, buying a ranch near Abby's pa's spread. The only thing stopping him was Abby. If she wanted him to stay, he'd stay. If not … The only thing holding him to Texas now was Beau.

"Reckon I'll see you back at camp." Lance moseyed into a saloon.

At least three more weeks in Abilene. They'd been here a month already, and Abby needed him more than ever.

He clenched his fists. With that brother of hers, she didn't know how much she needed him.

A big man riding past on a gray kicked up a dust cloud. Weaving past a loud group of men outside a saloon, Wade stepped inside. He searched the smoky room for Gordon as he had done every evening on his walk back to the herd. Not there. He checked another saloon without finding him. Maybe the boy had learned his lesson. Abby gave him money last Sunday—he'd been waiting for her when Wade walked her home from church. Abby'd politely dismissed him upon spotting her brother lounging on the outside steps.

He tried not to let it bother him. Fact was, she'd been nothing but polite since that day over a week ago when he'd almost kissed her. She'd accepted his escort to church then lit up like a firefly upon seeing her brother.

Not that Wade didn't understand the need for family. He missed Beau something fierce … at least, the way he'd been before losing their pa to a Yankee bullet and their ranch to Uncle Buck's poker game.

Those losses had come too close, too hard. They'd reeled from both blows. Beau had spun out of control, at least for a time. He still wasn't the man he could have been, should have been, but time was on his side. It had to be. *Please, God, save my brother.*

Approaching the last saloon on this side of Texas Street, he greeted one of Abby's regular customers. One more saloon to search. Then he'd head back to sleep under the stars just beginning to twinkle in a darkening sky. He flexed his tired shoulders. They'd been busy today.

He entered the smoky room. Chuckles. Raised voices. Brittle female laughter. Just like the last one. Just like all of them.

He stopped short of the gambling tables. It wasn't Gordon at the poker table who set his heart pounding. It wasn't the small stack of bills against his chest or his feverish stare locked on a haphazard array of bills in the middle of the table. It was the man across the table from Gordon. The man with a larger stack of bills.

The man with their father's square chin and brown eyes, their mother's blond hair. Beau.

# Chapter 11

WADE'S WORST NIGHTMARE. THE brother of the woman he loved learning the seedier side of poker from Wade's own flesh and blood. At least Uncle Buck didn't sit at the table with them. Small comfort.

Sweat broke out on Wade's forehead. He should get them out of there, but neither would thank him for interrupting. He stepped into the shadows. The noisy crowd might hide him until he could figure out if the pair knew each other.

Four other men filled out the table. Before the final bets, two men dropped out. Gordon and Beau stayed in. A fellow with his back to Wade won with two pair, sevens and deuces.

Crestfallen, Gordon counted his remaining cash. Four dollars.

"Cost you five to ante in, laddie." A red-haired man looked at Gordon, who picked up his cash and stood.

A bearded man slipped onto the vacated seat.

Beau stared at the winning hand.

Wade's blood ran cold. He recognized the look—his brother'd caught the man cheating. With no law in Abilene, more than one gambler had ended up on the wrong end of the gun here. Dead-wrong end. He stepped into the lantern's light, his gaze fastened on his brother.

Beau glanced up.

They didn't greet each other. The moment demanded more. *Don't challenge him, Beau. It's not worth your life.* Wade tensed.

"Since my friend here had to leave"—Beau gathered his cash as if he had all night—"I'll give my seat to one of the gentlemen waiting." Without counting it, the money went into a pouch.

Gordon moved closer to Wade.

A cowboy, glass of beer in hand, pulled up the chair vacated by Beau. "Don't mind if I do."

"You didn't play badly." Beau strode over and clapped Gordon on the back. "Gotta know when to walk away."

They knew each other. Just how long had Beau been in Abilene?

Wade's chest deflated. The kid was fourteen. No need to thrust him into the world of gambling.

Beau extended his hand. "Wade, old boy. Just the fellow I wanted to see."

Wade clasped the uncallused hand. His brother's Texas drawl never sounded so good. "Missed you, brother. Let's get out of here."

Outside, a fresh breeze blew the smoky smell from Wade's nostrils. "How long you been in Abilene?"

"Couple days." Lantern light revealed Beau's lazy smile.

Gordon shot a look at him before lowering his head toward the dusty street.

Wade winced. Lies were starting already. "Gordon here is the brother of my boss, Miss Abigail Cox."

"A woman?" Beau's brow furrowed. "Thought Lance Nye was trail boss." He quirked an eyebrow at Gordon.

Intercepting the look, Wade's chest tightened. Beau already knew. Why hide something like that? "Lance is still trail boss. Don't need as many cowboys to watch the herd off the trail. This job with Abby has been a godsend."

"You eat good, don't you?" Gordon's chin jutted forward.

"Yep." It wasn't really a question. "Haven't eaten this good since Ma died."

Beau's eyes widened before he looked away.

"Worse part about leaving the restaurant is missing Abby's meals." Gordon rubbed his belly. "Bet there weren't no chicken left from supper."

Wade folded his arms. "Nope."

"Anything left? I'm starving." He turned toward the darkened restaurant.

"Took some cabbage and beet soup to the cellar tonight." It was plain that Gordon hadn't been at his pa's ranch. The question was, where had he been?

Beau poked him in the side with his elbow. "They'll feed you at the boarding house."

"Boarding house? Aren't you staying at your pa's ranch? That's where Miss Abby believes you are."

Dim lantern light didn't hide the boy's flushed face. "What if I ain't? It's no concern of yours."

Beau shifted his weight.

"How'd you two meet?" Wade asked.

Gordon glanced at Beau. "I saw Beau playing poker. Asked him to teach me the rules."

Abby'd never forgive him now. His gambling brother taught her school-aged brother to play poker. His dreams of marrying her slipped through his fingers like the dust blowing on Texas Street. Wade swiped his hand across his brow. "Where are you staying?"

"Hotel." Beau kicked up a dust cloud.

"Which one?"

"Winnesheik House."

A cheap lodging favored by cowboys. Was that where Gordon stayed too? He'd seemed surprised by Beau's reference to a boarding house. "I bed down near our herd about a mile outside of town. I have a tent, but most nights I sleep under the stars. Stay there. Save your money. Be like old times."

"Maybe in a few days." Beau didn't look at him.

When his money was gone. Wade sighed.

"You're full of questions." Beau grinned. "We gonna stand on this boardwalk all night?"

"What did you have in mind?"

"Saloons are lively places. How about a drink?"

"It's late." Stars lit up a canvas of black sky. Wade's shoulders slumped. Uncle Buck's actions had turned one brother away from drinking and gambling and the other one toward them. "Gotta be at work before sunup."

"You always did work too hard." Beau brushed dust from his black coat and blue vest. "Aren't you gonna ask why I'm here?"

Wade eyed him. "What brings you to Abilene?"

"You." Laughing, Beau clapped him on the back. "I came to see my big brother."

Lately that meant only one thing. Wade squelched a groan behind a grin.

Beau needed money.

# Chapter 12

"INSTEAD OF GOING TO a saloon, let's walk along the Smoky Hill River."

"That muddy river?" Gordon snorted.

"True." Wade raised his eyebrows. "The cottonwoods lining both sides of the riverbank provide welcome shade during the day." Maybe Abby would stroll along the town's river with him on a Sunday afternoon. Maybe learn to trust him. He gave a slight shake of his head. Who was he fooling? Beau hammered a nail on those dreams when he taught her brother how to gamble.

"Once you've lived beside the mighty Mississippi, nothing else measures up." Gordon peered at the eastern sky.

"We've seen the Mississippi. During the war." Beau widened his stance. "I'd like to see it again. Maybe ride a steamboat. Might be fun to gamble on the Mississippi. Make better memories on that river."

"That's no way to create good memories." Wade frowned. No need to turn Gordon's head any more than it was. "You two ready to go back to your hotel?"

"Reckon so." Beau gave him a lazy grin.

"I'm heading back to the herd. Come by the restaurant tomorrow, Beau. I'll buy your meal." They needed privacy. His brother wasn't going to speak his mind with Gordon around. "Lunch or supper or both?"

"Maybe both. See you tomorrow." Beau tipped his hat. "Let's go, Gordon."

The pair strode in the direction of the hotel.

Wade ambled away from the crowded street. Doubts about Beau going straight to his hotel had him doubling back before the noise of town was behind him. If both Beau and Gordon were low in cash, they might gamble for smaller stakes.

He strode through Texas Street twice without finding them. Maybe they went back to the hotel after all, but Wade had a bad feeling. He didn't know what the pair was hiding, but he intended to find out.

There it was again. Abby sat straight up in bed. A footstep. On the boardwalk?

Someone breaking into the restaurant? If so, was this the real thief? She so wanted it to be someone else—anyone but Wade. In her heart, she knew he'd never do anything to hurt her.

Another footstep. Her heart leaped then pounded against her ribs. She had no rifle to defend her property. Wade would protect her, but he wasn't here.

No marshal to appeal to for help.

She scrunched the sheet to her chin. The lantern beside her bed had been dark for what seemed like hours. Wishing her brother still slept in the bedroom across the hall wouldn't make him appear.

A door creaked. The cellar door. A thief coming to steal the money?

Tossing the sheet, she swung her legs over the side of the bed. She'd hurry down and throw the cellar door closed and secure it with heavy crates and skillets, trapping the thief inside until … until what?

She halted at her bedroom door. No one would know her plight until Wade or Mr. Hixson arrived in the morning.

Dangerous at worst. Foolhardy at best.

At least her money was safe under the floorboards.

She sank onto her bed. Dishes clanked from below. Was someone eating in her kitchen?

She crept off the bed. Placed her ear against the rough floor. A spoon or fork scraped against a porcelain dish—a familiar sound.

She pushed herself up and rested on her knees. A hungry man who couldn't afford the price of her meals?

That possible explanation slowed her rapid heartbeat. She'd be safe if she just stayed put. No one could get to the second floor from inside the restaurant.

She prayed for protection until the muted noises stopped.

# Chapter 13

NEARING THE RESTAURANT BEFORE dawn, Wade rubbed his eyes. As late as it was—or as early—some saloons still had a few customers. His jaw cracked on a half-smothered yawn.

The tempting aroma of baking biscuits seeped through the closed kitchen door. Funny. They kept the door open to coax in a fresh breeze at all hours. He tapped on it.

Abby opened it. "Glad you're early." She grabbed his arm, pulled him inside, and closed the door behind him.

He'd come early to fry bacon or sausage on the outdoor fire the past three weeks. Her fingers trembled against his arm. "What is it?"

She pointed toward the counter. Two bowls. An empty soup tureen. "Somebody broke into the restaurant last night."

He rubbed the back of his neck. Gordon had complained of hunger. "You check the dining room?"

"Not yet." Abby flapped her hands toward her face. "What if he's still here?"

His jaw set, he touched his six-shooter. War had taught him how to use it if he had to. When was this town going to hire a marshal? "Stay in the kitchen. If you hear shots, run to the Hixsons."

She tugged on his arm. "Can't we wait until the sun rises? Give the thief time to sneak away?"

"Best do it now." He covered her hand with his. "I doubt anyone's in there."

"Be careful." Her troubled green eyes met his.

Tempted to kiss her, he stepped back instead. "Remember what I said."

Abby, a knot in her throat, glanced at the closed back door—her escape if the worst happened. This town was too dangerous when a woman alone didn't feel safe in her own home.

Wade had been gone only seconds. What if the robber overwhelmed him, took him to the floor before Wade drew his gun?

Her fingers closed around a kettle's handle. A wallop on the head with this sturdy kettle ought to end a fight if Wade had trouble.

Raising the kettle over her head with both hands, she crept toward the dining room door.

A knock on the back door. Abby swallowed. "Who is it?"

"Brian Hixson."

Legs wobbling, she ushered him inside. "Someone broke into the restaurant last night," she whispered, pointing to the dirty dishes, "and Wade's checking the dining room."

He straightened his shoulders. "I'll help him."

"Here." Abby offered the kettle. "Whack him in the head with this."

Mr. Hixson frowned. "That could kill someone. Wait here."

He reached for the door as it opened. "Wade. Find anyone?"

Entering the room, he shook his head. "Maybe he just ate and left."

"I don't like this one bit." Mr. Hixson glanced at Abby. "She's scared to death. We can't ignore this."

"You're right." Wade studied her. "I'll sleep in the kitchen. Starting tonight."

"I can't ask you to sleep on this hard floor." Abby held her breath. If only he'd insist.

"Ain't nothing after sleeping on the hard ground for months." He met her gaze squarely. "I'd not sleep a wink for worrying about you."

Her face flamed. He must have some feelings for her. And he couldn't be the thief. Last night's visitors proved it.

"Seems best to me. Living quarters are closed off to the restaurant. No one can get to you that way, Abby." Mr. Hixson glanced from Wade to Abby. "Try it for a night or two."

"I'd feel safer." Wade was a good man after all.

He smiled. "Consider it done."

Her tension eased. Perhaps her loneliness would ease as well.

Breakfast preparations refocused Abby's thoughts from last night's break-in. While clearing the tables afterward, a tall man with thick auburn hair came in. "We're closed until eleven o'clock."

"Not here for breakfast, miss." The man handed her a paper. He wore a badge. "I'm Tom Smith, the town's marshal."

"Miss Abigail Cox. I'm very happy to meet you."

He inclined his head. "If you'll just follow my instructions ..."

Scanning the page, Abby gasped.

"That's right, miss. Guns are not to be carried in Abilene." He rocked back on his heels. "Our town has a new ordinance. If you'll just post that notice and collect your customers' weapons, I'll be obliged."

"Marshal Smith, I don't even like guns. What am I going to do with them?"

"Lock them up." His alert eyes scanned the empty dining room. "Return them when the visitors leave town."

Her stomach lurched. The lawman made it sound easy. "When does this begin?"

"Today." He gestured to the dishes on the table. "Breakfast crowd is gone. Start collecting at lunch. Get the notice in the window right away."

Today? She'd built a rapport with regular customers over the past weeks. They might comply, but how would new customers take this request? Shoot up her dining room?

He strode to the door. "Much obliged, Miss Cox." He tipped his hat and strode away.

She glanced at the paper in her hands: *ALL FIREARMS ARE EXPECTED TO BE DEPOSITED WITH THE PROPRIETOR.*

She rubbed her clammy forehead. Didn't she have enough to contend with?

# Chapter 14

AFTER WRESTLING WITH WHETHER to tell Abby about finding Gordon playing poker, Wade decided to wait and talk with Beau first. But while Gordon showed up for meals, Beau didn't.

Every time Abby collected another firearm, she brought it to Wade, which he appreciated because of her inexperience with guns. What had the new marshal been thinking? Placing the responsibility for collection of weapons on business owners seemed unfair—especially if other proprietors reacted like Abby.

But no one asked Wade's opinion.

He'd stood beside the dining room door when Abby made the first timid requests for firearms.

Folks had looked at each other. Then someone commented, "Bein's somebody's gotta take ma gun, I'd ruther give it ta Miss Abby."

Others agreed. She tagged the guns and gave them over to Wade's care. He stored them in a small trunk in the cellar.

A busy afternoon included toting multiple buckets of water. He stole a glance at Abby as she placed another apple pie in the oven. She caught him staring and blushed so prettily that his heart sang … until he remembered his brother.

Christina worked with them all day. He didn't have a moment alone with Abby until the girl left at five o'clock. Then the supper crowd arrived. Between collecting and tagging firearms and serving the meal, Wade barely had time to watch for his brother.

If Beau didn't come, he'd search for him. Tonight. The longer Gordon kept deceiving Abby, the more he'd hurt her when she finally discovered it. And the potential for the gambling way of life to take root in the boy.

What was Beau's motive?

To be fair, Gordon had already discovered faro. And if he exposed Wade's knowledge of his gambling to his sister, the trust Wade had worked hard to nourish would wither before his eyes.

She loved that boy.

He plunged another stack of plates into soapy water with a glance over his shoulder at the clock. Fifteen minutes until closing time. Where was Beau?

Abby pushed open the dining room door. "A new customer just came in. Says he wants to give his gun to you."

"Who is it?" Wade wiped the sweat from his brow.

"He has your eyes, your square chin. Same blond hair." She put her hands on her hips. "Says his name is Beau Chadwick. That you invited him here."

Wade gave a slow smile. Beau came. "Yes, I saw him last night. Today's been hectic."

"I reckon that's so. Collecting firearms for the new ordinance has me all aflutter." Her face relaxed into a smile. "Collect his gun and then eat supper with him. He's on his own."

"Mighty kind of you." Her observation was truer than she knew. "Can you finish up? I need a long talk with Beau."

"You haven't told me much about him ... other than he makes his living as a gambler."

"He wasn't always this way. The war and our uncle changed him." Her words filled him with shame. Their mother must weep from heaven for her son. "I'll come back to guard the restaurant tonight. Do you know what the thieves took?" He rinsed and dried his hands, tensely waiting for her answer.

She sighed. "A sack of food—vegetables and cans. Not sure what all. I'll make an order for Hixson's Groceries tonight. Spend the evening with your brother. No charge for his supper."

He clasped her hand to his chest. "Thank you, Abby."

Her green eyes glowed up at him. "My pleasure ... Wade."

Abby finished cleaning the kitchen an hour after locking the doors behind the last customer. Wade had introduced her to his charming brother before they left.

A consistent hot breeze blew her skirt around her legs as she gathered napkins from the clothesline. Shaking the Kansas dust from them, she peered in every direction, squinting to the west against the setting sun. No sign of Wade yet. The brothers must have lots to discuss.

Men's laughter and boisterous talk from the street seemed quieter this evening. There hadn't been any shots fired all day. Contentment washed over her. It must be that new marshal. Maybe it was worth the extra bother to collect the guns for him.

That wasn't all that caused her smile this evening. Memories of Wade clasping her hand to his chest brought a heated flush to her face. He was a good man … and he seemed to reciprocate her feelings.

He'd return tonight. Sleep on a pallet she'd prepared for him in her kitchen to keep her safe from robbers. She'd have to give him his wages when he returned. He'd left without them. Probably distracted with his brother here and all.

At least her money was safe. Gordon had stayed around after eating lunch today. Pa needed as much money as she could spare, and he'd sent her brother a day early to get it. Father and son working as a team had made lots of progress digging holes for new fence posts. Taking him upstairs to her room, she was able to give him eighty dollars. Putting money into their ranch made her brother's face light up.

Her hard work had paid off. Anticipation of her pa's pleasure enhanced the glow in her heart that Wade had begun. She'd proven that she could run the restaurant. Pa must be pleased.

And he'd be pleased when he came to town and met Wade. Gordon said that Pa was happy she'd hired him.

She was happy he'd proven himself to be a good man.

She loved him, and he'd given her reason to believe he returned her love. She twirled around in the kitchen then looked out the window to be sure nobody had seen her. What would people think? That she was happy. She laughed and finished putting the kitchen to rights.

As twilight turned to darkness, she climbed the stairs to her living quarters, glad she'd given Wade a key to the restaurant after supper. A smile touched her lips at the brothers' reunion happening somewhere in Abilene.

"Abby? That you, girl?"

The key in her hand slipped to the landing. "Pa!" Picking up her skirt, she ran down the stairs and threw herself into his arms. "Pa, I've missed you."

"I've missed my Abby girl." John Cox hugged her and then stepped back. "Let me look at you. Ain't you a sight for sore eyes. Gordon already up there?"

"No, he ate lunch here today and left." She bit her lip. "He should have been back at the ranch hours ago. It's been a good week, Pa. I know the two of you have been working hard on those fence posts, but I'm busy too. Besides the seventy-five dollars I sent with him last Sunday, there's another eighty dollars you'll get from him today. Isn't that wonderful?"

His face turned ashen in the moonlight. "Gordon's not working with you here?"

"No." A chill washed over her despite the heat. "He's been with you on the ranch." Her voice rose. "I hired Wade Chadwick and Christina Hixson to help me. Didn't he tell you?"

"No." His voice came in a raspy, hoarse monotone. "He hasn't been with me. He brought me twelve dollars twice in the past month."

They stared at each other.

Pa reached for the banister, his knuckles white.

"If he wasn't on the ranch, where was he?" The chill spread to her core. Her brother had lied to her. Repeatedly. Stolen from their father. Why?

"That's what I'm going to find out." His expression grim, he turned toward the street.

"I'll go with you." She climbed to retrieve her key from the landing and dropped it in her pocket.

He shook his head. "Ain't proper for a lady to go where I believe I'll find him. I'll bring him back here. Then we'll decide what's best to do."

The slump of her father's shoulders and the heavy clump of his boots against the boardwalk tore at her heart. He'd been so happy to see her. Oh, what had her brother done?

Throat tight with unshed tears, her mind traveled back to that evening when Wade had found Gordon at a saloon. She'd given him the benefit of the doubt, believed it to be the first and only time he'd been inside such an establishment.

Had she missed the signs? He'd been in her care. Her chin quivered. Wade. Had he known?

Better if Pa didn't have to deal with this matter alone.

She faltered on the bottom step. Things had turned ugly the last time she'd ventured out after dark. Wade and Gordon had saved her that night.

No. She'd made too many mistakes already. Pa asked her to stay. Best wait for them here.

# Chapter 15

AFTER SPENDING TWO HOURS meeting Beau's new buddies in two different saloons, Wade was done with his brother's stalling tactics.

"Let's go to the Alamo next." Beau indicated three sets of glass doors.

"Later. How about we find a quiet place to talk first." They hadn't seen Gordon. "See the stockyards? They're down from the Drover's Cottage."

Beau shrugged. "Yeah. We should talk."

That sounded ominous. He'd heard it before. He led them toward a lesser populated section of town along the railroad. "What about?"

"I still owe Maury Fowler that twenty-five dollars." A train's whistle blew, then blew again while Wade gathered his thoughts.

"Don't you mean fifteen? I gave you ten of that before leaving Texas."

"Lost it at poker."

They strode past the depot. "That was about all the money I had, and you threw it away." Wade clenched his jaw.

"No, it wasn't enough. Thought I could at least double it." His tone lost its bravado.

"Then you left Texas."

"Followed my big brother up the Chisholm Trail." He grinned. "Stopped in Ellsworth and Wichita. Won there but not enough. Then I came to Abilene. Been losing again."

That all had the ring of truth. They were getting somewhere. "How long have you been here?" Wade rubbed coal smoke from his eyes. He'd never been in a town where one train pulled out, and another took its place.

"A week."

"Did you know where I was?"

"Met Gordon the first day. He told me all about himself, his sister's restaurant, and where she hid her money."

Wade stopped outside the Drover's Cottage. "Tell me you didn't—"

"I didn't." Beau faced him, the lantern from the building's porch illuminating his vulnerable expression. "Anyone could see Gordon was wet behind the ears. He told me he lost thirty dollars the day before at poker. He was like a sheep heading to slaughter. I suddenly saw myself at his age."

"Before Uncle Buck taught you everything he knew."

"Yep."

The back of Wade's neck burned. "I tried to save you from him."

"I know. I was too bullheaded." He followed the dirt road. "I'd fought two years. Lost the war. Lost Pa. Uncle Buck lost us the ranch. I was done losing."

"Even the best gamblers lose sometimes." Wade fell into step beside him.

"And the cheaters eventually end up on the wrong side of a gun. Witnessed that early on." Beau kicked a rock. "Uncle Buck neglected to teach me that truth. Never cheated again. But I recognize it easy enough." He stared at Wade. "Why'd you stop me from confronting that cheater last night? Between us, he stole twenty dollars from Gordon and me."

Wade clasped Beau's shoulder and stopped in the middle of the road. "Is twenty dollars worth your life?"

Beau sighed. "Reckon it is until I get enough to pay Maury Fowler."

"You're worth far more than a gambling debt, Beau. Jesus died on a cross for you. Don't you remember what we learned from Ma reading the Good Book to us?"

"Reckon I forgot that for a time." Moonlight illuminated his flushed face.

"I'll have eleven dollars saved from my job at the restaurant once I get paid. How much do you have?"

"Six dollars." He sighed. "Not enough."

"I'll earn enough to add to that in three weeks. Then we'll send the cash to Maury in Texas."

"You'd do that for me?" Beau's face crumpled. "After all I cost you?"

"You're my brother." Wade squeezed his shoulder. "What do you say to you having a conversation with Gordon?"

Beau looked him squarely in the eye. "I figure I got something to say to him. Now."

The air inside the kitchen stifled Abby as she paced. Patience had never been her virtue.

She stepped outside the restaurant to peer in the direction Pa took. The new marshal rode by on a big gray horse, his stalwart presence a comfort.

Folks moved about on the street and boardwalk in the darkness. Eyes straining to penetrate dim lantern light from buildings, Abby searched for Pa's purposeful stride, her brother's slumped figure.

No one she recognized.

With a sigh that came from her soul, she turned to step back inside.

A hand snaked around her waist from behind. "Gotcha now, Miss High and Mighty."

Her stomach dropped to her knees.

Wade and Beau found Gordon sitting at a poker table. A tall man, hand pressed to his stomach, watched the boy from the shadows. Gray sprinkled his brown hair. Worry lined his square face, so similar to Gordon's that it had to be his pa.

The game ended. Gordon scowled when the cowboy on his right raked in bills and coins.

Abby's pa waited for his son to catch his eye and then motioned him outside.

Cheeks scarlet, Gordon picked up a small wad of bills and followed.

Wade and Beau hung back while the pair had a private conversation a few feet from the saloon. Gordon averted his gaze in the brothers' direction and waved them over. He introduced them to his father.

"Gordon tells me you work for my daughter." Mr. Cox shook his hand.

"Yes, sir." Wade nodded, liking Mr. Cox's controlled stance. "For the last month."

"Doing a good job by her." They stood eye to eye.

"Thank you, sir."

Mr. Cox's face tightened. "And this is your brother who taught my son the rules of poker. Gordon is fourteen years old, Mr. Chadwick."

"Yes, sir." Beau pushed his hat farther down his forehead. "Since he was playing anyway, I tried to keep him from losing every cent he owns. I'm sorry for my part."

"I'd have won it all back." Gordon's face hardened.

A woman screamed from the direction of—

Wade tore down the street toward the restaurant.

The cowboy cut off Abby's scream with his other hand. "I told you I'd get you if you came out alone after dark. I've been watching you."

Gasping for air, she kicked his shins, the building, and then ground her heel on his toes.

He squealed like a pig. "Now you've done it." He lifted her off the ground. "Where's your beau now?" His lips were on her ear.

"Right here."

Strong arms jerked the vile man away from her.

One blow from a mighty fist took the cowboy to the ground. He collapsed into an unmoving heap.

Pulse racing, Abby sagged against Wade.

Gathering her to his chest, Wade whispered hoarsely, "He hurt you?"

"No."

"Abby girl?"

Wade's arms dropped away.

"I'm unharmed, Pa." She hugged him and stepped back to look up at him.

"What happened here?"

She turned at the gruff question. The marshal dismounted and stood over the prone man. She explained.

"I'll just have a little talk with him, Miss Cox." Marshal Smith pulled the cowboy up by the scruff of his neck. "He won't be botherin' you again."

The cowboy shook his head, rubbing his jaw as the lawman half-dragged him away.

"I should never have left you and Gordon here alone." Hands shaking, John studied his children.

"No, Pa. I asked to stay here. Make as much as I could to put toward building the ranch."

"No ranch is worth what my children have gone through."

"But I get more customers every day." Abby's hands covered her face at his torment. "I did well."

He turned to his son. "Abby gave you eighty dollars today. How much is left?"

Wade sucked in his breath.

"Is that what she told you? She gave me twenty-two dollars." Gordon lifted his chin. "Who you gonna believe, her or me?"

"What, now I'm a liar, Gordon?" Abby took a step closer to him. "I trusted you. I suspected Christina or Wade." Cheeks flaming, she looked at Wade. "Forgive me for doubting you." Her gaze returned to her brother. "I knew money was missing."

Gordon stiffened. "You're no good with figures is all."

"How long, Gordon? How long have you helped yourself to our profits?" Abby's green eyes darkened.

"I had a right to it. I worked as hard as you. No one ever listened to me until Beau taught me to gamble."

A dull flush spread across her face.

"Mr. Cox, may I speak with Gordon privately?" Beau spoke softly. "I learned some things about myself, my mistakes that may help."

"Why should we trust you?" Abby burst out. "Haven't you caused enough pain, Mr. Chadwick?"

Wade winced for his brother's sake.

"Understood." Beau straightened his shoulders. "Can't blame you. No one has trusted me for a long time except Wade … and Gordon." He turned on his heel and strode away.

Wade's heart broke for his brother's pain. "Miss Abby, you don't know Beau. You also don't know how hard I've fought to save him from the path he's walking."

Eyebrows raised, she tilted her head up at him.

He hated that she hurt for her brother. Hated that his brother had a hand in his downfall. Hated that he must put away his dreams of marrying her. "Don't destroy my brother while trying to save yours."

Emotionally spent, he strode after Beau to pick up the pieces yet again.

# Chapter 16

ABBY DRAGGED HERSELF OUT of bed, every muscle crying for more sleep. The first Sunday morning in weeks with her pa and Gordon sleeping in their rooms across the hall. The realization should have brought happiness—but yesterday had drained her joy.

Pa and Gordon had talked late into the night, their voices sometimes rose to her room above the kitchen.

Did their conversation resolve anything? Her mind so befuddled with Wade's last comment, Abby scarcely knew what to think. Had her words destroyed his brother?

She washed with water from her pitcher and basin and then made her way to the kitchen. No Wade. It was Sunday, but he'd offered to sleep in the kitchen to keep thieves away.

Wade hadn't stayed. Pa's presence made his sacrifice unnecessary. Before Abby went to bed, Gordon had confessed to "helping himself" to the food. He'd slept in the dining room most nights or slept in his own room during the day while she worked.

If only she'd known.

Pa and Gordon had consumed an apple pie that had been stored in the cellar and made themselves a pot of coffee. Grimacing at the mess, she gathered the things needed to make breakfast. She hated cooking on Sundays and had fallen into the habit of eating biscuits, cobbler— whatever food was left over from the week to avoid preparing a meal. But Pa would expect more.

Out of water. Wade's task during the week. He'd never complained about multiple daily trips to the well. He'd spoiled her.

She set the fourth bucket on the kitchen floor and mopped her brow.

If only Wade had told her of Gordon's continued gambling. She pondered his reasons for concealing the truth as sausage sizzled on the outdoor fire pit. The aroma of Pa's favorite breakfast ought to awaken him soon. She brought the cooked meat inside.

Emotions warred within her as she rolled biscuit dough—anger, frustration, doubt, shame. How could she trust Wade again?

Footsteps thumped outside the door. The dough dropped into a pile of flour in a cloud of white. Wade?

Pa stepped inside. "Sausage smells good." He stretched. "Hard night."

"How long did you talk?" Abby rolled the dough.

"Couple of hours after you went to bed." He touched the coffee pot. "Cold. Reckon I'll make it."

"How's Gordon?"

"Unremorseful. He'll work on the ranch with me. But we'll return here each day by sundown. My mind's made up on that one." His jaw set. "It was wrong to leave you here while I worked the ranch."

A weight lifted from Abby. True, she'd talked him into concentrating on the ranch while she earned money for their expenses, but she hadn't anticipated Gordon's unhappiness. Or his deceit.

Pa dropped a handful of roasted coffee beans in the coffee grinder on the counter. "He hates working in this kitchen."

The aroma of freshly ground coffee wafted over, making Abby thirsty. "I tried, Pa." She sighed. "I didn't know what to do. He wanted to go to the ranch. I sent him to you, never dreaming he'd go to the saloons instead."

"I was too mired in my grief to notice." His shoulders slumped. "I wanted to give my children a home. Build a ranch near a new, growing town, but purchasing the land took all our money. The restaurant's profits have to pay for the fencing, a new home. Is it too much to ask of you, running this business?"

"No. I like it. And I've hired more help." She placed the prepared biscuit pan into the oven, grimacing as the heat struck her face. "Gordon needs to be with you." She dusted the flour from her hands on her apron. "Earning a wage for a new hat, a new frock now and then would make me happy."

"You paid Gordon but not yourself?" He poured water into the blue coffee pot. "I didn't think it through. Start paying yourself a wage."

"I will." She gave a shaky laugh.

He met her eyes. "Save money for your future. You might want to get married someday. Maybe to a man like Wade."

Blood drained from her face. "No, I ... I mean, not that I wouldn't like ..." Recalling the desolation in his eyes when she scorned his brother's help, Abby covered her face with her hands. "Oh, Pa. I've made such a mess of things."

"By not trusting Wade."

She nodded.

"I don't know him well, but he strikes me as a fine, upstanding man worried about his brother *and* yours." He patted her shoulder.

She tried to swallow the lump in her throat. "He didn't even mention Gordon was in town."

"Probably meant to protect you."

It matched what she knew of him. Like all the little things he did to make her job easier. "It's too late. I hurt him and his brother."

"Reckon you did." Pa moved the coffee to the stove. "Letting Beau talk to Gordon will go a long way toward healin' that blow."

Her chin lifted. A gambler talking Gordon out of gambling? Not likely. "That'd be jumping from the frying pan into the fire, that's certain."

"Been ponderin' it all night." Dark shadows lay thick under his troubled eyes. "Gordon ain't himself. If anyone can bring him around, it's someone who's walked his path and come out on the other side."

"Or push him further away."

He rubbed his gray-streaked hair until it stood on end. "That's a chance I'm willing to take to save my son." He raised pain-filled eyes to her. "Are you?"

Gambling had such a hold as that on her brother? "I trust Wade."

He nodded. "And Wade trusts his brother to say and do the right thing."

Wade's words came back to smote her. *Don't destroy my brother while trying to save yours.* "Wade's been escorting me to church, but I doubt he'll stop here today."

"We're going to church as a family today. I'll get Gordon up while you finish breakfast." His expression was grave. "Hope the Chadwick brothers meet up with us there."

# Chapter 17

"You promised him what?" Wade took a step backward, jostling a dining room chair.

"One more game." Sweat beaded on Beau's forehead. "All in. I put up all my money for everything he has in his pockets."

"That money ain't his." Mr. Cox's lips thinned. "No telling how much he's already lost that's rightly mine. 'Spect it's better than two hundred dollars."

Slumping into a chair, Wade didn't doubt it. He'd given most of his hard-earned money to Beau over the past four years.

Abby folded her arms, an inscrutable expression crossing her face.

"Gordon's got the fever. Bad." Beau put his hat on the table where the rest sat. Pulling up a chair, he sat beside his brother. "It took a lot of persuading, but he's promised that this will be his final hand—if he loses."

A chill formed in the pit of Wade's stomach.

"Wh-what if he wins?" Abby's hands shook.

"Then he'll gamble again in the future."

Silence.

"I don't intend to lose. It's too important." Beau met Mr. Cox's gaze squarely. "But if I do, I've bought you some time. He'll work on the ranch with you. Build your home. Put up fencing around the property. For two years."

"A lot can happen in two years." John Cox leaned back in his chair. "I talked with my son for hours. I agree with your assessment. Can't forgive myself for not seeing the danger to him by leaving an impressionable boy in the middle of all the shenanigans in Abilene." He clutched the edge of the table. "I'll agree to this."

The tension didn't ease from Beau's face. "Wade, I had to include that eleven dollars you gave me toward my gambling debt."

That ranch he dreamed of building for Abby never seemed so far away—but supporting his brother might save his future. If Beau lost,

Wade would quit his job and leave Abilene when the longhorns sold and he drew his last pay. He'd barely been able to meet her eyes since her scornful refusal of Beau's help last night. She must scorn Wade also, for his part in hiding the truth about Gordon. "Agreed." He extended his hand.

Beau grasped it. "I'll make you proud of me."

"You already have."

Mr. Cox stood. "Let's see about getting Gordon in here." He shook Beau's hand. "Much obliged for all you've done."

Abby wrung her hands. Waiting in the kitchen while such an important card game played on Sunday—in her restaurant—stretched her nerves to the breaking point.

She had exchanged a quick greeting with Wade after church services ended hours ago. He avoided her eyes as they all ate leftover sausage and biscuits for lunch. Gordon and Beau took a walk. Pa and Wade sat in the dining room and talked about his paying his brother's gambling debts multiple times. She learned that his uncle gambled away his family's property, and then taught Beau how to gamble.

It seemed to run in the family. Did she want to align herself with them? But then, it was in her family now too.

Too agitated to sit still, she had started a grocery list and then set it aside unfinished.

Now she simply wanted the card game to be over. What was happening in there anyway? Abby pressed her ear to the dining room door.

"I'll take three cards." Gordon's voice had lost its arrogant tone.

Paper scraped across wood.

"And I'll draw two cards." Beau sounded casual as if asking for a second biscuit at a family dinner.

Three cards, two cards. What did that mean?

She stepped away from the door. Pa had never gambled to her knowledge, and she'd never been around poker, so the rules made no sense to her.

Clasping her hands together, she stared at the closed door. Gordon's promise to quit gambling forever if he lost showed his confidence in his abilities.

This was Beau's last game. Wade's worries were coming to an end.

Was her nightmare just beginning? Snippets of Wade's conversation with her father haunted her.

No matter the outcome, she owed Wade an apology. He'd supported her throughout this ordeal. Sprang to her rescue several times. Heat rose at the memory of how tenderly he held her in his arms after rescuing her from the cowboy. He must love her.

If he didn't tell her, she'd ask him. Point-blank.

There'd been too many secrets for too long. It was time to expose the truth.

Wade's stomach lurched when Gordon triumphantly showed a pair of queens. Good hand. Hopefully not good enough. His brother's face was devoid of emotion. *No. Just this once more, I'm pulling for you to win.*

Beau turned up a four of hearts. Then a four of clubs. Then a four of diamonds.

He'd done it. A four-year-old burden lifted from Wade's heart. Beau had a better idea of the tragedy he averted that day than either man standing tensely around him.

"I lost." Gordon's face crumpled. "I can't believe it."

"If you only knew how many times I've lost everything." Beau gave an understanding nod. "Gordon, you've got a second chance. A family that loves you." He glanced at Wade and back at Gordon. "Don't toss that away."

"I said I'd quit, and I will." Gordon shoved his chair back. He stared at the cash still in the middle of the table. "I'm done. Sorry, Pa. I lost more than you know."

"And you just gave me back more than you realize." John Cox put an arm around his son's shoulder. "Let's tell your sister." They went into the kitchen. The door swung shut behind them.

Beau stared at the money at the table. "This is the first time … in a long time … that I felt good about winning. And it's my last time to play."

"You mean it." Wade hardly dared to hope. What he'd prayed four long years to hear.

"This isn't enough to pay what I owe you." Closing his eyes, he shook his head. "All the money on this table is only a down payment on it."

"Pay off your debt to Maury. Then maybe you and I can combine our money and buy property for a ranch." He smiled at the hope rising in his brother's eyes. "Land is cheap around Abilene though it will take years to build a herd."

"Feels good to have a future again." Hope dawned in Beau's eyes. "What if one of us gets married?"

"A section of land is six hundred forty acres." Wade certainly hoped he'd marry sooner rather than later. "We'll build two houses at opposite ends."

Grinning, Beau leaped to his feet. "That ought to be enough land for two brothers and their families."

"If it's not, we'll buy more." Wade shook his hand and then pulled him close, thumping him on the back. Beau had finally come home.

Now he had to find out if Abby loved him enough to build that home with him.

# Chapter 18

ABBY'S BROTHER HAD LOST the game. He'd promised to make it his last. More than anything, Gordon needed time with his father. They'd disappeared out the back door of the restaurant a few minutes ago.

And Pa had put his grief for his wife aside long enough to see it. Abby couldn't be more thankful to the Chadwick brothers. Especially Wade.

High time for *her* cowboy to pay attention to her.

She pushed open the dining room door. "Wade Chadwick, I need a word with you." Beau gave his brother a stack of bills. She raised her eyebrows.

"I'll settle with my hotel. And I've got a letter to send." Tipping his hat at Abby, Beau strode outside.

"Looks like your brother saved my brother." Abby stepped closer to Wade. "And you saved both of them."

"I'm sorry my silence about Gordon hurt you." His face flushed.

"You meant to protect me." Smiling, her eyes searched his.

"It wasn't right to speak to you before"—he touched her face—"with too many secrets between us. I thought I could save Gordon without involving you in the pain."

She kissed his fingers. "I suspected you of thievery. Forgive me."

"You'd sooner suspect your own right hand than your brother. I understand."

"You and Christina were the only ones who went into the cellar every day." She leaned her face against his strong, calloused palm. "I never dreamed that Gordon ..."

"I know." He gathered her into his arms. "I tried to talk with him. He wouldn't listen."

"Thank you for that. I wondered why you were often in a hurry to leave." She sighed. "I had a hard time trusting a man who seemed to be stealing from me."

"Had I told you my suspicions about Gordon, you wouldn't have believed me."

"I'd have fired you." Cheeks blazing, she met his troubled eyes. "I wish you'd told me more about Beau."

He looked away. "I failed him. Nothing to brag about."

"You didn't give up on him." She held his face and stared up at him. "That is something to be proud of."

His gaze searched hers. "Can you give me hope that you'll learn to love me as I love you?"

He loved her. Her heart skipped a beat and then thundered on. "Oh, Wade, I love you."

No sooner had the words left her mouth than he kissed her. Her arms wrapped around his neck. She pulled him closer and kissed him back. Then she smiled up at him. "Well? Aren't you going to ask me to marry you?"

His laugh filled her with joy. "A mite forward, aren't you?"

She laughed.

He got down on one knee. "Miss Abby Cox, will you marry me?"

"Oh, yes." Happiness radiated from her. "I will marry you, Wade Chadwick."

He stood and clasped her against his heart.

"I've decided I like running *Miss Abby's Home Cooking*. And my family has searched for a place to settle since the war ended. The windy plains of Kansas have become my home. You won't try to uproot me to Texas, will you?"

"Nope." He grinned. "My trail ends in Abilene."

# AUTHOR'S NOTE

BEFORE I EVER DREAMED I'd pick up a pen again, my family took a vacation to Kansas to visit my brother and his family. We visited Abilene one afternoon. I learned a bit about the history of that wild western town … enough that I wanted to know more.

My sister-in-law has family ties to Abilene—another reason for my fascination. In fact, one of her ancestors was a friend of Wild Bill Hickok, who was marshal of Abilene in 1871, the year after our story. In 1870, Marshal Tom Smith insisted that the cowboys be disarmed. Storekeepers, saloonkeepers, and hotel owners were asked to post a sign and collect the guns of their customers. Marshal Smith knew what he was doing. He made the town a safer place. Sadly, he was killed later that year.

Stuart Henry's *Conquering Our Great American Plains* was a great resource for my story. Henry lived in Abilene from 1868–1872 as a boy. I *love* finding treasures like this author's book that allow me to take my readers back to 1870 Abilene, Kansas. What a gift.

When my editor approached me about writing a cowboy story set in the West, it did not take long for my imagination to take me back to Abilene. Who'd have guessed that a family vacation that took place before I decided to pursue a writing career would lead to a story?

I hope you enjoyed traveling back to the Wild West with me as much as I loved taking you there.

*Sandra Merville Hart*

# Acknowledgments

THIS IS NOW THE author's third adventure working with her talented editor, Pegg Thomas. She makes the journey fun even as I continuously learn—and alas! relearn—to become a better writer. Writing and editing is a lot of hard work. It's a wonderful blessing to find a friend along the way. Thank you for your patience, Pegg!

Thanks to Eddie Jones, Lighthouse Publishing of the Carolinas, for his continued encouragement. I've learned much from him.

Thanks also to my agent, Joyce Hart of Hartline Literary Agency, for believing in me first. Thank you, Joyce, for your support and enthusiasm along this journey.

Thanks to Stephanie, Brian, Kathy, Kristi, Jay, and Charlotte, who all inspired bits of this story. Love you!

Award-winning and Amazon bestselling author Sandra Merville Hart's debut Civil War romance, *A Stranger on My Land*, was IRCA Finalist 2015. *A Rebel in My House*, set during the historic Battle of Gettysburg, won the 2018 Silver Illumination Award and is a 2018 Faith, Hope, and Love Finalist. *A Musket in My Hands*, where two sisters join the Confederate army with the men they love, is the 2019 Serious Writer Medal Fiction Winner and a 2019 Selah Awards Finalist.

Sandra loves to uncover little-known yet fascinating facts about our American history to include in her stories. Whenever possible, she and her husband travel to the location of her stories. Visiting local museums, shopping, and eating at local restaurants gives her a sense of place and setting. Walking the same streets as her characters allows her imagination to soar, adding depth to her stories.

Connect with Sandra on her blog, Historical Nibbles:
https://sandramervillehart.wordpress.com/
Facebook: https://www.facebook.com/sandra.m.hart.7
Twitter: https://twitter.com/Sandra_M_Hart
Pinterest: http://www.pinterest.com/sandramhart7/

# Loving a Harvey Girl

By

Linda W. Yezak

# Dedication

*Dedicated to my old college buddy, Jerry Lee (gig 'em!).*
*His grandmother, Blažena Buček, came to America through Ellis Island*
*from a small town southwest of Prague in 1910 and became a Harvey*
*Girl around 1916. What an amazing part of history she was!*

# Chapter 1

*Texas, 1889*

CAL STEPHENS GAVE HIS reins a quick wrap around the hitchin' post in front of the mercantile and stepped up to the walkway, his first Saturday in his hometown since the cattle drive to Abilene. The *thunk* of his boots on the wooden planks accented the jingle of his spurs. Strange sound, leather soles on old wood, but he got used to it fast. He matched stride to the tinny beat from the saloon's old piano and *thunk-chinged* his way toward the barbershop.

Up ahead, the four Malone sisters huddled together in front of the post office, tittering over something or other. Cal tipped his hat, and Miss Melody Malone wrinkled her nose and fanned away his odor. No doubt it was strong. He couldn't remember when he'd bathed last.

A pretty blonde skirted the mass of sisters and plowed right into him. Her yellow hair wisped carelessly out from under a frilly hat that had probably seen better days. Long lashes fluttered over eyes bluer than the Texas sky, and cheeks flushed a rosy red.

"Pardon me," she muttered and stepped around him.

"My fault," he answered, tipping his hat to her back as she scurried down the walkway.

She grasped a worn leather satchel in front of her with both hands as if it were a mite heavy, and her dress bore the wrinkled look of someone who'd taken a long journey. Since the train was still drawing water from the tower, she'd probably stepped down from it not long ago. He'd never seen her before. But he sure wouldn't mind seeing her again. Soon as he got rid of the prairie brush on his jaw and the rank odor the sisters had scowled over.

Apparently, they'd never seen the blonde before either. Murmuring about her behind their hands, they watched as she marched with an unladylike stride toward the town's hotel. Wouldn't be long before they knew everything there was to know about the poor girl—and if they couldn't find it out, they'd make it up.

He crossed the threshold to the barbershop, giving way to a freshly-groomed townsman walking out.

Walter Neville swept up what looked like a half pound of hair and sent a stream of tobacco juice toward the spittoon. "Afternoon, Cal. Be right with ya."

"Ain't in no hurry." Cal rubbed his jaw and studied the handwritten sign over the fancy new National cash register. Walt had gone up two bits on both haircut and shave. Three bits on a bath. And heaven help anyone who needed a tooth pulled. "Folks round here get rich while we was gone?"

"Nope." Walt grabbed a fresh towel from a shelf stocked full of cloth, liniments, ointments, and other whatnots. "Took a little trip to Austin not long ago and discovered I've been going cheap."

"You figure we can do the big city prices?"

"These ain't big city prices. Just higher than my others." Walt glowered at him. "You here to gripe about how I do business or do you want me to shave that mess off your face?"

Cal pulled his silver from his pocket and turned his back to count it. He had enough for the works here, some new duds from the mercantile, and a quick beer at the saloon, but he didn't want Walt to know that. What Walt knew, everyone would know sooner or later. "Ain't gonna break me, I guess. Shave it, cut it, and set me up with a bath."

That seemed to please the old man. He bobbed his head and limped toward the bathhouse out the back door. "Ernesto, get a tub ready!"

By the time the piano player hit the final notes of a jaunty tune, Cal had drained his mug. He lowered it to the bar and winced inwardly. Didn't matter whether it was Pearl or Lone Star, he still hadn't developed a taste for beer. Never hurt to be sociable with the other cowpokes—all of whom had bypassed the barber in favor of blowing their wages in the saloon—but one brew was 'bout all he could stomach. He preferred to spend what was left of the amount he'd allotted himself on a meal better'n the grub they'd been fed on the trail.

He flipped a coin to the bartender, slapped the backs of buddies still sober enough to recognize him, then headed for the swinging doors. And collided with the pretty blonde barging her way inside.

She stumbled, and he caught her around her tiny waist. If anything, she looked more disheveled than she had an hour ago when she ran into him the first time. Her hat sat askew on her head, releasing more cottony curls, but her grip on the satchel hadn't relaxed.

He let her go and whipped off his Stetson. "Nice to bump into you again, miss."

She widened her baby blues, then blinked at him. Considering how he'd looked the first time they met, he understood why she was confused. But he didn't care to clarify.

He waved his hand toward the doors and invited her to precede him from the saloon. "After you."

"No thank you," she said, her prim voice somewhat harried. "I must speak with the owner of this establishment."

Behind him, Curtis Riggs got riled and upturned a poker table, sending cards and coins flying—followed rapidly by fists and language that weren't fittin' for a young lady.

Cal urged her outside with a hand on the small of her back. "No ma'am, there ain't nobody in there you need to see."

She stared up at him and blinked again. Then the water started pouring from her eyes like she was trying to fill a steam engine.

"Whoa there! I didn't mean to make ya cry." He fluttered his hands around her, not sure what he was supposed to do with a bawlin' female. He shouldn't touch her again. They weren't formally introduced. But she looked so pitiful with those huge drops streaming down her cheeks. He finally reached into the pocket of his new vest and pulled out a cotton kerchief for her.

She sniffed and accepted it, apparently trying to offer him a smile, but her lips were so twisted, he couldn't really tell if that was what she meant. Finally, after a sniff or two and a hefty honk into his new kerchief—well, her new kerchief now—she settled down enough to thank him.

"I'm sorry." The smile she gave him this time was undeniable and apologetic as she tried to return his kerchief.

He waved it off, then tipped his hat again. "Let's start over. I'm Cal

Stephens. I work at the Rolling Oak Ranch outside of town."

"Nice to meet you, Mr. Stephens. I'm Eva Knowles, and I'm … I'm …"

Her eyes welled up again, and before she could start to wailin' a second time, Cal said, "You hungry? I'm hungry. Why don't you come and have some grub with me, and we can have a nice talk? Would you like that?"

"I-I …" She sniffed and nodded, and her cheeks flushed rosy. Then, as if she'd remembered her manners, she straightened her shoulders and nodded once more. "I would appreciate that. Thank you for your kindness."

He walked her to the restaurant in the Harvey Hotel, close to the train depot, and soon they were breathing in the beefy scent of roast, with mashed taters and carrots. But nothing could top the smell of the fresh-baked bread. No sooner had the aproned Harvey Girl set their plates in front of them, Cal grabbed his fork—but Miss Knowles cleared her throat.

She sat with her hands in her lap and her head slightly bowed, glancing up at him from under her cockeyed hat. "Aren't you going to thank the Lord for our food?"

"Oh. Umm, yeah." He scrubbed his hands down his britches. He'd never prayed for eating. Not to say he never prayed at all, just not usually before a meal. He bowed his head. "Thank you, Lord, for this grub and the fine young lady I get to share it with. Amen."

He peeked at her for her approval, and at her nod, reached for his fork again. Now that she was calm and they was settled in somewhat, might be he could get some answers from her. "So, what brings you to town?"

"I have to find work." Miss Knowles picked at a carrot. "Mama died and Papa's sick. I have four brothers and sisters who are going to go hungry if I don't find some way to feed them."

Ladies didn't usually speak that frankly—at least none he knew of—but this one bore such a weight on her shoulders, all that cryin' made sense now. "What are you going to do?"

"I don't know." She rested her fork and returned her hands and gaze to her lap. "I used up most everything we had just to get here. What's left ain't enough for a room at either of the hotels or the boarding house, and no one's hirin' women. I was about to beg a job at the saloon and maybe get a room there when—"

"Pardon me for sayin', ma'am, but you ain't got no business working in a place like that." He took in her plain cotton dress with its frayed cuffs and almost too-tight collar buttoned at her throat. "You ever live in a city before?"

"No, and I ain't sure I'm going to like it. But better here than Austin, where Pa said I should go."

"Yes'm. Better here." He reached for his tea. "Austin's too big, but it seems like we're in a race to catch up."

Seemed she didn't have much more to say. She picked up her fork and took a halfhearted stab at her food.

"Miss Knowles, it ain't none of my business, but I figure you oughta eat them taters."

She sighed. "Yes, I suppose I should."

He squinted at her, watching her take a bite or two. Sometimes when she spoke, she sounded just as country and rough around the edges as he did. Other times, seemed she had a bit of learnin' in her head. If she did, then the answer to her problem was right here, in this very diner.

"You know what kinda work you want to do?"

Having just filled her mouth with a bite of the roast, she nodded. Then, she swallowed and said, "After Ma got sick, I did all the cookin' for Pa and the young'uns. Washed the clothes too. Did the mendin' and ironin'. My sister does it all now, so I can find a job here, doin' the kinds of things I did at home."

"What about school? You got any schoolin'?"

"Finished all eight grades. Got high marks too." She took another bite and studied him as she chewed. "You got something on your mind, don't you?"

Cal leaned toward her. "You oughta be here instead of the saloon. That's no place for you."

"But I already asked for a room here. They're full up."

"I don't mean askin' for a room. I mean askin' for a job."

Considerin' the look she gave him, he might as well've told her to work over at Madam Dallie's. When she finally found her tongue, she exclaimed, "Oh, goodness! How could you suggest such a thing? I could never! Back home, Pastor Roberts has been preaching against ladies leaving hearth and home and going to work at these"—she lowered her voice and leaned toward him—"at these kinds of places. Why, he says places like this are where young ladies lose their virtue."

"That ain't so. They're more likely to find husbands here." Cal speared a chunk of his roast. "Besides, wasn't you just tryin' to get a job at the saloon?"

She flushed again and lowered her eyes. "I wasn't thinking straight at that moment."

"I reckon not. Reckon it can be kinda scary for a young girl all alone." He sawed off another hunk of beef. "Your preacher is wrong, though—meanin' no disrespect. But there's a housemother or something here that keeps them girls in line. You break one of the rules, you're likely to get yourself fired."

"A housemother? Would I have my own room? How much would it cost?"

"That's just it. Don't cost ya nothin'. You go to work here and get room and board on top of your wages." He popped the bite into his mouth and chewed while he watched her cogitatin' all he'd told her. Wouldn't hurt to sweeten the deal a little with another bit of information. "I happen to know the housemother here—Miss Henrietta Bacon—and I bet I can get you on. If you want the job, that is."

For the first time since he'd met her, her eyes lit up with her smile. Great howlin' coyotes, he wanted to see that happen more often.

# Chapter 2

WHO KNEW THERE COULD be so much involved in setting and serving a table? If a cup was upturned with the handle one way, the Harvey Girls were to give the customer coffee. Turned the other way, they were to provide tea. Upside down meant he didn't want a hot beverage at all, and the waitress had best see what he *did* want.

Four full plates could be stacked up the left arm, freeing the right hand to deposit each of them in front of the hungry travelers. The trick, of course, was in not bumping that left arm and dumping the entire load of creamed corn and baked chicken atop the heads of those dining nearby. Miss Henrietta swore that was the exact reason the last Harvey Girl got fired, though Eva heard other stories—like she'd been caught smoking behind the outhouse.

The rules were strict, and Miss Henrietta enforced them to the letter, but Eva didn't mind. She'd learned them during her six weeks of training in Newton, Kansas, but, aside from the particulars of cup placement and such, it wasn't much different from living at home under Pa's roof. The Harvey Girls weren't to go out after ten at night, and no gentlemen callers were allowed in their presence after that time. Catching a man upstairs meant prompt dismissal for the young lady who'd violated the rules.

Only one thing Mr. Stephens told Eva turned out not to be so. She didn't have her own room. Each of the girls squeezed four to a room on the hotel's third floor. Eva's quarters were so tiny they had to crawl over each other to find their places in one of the double beds. Even with all the windows open, the room was often stifling. She'd put up with it for a solid week before climbing out the window with her pillow and a light quilt to sleep on the balconet.

They didn't work on Sunday mornings but were expected to be in church regardless of how much rest they needed from a week's worth of work. Six days, ten hours a day—most of them spent on their feet— could render a girl bone-weary come Sunday, but Miss Henrietta herded them like cattle down the street to the white clapboard building that doubled as the local school. There were an even dozen Harvey Girls, and they occupied the same pews each Sunday morning. Miss Henrietta sat with three girls to her left, three to her right, and six on the bench in front of her. If anyone dared doze off, she'd likely get a thump on the shoulder for her rudeness.

If only someone would thump that Melody Malone for her rudeness, maybe things would be better for the Harvey Girls. Bad enough that the preacher spoke of them as if they were all destined to become harlots, causing the entire congregation to look askance at them as if they already wore red satin and a scarlet A. None of the Malone sisters was particularly kind, but Melody seemed to have cut Eva out like a calf from the herd and branded her as her personal target for meanness.

Once the sermon ended, Miss Henrietta ushered the girls past the snobbish Malone clan and toward the entrance, where Rev. Jeremiah Watkins stared down his nose at them from behind his spectacles.

"Fine sermon, Reverend." Miss Henrietta clutched her Bible to her bosom and gave him a smile that bordered on a sneer. "Right fine sermon."

"All God's words are fine to the right ears, Miss Bacon." The reverend dipped his head ever so slightly. "I'll be praying for your soul—yours and those of your girls."

She smirked. "And we'll be praying for yours." With that, she swept them past him. "Come along, ladies."

Eva lagged behind the others and sneaked a glance back at the preacher. She had been to church service the past two Sundays since returning from Kansas, and both times, he'd made it a point to denigrate them. The Harvey House Hotel had been in business in this town for a couple of years; a body'd think the man would be educated about the girls by now.

She lifted her skirt and hurried to Miss Henrietta, then slowed her pace to match the older woman's steps. "Rev. Watkins doesn't seem too fond of us, does he?"

Miss Henrietta's cinnamon-colored curls bounced as she marched away from the church at a quick clip. "He's just ignorant of the facts, as are plenty of the other townsfolk around here. But until this town builds another church, he's our pastor, and as such, he deserves our respect and attention."

Eva hunched her shoulders. "Wouldn't matter if there were another church. Our preacher back home said the same things about the girls, and he didn't live anywhere near a Harvey House."

"Until attitudes change, there's nothing we can do but keep our heads up and our backs straight." She poked Eva's spine, forcing her upright. "People will come around. You'll see."

Penelope Mayflower caught up with them and rested a hand in the crook of Eva's arm, slowing her gait to let the others go around.

"Isn't Cal Stephens the one who got you this job?" She shifted her eyes toward something over Eva's left shoulder. "He doesn't go to church, so I wonder why ... Oh, I bet he's looking for you!"

"Me?" She twisted around, but Penelope yanked her straight again.

"Don't look. That's too forward."

Melody Malone didn't mind being forward. In the brief glimpse Eva had of Mr. Stephens, Melody was already fawning over him. Not that it mattered. After he put in a word with Miss Henrietta and got Eva her job, he'd disappeared. This was the first she'd seen him since. Her own absence for training hadn't helped anything, but still, it would've been nice had he met her when she returned.

As she and Penelope approached the side stairs to the hotel, they both looked back. Penelope heaved a sigh. "He's so handsome. Do you think he'll come calling on you?"

"I don't care one whit whether he does or doesn't. We hardly know each other." But the image of him with Melody's hand tucked in his arm didn't set well with her.

Eva deposited a stack of plates with the dishwasher, a widow with shocks of silver streaking her chocolate-brown hair. "We're about done until this evening, Liza. Just a few more diners lingering over their coffee."

Liza Stafford brushed a strand of dark hair off her brow with the back of a sudsy hand. "That's good news. Maybe I can take a quick nap before the next train rolls in."

Eva gave her shoulders an affectionate squeeze. "I'll see that no one disturbs you."

As she turned toward the dining room, she caught a glimpse through the window of Penelope resting on the back stairs with a shoe in her hand.

Eva pushed open the screened door. "What are you doing out here? Miss Henrietta will have your hide if she catches you sitting during your shift."

Penelope rubbed her arch and gave her a woeful look. "My feet are killing me. I don't think I can stand another minute."

"Serves you right for buying a size too small. New shoes are hard enough to break in without you having to squeeze your toes into something not meant for them."

"I know, I know. I wish I had dainty feet like yours instead of these boat paddles."

Eva *tsked*. "There's nothing wrong with your feet that the right size shoe wouldn't solve." She peeked over her shoulder. Miss Henrietta was nowhere in sight. "I'll cover for you for now, but when the new train pulls in, you'd better have your old shoes on."

With that, she scurried through the kitchen and into the dining room. Only a dozen or so patrons lingered, most at tables not her own and attended by others. Considering how casually they squandered their time, they weren't in a hurry to catch the train that would soon depart. These must be townsfolk, though she didn't recognize any of them. At least not until the reverend turned his head. He'd been sitting at one of Penelope's tables with two other men.

How ironic that the same women he preached against this morning had served his plate and refilled his cup. Had Eva realized he was there, she wouldn't have been so willing to cover Penelope's tables. But she tilted her lips upward and, holding her back straight and head high, glided toward him with the china coffeepot. Though the temptation was strong, pouring the brew over his head wouldn't likely convince him he was wrong about the Harvey Girls, so she'd have to be honey-sweet until his attitude changed.

Who knew when that would be?

Approaching from the right, as she'd been taught, she offered the first gentleman a smile and a refill. He and the second accepted her hospitality and returned her smile with genuine appreciation. Aside from raising his cup for her to fill, Rev. Watkins didn't acknowledge her presence but continued pontificating upon whatever topic he felt was spellbinding to his captive audience.

Squelching a huff and a smart retort, Eva left the men as gracefully as she'd arrived. But oh, how satisfying it would have been to anoint that arrogant man with the contents of the china pot.

"Miss Eva, is that you?" Cal Stephens stood near the doorway with Melody Malone's proprietary hand locked on his arm. He held his

Stetson between his fingers and looked at Eva with his bright green eyes, smiling as if he were truly happy to see her. His broad shoulders did wonderful things to the Sunday suit he wore, though he hadn't been in church that morning. Being so dressed up, he looked both handsome and uncomfortable.

Melody cleared her throat. "Yes. Hello, Eva. So nice to see you again."

Eva realized she'd been gaping and recovered with a quick nod. "You too, Miss Malone, and you, Mr. Stephens. How thoughtful of you to remember me. I returned from Kansas a couple of weeks ago." With a wave of her hand, she offered them a seat anywhere in the large dining room. "Would you like a meal? A cup of coffee?"

"Oh, no ma'am. I just, uh, we were ..." He looked her over from the smart cap topping her curls to the hem of her aproned black dress. "I forgot how purty you are."

She flushed and turned her head—directly toward Rev. Watkins' disapproving gaze. How dare he judge her? For all he knew, Mr. Stephens was a customer or an old friend. What was she supposed to do? Ignore him?

"Just saw you through the window, and thought we'd drop in," Mr. Stephens was saying when she finally ripped her focus off the irredeemable clergyman. "I been wonderin' how things turned out with you, and now I know. I'm right happy for you."

She brought her shoulders back, though her grip on the china pot threatened to snap the handle. "Yes, I successfully completed the training and am now proud to call myself a Harvey Girl." She raised her chin and added, "And I owe it all to you, Mr. Stephens."

The reverend cocked an arrogant brow, Melody scowled, and Cal Stephens blushed bright pink under his tanned skin. And she, stiff from standing so erect, wanted to kick herself all the way back to the kitchen for opening her mouth. Being a proud Harvey Girl was one thing, but being indebted to a cowboy—and admitting as much in front of the one man who had no respect for her or her profession—was quite another. Heaven help her if Mr. Stephens got the wrong impression of her admission, but heaven help her more if she became the central focus of Rev. Watkins' next sermon.

Melody shifted her attention to the preacher and flounced to his table. "Hello, Reverend. I didn't expect to see you here. I so enjoyed your sermon this morning."

Rev. Watkins and the men with him stood as she approached, and the reverend took her extended hand in both of his. "Why, thank you, Miss Malone. Despite the questionable morality of the women who work here, I have yet to find a better braised chicken anywhere else."

"I'll have to try it someday just because you recommend it so highly." She patted the air, indicating that the men should resume their seats. "Please, don't let your coffee get cold on account of me."

*Oh, good grief.* Eva raised her eyes heavenward before she dipped her head. "If I am no longer needed here, I should return this pot to the kitchen. Its contents are getting cold."

Mr. Stephens stepped forward. "Maybe I could walk with you?"

"To the kitchen?" What an odd request.

He gave her a sheepish grin. "I mean later. If you're free later, we could go for a walk."

Melody gasped, and Eva bit back a grin. How delicious! He'd asked her out for the evening right in front of the woman who'd been clinging to his arm. Maybe that would knock her down a peg. Eva ought to accept the offer out of sheer meanness.

But that would put her on the same footing as the Malone sisters.

She lowered her lashes. "I appreciate the offer, Mr. Stephens, but I'm afraid, given the current circumstances, that wouldn't be appropriate."

"Appropriate? Circumstances?" He gave her a quizzical look. "What circumstances?"

Eva shifted her eyes toward Melody, who bustled back to his side and reclaimed her possession.

Cal frowned at her hand on his arm, then apparently realized its implication. "Oh, no. This isn't what it looks like—"

"Come along, Cal." Melody aimed him toward the door. "We mustn't keep everyone waiting."

As she ushered him out, he twisted back toward Eva. "I'll come by later and explain."

Chairs scraped the hardwood floor to her left as the preacher and his friends got up to leave. Rev. Watkins tossed a few coins on the table, then smirked and added another. "For the show."

One of the men—a church elder, she realized—offered her a sympathetic smile and laid another coin on the table. "For putting up with us."

His kindness created a lump in her throat that she choked down. "Oh, no sir. It was my pleasure."

She shook her head as they left. Rev. Watkins would be a hard nut to crack, but at least his attitude hadn't permeated the entire town.

As for Mr. Stephens ... she had no idea what to think of him.

# Chapter 3

COULDN'T GET BY WITH just choppin' locoweed—it would always come back. Cal, along with Edmund Cavender and Curtis Riggs, had to dig it up from the new pasture and burn it before a horse or cow could feed in this lot. Cal'd seen horses crazy on the weed, groanin' and foamin' at the mouth. Great howlin' coyotes, it was horrible stuff.

Ed leaned on his spade and scrubbed his sweaty face with his kerchief. "This is a rotty job. How did we manage to get tossed out here?"

"I say, old chap." Curtis brought himself upright, looking down his nose at Ed and mimicking his accent. "Don't they have this particular botanical beauty in jolly old England?"

Ed jabbed his spade into the soil and tossed the dirt at Curtis. "Careful, or I shall burn you with the rest of the weeds."

Cal shook his head. What a pair. Curtis worked for the sole purpose of funding his next poker game, and Ed worked because, despite his family's fancy title back in England, he was stone-cold broke. Curse of being a third son, he'd said. Called himself well educated, yet good for nothing. At least in his father's eyes. He intended to make his fortune and return home in style. That's what he'd said three years ago, anyway. Cal didn't know where Ed's wages went, but he hadn't seen any evidence of style.

After a moment, a spadeful of dry dirt landed at his feet.

Curtis grinned at him. "Heard that pretty new Harvey Girl turned you down for an evenin' walk last Sunday."

"She didn't rightly turn me down." With a final grunt, he upended the weed he'd been working on and tossed it toward the pile of others they would burn later. "My timin' was just off is all."

"I cannot imagine it is ever a good time to ask a woman out when another is gracing your arm," Ed said. "I thought even you vulgar Americans knew better than that."

Cal spotted and attacked another weed, this one farther from the guffawing cowpokes. They were right. He'd shown about as much sense as a horse on locoweed when he'd stumbled all over his tongue last Sunday. Miss Eva hadn't even come to say hello when he asked Miss Henrietta for her later. Sent her apologies instead. He was the one who needed to apologize.

Since today was payday, he might get his chance. The ranch boss usually let the boys off early on a payday so they could get to the bank before it closed—not that many of them went to the bank. But Cal did. Put a little in his account every time he got paid. Maybe this time, though, he'd save out enough to treat himself to supper at the Harvey House restaurant. And then, maybe he'd be able to talk Miss Eva into taking a stroll with him. After the train left, of course.

Where would they go? What would they talk about? His experience with women was fairly limited, considering he spent most of his time in the saddle. Other than Ma and his sisters, Melody Malone was the only proper girl he associated with. The other women he knew worked at the saloon, and he'd always made it a point to get outta there as quick as—

"Ain't you gonna eat?" Curtis was staring at him like he'd gone loco. "Cookie's been ringin' that bell for nigh unto twenty minutes now."

Back of Cal's neck grew warm as he scowled at him. "Iffen it's been twenty minutes, what's takin' you so long to get in line?"

"Come on, fellows." Ed propped his spade on his shoulder. "If we do not make haste, there shan't be anything left but bean gravy and biscuit crumbs."

Ed and Curtis raced their horses back to the ranch house, with Curtis in the lead. He got there first and pulled back on the reins right in front of the feed line. His sorrel skidded on its haunches in a cloud of dust that had Cookie spittin' out some spicy words. Curtis was out of the saddle and in line before the gelding could raise its rump again, and Ed wasn't too far behind him. Cal just shook his head. Cookie's grub weren't bad, but it weren't worth injurin' a horse over either.

He tossed his reins over the hitchin' rail at the bunkhouse and ambled to the end of the line. The guys didn't eat inside anywhere, just grabbed a hunk of shade from whatever was casting it and settled there. If they were lucky enough, the shade came with a place to rest an aching back. He glanced ahead at the steam rolling off Cookie's pots sitting atop an old wood table. Cookie, wearing an apron almost as long as the Harvey Girls' and five times dirtier, dipped a ladle into a pot and waved the cowpoke he was serving on ahead. Whatever was being plopped onto the tin plates was nothing compared to what Cal would be chewing on tonight, if he got his way—and judging by the looks of the bossman marching toward him, he'd get his way.

Milt Wiley, the freckled, redheaded ranch boss, gave him a sharp nod. "Get your grub and c'mon up to the house. Got a thing or two I want you to do."

"Sure thing, Boss."

Milt headed to the stone and wood structure he lived in with his purty wife and three little kiddies. Wouldn't expect a man that young to be responsible for runnin' a spread as big as the Rolling Oak, but the owner had faith in him, and he'd proved himself worthy. Owner and his wife would come up from Houston two or three times a year, lookin' all rich and snobby. They'd stay a week or two, making ever'body edgy while they played at being boss, then go back to the city. Meanwhile, Milt did his job and made sure everyone else did too.

Cal bounced on his toes, all antsy like, and drummed his fingers on the bottom of his empty plate. Seeing Miss Eva again yanked at his longin' a lot harder than filling his belly. If that line moved any slower, he might just bypass the usual grub and head straight to the house. See what the boss wanted. Whatever it was, he'd bet his biscuit it meant a trip to town.

He returned his plate to the stack of them sitting on the end of the table and moseyed on up to the house. A quick knock brought the boss to the door.

"You eat already? That was fast."

"Weren't that hungry," Cal lied. He was half starved, but he could wait till he got to the restaurant—and Miss Eva. "You wanted to see me?"

Going to town was a good thing. A stop at the dry goods store for Miz Wiley, another at the bank for the boss and himself, then he'd be on his own to do whatever he wanted—which meant he'd have plenty of time for strolling with Miss Eva. That thought had dominated his mind the entire ride into town.

On the other hand, havin' to make a stop to see Rev. Watkins didn't rank high on the *favorite things to do* list. Cal rarely made it to church, couldn't stand to spend a couple of hours squirming on a hard, wooden bench. But this weren't Sunday. He could deliver what he needed to deliver and get gone.

Might as well do the worst first.

He pulled the wagon to a stop in front of the parsonage, a sad-looking white house as cheerless as the one who occupied it. The previous reverend had a wife to keep the place all purtied up with flowers and such, but Rev. Watkins didn't have a wife, just a few women from the church who took turns cooking, cleaning, and washing his clothes.

Cal grabbed the picnic basket from the wagon seat and headed toward the preacher's door. Once in a while, the smell of the fried chicken, mashed taters, green beans, and fresh bread would waft his way as he drove to town and get his mouth to watering somethin' fierce. Seemed a right shame the cowpokes ate a steady diet of beef stew or chili or beans and cornbread while everyone else had a little variety. Onliest time he got fried chicken was when he came to town, and even then, it was rare.

The preacher opened the door before he could knock. "Oh, good. I've been looking forward to Camelia's home-baked bread all day."

"Yessir. Best in town." Cal handed over the basket.

"Glad we're in agreement. Why don't you come in and share a slice with me?"

"Oh, no sir. I got errands to—"

"Nonsense! How could you pass this up?"

In truth, he couldn't. His protest didn't have much conviction behind it, so when the reverend pressed, he didn't turn down the offer a second time.

He trailed Rev. Watkins through a sparsely furnished house to a simple kitchen and stood with his hat in his hands while the preacher scouted out a cuttin' knife.

"Saw you in the Harvey House last Sunday." Rev. Watkins' voice barely contained a chuckle. "If I remember correctly, you were there with one young lady and eyeing another."

The knife slid back and forth through the fresh bread, and Cal watched as if givin' it a good stare would make it slice faster. The aroma 'bout made him weak-kneed, but he remembered his manners well enough to respond. "Miss Melody's just a friend. I knowed her back when she wore her hair in pigtails."

"And you haven't noticed she styles it differently these days?" Rev. Watkins retrieved a couple of plates and a jar of honey, then nodded Cal toward a chair. "She's a fine-looking woman now."

"Yessir, but she's still more like a sister to me." He couldn't keep his eyes off the thick slice the reverend placed in front of him, but he didn't dare pick it up. If he knew anything about preachers, the man would have to pray before anything touched his tongue. And sure 'nough, this time weren't no different.

Rev. Watkins bowed his head, and Cal followed suit. Once the preacher'd said his words, Cal still tried to mind his manners. His ma had taught him right, but he sure would like to nab the honey jar and get to chawin' on the bread.

The reverend nudged the jar toward him. "You'd do far better with Miss Malone than you would that woman at the restaurant, you know. Miss Malone is a good Christian woman and a good cook, and the art of sewing didn't escape her either. She'd make a fine wife and mother."

*Wife and mother?* Cal about choked. Miss Melody had a temper bigger'n Dallas, and it had a hair trigger. She could fire it off faster'n Jesse James could clear his holster. And *bossy!* Lands, that woman gave orders like a range boss.

He shoved a huge bite of honeyed bread in his mouth to keep from responding. Best not to argue with the preacher. Best not to say anything at all.

"And from what I understand about the Harvey Girls," the reverend continued, "they tend to be on the loose side. Not much better than a saloon girl, if you ask me."

That comment *did* make Cal choke. He sputtered and swallowed and coughed until his face grew all hot. When he could finally speak, his voice wasn't much better'n a croak, but he couldn't let the reverend say what he did without saying somethin' in return. "Miss Eva is a nice Christian woman too. In fact, all them girls are. They're in your church ever' Sunday morning, ain't they?"

"They are indeed, but—"

"And you're puttin' the fear of God in 'em, right?"

"That's the effect of most of my sermons, yes."

"So, seems to me, if them girls ain't good Christian women yet, you ain't got no one to blame but yourself."

It was the reverend's turn to choke.

While he sputtered, Cal finished his bread and stood. "Thank you right kindly for sharing with me. I reckon I oughta get to the bank before it closes."

By the time he'd finished all the banking and Miz Wiley's shopping, the train had left the station, and an almost-empty Harvey House

Restaurant lured him to its doors. He stepped inside, jerked his hat off, and looked past the locals sippin' coffee till he found Miss Eva. She was scrubbing a table at the far right of the restaurant, near the windows at the side street. Freed from her black cap, strands of cottony hair danced in the breeze and sunlight like they was old friends. She looked up and smiled at him, and his heart galloped through his chest like ol' Curtis' gelding. Weren't no angel in heaven purtier'n her.

"Good to see you, Mr. Stephens." She wiped her hands on her towel as she approached. "Would you care for a plate, or are you here simply for refreshment? Coffee? Tea?"

His stomach answered before he could, and she laughed. "A plate it is, then. Today's special is creamed chicken with carrots and peas, served over mashed potatoes, and with a side of sweet sugar beets. Dessert is one of my personal favorites, a berry pudding topped with a fluffy cloud of whipped cream."

"Sounds right good, Miss Eva." He followed her to a table and took a seat, hanging his hat on a spindle chair next to his.

"Would you like coffee or tea?"

"Coffee's fine, ma'am."

She turned his coffee cup, then folded her hands. "I'll send Penelope out to wait on you. Shouldn't take a minute."

"Penelope?" He bounced out of his chair like a jackrabbit and caught her before she'd walked too far. "Excuse me, Miss Eva, but I thought you'd wait on me."

"My shift is over, and I'm done for the day. But Penelope is quite good at her job."

Her shift was over? His luck couldn't get any better'n this. "Have you eaten? Maybe you could join me."

"I have eaten, but thank you for your offer." She turned to leave again.

"Then what about dessert and coffee? You said the berry puddin's your favorite."

She hesitated, tilting her head at him as if considering.

"Please? I'd sure appreciate your company." He gave her his best hangdog look. Lost some of its effectiveness without his hat brim between his fingers, but it seemed to work well enough.

She released a golden laugh. "All right. Just let me give your order to Penelope."

By the time he finished eating a meal he didn't remember and hadn't tasted, he'd told her everything about his week and all the work he'd done during it. Now he was purty much talked out but not willing to leave her company.

He paid the bill, leaving a nice tip for Penelope, then retrieved his hat. "Miss Eva, it promises to be a right fine evenin'. Care to take a walk with me?"

His buttons threatened to pop off his chest when she accepted his arm.

The evening air weren't that much cooler than the daytime air, but the shadows ran deeper, and that helped a mite. The stores had closed up, and lights flickered in the second-floor windows all along Main Street. Not many folks were out. The competing pianos from the saloon and Madam Dallie's house at the opposite end of the street made the most noise—raucous music with the occasional sour note. Cal nodded and wished a good evening to another couple strolling toward them on the sidewalk slats, but that was about the only thing he'd done right since opening the door for Miss Eva when they left the restaurant. Why was it he could talk up a blue streak in the restaurant, with her lookin' right at him like she was gobblin' up every word, but out here, his tongue shriveled?

He fumbled around his brain and came up with, "How's your pa and them doin'?"

"I got a letter from my sister Sarah Ann just this week. She said Papa's getting better, but he didn't like the notion of me working as a Harvey Girl. She told me he calmed down when he saw the money I sent home. It was just a little from my tips, because I haven't been paid yet, but—Oh, would you look who's coming toward us!" Miss Eva lowered her head as she spoke and peered up through her long lashes. "If it isn't the good Reverend Watkins. Heading in to see Miss Henrietta again, I'd wager. If that's not hypocritical, nothing is. Speaks ill of us Harvey Girls on a Sunday morning, and visits our very housemother during the week. Downright hypocritical, I say."

On the other side of the dirt road, Rev. Watkins strode toward the restaurant at a fine clip. How could he still be hungry after eating Miz Wiley's fried chicken? She'd packed enough to last him the day at least. More, if he stored it right.

Rev. Watkins crossed the street, flashed them a smile, and carried on toward the restaurant. Miss Eva watched him over her shoulder. "He seems to be pursuing her."

"Is that so?" Weren't Cal's place to say anything, but hypocritical would be a good word for it, after what the preacher'd said about her and all the girls, not more'n three hours ago.

Lightly holding the crook of his elbow, she continued their walk. "Oh, he tries to be discreet about it, but when he comes alone, he always requests her service rather than one of the other girls', and he always invites her to join him."

"And does she?"

"Mostly." She giggled. "You should hear some of their discussions. She debates Scripture with him as if she were the preacher and he a heathen. If they ever got married, he'd have to change his sermons."

Now, that would be something to see. If he could think of a valid excuse, he'd turn around to watch the show. They stopped at a crossroad to see the sun setting beyond the town. "Not likely they'd get married, but whoever weds him will need the patience of a mule skinner."

She giggled again, and the sound of it gave him a sense of joy and lightheartedness he hadn't felt before. And just then—just that moment—the sunset's orange glow caught in her hair and stole his breath away.

With his heart soaring sky-high on the wings of an unlikely hope, he studied the depths of her sweet blue eyes. "What about you? Do you think you'll marry someday?"

"Marry?" She gaped at him like a stock-pond bass. "I have no intention of marrying. Ever."

The sun sank below the horizon in a glorious crimson blaze. Weren't no point watchin' it anymore.

He caged his pounding heart behind his ribs and turned with her toward the hotel. "Reckon I oughta get you back home."

# Chapter 4

"OF COURSE, I TURNED him down, though he wasn't asking for my hand." Eva lined the breakfast plates up her arm while she whispered to Penelope, so the other girls couldn't hear. "I shouldn't string him along if I don't intend to marry."

Penelope filled the china coffeepot. "I don't understand you at all. The prospect of getting married is one of the reasons I became a Harvey Girl. Clara and Prudie will be married before you know it."

"If they keep coming in after curfew, they're more likely to lose their jobs." Eva glanced at the porcelain-pale Clara and the olive-skinned Prudie, the other two who shared Penelope and Eva's room. Neither looked overly tired, considering the hours they kept. She had expected yawns and dark rings under their eyes. "Do you know about the men who've captured their affections?"

"Clara has been seeing a cattle baron who comes through from Oklahoma, and Prudie caught the eye of a banker who has traveled all the way from New York. He has business around here and will be staying at the hotel awhile." She held the pot with both hands and released a dreamy sigh. "New York! Can you imagine?"

"I don't want to imagine it. Not if I have to see it as a married woman." She picked up the fifth plate. "I don't see the point of leaving my father's house and rules to live under the roof and rules of another man."

Penelope followed her out of the kitchen. "Do you intend to work for the rest of your life? Serving strangers and waiting tables?"

"No, of course not. I want to make sure my family is financially comfortable, so Papa doesn't have to worry, then I want to travel. See things. Go places. Taste the world."

"Huh. And you think *we're* romantic! Don't you think seeing the world would be more fun with someone to share the experience?"

"I suppose." Eva paused before heading to her table. "But if I go on my own, I get to decide where and when and for how long. That's what

I want, you know? Independence. Freedom. And I'm willing to wait on strangers and clean tables until I earn enough to go."

She put a smile on her face and approached the family of five who awaited their breakfast. Porridge and berry muffins for the two youngest, definitely twins. A large stack of griddle cakes for the older boy. Shirred eggs and toast for the missus, and fried eggs, griddle cakes, and a large steak for the mister, who looked like he could eat it all in an instant and return for more. She'd hate to have to feed the man on a regular basis—she'd never be allowed out of the kitchen.

"May I bring you anything else? More coffee perhaps? More milk for the little ones?"

Early in the morning, and the missus already looked harried. But she managed a smile. "I believe we have all we need. Thank you."

Eva turned to the next table and asked the same question of three affluent gentlemen, judging by the fine fabric of their suits and the shiny gold chain of one's pocket watch. The three treated her with respect, but she never quite shook the feeling of their eyes on her as she took the order of another family who had just taken seats.

She had no doubt the men watching her were married. Why would anyone want such a creature with a wandering eye and a voracious appetite? Men occupied most of the tables surrounding her, and the few women in the room were here with their husbands. The choices were clear. She could marry and remain home while her husband hunted new game in faraway restaurants, or she could travel with him and never have a moment's peace. Cal Stephens supplied the third option—just as distasteful as the others. She could marry a man who never traveled beyond the cattle trail.

No. None of the options would do. Not for her.

"Why, Cal Stephens! You're just the man I wanted to see."

He stepped off his horse and tossed the reins over the post. "Mighty good to see you too, Miss Melody. What can I do for you?"

"I had a hankering for one of Miss Gertrude's lemon phosphates. Come have one with me."

Always pretty as a spring flower, Melody had dressed up right nice for a Saturday afternoon. Any man'd be proud to have her on his arm. One of the locals should've snatched her up by now. He had a few pennies in his pocket from last night. Might as well spend them on an old friend.

He offered his hand to help her off the sidewalk, then tucked her fingers in the crook of his arm as they crossed the street to Miss Gertrude's Phosphates and Sarsaparilla Emporium. Next to the emporium, Lillie Daniels hung a sign in the window of the library. Somebody or other would be in town tonight, reading from some book or other. Not the likely way Cal'd spend his Saturday off.

But it caught Melody's attention. She stopped in front of the library. "I've heard of that author. Wonderful work. Maybe you could take me tonight?"

"Aw, now, I don't know about that. I ain't that interested in books and stuff."

"Oh, but this man has been all over the world," she said as they continued to the emporium. "I heard that his latest book is all about Singapore."

Singapore had never struck him as a place he'd wanted to go. But the idea of traveling the world had always held his attention.

Miss Gertrude's emporium was bright as a summer day, all yellow inside—yellow checkered tablecloths and curtains, yellow on the walls, and all trimmed in white. She had a counter as high as the one in the general store and a soda fountain and one of those fancy cash registers like ol' Walter had in the barbershop. Perked up a body's spirit just walkin' inside.

Cal carried their drinks to a small table near the window and helped Melody get settled in her chair. She sipped her lemon phosphate with her drinkin' straw, regarding him from beneath her lashes. "I saw you with that Harvey Girl last night. What was her name?"

"Eva," he said. "Eva Knowles." Saying her name dried out his tongue, despite the sassparilla.

"You seemed quite lovestruck."

Just thinkin' about it soured his stomach. "The feelin's not mutual."

Melody's eyes widened as if he'd smacked her with a bull's tail. "That can't possibly be right. Any woman would be smitten with a handsome man like you. Why look at you! Tall and strong and quite dashing."

Maybe not dashing, but he did have his Saturday bath earlier, and he'd ragged out right proper in the new clothes he'd bought the week before. "I don't think it's me that's the problem. She talks like she don't want nobody. I guess she likes makin' her own money and bein' independent."

"Fiddle-faddle. That's just silly. Every woman wants someone to love. Someone to love her." She tapped her finger on her cheek, staring past him and considering whatever thought had entered her head. Then she shifted her gaze to him and smiled real slow-like.

"Now, Miss Melody, you look like you're ready to raise someone's bristles with whatever you got in mind."

"I think the best way to get Eva to notice you is to make her jealous. And if that raises her bristles, then so much the better." She took another sip from her straw, then said, "I think you should take me to the library tonight. In fact, you should probably take me to dinner at Harvey House Restaurant just to make sure she sees us together."

"I don't know 'bout that idea. Isn't it a little—"

"Dishonest?" She grinned. "All's fair in love and war."

"Well, I ain't sure I'm in love with her." But if not yet, he would be. Given enough time. "Ain't seen her but once or twice."

"You'll never get a chance to know how you feel unless you test the waters, right?"

He stared out the window at an old brown cur nosing something under the sidewalk.

Miss Eva was the purtiest thing he ever saw, and she seemed nice too. Kind. The way she wanted to care for her family was right admirable. She seemed like a fine woman. And the way he figured it, he needed to find himself a good woman. Bank account had climbed some, and he sure weren't gettin' any younger. If he wanted to start making his own dreams come true, he'd better look for a wife to share 'em with.

He grabbed his hat off the chair next to him. "What time do you want to eat?"

Eva swept the back of her hand across her brow. Her bangs were damp enough to wash dishes. "I swear, the passengers on that train must've been packed in like cattle in a pen. There are so many of them tonight! I don't believe I've ever seen the restaurant so full."

"They're not all from the train. A lot of them are townsfolk having an evening out on account of that author speaking at the library tonight." Penelope set a load of china and silverware next to Liza and patted her on the shoulder. "You're going to have a lot of dishes, judging by that crowd out there."

Liza gave her a weary smile. "Maybe Miss Henrietta will have one of the girls start up another dish tub soon."

Eva dipped a serving of escalloped cabbage. "I heard that a woman up around Chicago has invented some kind of machine that washes dishes. I wonder if Mr. Harvey would—"

"Girls, girls—gather round! You won't ever believe this!" Prudie scurried across the kitchen floor, holding her hem off the ground. "Clara didn't come back from her break this afternoon!"

Eva stared at her. "I don't understand. What does that mean?"

As Eva and the others huddled around her, Prudie leaned forward to whisper, "She ran off with that cattle baron. His train left for Oklahoma not two hours ago."

The sudden intake of breath stole the air from the room. Prudie raised her chin a notch, proud of being the first one to share the gossip.

"How can you be sure?" Eva asked.

"Well, the porter told one of the Malone sisters, and she told Rev. Watkins, and he told Miss Henri—"

"*Ladies!*" One scowl from Miss Henrietta sent the women dashing about, returning to their work.

Eva held the plate with the now-tepid cabbage. She could either throw it out—such waste!— or serve it as it was. Or ... She glanced around at the others busying themselves with their tasks, then scooped the cabbage back in its bowl, stirred it around, and dished out a warmer serving. There. No harm done.

She prepared all the plates for her table order, lined them up her arm, and glided from the kitchen. The dining room seemed packed beyond capacity, requiring much concentration to avoid dropping her plates. But once they were safely deposited, she took a moment to glance around the room. Sure enough, Rev. Watkins sat at his regular table, accompanied by none other than the Malone sisters themselves. And Cal Stephens! Why, she'd never seen him step one booted foot in church, and here he was, seated at the preacher's table as if they were old friends.

At that moment, Miss Melody Malone turned, caught Eva's eye, and with a sly grin, rested her hand on Cal's arm. As if Eva cared one whit!

No, what she cared about was the tongue-thrashing the Harvey Girls would receive from the pulpit in the morning. Clara's leaving would most assuredly unleash the reverend's fury against them. She could practically feel the brand on her skin now as he accused all of the girls of harlotry.

With her face hot enough to heat the cabbage, she returned to the kitchen. If only there were some way to sway Rev. Watkins' opinion of the girls.

Cal had figured wrong when he thought he'd snore his way through the author's speech. That man had been *everywhere*. He talked about pyramids one minute and boomerangs the next. Mounts Kilimanjaro and Fuji in the same breath. Places Cal wanted to see. Places he'd never heard of. More places to add to his list. Too bad he couldn't buy the man's book. He needed to save his money for his extended travels. The library would have it soon enough.

"Fine speech tonight." Rev. Watkins topped his head with a tall derby, then extended his hand to Cal and drew him aside. With a wink and a nod toward Miss Melody, who was talking with some other lady, he muttered, "Good to see you took my advice. She's quite a catch."

"Oh, this ain't what you think."

"Nonsense, boy. Give it time." The reverend tipped his hat to her as she joined them, taking ahold of Cal's arm. "You two have a nice evening, now. Hope to see you in church tomorrow."

Melody placed her hand over her heart. "You know I never miss."

"Maybe you could coax your young man into coming with you this time."

She smiled up at Cal. "Maybe I shall."

When the reverend bid them good night and strolled away, she said, "You really should go to church with me tomorrow. Eva is always there."

"Can't. My turn to watch the herd." He walked with her toward her parents' home, a big two-story house on one of the side streets. "Besides, you know I never go to church."

She pouted. "Not even for me?"

"Like I said, I can't."

A different preacher at a different time had spoken over his father's grave, and the words he said weren't kind. Pa might not have been a church-goin' man, but he believed in God. Just never got the urge to prove it to anyone. Cal figured if a private belief was good enough for his pa, it was good enough for him.

"Eva looked quite upset to see us together at the restaurant tonight." Melody sounded proud of herself. "I wish she'd come to the library. I felt certain she would."

"I'm sorry she got upset. That weren't the plan."

"But of course it was! When a girl gets jealous, she can't help but get upset."

"I reckon so." He rubbed the back of his neck. "But this don't seem right."

"Oh, *pshaw*. This will work. You'll see." They stopped on the sidewalk in front of her house. She stood, holding her reticule in both hands in front of her and swishing her skirt side to side. With a devious smile, she said, "You know, what will really turn her green with envy is for you to kiss me."

Cal rubbed his neck again. "Don't know how that'll make her jealous. She ain't here to see it."

Melody stepped closer. "I'm sure word would get back to her."

A curtain shifted in one of the upstairs windows, and Cal grinned. "I'm sure it would."

He tapped his hat brim, said good night, and ambled off to get his horse.

# Chapter 5

As expected, Rev. Watkins delivered a blistering sermon Sunday morning. His stern threats and veiled accusations had been bad enough to cause Miss Henrietta to stew all the way back to the hotel—after smiling and telling him it was a "right fine sermon." Why she felt obliged to compliment him every Sunday was beyond Eva's understanding.

Kneeling on a blanket in the shade of an old sycamore tree, Eva lifted a napkin-covered plate of chicken salad sandwiches from the picnic basket and set them out for the other girls. "Isn't there some way we could change Rev. Watkins' attitude about us? Miss Henrietta told him Clara and her beau planned to marry, but that didn't stop his sharp remarks this morning."

Penelope frowned. "He's always so mean. Not at all like Rev. James, our other preacher. He and his wife were the sweetest people. They'd never speak of anyone like that."

"I wish I could have known them." Eva filled glasses with lemonade from a pitcher and offered them to Louise and Grace, two of the young ladies who shared the room next to the one she and Penelope shared. "It's hard to smile and nod at a preacher who believes you're morally corrupt."

She joined hands with the girls next to her and took a moment to thank God for their bounty. Whether He heard them despite their grousing was another matter, but she still wanted to voice thanksgiving.

After the amen, Grace lifted a sandwich from the plate. "I'm just glad Clara wasn't here to listen to the indictment against her. You know how sensitive she can be."

"There ought to be something we can do to change the preacher's opinion." Eva took a bite of her sandwich and watched the bees buzzing the nearby primroses and the butterflies gracing the lavender stars. A soft breeze rustled the leaves over her head, making the sunlight filtering down dance with the shadows on the blanket. All perfectly wonderful and relaxing. All totally ruined by the harsh words delivered from the pulpit this morning.

Men courted women, and women enjoyed being courted. That was a plain and simple fact. Why, how else could couples get married and have families? And what was wrong with men courting the Harvey Girls? Just because she wasn't interested in marriage didn't mean the other ladies weren't. It was an honorable institution, created and sanctioned by God Himself, so what could a preacher possibly have against it? Unless …

"I know!" She interrupted whatever Penelope was saying to Grace. "I bet Rev. Watkins doesn't approve of us because he doesn't know the men who have captured our affections—well, the other girls' affections anyway. We need to get them to take their beaus to church so the reverend can meet them. If the fellows joined them for the service like good Christian men, Rev. Watkins would have very little to say. Don't you think?"

"Not all the girls in the group are seeing God-fearing men," Louise said. "If you ask me, they're the ones Rev. Watkins aims his comments at."

"Perhaps, but we all feel the sting."

"We certainly do." Grace brushed crumbs from her gingham frock. "The men may not all be godly, but it's still worth a try."

Penelope nodded, making her bonnet bob. "That's a perfect idea. Prudie would jump at the chance to get her banker inside the church house. He's apparently quite a catch."

"Ada would bring her young fella to church too if he'd stay long enough," Grace added. "He's from Atlanta and doing business around hereabouts. But he's not often here on weekends."

"Perhaps it would be enough for her to introduce him to the preacher somehow." Eva smiled. This could work. If enough of the girls showed the reverend they weren't embarrassed about their relationships, he might realize they were all engaged in respectable activities. A woman doing what he accused them of would try to hide it, wouldn't she? At the very least, she wouldn't flaunt it in front of the town's only preacher—or in front of Miss Henrietta, who would send her packing in a heartbeat. So the preacher would have to believe the best of a Harvey Girl who brought her beau to meet him. Wouldn't he?

"What about you?" Penelope nudged Eva's shoulder with her own. "You should take Cal. He's local, but I don't remember ever seeing him at church. But I've seen the way he looks at you, and it wouldn't be so difficult for you to convince him to go."

Louise gave a slight shake of her head. "That Melody Malone has her claws in him."

"They're just friends," Penelope said. "He has his eye on Eva."

"He may have his eye on Eva," Grace countered, "but Louise is right. Melody staked her claim on him long ago. I saw them at the library last night, and she kept a hand on his arm during the entire lecture. He may think they're only friends, but she has other ideas in mind."

Frowning, Louise swallowed a bite of her sandwich. "What is it about the man that would attract someone as cultured and privileged as Melody Malone? She and her family are the closest things to high society we have in this town, and he's just another cowhand."

Eva understood the attraction. Cal was kindhearted and funny—not to mention the best-looking man she'd seen in all her born days. He was polite and respectful, even if he wasn't quite polished. Why, when they first met, she wasn't quite polished either. Six weeks in Kansas had sanded off her rough edges, but she hadn't become so snobby that his roughness bothered her. If she were to marry, if she hadn't held dreams of world travel and adventure, she'd want someone like him.

"All I'm saying is Rev. Watkins has been trying to get Cal to go to church for a long time," Penelope said, "and if Melody can't get him to step a boot over the threshold, maybe Eva can."

"I don't know whether I can, but I'm certainly willing to try. Especially if the other girls agree to do the same."

Grace tilted her ear to the wind. "Train's coming. We'd better hurry back."

The whistle sounded far off, but the steam engine could bring hungry passengers to the restaurant faster than they could say Jack Spratt. Eva retrieved the glasses and folded the napkins around them.

Was Cal a godly man? He prayed before the meals they'd shared together, but only at her prompting. Frankly, she had no clue where he stood on the subject. If he wasn't already predisposed to faith and godly living, getting him into the sanctuary might be harder than it sounded. But she was certainly willing to try. If she could pry him away from Melody long enough.

Eva couldn't help keeping an eye on the door every time it opened. At one point, she'd come precariously close to pouring hot tea in a customer's lap. Cal should've been here by now. He always came around suppertime on Sunday nights—at least the early supper at five. Here it was, nigh unto six thirty, and she hadn't seen so much as his shadow.

She slipped the coins from the table into her pocket—having the silver softly jingle when she walked served as a reminder to others to also be generous—then stacked the dirty dishes. The change she sent back home would be more than her first paltry sum, but she couldn't send anything substantial until the end of the month when she got her first paycheck. Then, at least Papa would think more kindly of her being a Harvey Girl even if the reverend didn't.

The bell chimed on the door again, and the china clattered in her trembling hands as she jerked around to look. Not Cal. Again. Where was that man?

Releasing a huff, she carried her load back to the kitchen and set it on the counter beside Liza.

Liza eyed her. "You look as frazzled as an old shawl. Are you well?"

"Oh, I'm fine. I don't know what has gotten into me." She clamped one hand on the countertop and propped the other on her hip. If she didn't gain control of herself, she surely would drop a stack of china and be obligated to pay for it. Why was she so anxious to see Cal Stephens anyway? It wasn't as if she'd figured out how to approach him.

"Hand me that pitcher, would you?" Liza nodded toward it, and Eva scooted it closer to her. She didn't dare pick it up. It would crash to the floor.

Penelope swept into the kitchen and grabbed the coffeepot. "You have customers at one of your tables, Eva. You'd better get out there." As she headed out again, she warned, "Brace yourself."

*Brace myself?* Had Cal finally shown up?

She adjusted her hat and smoothed her apron, feeling as taut as the piano wire at the saloon. Before she stepped into the dining hall, she pinched her cheeks and adorned her face with her best smile. Which immediately faltered when she discovered who she was to brace herself against.

With her hands clasped at her waist in a grip tight enough to stop the blood flow, she greeted each of the Malone sisters by name, in order of age, ending with, "Miss Melody. Always a pleasure to see you."

Melody batted her eyelashes. "Oh, I wouldn't have anyone but you serve us. You know just how to do it."

"Mr. Harvey taught us all how to do it. He's very particular." The lessons about keeping her demeanor pleasant but neutral while with a disagreeable patron were serving her well at this very moment.

"Still, I do prefer your service. As does Cal, when he's here." Melody studied her fingernails a moment, then slanted a glance at her. "The waitress where he took me for lunch wasn't nearly as good."

Melody's smile might have been all sweetness and innocence, but her intent made Eva doubly happy she'd mastered her features. She shifted her gaze to the eldest Malone sister. "What is your pleasure this evening, Miss Mimi? Our Harvey chef has prepared a wonderful veal shoulder—"

"We've eaten, and I believe we all want the same thing now." Melody glanced from sister to sister. "Lemon cake and tea, everyone?"

At their nods, Eva said, "I'll bring it right out. Extra lemon for the tea, ladies?"

By the time she finished taking their request, her smile had begun to cramp her cheeks. She exited the dining hall gracefully and walked through the door to the kitchen without the satisfaction of a chandelier-rattling slam, but she wanted to slam *something*. If she couldn't at least scream, she would explode, right on the kitchen floor in front of God and everybody.

She marched out the back door and kicked the first stair to the upper floors. "Oh! That woman! What she needs is a good, strong kick in the—"

"Temper, temper!" Miss Henrietta waggled a finger at her. Her other hand was tucked inside the crook of Rev. Watkins' elbow. An amused Rev. Watkins.

Whatever was left of Eva's temper evaporated, and she bowed her head. "Yes, ma'am. I'm sorry."

Miss Henrietta offered an understanding smile. "Rough night?"

Eva peeked up at the reverend. The Malones were his personal friends, and she dared not say a word against them. She shouldn't anyway. "No, ma'am. Just a moment of frustration."

"You know what the Good Book says about temper, don't you?" The reverend's tone gave the question the hint of challenge.

"'Be angry and sin not,'" she recited, then raised her chin. He could never say she didn't know her Bible—but before her temper flared again, she had better part ways with him. "If you will excuse me, I must return to my work."

The preacher dipped his head and Miss Henrietta smiled her

consent. Eva scooted back inside. Given the choice of facing Melody Malone or Rev. Watkins again, she'd choose Melody every time. The anger she often felt toward him was curbed by respect for his position as their pastor, but, oh, the number of times she'd about bitten her tongue in two!

How could that man preach against the Harvey Girls in the morning and take their housemother on a stroll that very evening? And if Miss Henrietta hadn't changed his mind about the girls by now, how could Eva?

But the ladies from the picnic had already told the others of their plans, and the only thing she could do was try to sway Cal toward the church. For now, however, she had to don her smile and take dessert and tea to the table before she lost her most-preferred-servant status.

She delivered the cake, then returned long enough to retrieve the teapot, which she should've done first. The ladies had been sitting all that time without their beverage. Not an intentional slight, but—well, she didn't feel too bad about it.

Eva poured the tea and watched Miss Mimi enjoying her cake. The woman slipped a bite into her mouth and slid the fork from between her lips slowly, eyes closed, a radiant smile adorning her face. And once she swallowed, she released a sigh of utter pleasure.

"Isn't this the best?" she exclaimed.

Similar murmurs erupted from around the table and ended when Melody said, "Cal was absolutely right when he pronounced this to be the Harvey House's best dessert." She made eye contact with each of her sisters. "So, it's settled?"

With a nod, Mimi dabbed her lips and turned to Eva. "Is it possible for the cook to bake this wonderful cake for our ladies' gathering Wednesday morning?"

"I'm certain that could be arranged. The cook will view it as a great compliment."

The door opened again. Not Cal. How could she invite him to church if he wasn't here? He never came to town during the week, and come Friday, there was no guarantee she'd see him. Especially if he was courting Melody.

Eva hid her disappointment behind her professional smile. "Where would you like the cake delivered?"

The answer to her dilemma came as quickly as Mimi's response. "The Rolling Oak Ranch. We'll need it there by ten."

"Perfect." In more ways than one. Despite her cool exterior, Eva squealed like a school girl inside. On her order pad, she wrote, *2 lemon cakes, Rolling Oak, Wed. 10 a.m.*

# Chapter 6

EVERY NEW PASTURE REQUIRED a fence and windmill, and now that they'd cleared the pasture of locoweed, Ed, Curtis, and Cal worked the fence. Cal kept an eye toward the road. If the windmiller came soon, they could get a break from clearing a fence line and driving posts into the ground to follow the miller around. They'd been working since around seven this morning, and in the past three hours, they'd planted a half-mile's worth of posts. Only twenty-three more miles to go before they turned west to meet up with the other fence-building crew.

Yep. Best part of the job.

Cal snorted at his own sarcasm and glanced at the road again.

Low spots at this end of the pasture would be surefire bets for water. Down at the bottoms of the ruts and ravines, where the trees still grew along dried-up creek beds. Be interesting to see if the windmiller agreed with him.

"Hey, lover boy." Curtis scowled at him. "You gonna sink that post or just stand there dreamin'? It'll be a great while afore them women show up for Miz Wiley's meetin.'"

Cal's neck heated. "It'll be a great while afore the miller shows up too. That's what I'm watchin' for."

"Don't even try it, mate. Nobody here to believe you." Ed put the machete in the back of the wagon and exchanged it for a small ax to take out the thick sapling up ahead. "Any man who holds the hearts of two women deserves the title of lover boy."

"Ain't got the hearts of two women," Cal muttered. He dropped the post in the hole and tamped the dirt around it, then shouldered a new post and strode to where Curtis dug another hole.

Truth be told, weren't a single cowhand not keepin' an eye on the road—and not for the windmiller, neither. Ever'one knew that Wednesdays, Miz Wiley held her Bible study meetin' and feedin' for the ladies from the church. The hands not watchin' the herd were finding chores close to the house, or at least the road leading to it. The onliest lady Cal wanted to see worked during the meetin' times, so he had no reason to get excited.

Ed nudged Curtis and pointed down the road. "Here comes one of the ladies now."

Curtis leaned on the post-hole digger and watched. "Unusual for any of them women to come by themselves."

"This ain't getting the fence built. Best we keep workin'." Cal dropped the post and glanced toward the road. "Them women ain't never looked at the likes of us any—"

He did a double take. He'd know that cottony blond hair anywhere. Great howlin' coyotes. When did Miss Eva start comin' to the meetings? All of a sudden like, he had a powerful need for something at the bunkhouse. He didn't know what, but he'd figure it out on the way there.

Glowering at the others, he said, "Looks like I ain't gonna get another lick o' work outta you two. I might as well …"

He grabbed the reins of the horse tied to the back of the wagon and swung up into the saddle.

Miss Eva was reining the buckboard in the front of the ranch house by the time Cal arrived. He tied the roan by the bunkhouse and headed toward her. He hadn't thought much about what he'd say. Hadn't thought much about what he was doin' a'tall. Not the smartest thing, takin' off like that. Curtis and Ed weren't much likely to let him live this down, but when it came to Miss Eva, his brain just seemed bent on ruination.

"Hello, Mr. Stephens! I was hoping I'd see you here this morning."

He snatched off his hat and tried to keep his jaw from dropping to his boots. "You came to see me?"

She ducked her head. "Well, not to see you specifically. I have to make a delivery to Mrs. Wiley. But I knew you worked here, and I–I …"

Her cheeks turned the purtiest pink he'd ever seen. He wanted to take her hand, let her know she didn't have to be so shy with him.

"I'm right honored you wanted to see me, Miss Eva. I've kinda been thinkin' about you too." Puttin' it mildly. She'd occupied his every thought for quite some time now.

She offered one of her heart-stealing smiles, and his ol' ticker just about thumped right out of his chest. "Let me take this in to Mrs. Wiley, and I'll come right back. I have something for you."

"Here, let me help you." He slapped his hat back on and grabbed a covered cake plate that smelled of lemony sweetness. "I bet I know what this is. The ladies are sure in luck this morning."

She giggled. "If they are, you are."

He didn't have a chance to ask what she meant before she led the way up to the ranch house porch. He trailed along behind her, sniffing the lemon cake and watching the sunlight dance on her hair. And within minutes, he trailed her back out to her wagon again.

Her being at the ranch house signaled the hands to start meandering in from their work. The church ladies from town would soon arrive. Besides, Cookie'd be dishin' out grub before too long. Another coupla hours. Cal had heard it all before. Ever' Wednesday, they gathered around the house, hoping one of the purty girls would flutter their lashes at 'em. Sometimes they did.

But this time, the purty girl was here to see Cal, and he didn't much appreciate the others hangin' around and gawkin' at her.

He escorted her to her wagon, keeping his voice low as he did. "Right nice of you to come all this way. Usually someone else from town makes the delivery, or Miz Wiley does her own bakin'."

"I wanted to make the delivery this time." Miss Eva reached under the seat and pulled out another cake, just like the one she'd given to Miz Wiley. "I wanted you to have this as a thank you."

He accepted the gift and his mouth watered. "I sure appreciate it, Miss Eva. But what are you thankin' me for?"

Her cheeks turned all rosy again as she studied the pebbles at her feet. "You have been so good and helpful to me. If it wasn't for you"— she raised her eyes then, beautiful blue pools that mesmerized him—"I wouldn't even have a job. I'd be living in Austin, doing who knows what. But you found the perfect alternative for me."

Now it was his turn to study the pebbles. "It weren't nothing. I just couldn't see you workin' at the saloon is all."

I was wondering …" she began, then started over. "I have Saturday night off this week, and I was wondering if you—"

"Yoo-hoo!" A carriage pulled up and stopped right close to Miss Eva's buckboard, and all four of the Malone sisters greeted them. Melody scrambled out and hotfooted it over to him and Miss Eva.

"Why, Cal, I was hoping to see you again." She latched on to his arm and gave him a too-bright smile. "We need to go out again. Soon."

Then, she turned that smile on Eva. "It's good to see you again too, but aren't you missing your shift? Wouldn't want you to lose your job."

Miss Eva stiffened ramrod straight and plastered on a smile even Cal recognized as forced. "You're right, of course. I should be heading back."

Cal stared from one to the other in the instant before Miss Eva started clambering up to her wagon seat. He offered her his free hand to help her up. "What were you going to ask me?"

She gave him the same strained smile she'd given Melody. "It doesn't matter. Enjoy your cake."

While her sisters bustled inside, Melody stayed rooted at Cal's side, shading her eyes as she watched Miss Eva drive the buckboard toward the road. "I wasn't expecting to see Eva here. What did she want?"

"She brought me this cake. And she was about to ask me something before you nosed in."

"Looks like I got here just in time to save you. If you want to catch her, you can't appear to be too eager or available. Best stay with the plan."

"I don't much like that plan," he said. "It seems dishonest."

"Remember what I told you." She patted his cheek. "All's fair …"

She left him then, sashaying to the house with a little extra swing to her hips, making her dress swish and the cowpokes stare. Once she reached the porch, she peeked at him over her shoulder with a sassy look on her face, then disappeared into the house.

That look was mighty bothersome. Was she really trying to help him win Eva, or did she have somethin' else in mind? Maybe her pigtails weren't the only thing 'bout her that changed, not that it mattered. He'd never be able to think of her the way he did of Miss Eva.

Right after his Saturday bath, Cal hoofed it over to the Harvey House. Miss Eva'd said she had the day off, but never got a chance to tell him what she wanted to do with it. He had an idea or two that just might work—and had paid more'n half a lemon cake to get the day off. The way rotation worked at the ranch, he wasn't due another Saturday off until next month, but at least he'd had something to barter for it. But he was free today, and Miss Eva'd said she was too, so might be she'd want to go with him to the barbecue and dance at the Crooked Creek Ranch.

He entered the hotel and crossed to the desk. Ever' time he'd seen Eva, she'd been in the restaurant. He wasn't quite sure how to find her when she wasn't working, but as he approached the desk, he recognized the clerk. "G'mornin', Miss Henrietta. I didn't know you worked the hotel side too."

"Good morning, Cal. Haven't seen you in a while." She sorted through mail and slipped notes into the pigeon holes. "Today is Mr. Abernathy's day off, so I'm filling in for him."

"How you gettin' along with that brother of yours?"

"Oh, he's stubborn as ever. Hard to believe we came from the same parents." She inserted the last letter, then turned to face him. "Now, what can I do for you?"

"I'm lookin' for Miss Eva. Is she around?"

"I haven't seen her yet. Is she expecting you?"

"I'm not right sure, but she told me she'd be free today."

Miss Henrietta gave him a knowing smile, then looked around at the empty lobby. "It's not busy right now. Let me look in on her, and I'll send her to you when she's ready. Why don't you wait in the restaurant? We have some pork sausage and fresh biscuits this morning, and molasses all the way from Louisiana."

Sure sounded better'n the cornmeal mush Cookie had served earlier, but … "I'll wait until she joins me."

"It will be a few minutes, then. Have some coffee while you wait."

Cal took her up on her offer, finding a table close to the entry between the hotel lobby and the restaurant. The chair facing the lobby suited him right fine.

After a moment, Miss Penelope came to the table, fancy coffeepot in one hand and the local Saturday newspaper in the other. "I almost didn't see you. Are you having breakfast today?"

"I'm waitin' for someone, so just coffee for now. Thanks."

She filled his cup, then glanced into the lobby and back at him with a smile that made him think she knew somethin' he didn't, but all she said was, "Let me know when you're ready to order."

As she walked away, he settled in with his coffee and paper. Ol' Cecil's milk cow got loose again and trampled Miz Ophelia's flowers. Showed how big the town was getting. Cecil used to live a mile away from anything resemblin' a flower garden, and he weren't the one that moved.

He wrapped his hand around his coffee cup—no point using the handle; it was too tiny in his clumsy fingers—and took another sip, casting a glance toward the lobby. Nothing to look at, so he returned to the paper. Library was boasting about gettin' a new book. *A Connecticut*

*Yankee in King Arthur's Court.* He'd read all 'bout King Arthur and his round table when he was a boy. Didn't remember reading about any Yankee there. Mr. Twain sure knew how to spin a tale.

Another sip, another glance—and a double take. Miss Eva glided toward him like she was floatin'. The tails of her blue ribbon drifted down the length of her hair and matched the bright blue dress she wore. Her face looked fresh-scrubbed and rosy, and her soft lips were lifted in a smile that told him she was glad to see him. For a woman who didn't intend to marry, she sure knew how to bring the matter to a man's mind.

He stood and pulled out a chair for her, losing himself in her eyes. She'd be the purtiest girl at the Crooked Creek barbecue, and he'd best start now makin' sure she saved ever' dance for him.

# Chapter 7

WHEN EVA ASKED ABOUT leaving with Cal, Miss Henrietta had said nothing more than, "Don't forget your curfew." Eva had never asked how the two knew each other, but they seemed to be easy friends. She treated him like a kid brother. He treated her with the same respect he treated everyone.

While he told Eva the particulars about erecting a windmill, she fingered the buttoned seats and fine, polished sides of the carriage. Although she'd expected to be riding to the Crooked Creek in the Wiley's buckboard, Cal had hitched up his horse to a rented carriage with padded, black-leather seats and a fringed cover. She'd never ridden in anything so fine. How could he possibly afford it on a cowboy's wages? The man was full of surprises.

She peered at him from the corner of her eye. For all his nervous chatter, he seemed relaxed, holding the reins loosely in strong, tanned hands. Dark hair not hidden by his hat curled around his collar and stuck to his damp forehead. The white shirt stretched across his broad shoulders had been starched stiff when she first saw him this morning, but with the heat of the day, it had softened and looked far more comfortable. She could certainly see why Melody found him attractive. Any woman would consider him so. Why, most of the young ladies in town probably wished he'd glance their way. If marriage held any appeal for her, she'd be flirting with him as shamelessly as Melody did and keeping a possessive hand on him.

But her goal was to get him into that church, so maybe a little flirtation and possessiveness were appropriate.

Cal clicked to the horse and turned it off the dirt road to another dirt road, and before long, they crossed under a metalworks sign at the entrance to the Crooked Creek Ranch. Eva could smell the smoke from the barbecue, and despite having a late breakfast, hunger gnawed at her.

Cal found a place to park the carriage among the other buggies and wagons. "Looks like a good turnout. But then, the McMasters always throw a great shindig."

He secured the horse, then came around to help her down. She gave him her best smile and latched her hand on to his forearm. "Don't leave me. I'm not certain I'll know anyone here."

"Sure you will." He patted her fingers. "I bet you see most of 'em ever' Sunday mornin'."

Oh, she hadn't thought of that—and no tongues wagged faster than those in the mouths of church ladies. But that could work in her favor. If they saw her on Cal's arm today, they'd expect him in the sanctuary with her tomorrow. And if he didn't come, more than just her would be trying to encourage him.

The McMasters' house was a low, wide affair with tall cedar trunks for porch pillars and clay tiles for the gently sloped roof. After coming from town, with its dignified two-story homes and carefully maintained lawns, Eva thought this place hinted of a harsher life. But it seemed more appropriate for a ranch, with all this ruggedness. Off to the left, the menfolk hovered near the barbecue pit—a ditch dug into the soil that held the fire cooking the beef that rotated on a spit above it. Dressed in bright, colorful cotton, the women worked together to the right of the house to set up the tables with red-checked cloths. Children chased each other or huddled together in little groups, and blankets spread beneath thick-leafed trees held little ones napping under the watchful gaze of the older girls.

A huge man approached and slapped Cal on the back as he offered to shake his hand. "You slicked up right nice for a day of grubbin', didn't you?" He turned hazel eyes on Eva and winked. "Or maybe you slicked up for a bit of sparkin' at the dance tonight."

With his hand lost in the other man's, Cal flushed. "Aw, just my usual Saturday bath 'n' shave." He nudged Eva forward. "But maybe I plan a little sparkin'. This here is Eva Knowles."

The older man laughed and shoved his hand out to her. "Bart McMasters, ma'am." He pointed to a willowy brunette in a moss-green dress strolling toward them. "That's Lydia, my bride of thirty years."

"Pleased to meet you," Mrs. McMasters said. "So, Cal, have you finally found someone who wants to travel as much as you do?"

He wanted to travel? What else didn't she know about this amazing man?

"We haven't actually talked about it," he said.

"Perhaps we should." She tightened her grip on his arm. "I'd love to see the world."

Another carriage clattered down the drive, and Mr. McMasters excused himself. His wife smiled at Eva and Cal. "Sounds like you two have a lot to talk about. I'll leave you to it. Enjoy the barbecue—we'll be serving soon."

As she trailed her husband, Cal gave Eva a look akin to awe. "You want to see the world?"

"Eva! Eva!" Prudie charged toward her with an overdressed dude in tow. "I didn't know you'd be here. Why didn't you say something?"

"I didn't know either until just this morning." She offered her friend a quick hug but couldn't help eyeing the man who looked so out of place. In his three-piece suit and bowler hat, he could be none other than—

"Theodore Hanover, the third." He introduced himself to Cal and tipped his hat to her. "Pleasure to meet you."

As Cal struck up a conversation with Theodore, Eva whispered to Prudie, "Is that your banker?"

"Yes. Isn't he handsome?" she whispered back, then entwined her arm with Eva's and drew her away, calling over her shoulder, "We need to help the other ladies. Why don't you two go talk with the men?"

Eva stumbled along beside her, glancing back while Prudie said something about getting him to church. Whether she meant Theodore or Cal, Eva did not know.

Cal wandered toward the barbecue pit with Theodore in tow. He didn't have much in common with the New York banker—no one here did—but he seemed a nice enough fella. As long as Cal could get back to Eva soon, everything would be all right. He hadn't dandied up so he could swap tales with a bunch of sweaty men. He could do that anytime. Thoughts of spending today with Eva had taken up the better part of his brain ever since she said she had the day to herself.

Across the wide lawn, she pitched in with the womenfolk, totin' this bowl and that to the tables, fussin' over what was already there, and pausing to talk to whoever caught her attention. She seemed to fit right in. She'd make a great wife. And she liked to travel. What more could he ask for?

A tap on his shoulder distracted him. Melody smiled up at him and batted her lashes. For some reason, her being here put a burr under his saddle. He was done tryin' to make Eva jealous.

"Hello, Cal." Her voice held a singsong lilt. If he didn't know better, he'd think she was flirting with him. "I didn't know you were coming to the barbecue."

"I didn't know you were either." He didn't much like the tone he'd used—she was a friend, after all. He tamped down his irritation. "Who'd you come with?"

"My sisters." She waved a hand toward the other Malone girls, then clamped it on his arm. "Since you're here, we could eat together."

"Not this time. I came with someone."

"You did? Who?" She took a gander at the cluster of women across the way and must've caught sight of Eva. "So my little plan to make her jealous worked, didn't it?"

Eva wasn't looking back at them, which suited him right fine. "I can't tell whether your plan worked or if she just had a day off to spend with me. But whatever it was, I'm done tryin' to make her jealous." He rescued his arm from her grasp. "You ought to find some other fella to eat with. There be plenty of 'em here."

Her bottom lip stuck out, and she looked up at him with damp eyes as if he'd hurt her feelin's. "But I never wanted anyone but you."

He stared at her like she'd dropped from the sky. "I knowed you all your life, girl. I could no more court you than I could my own sister."

"And I've known you too, since before your sisters married and moved away and your parents got killed. I've had my heart set on you since I don't know when. I just always assumed ..."

"Aw, Melody, I never meant for you to think that." He rubbed the back of his neck. How could things get so all-fired messy? "I'm sorry, but I got my eye set on Miss Eva."

"How do you know she's not after you for your money?"

"Keep your voice down!" He took her arm and pulled her farther away from the group crowded around the barbecue pit. "She don't know about it. Nobody does other'n my sisters and you—and I shouldn't've told you."

She glared at him. "You can still trust me, Cal Stephens. I could never do anything to hurt you. You know that."

"Yeah, you're right. I know that. I'm sorry." He kissed the top of her head. "Now why don't you go join the other women. Let the menfolk get an eye of you walkin' in that purty dress, and I betcha one of 'em'll be beggin' to sit beside you."

"I'm not a child. You don't have to distract me with candy every time I don't get my way." But she sauntered off without a backward glance, yoo-hooing Miss Prudie as she neared the picnic tables.

Cal headed back to the pit. The fellas were taking the meat off the spit and settlin' it in huge roast pans. Enough beef to feed ever'one there a few times over and smelled better'n anything in a fancy restaurant. He grabbed a couple of rags and took up a pan in each hand to take back to the tables.

Mr. McMasters strode beside him with two pans of his own and a wide grin stretched between his cheeks. "I been hearing about you and all your lady loves. Some of the boys want to know your secret."

Cal's neck heated up under his collar. "I don't have a lady love, and I don't rightly have a way with women like they been sayin'. You know how long I've known the Malone sisters. There ain't nothin' to that rumor."

"Glad to hear it. That'll leave more girls for the rest of the fellas here." He pointed at Eva with one of the roast pans. "That young lady you came with is a mighty handsome woman. Is she special?"

"It's a mite early to tell." But oh yeah, she was special.

She caught his eye right then and watched him come toward her as if there weren't nobody else around. Might be she thought him special too.

Dancin' by campfire and torchlight should've been more romantical, but "Buffalo Gals" weren't right for sparkin'. After that one, Mr. McMasters called the dosey-does and swing-your-partners, and Cal didn't get to hold Eva's hand for an instant before findin' himself with someone else. But he still caught glimpses of the firelight shining in her hair and caught the sound of her laughter, light and happy, as someone else swung her around and back to him. She'd smile up at him from a flushed face, and all he could think of was how he wanted to kiss her. Then they started a lively reel, and she was gone again. He never really saw the ladies threadin' the lines with him, just always watched for Eva.

Before the musicians could start another tune, Cal caught Eva by the elbow. "That was some mighty fast dancin'. Enough to take the spit right out of a body. Would you like something to drink?"

She nodded and let him escort her to the refreshment table. One of McMasters' daughters tipped some lemonade into a glass and handed it to Eva, then did the same for Cal. He found a quiet place for them, away from the heat of the fires, but still visible to the crowd, keeping the distance respectable.

"You havin' fun?"

"Oh yes! Our gatherings back home were never quite so lively. For some reason, our church socials tended to be more ... *proper*, I suppose." She waved her lemonade glass toward the group. "We never did anything quite that exuberant."

Whatever *exuberant* meant must've been a good thing, because laughter played in her eyes and rolled off her tongue while she watched the dancers line up and start another one.

"If you never been to a shindig like this one, how come you to know all the steps?"

She giggled. "I'm afraid I've been faking it. I just bounce in time with the music."

"Truth be told, that's what I do too."

Now that they were away from the crowd, his tongue failed him. He didn't have much trouble when they were riding out to the McMasters' ranch, pro'bly 'cause he was excited about havin' her with him. Made his nerves jitter and his mouth run, just like it did when she'd joined him for supper that time at the Harvey House. During supper tonight, they'd been with other folks who kept the conversation from laggin' like a stray. Then there was the dancin'. But now ...

He scratched under his hat and glanced down at her. Their eyes met for an instant before she darted hers back to the dancers. When'd his brain get so empty? Some *lover boy* he was. Couldn't even talk to a—

"You said you want to travel." She looked up at him from the corner of her eye. "Where do you want to go?"

"Ever'where. I want to see California and then go back east and see everything in between. Then I want to go to Europe."

"Oh, I do too!" Her eyes brightened in the torchlight, lively as the folks dancin' the reel. "I want to see England and Ireland and Scotland and Wales—"

"And then head to Norway and Sweden—"

"And south to France and Italy!"

"What about Egypt? Maybe even the Far East?"

"I'd love to go to all those places."

"I don't want to just go," Cal said. "I want to stay a while. Spend time."

"And learn the culture and history." Eva bounced on her toes like an excited young'un. "I'd love to write about each place. Tell stories and sell them back home."

"I can't write good. I can't even talk smart like you can, but I can draw."

"You could be my illustrator." She took his hand like it was the most naturalest thing to do. "We could be partners in travel. And I'd write, and you'd draw, and we'd live off the money we earned from books and magazine articles."

"Just like that guy talkin' at the library—"

"Yes, the speaker you took me to hear." Melody had blindsided him and slipped her hand into his—the one Eva wasn't holding. "Hello, Eva."

Cal'd seen the look Melody gave Eva on one of the ranch curs when it was facin' down a rattler. He gave her hand a warnin' squeeze before breakin' loose if it. "I thought I seen you with Mr. McMasters' youngest. Did you get tired of dancin'?"

She sneered at Eva one more time before shifting her attention to him. "Actually, I was talking with Prudie. Seems she and the other Harvey Girls have a bet going."

"A bet?" Beside him, Eva tightened up like a tense mare. He stared at Melody. "What kinda bet?"

"They're all betting on who can get their beaus to church tomorrow. Prudie is taking Theodore, and this one"—she shot another glare at Eva—"intends to take you. All she's doing with you tonight is trying to win a bet."

"Now, that's not true," Eva cried. "It's nothing like that!"

"Then what is it like?" Melody's honeyed voice held a bitter edge of accusation, and Cal didn't like it one bit.

"Now, look, Melody. Miss Eva ain't said a thing to me about going to no church—"

She waved her hand toward Eva. "She's standing right there. Ask her!"

Miss Eva let loose of Cal's hand and went to wringin' hers. Cal's gut twisted with every second she didn't say somethin', till finally she blurted, "It isn't like that! It's not a bet."

Melody raised her chin like she'd done won the battle. "But you *do* intend to get him into that church, don't you?"

"Well, yes, but—"

"And before this event, you weren't really interested in Cal, were you?"

"I can't say that is true. He is a truly sweet and special man, and—"

"But you didn't want him courting you, did you? Prudie said—"

"Prudie has a big mouth." Eva crossed her arms over her middle and scowled. "And she doesn't know a thing of how I feel about Cal Stephens. Why, if it wasn't for him, I wouldn't be working at the Harvey House Restaurant."

Melody matched her pose. "And that's something else Prudie said. You Harvey Girls are only doing this so you can get on Rev. Watkins' good side."

At that, Eva hung her head. "That's not the only reason, but it is true. The reverend doesn't think very highly of us, and we thought …"

Instead of finishin' what she was going to say, she sank her fists in her skirt and raised it high enough to run away.

"Miss Eva, wait!" Cal started toward her, but Melody grabbed his arm.

"Don't go after her, Cal. She's using you. Don't you see?"

"I don't know what's going on, Melody, but it's between her 'n' me. I told you to stay out of it."

He left her standin' there gapin' at him and took off into the shadows.

# Chapter 8

WHAT A HORRIBLE, HORRIBLE person! Why, Melody Malone was probably the worst person in the whole county! She'd made Eva and the other girls look just awful. And Prudie certainly hadn't said a word about a bet being made. She wasn't the sort to make up tales like that.

Eva found a wagon and gave the wheel a swift kick, earning a rustle and a nicker from the horse attached to it.

Oh, why had she come to this stupid dance? She should've known Melody would be here. Seemed that girl was *everywhere,* and she apparently took pleasure in being rude. Especially to Eva. And Eva had yet to understand why the intense disliking. She'd never done anything to any of the Malone sisters, least of all Melody.

She kicked the wheel again, then searched the torch-lit grounds for the carriage. Perhaps she could send word to Cal that she'd taken it into town. He knew more people here than she. He could find a way back. Surely, there was someone nearby to ask.

She whirled around to find someone and collided with Cal.

He caught her by the shoulders and steadied her. "I've been huntin' for you ever'where."

His strong, gentle hands had the same effect they'd had when she was new in town and first stumbled into him. Numbed her mind and sent her senses reeling until her head got all dizzy and she could scarcely think. She turned from him and broke contact.

"I-I was looking for a way to get home."

"Don't reckon you oughta take any of these wagons. Owners don't look too kindly to havin' their horses stolen."

She huffed. "I wasn't going to steal one. I was looking for the carriage."

He took her by the shoulders again and turned her around. "You passed it back thataway."

His voice held a maddening humor as if this were some laughing matter. How could he not be furious with her after Melody's lies and accusations?

Just when Eva was growing truly fond of him. If ever there'd been a time for her to think of marriage, this would've been it, and Cal would've been the one to set her cap for. He was handsome and kind and gentle, and they had the same dreams …

And he was a cowhand. How would he pay for world travel?

"Well?" he asked.

She blinked. "I'm sorry, what did you say?"

"Do you want to go back to the party or do you want me to take you home?"

"I … Don't you want to hear what that so-called bet is about?"

"Is there really a bet?"

"No, of course not, but—"

"But you and the others think that gettin' us fellas to go to church will make Rev. Watkins be nicer to you."

She scuffed her shoes among the pebbled drive. "Yes. That's what we were hoping, just as Melody said."

"Is that the only reason you came with me?"

Heat flamed her cheeks, and she kept her eyes downcast while she nodded.

The sigh he released held enough sadness to break her heart. "Let's go say our goodbyes to Mr. and Miz McMasters, and I'll take you home."

The full moon had guided them back into town and might as well have been Eva's only company. Cal didn't utter a word the entire time. He pulled up in front of the hotel and helped her out of the carriage, then quickly withdrew his hand as he walked her to the veranda.

At the door, he took off his hat. "I had a right nice time, Miss Eva. I'm sorry for the way it turned out. Melody had no call to upset you the way she did."

As he turned to go, she touched his arm. "Cal, I may have accepted your offer to go to the party under false pretenses, but I really had a nice time. I …" She lowered her eyes. "I liked being with you and talking about all the traveling we'd do, even if we never get to do it."

"I liked bein' with you too." He replaced his hat. "I'll come get you for church in the morning, for what good it'll do ya. Rev. Watkins ain't never gonna change his mind about the Harvey Girls. At least, not as long as his sister's one."

She peered at him, unable to see his eyes in the shadow of his hat brim. "Who is his sister?"

"Miss Henrietta," he responded with a tinge of surprise in his voice. "I thought you knew."

"No, I didn't have a clue. What happened?"

"That's her story to tell." He stared at the porch slats. "Well, I best be goin'. Like I said, I'm sorry about tonight."

He plodded his way to the carriage and climbed in, then clicked his tongue. The horse pulled the carriage toward the livery stable with a soft clip-clop on the packed dirt.

She'd hurt him. The nicest man she'd ever known, and she'd hurt him. Amazing that he agreed to go to church with her, but after him being such easy company tonight, what would he be like tomorrow?

She walked into the empty hotel lobby and flopped onto the settee. For someone who'd sworn she'd never marry, she'd sure lost her heart quick enough. And she'd really made a mess of things. Being with Cal would never feel comfortable again, and she had no one to blame but herself.

And Melody Malone.

Maybe it was for the best. She needed to be concentrating on keeping her family fed and Papa out of debt until he was well enough to find work again. Any thought of her marrying—let alone traveling around the world—would have to wait until he was back on his feet.

Carrying a turkey-feather duster, Miss Henrietta stepped around the corner from the hallway into the main lobby and whisked off the bronze bust of Fred Harvey, founder of the Harvey House Hotel and Restaurant, then swept the duster down the length of the pedestal the bust sat upon. All those evenings Eva thought Rev. Watkins was courting Miss Henrietta, and it was just sibling affection. But if that were true, then why the hostility on Sunday mornings?

Eva watched her a moment longer. She knew of no polite way to ask about something that was distinctly none of her business, but she couldn't share the quiet room with the woman and not acknowledge her presence.

"Miss Henrietta, it's awfully late for you to be doing that. Isn't Mr. Abernathy back yet?"

"He isn't due until tomorrow evening, and I must do something to keep myself awake until the last scheduled train passes through, or I'll be caught napping at the clerk's counter." She gave the bronze Mr.

Harvey a final swipe, then joined Eva on the settee. "It might be late for me, but it's early for you. Didn't you have a good time with Mr. Stephens?"

Eva decided she could use the guidance of a more mature woman about now, so she told her everything. She told about how the reverend—Miss Henrietta's brother, though Eva didn't mention it—upset her and the other girls with his sermons. About their plan to win him over. About the jumble she'd made of her relationship with Cal, even though he said he'd go to Sunday's service with her. But she'd been careful not to mention Melody's name. No point adding gossip and backbiting to her list of sins.

Chuckling, Miss Henrietta shook her head. "All that, just to get on Jeremiah's good side. I wish you'd talked to me earlier. Trying to impress the good reverend is pointless. My brother is never going to change his mind about the Harvey Girls."

"Your brother?" She feigned surprise for Cal's sake. "Rev. Watkins is your brother?"

"Yes, and I am the reason he is so against the Harvey Girls."

"I can't imagine what you could've done to earn such ire from him."

"It's not that big of a secret, I suppose. No longer much of an issue." Miss Henrietta huffed a breath. "Several years ago, I divorced my husband in Oklahoma on the grounds of drunkenness and infidelity. Afterward, I lived with Jeremiah awhile, trying to take care of him while he took care of his flock in our church there. But he kept pushing me to go back to my husband. Divorce is a sin, he said. Forgiveness is a commandment of God."

"Even God allows divorce for infidelity. As a preacher, he should know that."

"Oh, he does. But my being divorced is an embarrassment to him." She fiddled with her cuticles as she talked. "I finally got aggravated with his fussing, so I decided to move out. I had no intention of going back to that man I'd married, but I also had no means of supporting myself, until a friend told me of Fred Harvey and what he was doing all across the nation. I went to work for the Harvey House and eventually came here. Then Rev. James retired, and Jeremiah came here too."

"It must've been like a fresh start for both of you. New town, new people." Eva searched her eyes. "I assume you never told anyone of the divorce."

"Not at first, but when Jeremiah came, I had to squelch inappropriate rumors and admit that we were related, which meant I also had to admit why we have different last names." She wrinkled her nose. "I could never lie and say I was widowed."

"But that still doesn't explain his attitude about the Harvey Girls."

She sighed. "At first, his sermons were aimed at me. Though he never said so from the pulpit, he faulted me for going to work and becoming self-sufficient instead of returning to my former husband. Then, as some of the girls began flirting with the men who came through and getting involved in unseemly activities, he considered it his mission to put the fear of God in their hearts."

He certainly did that well. "He seems to have forgiven you. The two of you spend quite a bit of time together."

"And we fight a lot too. I'm sure you've heard our rather spirited debates in the restaurant."

"I'm afraid so. It can be quite entertaining." Eva laughed, but then the smile fell from her lips. "I suppose our plan to bring the men into the church would be as likely to fail as it would to succeed. There is simply no way of knowing. If his attitude is derived from girls being courted by men from the trains, then it wouldn't be wise to flaunt them in front of him."

"Or, it could work exactly as you planned. Courtship is different from what he'd witnessed before. And though there are still girls with Harvey House who behave as if they should work in a saloon, none of them are in *this* house."

"But Clara—"

"Clara and her intended spoke to me and received my blessing long before they left." She lowered her head. "I was disappointed, of course, to hear she would wed without any of her friends here as witnesses. But with his large family, it proved much easier for her to go to his town than for all of his kin to come here. Though I still wish she'd told everyone good-bye. She said she hated farewells and would write us later."

Miss Henrietta rose from the settee and tapped her feather duster against her palm. "Now, I suggest all of the ladies bring their beaus to church in the morning as a show of force. Take up the entire front row and show the good reverend they have nothing to hide. And if that doesn't change his tune, I know of something that will."

# Chapter 9

CAL RAN HIS FINGER under the collar of a too-tight shirt made tighter by the string tie wrapped around his neck like a noose. Great howlin' coyotes. This getup was gonna strangle him afore he could get to the hotel. He'd dirtied his only good shirt at the dance last night and had to borrow a Sunday best from one of the cowpokes in the bunkhouse. Too bad he was one of the littler ones. If Cal weren't careful when he moved his arms, he'd rip the sleeves right off. Flickin' the reins on the horse's back proved a mite challengin'.

He'd talked the smithy into rentin' him the carriage for one more day so he could take Miss Eva to church service in style. After he went to bed last night, he spent hours running the events of the evening through his head. Didn't matter that Miss Eva hadn't started out with honest intentions—she ended it with a right favorable opinion of him. Would've been the perfect night if Melody'd kept her nose to herself.

All them years he'd watched Melody grow up, and he never once thought of her as anything but a kid sister. And never considered she thought otherwise. He couldn't stay mad at her, but she'd better be clear about who held his interest. He hadn't thought of much more'n sparkin' with Miss Eva since he first knew that she'd come back to town. If she wanted him to wear tight collars and sit for hours on a hard pew, he'd do it. A time or two, anyway.

The hotel seemed to be right crowded this morning. But a closer gander told him it was the Harvey Girls swarming the porch, some with fellas lookin' just as choked and miserable as him. They must be the ones them girls talked into their scheme. Only Theo seemed comfortable in his full Sunday getup.

Cal stopped the rig in line with other carriages and buckboards. Seemed kind of fancy for them all to ride to a church they could just as easily walk to, but the girls must've wanted to put on a show. Cal didn't have much more to go on about the preacher except what Miss Henrietta had told him and what he'd witnessed himself the day he took the fried chicken to the parsonage. But that was enough to tell him them girls had a right to be upset.

Dressed in yellow gingham and purtier'n a daisy, Miss Eva waved to him. He hollered *whoa* to the horse, then hotfooted it to the porch, where he whisked off his hat and greeted those he knew and nodded at those he didn't. He stuck his elbow out for Miss Eva to rest her hand on, then escorted her to the carriage. All the ladies from the porch matched up with their fellas and followed Cal and Eva down to their rides.

"I'm so glad you were willing to come after everything that happened last night." Miss Eva kept her voice low and glanced around at the others. "I must apologize again for my behavior."

He patted her hand. "You ain't got nothin' to apologize for. I was right glad you came with me yesterday, and I figure the reason don't matter. Besides, I reckon we got a bit more in common than you thought at first."

She graced him with a sunny smile. "You're right."

Their carriage led all the others in a promenade down the dusty street to the front of the little white church, then they led the way inside it. Seemed ever'one wanted to follow Miss Eva's lead. Made perfect sense to him. Good woman like her was worth followin'.

They weren't exactly quiet when they crossed the threshold and marched to the front of the room. Folks in the pews to the right and the left stopped their gabbin' and gawked at 'em as they strode past and took their seats right up there on the front row. Melody's jaw 'bout dropped to the floor, but she recovered right quick and looked away. He'd have to make up with her later, but for now … Well, if she hadn't understood the way things stood before, she sure did now.

He and Eva took seats in front of Miss Henrietta, and she beamed her approval clear as day. The choir started "Bringing in the Sheaves," and purty soon ever'one else was singin' it too. Cal hadn't heard it since he was a young'un, but he pitched his voice into it and did the best he could.

The reverend came in from a room behind the pulpit, and Miss Eva clamped a hand on Cal's arm tight enough to turn her knuckles white. She didn't have nothin' to be a-feared of, though. The preacher stood up there gawkin' at all them women with their menfolks at their sides. Seemed he was the one caught without a saddle.

He stepped up to the pulpit lookin' as lost as a calf without its mama. Like he didn't know what to talk about. But he reminded ever'one that

Jesus loved 'em enough to die on that cross for 'em, and if they be wantin' to call themselves *His*, they best be lovin' each other and doin' what was right. *In Jesus' name, amen.*

Then he dashed out the back, leavin' the choir to sing "Rock of Ages" in a fit of confusion.

Once ever'one stood to leave, Miss Henrietta caught hold of Eva. "Your plan worked. I've never seen him so rattled. Last evening at supper, he told me his sermon would heap guilt upon the souls of those out dancing and reveling at the McMasters' party—with an emphasis on some of the Harvey Girls being there, of course."

Miss Eva raised her eyes heavenward. "Of course."

"But I believe having everyone here with their beaus threw him off course." Miss Henrietta giggled behind her fingers. "I would've paid money to see him squirm like that."

"It was entertaining, wasn't it?" Eva tilted her head. "What were you going to do if he hadn't changed his sermon?"

She waved her hand like she was brushin' aside the question. "I know something on him, a little embarrassment is all. But we don't need it now, do we?"

Rev. Watkins was shakin' hands and talkin' to folks at the front door by the time his sister and Cal and Eva approached. Miss Prudie introduced him to Theo, then asked him to hitch 'em together in a church wedding soon. For the second time in one mornin', the preacher gaped like a fish outta water.

Cal had figured to say good-bye to Miss Eva after church, her havin' to work and all, but soon as they'd settled in the carriage, she said, "We have time before the next train comes today, so some of us planned a picnic out under the sycamore tree. Would you—"

"Yes'm, I surely would."

He hadn't known where the sycamore tree was till now. Sure was a right purty place. Put a man's thoughts to love and romance. They'd landed at the site first, and afore he could help her spread the blanket, he had to loosen his collar and roll up his sleeves, or he'd rip 'em at the shoulders. Danged uncomfortable shirt, but he could put up with it a bit longer.

"This was a good idea," he said. "Can't ask for a purtier day."

"That's true." She smoothed a corner of the blanket and knelt on it.

"We decided a picnic would be the best thing to do after church today. Sort of a celebration if things went right with Rev. Watkins or a way to perk ourselves up if they didn't."

"I'm plum tickled they went your way."

"I am too." She looked up at him. "I just wonder what Miss Henrietta has on the preacher that she intended to use on him if things hadn't gone well."

Cal swallowed a chuckle. Back when Rev. Watkins first arrived in town, he fell hard for a purty little thing and commenced to courtin' her before he found out she was one of Madam Dallie's girls. 'Bout near caused the scandal of the lifetime in this little town. But that weren't his tale to tell. "Aw, you know how brothers and sisters are. They always got somethin' or other that'd come in handy to get their way."

"Yes, I suppose. My brothers and sisters and I are the same." She patted the blanket beside her, an invitation for him to sit down. Weren't no need to ask him twice. "What about you? Do you have family?"

"A couple of older sisters. They married and moved off after Pa died."

"So you're from here originally?"

"Yep, not too far from where the hotel is now. We sold the house and land and divided the money three ways so the girls could have a dowry of sorts and I could have a stake to go off and see the world if I want."

"I'm surprised you haven't left yet."

"Just feedin' the kitty a little more. I want to travel much farther and longer than that stake can handle."

Another wagon kicked up dust on the road, then pulled onto the grass. Two more couples joined them, Miss Prudie and Theo, and Miss Penelope and … Ed?

Soon as Ed cleared the buckboard, Cal drew him aside. "How you come to know Miss Penelope?"

"It's all your fault. You talk about that restaurant all the time, and after trying the cake, I decided to try their food."

"Yeah, but how'd you come to be here with Miss Penelope?"

"I asked."

Cal grinned. "You're a sly one. Did Curtis go to the restaurant too?"

"No. Of course not. Someone had to cover your lazy arse while you went out a-sparkin', as you say."

Theo joined them as the ladies set up the picnic. He'd shed his coat, vest, and tie and looked a little less like the banker he was. He stood between Ed and Cal and propped a hand on their shoulders. "Just look at those lovely creatures, gentlemen. I believe we are the luckiest men on earth."

Cal watched Miss Eva fussin' over plates and talking with the other girls—all excited over their little victory today—and his chest swelled. "Yessir. I believe you're right."

Feelin' fuller'n a fat tick on a husky dog, Cal went walking with Miss Eva in a meadow of flowers and fresh grass, leaving the other picnickers behind. More'n anything, he wanted to hold her hand while they walked, but he busied his paws with a blade of grass instead.

At least this time, he knew what they could talk about. "Where do you reckon you want to travel to first?"

"I can't go anywhere for at least a year. I want to be sure Papa and my family are doing well." She stooped to pick a wildflower.

"I reckon I can understand that. You got a duty to your family. I admire ya for your commitment."

His comment brought a blush to her cheeks, but it seemed to please her. "I always think about seeing the world, though. When it's time, I want to go west. I want to see the Grand Canyon and California. And I heard of a geyser that squirts water way high in the air, and I'd love to see the Tetons."

"That sounds nice. Right nice." Perfect, in fact.

He picked a purty yellow flower and handed it to her. She smiled as she took it. "Where do you want to go first?"

Her smile stole his heart and sent it soaring. "I want to go wherever you want to go, whenever you're ready to go there, and for however long you want to stay."

She took his hand, and all of a sudden like, he couldn't feel the ground under his feet. Then she gave him the kind of smile that melted his heart and said, "Then we should start planning."

# Author's Note

Back when the Atchison, Topeka, and the Santa Fe Railroads were the travel mode of choice, restauranteurs learned how to get more than their fair share of the passengers' coins. As the trains took on more water for their steam engines, hungry passengers would file to the establishments in search of food and refreshment. But often the locals got dollar signs in their eyes and honesty floated out the window. Special tricks included overcharging the out-of-towners, scraping leftovers together and serving them to the next crowd, and accepting pay in advance for food that wouldn't be served before the train left the station.

That's where Fred Harvey came in. Around 1870, he approached the president of the ATSF railway, Charlie Morse, about an idea to open Harvey House restaurants and hotels all along the train's stops to assure great food at a fair price to the passengers. Within fifteen years, he had seventeen Harvey Houses, all staffed by women he picked, generally from "back east," and trained in Kansas.

Around that same time, women weren't allowed much in the line of honest work. They could take in laundry, work in kitchens, or teach—a position that generally ended once they married. Pay was barely enough to support them. Working women were frowned upon and whispered about. They were either spinsters—the poor dears—or too independent for their own good.

So when Fred Harvey provided a way for women to become financially independent at a decent wage ($17.50 per month plus tips at one point), room, and board, many of the men of the era saw this as a threat to their male dominance. No decent woman would wait tables and serve strangers! Preachers taught against them in the pulpits, especially when promiscuity accompanied independence.

Not all women were promiscuous, though. Most married and left before their contracts with Harvey House were up, leaving Fred Harvey always scrambling to fill positions. That didn't cause too big of a problem for his enterprise, though. At one point there were eight-four Harvey Houses across the nation, and the Harvey Girls brought hospitality and gentility throughout the Southwest as far as Arizona.

As I wrote this novella—my first historical romance—I had to double-check things. Like the cash register. Although it has virtually disappeared today, the old key register has been around since at least 1878. While soda fountains were invented in 1832, the paper straw didn't show up until 1888.

My best finds? Women inventors whose products were patented. The turkey-feather duster was invented by Susan Hibbard, who had to fight her own scheming husband for the patent. But the court awarded it to her in 1878. Josephine Cochran invented the first dishwasher. Her primary problem was getting someone to make it. "I couldn't get men to do the things I wanted in my way until they had tried and failed in their own," she said. She got her patent on December 28, 1886, and began selling to hotels. A cold call to Sherman House hotel landed her an $800 order. Not too shabby for her era.

These inventors, along with the Harvey Girls, are true heroes among American women. The "man's world" we live in now is nothing compared to the one they battled.

# Acknowledgments

WHAT WOULD I DO without my amazing Caffeine Dream Team? Someone is always available to help me and put their eagle eyes to work. This novella wouldn't be what it is without my sweet friends and readers. Special thanks to team members Lora Mayfield, Sally Shupe, Cecilia Marie Pulliam, Janet Kerr (my beloved Comma Mama), and Sylvia Stewart, guardian of accuracy for all things historical.

I don't know much about Great Britain, historical or otherwise, so when I stuck an Englishman on the ranch, I needed to know how he would speak. Thanks to author Michelle Griep, historian extraordinaire when it comes to Brit characters, who upgraded Edward's speech patterns to something more fitting a son of title.

To Pegg Thomas for getting me into this and for her encouragement and friendship. She's in the handheld few of my mostest special friends and snort-laugh buddies.

For Billy, of course, not only because he puts up with me, but because he has the whole collection of Time Life Books called *The Old West*. Quick references right in my own home! And for Mama—Joyce "Dusty" Wrenn—who catches things as I read to her. What the eye can no longer see, the ear can hear, and she's done a great job proof-hearing my work.

As always, to God be the glory. Without Him, I could do nothing.

Linda W. Yezak lives with her husband and their funky feline, PB, in a forest in deep East Texas, where tall tales abound and exaggeration is an art form. She has a deep and abiding love for her Lord, her family, and salted caramel. And coffee—with a caramel creamer. Author of award-winning books and short stories, she didn't begin writing professionally until she turned fifty. Taking on a new career every half century is a good thing.

Website: http://lindawyezak.com
Newsletter: http://dld.bz/CoffeewithLinda
Facebook: Author Page
Pinterest: https://www.pinterest.com/lyezak/
Twitter: @LindaYezak
Amazon Page: http://dld.bz/LWYAmazonPage
Goodreads: Linda W Yezak

SEP 2019

CPSIA information can be obtained
at www.ICGtesting.com
Printed in the USA
LVHW091556060819
626724LV00004B/596/P

9 781946 016904